Surviving Fate

By Kimberly S. Gettum

D1716894

ISBN 9798622532993

When I started this story, I was 19 years old.
When I finished this story, I was 25 years old.
When I decided it was time to release it into the world, I was 30 years old.
I am now 31 years old.
Thank you to my family and friends who have supported me the entire way.
Most of all, thank you to my husband, Phillip, who has believed in me from day one.
You are my biggest fan, my favorite person and my world.
I love you.

<u>Preface:</u> Open Door

Pain struck my body as I woke up in the middle of my deserted hell. I instantly felt the physical and emotional bruises on my body. Violated couldn't compare to the way I felt. I was alone again, left for dead. But a strange feeling came over me as I opened my eyes to look up at the broken ceiling of my prison; determination. For the first time in days I felt the will to live. I wanted freedom now more than I ever had in my entire life.

I would escape and I would see my family again. I wasn't just optimistic, I was sure of it. My life was only just beginning. I had to live. I had to live for him.

Suddenly conscious of all my injuries, the pain in my chest pounded. Would I ever see him again? *What did his parents do to him after they left?* I shook my head and closed my eyes tightly, pushing the tears from my eyes.

I wiped my tears with my hands and noticed something out the corner of my eyes. I sat up slowly to see the door swing in the wind. *It's open.*

PART ONE

-1- Annabelle: Envelope

<u>Friday, December 12th</u>

Only one hour into my two hour exam and I had already finished my essay. I left the classroom, taking a seat on the floor outside of the door. I carefully placed two pen drawn hearts on the back of my hand. I sighed heavily and glanced at the clock. Spare time was the last thing I needed. There were too many bad memories to think about. *Damn it, Annabelle.* Here I go again, back to that night…

<u>*One Week Earlier*</u>

We finished getting ready for the small party at Billy-Jean's boyfriend, Ronnie's house. My boyfriend, Dolan, would be meeting us there, along with some other friends from work and school.

"I'm so glad that we only have one more week of college. I hope Ronnie picked up something good for us. I could use a drink." *Billy sighed into the mirror next to me. I smiled a little.*

"Yeah, but we have exams this week. That is the worst part of the semester. I am going to bomb Brillerson's essay exam," I said, thinking about all the studying I was going to need to do before Monday.

"Annabelle Dawn Rockart. Shut your mouth. You will do just fine on all your exams, like you always do," she told me sternly. "It's Saturday night. Relax. Have some beer and we will enjoy the weekend before hell week. Okay?"

"Yes, mom." I laughed.

Driving to Ronnie's parent's house was quiet. We listened to the radio, "And the National Weather Service is calling for snow late next week. Hope everyone has their snow gear ready, it's going to be a cold winter this-" *Billy turned the station so fast I thought she might take the knob off the radio. She muttered under her breath at the weather..*

"One more week Bills, you'll be in sunny, hot Texas with your Granny." I laughed at her.

"One more week," she whispered to herself reassuringly. We drove the rest of the way to Ronnie's in silence. The closer we got, the more Billy relaxed.

"So, when is Ronnie moving in?" I questioned as we pulled into the driveway.

"Monday, he wants to be settled in before I have to leave," she explained turning the car off and taking one last look in the review mirror. "Ready?"

"Let's go."

Once inside, Ronnie met Billy with a huge smile and kiss that I could have lived without seeing.

"Get a room." I took off my coat and hung it on the hooks by the door. I noticed Dolan's jacket along with a few others that I didn't recognize. I figured that Ronnie invited some old friends from high school. "Where's Dolan, Ronnie?"

"Try the kitchen. He went to put the beer in the fridge," Ronnie said with Billy-Jean still tangled in his arms. I shook my head and walked past them.

"Wait, Anna. I'm coming with you. Beer sounds amazing," Billy said grabbing my hand.

"You are such an alcoholic," I joked.

We walked into the kitchen and saw Dolan and a guy I remembered from high school. I smiled at Dolan as he walked towards me. Billy slid passed him and went to the fridge. Dolan wrapped his arms tightly around my waist. I kissed his lips gently. He pulled me closer and kissed me violently. I pulled away from him and glared.

"Dolan," I hissed. He laughed and shrugged his shoulders. He leaned forward and kissed the tip of my nose. As my cheeks burned, I smiled, hesitantly, and got a drink.

A few hours and a couple drinks later, Billy and Ronnie had disappeared upstairs. Most of the guests had gone home a long time ago. Dolan sat on the couch next to me, finishing his umpteenth beer. He set the bottle down and looked at me.

He leaned forward, kissing my neck. As he leaned forward, I leaned backwards, lying down on the couch. Dolan continued to kiss my lips, cheeks, neck and began to move farther down my chest. I pulled his face back up to mine and redirected his kiss to my lips.

"Want to go upstairs, Bell?" He smirked.

I had a few drinks myself but I understood exactly what he wanted. I looked up at him with an annoyed look.

"Dolan, you know exactly what I'm going to say." I repeated this line every time Dolan drank.

"Come on, Bell. You know you want me." His breath kissed my nose. I turned my head as he leaned forward to kiss me. Taking my

turned face as an opportunity, Dolan grabbed my chest. I pushed him off the couch.

"Stop it, Dolan, "I growled. I stood up from the couch and turned to walk away.

Dolan reached forward and grabbed my arm. He pulled me back to him and pressed his body up against mine. I pushed against him, in protest. Instead of letting go, Dolan pushed me onto the couch. Using his body to overpower me, Dolan got on top of me.

"Dolan, get the fuck off me," I yelled. My intent was to get Billy-Jean's attention. Dolan slapped me across the face.

I didn't waste time and I began to scream at the top of my lungs. A thunderous noise from upstairs came barreling down the stairs as Dolan wrapped his hand around my neck.

"Annabelle!" Billy-Jean's voice screamed. Ronnie charged at Dolan.

"Annabelle!" Billy-Jean said waving her hand in front of my face, waking me from my day dream. Or day "mare" is what I would like to call memories like that. "Earth to Annabelle, come in Annabelle."

"What?" I asked quietly holding back tears.

"What were you thinking about?"

"Nothing, just wondering how I did on the essay."

"Anna. Seriously, just relax. You turned in your final exam of your college career." Billy-Jean tugged on the strap of my bag, pulling me from my spot on the floor.

"But what if –" I started.

"No buts missy. Today is the start of a new life. You are Annabelle Dawn Rockart, a brilliant and beautiful 22 year old woman who needs a break!" Billy said pulling me, still, by the strap of my bag.

"'k Billy, you can let go now. I'm okay. People are staring," I said as she let go of me. She smiled but that soon turned into hysterical laughing. "Billy, quiet down! People are taking exams!" I whispered loudly, almost hissing at my best friend. This only made her laugh harder. I shook my head and pulled her out the door.

We left the college and met the fresh snowfall on the ground. It was such a welcoming sight for me, calming. I smiled inward and waited for Billy to notice.

Her laughter came to a screeching halt, "Damn it! I hate Maine!" I laughed out loud this time. Billy-Jean was from Texas and she had never gotten used to the weather here in Fort Kent, Maine. She moved here in the summer before our junior year in high school and we were now in our senior year in college. "I wish I was back in Texas."

"No worries Bills. You'll be leaving tomorrow," I told her sadly. She was flying to Texas for three weeks. Billy had spent every winter break, since she moved here, with her Grandma in Texas. This year I was really going to miss her. I looked down at my feet as we shuffled through the snow to her car.

"No worries Ann, I'll be home on January 2nd! That's only three weeks away. I'll be back before you know it." Billy put her arm around me and we continued walking.

"I can't believe we're graduating Monday." I laughed and shook my head. "And I can't believe you are going to miss your college graduation."

"Oh, please. It's a long, drawn out ceremony to celebrate something I have to continue next year anyway," Billy joked.

"Not my fault. You wanted to be a lawyer," I pointed out. She laughed and stuck her tongue out. "I'll still miss you. After Dolan–"

"You promised to never speak his name. He's not worth it Annabelle Dawn," she told me sternly, using my full name as if she was my mother. She smiled sweetly, "I'll call you everyday Anna. No worries, right?"

"No worries," I promised. I couldn't help but feel a little bit of my hope fly away from me with that promise. Of course there were worries. What if I see him at work? What about his parents? What do I say? Do they know the truth? Should I mention it to them to make sure they know the truth? *Slow down, girlfriend,* I told myself.

We hurried into Billy's car. I put on my seat belt and she started it. She shivered for the first five minutes until it warmed up. I was quite comfortable. I loved the snow. It always made me smile.

When I was little I would pretend that I was a Snow Princess. In a pink tutu and snow boots, I would go out into the snow and dance around the yard. My mom would always yell for me to come back inside and get bundled up properly. That is my mom, Mrs. Do-Everything-Properly. Even though I never understood her, I know now that she meant well.

"I have to stop at the store on the way home; Ronnie wants me to pick up a lint roller," she reminded herself out loud as we exited the expressway. "I don't understand why he needs one. Felix isn't shedding at all. Just normal cat hair." She shrugged.

"Well he just moved in Billy, he's not used to living with *any* cat hair. Give him time to adjust," I told her thoughtfully. With a nod, she sighed. I left it at that, avoiding any chance of an argument. I shook my head and focused my attention back on the falling snow. When I saw the neighborhood kids walking home from school, I smiled.

The traffic light turned red and Billy stopped her car right as the three kids, two boys and a girl, crossed the street. One of the boys, the taller, and chubbier of the two, scooped up a handful of snow and threw it at the girl's back. The snowball hit her small frame and she fell forward from the force of the boy's throw. She fell to her knees and dropped her books. The shorter, skinnier boy of the two stopped to pick up the girl's now soaking books and helped her up. She wiped off her tears and quickly grabbed her books from the skinny boy and took off running in the opposite direction they were headed. The light turned green and the last thing I saw was the skinny boy jump on the chubby boy. I laughed.

"What?" Billy-Jean questioned turning into the parking lot of the corner store. I smiled.

"Just watching the little kids …" I trailed off thinking about childhood. How easy, and worry free it was to be a child. *It would be nice to go back to that.*

"You're so out of it right now. Are you sure you're okay, Anna?"

"Not at all Billy," I began, feeling Billy's eyes on me. "I don't feel like I'm ever going to find a man who can actually treat me like a human being instead of an object to own or use and ruin. I want to find the one guy in the world that would risk everything including his own well being to make me safe and happy."

"Annabelle…" Billy's voice was sympathetic.

"Don't Billy, just leave it alone. I'm fine." I cut her short and unbuckled my seat belt. She shivered again when we got out of the car and I could hear her cursing as we walked towards the store.

"Good Afternoon, girls," Mrs. Anderson, the store owner, called when she heard the bell on the door ring.

"Hello," we said together, heading towards the pet aisle. Billy shoved her hands in her pockets trying to stay warm in the old store. It was easy to get frost bite in this old store; an icy draft swept through the aisles, even with the door closed.

"Hey, I'm going to go get the lint brush. Will you go pick up a bottle of wine? Something tells me that you need a nice glass of wine." She smiled. She was right, again. I needed something to calm me down and start the relaxation period of this break. *Nothing is better than a glass of wine and your best friend.*

"Okay, meet me over in the liquor aisle; you know how long it takes me to pick out wine." I laughed and headed in the opposite direction of Billy to the back corner of the store. I walked in the chilly air of the store and turned slowly down the aisle reading the labels on the bottles. I could hardly pronounce any of the names, but I knew the label of the kind I enjoyed most on a day like today. I continued walking with my eyes glued on the bottles.

As I approached the end of the aisle, I looked up just in time to see a tall, brown haired man facing the opposite direction. We were standing so close that if I wouldn't have looked up when I did, I would have ran straight into him.

"I'm sorry, excuse me," I said politely as he turned around. There in front of me stood none other than Dolan.

He didn't say a word; we just kind of stared at each other. I was speechless and immobile. I couldn't remember how to forms words or even how to think. Telling my legs to work was impossible and my mind went wild.

Relax Annabelle. But he's standing right in front of me.

Then the tears welled up in my eyes. *Keep yourself together. Don't let him see you cry.*

I didn't think I would feel this way when I saw him again. I have to say something.

No! Annabelle. You can't. Remember your promise to Billy-Jean. Never talk to him again. He is an asshole. But I still love him. Maybe he has an excuse. *Listen to yourself. What kind of excuse could there possibly be for trying to force your girlfriend to have sex with you?*

I had to turn and walk away. I had to figure out how to tell my body to move. I couldn't face him, not yet. Not here. *Take a deep breath and go.* Just go. I slowly gained control of my neck and turned my head away from him. It was as if that first movement triggered the rest of my muscles. I turned quickly and my tears fell fast, leaving salty, wet streaks down either side of my face. I moved steadily down the aisle.

It seemed like Dolan had stayed where he was until I heard him say, "I'm sorry, Bell."

The world stopped. I don't know if was anger or sadness, but a hurricane of tears ripped through my eyes. My body shook violently; I couldn't remember how to breathe. I pivoted my body and looked back at him, not a single breath escaped from my lips and no beat could be felt in my chest. Time stopped.

"W-what... I-I..." I was completely speechless when Dolan began moving closer to me. He walked slowly as if he were coming across a wounded animal, waiting for it to react defensively to any approaching creature. My body felt wounded. My mind felt defensive. But I couldn't react. He reached out to me slowly. When he touched my arm, lightning struck my body. I lost it. Ragged breaths escaped my lips, I quickly inhaled with whimper. I shook uncontrollably as he pulled me into his arms.

How could a mere embrace from this man cause such a terrible break in my heart? Was it because, deep down, I wanted to love him, but didn't know how? Or was it because I longed so sincerely to be with him and a promise made to the person who kept me grounded forbids me to even think of him? *So torn.* This is stupid. I need to talk to him. He said he was sorry. He was drunk, it was a mistake. But the emotions running through my mind and body prevented me from even forming a sentence.

"Anna, check out this lint roller. You can use your vacuum to-" Billy stopped in her tracks. To think what was going through her mind when she saw her hysterical best friend wrapped in the arms of ex-boyfriend is beyond my imagination. The look on her face turned to pure hatred and she stepped forward. I thought she might yell at me for breaking our promise, but instead she ripped me front Dolan's arms.

"How dare you touch her? Why can't you just leave her alone? You know, I stuck up for you for the longest time Dolan. What the hell gives you the nerve to even talk to her after what you've done to her?" Billy-Jean yelled, completely enraged. I put my hand on her shoulder trying to get her attention. She continued to yell things that didn't even register in my ears. With tears still streaming down my face, I looked

10

over to Dolan. The look on his face hadn't changed. He looked sad, not the slightest bit angry for Billy yelling horrible things in his face. He looked at me and I noticed a tear sitting at the edge of his eye lid. I had never seen him cry, or even close to crying. *You need to talk to him.* I need to talk to him soon.

"Billy, please. Let's go," I whispered to her. She stopped yelling and looked at me sadly. She put her hands on my face, wiping the tears from my eyes. It was pointless because they continued to fall.

"I'll leave," Dolan spoke quietly and walked swiftly past us. I turned to see him walk out the door. *You can call him later.*

"I'm so sorry Ann. I should have never left you alone."

"I'm not a child, Billy!" I snapped. I couldn't stand her babying right now. I was a mess.

"I'm sorry." She sounded hurt. "Let me pay for this and we'll go" And she walked to the counter.

"Is everything alright girls?" Mrs. Anderson asked curiously having just heard Billy's yelling.

"No, but it will be," Billy answered quietly. I looked down, avoiding Mrs. Anderson's eyes. News traveled so fast around this tiny town that my parents would know about this little episode by the time I got home later and there would be a message on my answering machine.

Billy paid for the lint roller and we walked quietly out to her car. There was about an inch of snow covering her car after only the short time we spent in the store. The heavy snowfall had turned into a light flurry and the wind had given up its fight with the winter air. I looked up at the clouds and let the snowflakes fall into my face.

"Anna, I'm sorry."

"Don't apologize, Bills. You were just looking out for me. I understand. I snapped; too much all at once." I gave her a weak smile. "I just want to go home."

"No worries Ann, we'll get you home right now." She smiled and we got into her car.

The drive from the corner store to my small, one bedroom apartment was short and quiet. In the car, the Christmas music whispered ever so softly through the car. Outside, the flurries danced across the windshield and the wind blew, carrying the dust-like layer of snow across the road in front of the car. The sky had no sign of life because the birds were long gone for winter. The clouds blanketed my little town, Fort Kent, Maine, like a quilt on a cold day. The weather was actually quite mild for December in Maine. By now the ground was usually covered in a foot of snow which was then covered by three inches of ice. There was barely five inches covering the ground.

Billy-Jean pulled into the parking lot of my apartment complex and parked in the spot next to my car.

"Do you want me to come in with you?" Billy knew my usual reaction would be to say yes and let her comfort my horrible mood.

"Not today. I'm just going to go inside and turn on a Lifetime movie to make my tears seem like they were caused by something other than a boy," I said as I grabbed my bag from the back seat. She looked back at me sadly. "No worries Bills. I'm okay. You don't have to worry about me. I will be 110% tomorrow morning when I pick you up for the airport."

"Good. If you need me, call. Nothing is more important than keeping you happy." She smiled and gave me a hug. "Until tomorrow?"

"Until tomorrow," I promised. She smiled and I got out of her car. I stood by and waved as she drove away. I looked through my bag for my keys as I walked to the door of the building. As I got to the door I noticed my neighbor, Grady, coming out so I didn't bother continuing to struggle with my big purse.

"Excuse me," he said politely, holding the door open for me.

"Thank you." I smiled walking past him and through the door. I went on my way to the mail boxes to grab my mail and go; nothing but bills, *just what you need.* I walked up the stairs to my second floor apartment, stopping at my door, B2. Sticking out from under my door was an envelope. When I picked it up and it had my name printed neatly on the outside.

I finally found my keys and let myself into the apartment. I locked the door behind me, dropping my bag on the floor. While I took my coat off, I pressed the answering machine button. I kept my eyes glued on the envelope that I had placed on the hall table.

"Annabelle, this is your mother. Please give me a call later. I stopped at the market today and heard some disturbing news from Mrs. Anderson. Call me as soon as you get this because I really think that you should-" I cut the message off and hit the delete button. I was in no mood to hear a lecture from my mother. *Maybe a couple drinks before you call her will do the trick.*

After I had my shoes and coat put away, I grabbed the letter and went to the couch. I finally realized whose handwriting it was, *Dolan's.*

I sat down on the couch and placed the envelope on the coffee table in front of me. *You shouldn't open it.* But I want to open it. *You promised Billy.* I promised her I wouldn't talk to him or about him. We never said anything about him writing to me. *Seems like a thin line to me.*

"Shut up!" I told myself. "Just open the damn thing. How far can I be pushed in one day?" I opened the envelope slowly, taking deep breaths. It's just a letter, right? *Wrong, you shouldn't open it.* But I want to, *your choice.* When I opened it I saw Dolan's neat handwriting that formed only four brief lines.

I have to talk to you. Nothing is more important than apologizing for my mistake. Please, give me the chance to explain myself.

I love you Bell. -Dolan.

My hand shook as I finished the note. I let a few tears roll down my cheek. *Don't let him fool you Annabelle.* I have to just give him two minutes to explain. *You don't have to give him anything.* I need to know the truth. I want to know the truth. With a shaking hand, I picked up my phone. I dialed the number that was so familiar to me after three years of dating him.

The phone rang once, "Hello?" Dolan's voice was calm and quiet.

"Dolan?" My voice shook and my throat was dry. Silence, "I'm giving you a chance to explain." More silence, "hello?"

"Can I come to your apartment? I need to talk to you, face to face." He asked softly.

Don't let him. He doesn't mean that. He will just hurt you again. Shut up.

"Yes. You can come here." I hung up the phone. I sat shaking and completely shocked. I got up from the couch and paced back and forth once or twice. *What did you do, Annabelle?*

I felt sick. I walked to the bathroom, in fear of losing my lunch. My chest tightened and I gasped for a breath. I put my head down; I choked out a few tears and braced myself on the sink. *You're a mess Annabelle.* I lifted my head to look into the mirror. My light brown hair hung, disheveled in my face. I took a deep breath and tucked my hair behind my ears. I wiped my tears dry and cleaned my mascara stained face. I looked back into the mirror; my once brilliant blue eyes were dull. *You aren't yourself anymore Annabelle.*

After only five minutes of emotionally preparing myself for the worst, my door bell rang.

"Hello Bell." Dolan said quietly from his spot in the doorway. The door frame acted like a boundary between two warring countries.

We stood in silence for a good two minutes, and my eyes wondered everywhere but his face. I felt his eyes burning into my skin. I didn't know how to feel. I didn't exactly know what to do. *Close the door in his face sounds like a good idea to me.*

Dolan broke the silence. "Thank you for giving me a chance."

"I'm giving you five minutes," I retorted.

We stood awkwardly at the door for a few more minutes before I shook my head and walked into my apartment, leaving the door wide open. I heard the door close and he followed me to the kitchen table. I sat down at one end of the table and Dolan stood quietly in the doorway of the kitchen.

"Well," I pushed. *What excuse can he come up with today...?*

"What happened last week was a mistake on my part."

"Clearly." I felt the anger begin to boil under my skin. Dolan closed his mouth tightly.

"I had been drinking."

"Typical answer." *What an idiot.*

"Bell, please, let me finish," Dolan pleaded, now sitting down in the chair across the table from me.

"Fine." I folded my arms across my chest and waited.

"I don't know what came over me. I should have never pressured you or hurt you the way I did." Dolan's brown eyes pierced through mine. I felt my eyes swell with tears. "I know I've done this before."

"To say the least," I added. Dolan sat quietly for a minute. He put his hand in his coat pocket and looked at me nervously.

"I was planning on giving you this that night." He placed a small, red velvet box on the table in front of me. *A ring?*

"Is that a-"

"Yes." Dolan avoided my eyes. "And I was ready to ask you, but then I got so nervous, I started drinking." Dolan's voice changed in a split second. I sat quietly.

"I love you, Annabelle." Dolan's words echoed through my mind.

I couldn't breathe. *Don't even do it, Annabelle.* I couldn't say yes to him. Not yet, it was too soon to even forgive him let alone accept a marriage proposal.

"Dolan, I-I can't s-say… I don't… you… It's too much," I stammered. He nodded.

"You don't need to say anything right now. I understand how you feel," Dolan sympathized. "You need time. I'll give you as much as you need. I'm always around, Bell," he reminded me.

I looked at him and he smiled sadly. I couldn't breathe again. The tears began burning my eyes and I put my head down. He stood for a moment, but then turned and walked from the kitchen. I heard the door open, then close slowly.

Wow, I don't know what you should do now. Maybe he was serious…

"Yeah, you think?" I spoke to myself out loud. *Damn it, Annabelle. Get him.*

I got up from my seat, grabbing the ring box, and ran out the door after Dolan.

"Dolan!" I called as I opened the door. He was at the end of the hallway. I paused in the doorway, and watched him turn around.

We stared at each other from the places we stood. I didn't exactly know what to say. *Tell him you love him.* No, not yet. I need to ease myself down. *Just tell him to come back.*

"D-do you … want to c-come back in?" I forced the sentence out, closing my eyes like I was in pain. *Why do you do this to yourself?* I hadn't figured that out yet.

"If you would like me to, yes I will." Dolan stood still in his spot at the top of the stairs.

"Yes," I blurted out. *Do you?* "Yes, come in," I repeated. He smiled and walked towards me. When he met me at the door, I stopped him by placing my hand on his chest.

"One thing, before I give you this chance," I began. I held out the little velvet box in my hand. "Take this back. I'm not ready for this yet."

He looked down at the box, then back at me. "I bought it for you."

"I can't accept it Dolan."

"But I have no use for it," he argued.

"Just take it, please, don't make this harder."

16

"But I-"

"TAKE IT!" My impatient anger got the best of me. Dolan seemed a bit shaken as he slowly took the box from my hand. As I watched his shaking hand take it from my hands, something inside me snapped.

Emotions poured out of my body, I felt the tears leave my eyes and my stomach turned into knots. My body shook and I couldn't control the sounds that escaped my lips. I whimpered, cries of agony rushed through my lips as I felt my knees shake beneath me. *You pushed yourself too far.*

"Bell? Are you okay?" Dolan's voice was concerned. I looked up into his eyes.

"Am I okay? What kind of question is that? One minute I have to hate you for everything you are and everything that I once loved. Now, you tell me that you want to marry me! And I'm just supposed to be okay?" My voice echoed through the halls of the building. Dolan stood, like stone, in front of me, speechless.

"Dolan, I was in love with you. I was so ready to be yours, for life. Now, I don't know what I want. I want to believe you are telling me the truth. I really do. But I'm so far passed trusting you. I'm so far gone…" I spoke so fast that my mind was having a hard time keeping up. *Girl, you did this to yourself.*

Dolan stood silently, waiting for me to make a move. I thought back to the first time I had accepted Dolan back into my life. It was over a year ago when he slapped me at the mall. My family never accepted him again. Billy-Jean and Ronnie had given him a second chance when they saw how much I wanted to make it work. I felt the same pain in my chest, longing to hold him.

"This is stupid… I am so sick of being unhappy," I stammered through my tears. I turned without another word and returned to my living room. After a few seconds, I heard the door close and Dolan followed me.

Dolan, still speechless, grabbed a blanket from the back of the couch and draped it over my body. I continued my blubbering speech. "Dolan, you can't even begin to imagine how much I have wanted to talk to you… I have been so lost without you, but I don't know how to believe that you won't…"

Dolan left the room, walked into the kitchen, and came back with a glass of water. He held it out for me to take. I didn't take it. Dolan sat down next to me still holding the glass.

"Why are you allowing me to yell at you?"

Dolan finally spoke. "Because I care about you Bell, you mean the world to me."

I stared at him for a minute. Though I had heard it time and time before, I didn't know how to react to his statement. I had never felt this torn in my life. *Tell me about it.* After a few minutes of silent staring, Dolan got up to leave. I grabbed his arm.

"Don't leave," I almost begged. *You are dependent on a man that doesn't deserve you.*

He sat back down on the couch next to me. This time, I moved closer. After having the mental break down, I needed him. I needed his arms around me and his heartbeat in my ear. I rested my head against his chest. I felt his hesitation to put his arms around me. When he did, something inside of me felt right. But at the same time, something inside of me felt wrong. *Billy-Jean will never forgive you.*

As that thought ran through my head, my phone rang. I nearly jumped out of my skin when the sound of Billy-Jean's ringtone hit my ear.

"Hang on," I told Dolan, reaching for my phone with a shaking hand. I opened it and put it to my ear. "Hello." I put my index finger to my mouth and motioned for Dolan to stay quiet. *You are in so much trouble.*

"Hey Ann, how are you doing?" Billy asked. *Ha, it would be easier to ask, "How don't you feel?" It's a shorter list.*

"I'm okay," I lied. *You're doing a lot of that, aren't you?*

"Are you sure you don't want to hang out tonight? You sound terrible Anna." *Gee, thanks Billy.*

"No. I'm okay, really. You need to pack and I just need some sleep." I looked at Dolan who rubbed my hand gently.

"Okay. But make sure you call me the second you want someone to talk to. I don't care what time it is," Billy reassured me. I smiled.

"Thanks Bills. No worries."

"Goodnight Annabelle." Billy yawned.

"Goodnight Billy-Jean." I laughed. She hung up. I closed my phone and placed it back on the table. I turned to Dolan.

"What now?" he asked with a smile.

"I'm not sure." I looked down at our entwined hands. "This shouldn't be easy. I should be angry. Shouldn't I?"

"I can't decide that for you."

I looked up at him and smiled. "I missed you."

Dolan smiled and squeezed my hand. "You don't know how good that makes me feel to here you say that."

"Good." I leaned my forehead on his shoulder. *Can't believe a day ago you were telling yourself to move on, now you're back in his arms.*

"I'm not going to rush you, Bell." He brushed my hair away from my face and pulled my chin up to look at him. I felt him leaning closer to me. As his lips closed in on their target, I turned my head and he kissed my cheek.

"Too fast," I whispered.

"I'm sorry."

"It's alright." I yawned. "I should be getting to bed. I have to take Billy to the airport in the morning."

"It's only 9:30pm," Dolan pointed out. I sighed.

"You should go Dolan." I hoped he would take the hint. "I have to call my mother."

"Are you sure you don't want me to stay?" He seemed persistent on staying longer.

"Dolan, don't push things. Please." I stood up from the couch. He grabbed my arm and pulled me into his grip. "Dolan, let go of me please." His grip tightened. I felt my skin twist under his grip. "Dolan." Pain swept through my arm. "You're hurting me."

I looked into his eyes and he seemed to be angry.

"Why can't I stay with you Bell? Don't you want to try and get through this?"

"Dolan. Let. Go. Of. My. Arm," I said sternly. His grip didn't loosen. *Punch him, kick his ass out.*

"No." He stayed calm, but his eyes still read angry. I had done this to myself. *Yes, you did.*

I stood up again, trying to force my arm out of his grip. He held his grip around my arm and twisted it behind my back. He stood up and pushed all his body weight onto my tiny frame. My body sunk into the couch cushion. *One wrong move and he will snap your arm like a twig.*

19

"Dolan, please stop. You're hurting me." I felt my voice straining with the sting of regret. He didn't say a word. I needed to use every ounce of strength in my body to push him off of me. *Kick, scream, and punch.*

I kicked my leg up at hard as I could. I must have aimed just right, his weight buckled over me. Adrenaline rushing through my veins, I rolled him off me. I stood up and grabbed my phone. I ran and stood behind the couch. I saw him roll off the couch, grab himself and groan loudly. *Bulls-eye.* I opened my phone, pressed speed dial to call Billy. *She's going to kill you.* I quickly closed my phone.

"Dolan, get out of my apartment before I call the police." My voice shook, but I yelled louder than I thought I could. He groaned again. "You have ten seconds until I call the police, Dolan." *You wanted to let him in.* Shut up.

He stood up slowly. "Bell, I'm so sorry. I don't know what came over me. Forgive me, please. I didn't mean it." As he moved around the couch, I went towards the doorway.

"Bullshit! You knew exactly what you were doing! Get the hell out of here, RIGHT NOW!" My anger shook through my body. My face burned crimson.

"Bell, please," he pleaded.

"Get. Out. NOW!" I opened the door for him to leave. He walked slowly towards me.

"I am sorry Bell-"

"Save it for someone who cares. I'm done with you. You've had more chances than you ever deserved! You ruined them all. I'm over it."

He was silent. He stared at me for a minute then he smirked. "Fine, but you'll be missing out."

That's it. I reached up and slapped him across the face. He raised his hand to retaliate when my brother's voice came from the hallway,

"Touch her and you'll regret it, Meyer." Evan didn't waste time pushing Dolan out the door and slamming it in his face. *Thank God for being the baby sister.*

I felt the tears burn my eyes. As the adrenaline drained, my body shook and my head spun. I reached out for Evan and he pulled me into his arms. His six foot three frame easily lifted my five foot two frame off the ground and took me to the couch. "Why was he here, Anna? What happened?"

I looked up at him and shook my head absently. "I-I... h-he was... I-I... and a ring... I-I was going t-to..."

"Okay, okay. Calm down. It's okay." Evan put his arms around me and rocked back and forth like our mom did when we were upset as kids. *You're lucky you have a brother.* I couldn't register anything that had just happened. I was so grateful that he showed up when he did. He let go of his embrace and he held me in front of him, with both hands on my shoulders, and looked into my eyes. "Now, why was Meyer here Anna, did you invite him?"

I nodded my head, but changed my mind quickly and shook it back and forth obsessively.

"Yes or no Anna, did he force his way in or did you let him in?"

I stopped shaking my head no and said, "I-I let him in. B-but he wasn't... he didn't... he was sorry." I felt like a child who has just been caught drawing on the wall in red permanent marker.

"Why did you let him in, Annabelle? He is just going to keep hurting you," Evan tried to convince me. *Where have you heard that before?* "You can be so naive."

"B-but he seemed so sincere. Evan, he had a ring. I was so sure I was doing the right thing." The tears streamed down my face. "It was my fault. I let him in. I should have been smarter. I'm sorry."

"Stop it. Stop apologizing right now." He pulled me into his chest and I started to cry harder. "Anna, it's not your fault that Dolan Meyer is a dick. Don't say you're sorry. You have nothing to be sorry for."

Evan was the perfect big brother. We never fought like average brothers and sisters did. We had always gotten along. He had protected me ever since I could remember. Believe me, no one messed with me in high school. Evan was six foot in his freshman year of high school. Now he is 6'3 and a devoted member at the local gym. *Permanent body guard...*

"Thank you." I told him, wiping my tears. "What brought you over here in the first place?"

"Well, mom called." That was all he needed to say.

"Say no more, I'm on it."

I opened my phone and dialed my parents' number; one ring and, "Hello?"

"Hi Ma," I sighed.

"Annabelle Dawn. Why haven't you called me? I've been so worried. I waited for your call and when you didn't call, I called Billy and she said you should be home. So I called Evan to go check on you. Are you okay? I talked to Mrs. Anderson today and she said that there was a problem in the store with that damn Meyer boy again. I told you that boy was bad news." I made sure she was done with her little speech and took my time to respond.

"Ma, I'm fine. Relax. Nothing happened. Everything is over. Dolan is out of my life." I gave Evan a look of complete exhaustion.

"What do you mean? Did you talk to that boy? Annabelle, he's bad news. Don't listen to anything he says." *She's your mother, be nice.*

"Yes mother, I know that now." I'm sure I sounded annoyed.

"Okay. Well get some sleep. It's nearly 10:30 and you have to wake up and take Billy to the airport at seven."

"Yes, mother. I'm getting off the phone right now and going to bed." I rolled my eyes at Evan.

"Goodnight sweetheart. I only worry because I love you."

"I love you too, Ma." I smiled inward.

"Buh-bye."

"Bye, Ma." I closed my phone and sighed heavily.

"That wasn't too bad." Evan joked. I punched him playfully. *He's right.*

"Don't tell her anything about tonight," I told him, begging with my eyes.

"I promise, Anna." Evan smiled. I relaxed.

"I do need to sleep now." I stretched and stood up. "Thanks Evan. I appreciate it."

"I know. I'm always here, Anna." He pulled me into a goodbye hug.

I winced as he hugged me tightly.

"Are you hurt?" he questioned, holding my shoulders.

"My arm, it's probably nothing," I said shyly running my left hand up and down my right arm.

"Let me look at it." Evan pulled my sleeve up. Nothing was there.

22

"See, it's nothing." I smiled up at him. He shook his head and we said goodbye. I shut and locked the door; turning around to lean against it.

"What a night." I sighed and walked through the living room to my room. When I walked into my room, I turned on the lamp near the bed and sat at the edge of my bed. *Don't even think about it now.* I turned down the sheets and changed out of my clothes into something comfortable for bed.

Sleep wasn't exactly my favorite part of the day like it is for most people. I hated sleeping. If my body didn't need sleep to rejuvenate every night, my life would be that much better. Sleep is lonely and you can't control what goes on in your dreams. I much prefer being awake, in the daylight, where I could normally choose what goes on in my mind. Sleep is dark, I hate the dark. Darkness is blinding. Not being able to see my surroundings, not knowing where I am is my worst phobia. *You worry too much.* I buried myself under the covers and turned out my light.

He's out of my life for good. *Isn't that what you said the last time?*

Saturday, December 13th

Buzz, Buzz, Buzz, *Reminder to self: Kill alarm clock.*

The morning came so fast it felt like I had never fallen asleep at all. I woke up in a haze. The sleep weighed heavily on my eyes as I stumbled to the shower. I lingered in the hot water as long as I could, *time to go.* The steam rolled out of the bathroom as I walked back to my room to change.

When I finished getting dressed, reality hit me. Billy was leaving today for three weeks. She doesn't know about what happened last night. *She is going to kill you.* I won't ruin her trip; I'll keep it to myself. *She won't be happy you kept it from her for so long either.* Damn it. I didn't have enough time to explain everything to her. *You have an hour car ride to the airport.* But I won't be able to really explain. *Stop making excuses.*

"I'll do it!" I yelled at myself. I sighed and finished getting ready. When I grabbed my brush to do my hair, I noticed it. *Now that's a bruise...* On my right forearm lay a dark purple stripe, the exact size of Dolan's hand.

"Awesome, more to explain," I told myself. *You will have a coat on.*

I finished my hair and grabbed my purse. It was ten to seven and I would be just on time to pick Billy-Jean up from her apartment.

I parked my car outside her building and got out. I knew she would have tons of bags to carry. *She never packs light.* As soon as I stepped up on the landing, the door opened. Billy smiled happily and hugged me. She pulled me inside and up the stairs to the third floor.

"Whoa girl, what's up?" I questioned finally getting my arm back from her. I rubbed the freshly painful bruise from last night. Billy squirmed around in front of me like she was a five year old waiting to sit on Santa's lap. She giggled and held out her left hand. A shiny rock had been wrapped around her ring finger, making itself a new, permanent home there.

"Wow." I felt happy for her, but an angry batch of envy brewed within my body. I felt as though I might turn green and give away my fake smile. "When did he ask you?"

"Last night after I got off the phone with you, Anna, you have no idea how cute he was. Fumblin' over his words, hands shakin' and sweatin' buckets," Billy explained in her southern accent and smiled brightly. *Just be happy for her Annabelle. She deserves it.*

"I am so happy for you Bills. You deserve this more than anyone I know." I was being completely honest; she was very deserving of this. Billy and Ronnie had been together since the beginning of our senior year in high school. I reached out to give her a hug. She gladly pulled me into her chest. I couldn't help but smile.

"Where is the lucky man?" I asked pulling away from her and looking around the apartment for Ronnie.

"Oh, he already left for work." She smiled, twirling the ring around her finger.

"Already? It's only 7am. Is he opening today?" Ronnie and I both work for Nancy and Matt Meyers at their bookstore, Meyer Books. *Yes, Dolan's parents.*

"Yeah, he picked up for D-... him." She stopped herself from saying Dolan's name. *At least someone sticks to a promise.*

"Are you all ready to go then?" I pushed the subject away from my mind. She smiled.

"Yep, my bags are right there." She pointed to a pile of two large suitcases, one carryon bag and a cat carrier with Felix fast asleep in it. I laughed and rolled my eyes. I went to pick up one of the large bags and winced at the pain that shot through my arm.

"Are you okay, Anna?" Billy asked. I shook my right arm a little.

"Yeah, yeah, I'm fine, just a little slip on the ice this morning. Fell on my hand, no big deal. That's why God gave us two arms, right?" I lied, using my other hand to pick up the bag.

"Let me take a look Anna. You should get it checked out to make sure you didn't break anything." Billy reached for my hand. I quickly moved it out of her reach.

"It's no big deal really. I'll be fine." I tried to convince her. *You are in for it now.*

"Annabelle. Let me look at your arm. What is the big deal?" She smiled at me and held out her hand. I bit my lip and sighed. I pulled my right arm out of my coat and set my hand in hers.

"Annabelle." She gasped. She traced the bruise with her thumb. "This isn't a fall injury." She looked up at me concerned. "Who did this to you?" I avoided her eyes. She put her hand on my chin and lifted my face to meet hers. "Who, Annabelle?"

"Dolan," I whispered. She dropped my arm.

"Yesterday at the store?" I heard the anger in her voice.

"No." I paused and looked down again. "Last night, in my apartment." I let a tear of shame fall. Billy was silent for only a few seconds.

"Why was he at your apartment?"

"Billy, I was stupid. That's why he was at my apartment. Okay, happy?" I let the tears fall freely now. I sat down on the couch and put my face in my hands.

"Annabelle. You're not stupid." Billy still sounded annoyed. She sighed and I felt her sit down beside me. "Maybe I should stay home."

"No, no. Billy, you are leaving. You don't need to stay here and babysit me. I am going to be just fine," I said sincerely. *She is an amazing friend.*

"You know I'm a phone call away right?" she asked. I nodded and smiled. She hugged me and got up from the couch. I grabbed the bag with my left arm this time and we left the apartment. I had her carryon over my right shoulder and the large bag over the other. We slowly made our way down the stairs to my car.

"Careful, it really is icy out," I cautioned her.

Once my little car was packed, and Felix was happily snoring in the backseat, we were on our way. The ride remained quiet most of the time. Billy kept sneaking glances at me. I knew she was concerned for me. I grabbed her hand.

"I'll be fine Billy. Please, have fun." I tried to convince her. *Or convince yourself...*

"I know you will. I just hate leaving you when you need me."

"I will be just fine. I have Evan and Allie. Madison will keep me busy. It's okay, really."

"All right." She smiled.

Convincing her was harder than convincing myself of things. *You've got that right.* I spent the rest of the drive wondering how I had become so impossibly dependant on the people around me. I clung to my friends and family as if they were my only hope for survival. Over the past year or so, I had lost myself in the mix of school, work and my poisonous relationship with Dolan. I sighed silently, knowing I needed help. Knowing I would lose myself completely if I was alone.

We arrived at the airport right at 8:10am.

"You have a good hour until your flight leaves," I told her opening the trunk of my car. She retrieved Felix from the backseat and set him on the baggage cart sitting on the sidewalk.

"I wish they would let you in there with me," Billy said standing in front of me. I saw the tears forming in her eyes.

"Don't you dare cry, Billy-Jean Miler," I joked at her as the tears formed in my eyes as well.

She wrapped her arms around me tightly. I did the same and tucked my face into her neck. I kissed her cheek and pulled away from her.

"Merry Christmas and Happy New Year and no making out with any boys, of course, don't want to make your fiancé jealous, do you?" I wiped the tears off her face. She did the same to me.

"Get going," I encouraged her.

"I promise I'll call when I get there." She waved. "No worries, Ann." She walked into the building. I watched her walk to the counter and then I got back into my car.

The way home was filled with cheerful music. Silence would make my mind wander too easily. I needed to get home and find something to occupy my time until work. It was 9:30am and I worked at 2:00pm. I wouldn't be out until 10:30 tonight. *Closing isn't the worst part of working there.* Today was going to be interesting.

I stopped at the light before my complex parking lot and felt my phone vibrating. I dug it out of my coat pocket and answered without looking to see who it was.

"Hello?" I asked hurriedly hoping I caught the call in time.

"Hey Anna," answered my brother's husky voice.

"Hi, what's up?" I asked as the light turned green.

"Well, I have a little favor to ask of you." He sounded like he might be begging.

"And what's that?" I smiled and pulled into the parking lot.

"Allie's car is in the shop and we need to pick it up before she has to work at 11."

"That's fine. Give me ten minutes and I'll be there."

"Thanks so much Anna." He sighed in relief.

"No problem Evan."

We hung up and I turned around in the closest parking spot. It took about five minutes to get to Evan's house when there wasn't any snow. The drive was easy and barely ever had traffic. I got to his house in less than ten minutes. The way to the front door was completely iced over. The one and only part of winter I've never enjoyed.

"Fabulous." *Just walk slowly.* I got out of my car and stood holding onto my car as I walked forward. *Not too bad.* I continued my voyage to the front door. I finally was only a few feet away from the door when I heard it.

"Oh no." *stay calm.* "Baby..." I regretted stopping when Evan's golden retriever, Baby, came barreling around the side of the house charging straight in my direction. Baby was so thrilled to see me that her split second decision to jump up into my arms was quickly intercepted by the large ice rink we were standing on. Instead of stopping, Baby came sliding into my legs which brought us both crashing down into the pile of snow sitting behind me.

"Great," I said out loud as Baby feverishly licked my face. "Yeah, yeah, nice to see you too Baby." *Dogs, gross.* I started to push her face away from mine when I heard a woman's voice from the front door.

"Baby! Back yard, now! Bad girl!" she bellowed and the dog galloped back into the yard. "Stupid dog," she muttered and turned to me. "Anna, I'm sorry about her, I told Evan to get a higher fence."

"It's cool. I love getting tackled by beastly, golden, hairballs."

Allie, Evan's wife and one of my best friends, reached her hand out to help me up off the ground. She had light blonde hair, a brilliant white smile and a gorgeous body that any girl would kill for. She was like looking into a mirror, only taller, lighter hair and green eyes. *So another words, you look nothing alike...* Her golden badge shined in the sunlight and I laughed.

"Reporting for duty, Sheriff Rockart," I joked.

"That's right missy. I am the law now." Allie laughed

"Congratulations! I heard about your promotion." I gave her a hug.

"Thanks, it's taking some getting used to." She smiled and sighed. "We're so glad you could come in such short notice, we appreciate it," she said as I brushed off the front of my clothes and followed her into the house.

"Evan's in the kitchen, I'll be right back down," Allie said running up the stairs.

I walked through the familiar house towards the kitchen. There was Evan sitting at the kitchen table eating what looked like eggs. The smell hit me as soon as I stepped toward him.

"Ugh, you and mushrooms, I swear, if you could have married a mushroom, you would have," I joked as I stood next to him.

"No, I married the next best thing." He laughed with a mouth full of food.

"What's that?" I gagged jokingly.

"I married a woman who loves them just as much or possibly more than me."

"Who could possibly love mushrooms more than Evan Rockart?" Allie questioned, walking into the room with her hands full; her three year old daughter in one arm, snow suit and bag in the other.

"There's my Maddy." I smiled happily. I put my arms out to her and she didn't hesitate to leave her mother's arms for mine. "Someone just woke up," I said to the sleepy child who immediately laid her head on my shoulder. She wiggled slightly and the small shift of her weight sent a wave of pain up my right arm. I winced.

"Are you okay? She's getting big isn't she?" Allie laughed running her fingers through Maddy's curly blonde hair. I smiled.

"Yeah, she's a big girl." I exchanged looks with Evan to make sure he kept quiet. He rolled his eyes and put his dishes in the sink.

I set Maddy down on the counter and took her snow suit from Allie. I slipped the little girls feet into the legs of the suit and picked her up off the counter.

"Maddy, I need you to stand up for Auntie. Can you do that for me?" I asked her. She nodded her head and I set her down on the ground. She helped me finish putting on her snow suit and then her pink princess snow boots. As soon as the last zipper was zipped and the last button was snapped she stuck her hands in the air for me to pick her up.

"You know, one day you're going to have to walk everywhere Madison," I told her. She shook her head and then set it on my shoulder. I laughed and shifted her weight to rest her on my left hip.

"Evan, will you help Anna put the car seat in her car? I am going to make sure I put everything in her bag. I forgot Mr. Ting-Ting and she went berserk on your mom last week." Allie stressed her laugh. She looked exhausted. *That's what being a police officer and a mother of a three year old can do to a person.*

Evan and I walked out to the car with Maddy beginning to fall asleep in my arms. Evan opened the back door and secured the car seat into place.

"Anna, you really should have someone look at your arm," he commented taking Maddy from me to put her in the car seat.

"Yeah, I know. I have to work until close today, tomorrow I'll go. I promise."

"You know, those Meyers are a real trip. I can't believe they have you working six days a week when their own son works two days a week," His older brother senses kicked in. He finished buckling Maddy in and closed the door. "Seems a little shitty to me."

"I know. Don't worry Evan. I need the money." I put my hand on his shoulder and said, "I know you're worried Evan, just trust me. I'm fine. I promise."

He just sighed and nodded his head. Allie glided out of the house with Maddy's bag in hand.

"Make sure Marie knows that she already had a nap, otherwise, she'll give her another one," Allie reminded me.

"We want her to sleep through the night," Evan joked putting the bag in the back seat.

"Thanks again Anna, it really helps," Allie said giving me a hug.

"No problem at all." I smiled patting her on the back.

"We will pay you back, I promise," Evan called as they walked to his truck. I got into my car and glanced back at the sleeping girl in the back seat. I decided no music would be the best not to wake her up. *Nothing worse than a grumpy three year old...*

It was ten am when I left Evan's house, the drive to my parent's house was fifteen minute drive in snowy conditions like today. By the time I got there it was almost 10:20. Maddy had begun to wake up when I pulled up the driveway to my childhood home. When I turned off the car, I turned around to look at the three year old. She yawned and smiled at me.

"Gama and Gampa?" she asked happily. I smiled.

"Yes. Grandma and Grandpa are going to watch you today until Daddy can pick you up later," I told her and she clapped happily. I unbuckled my seat belt and got out of the car. I was glad to see that the driveway had been shoveled and thoroughly salted. After he retired three years ago, my father had become a bit obsessive compulsive

30

when it came to keeping the yard neat during the warm seasons and the snow shoveled and cleared during winter.

I went around the car to the back passenger door and unbuckled Madison from her car seat. I set her down on the ground and grabbed her bag. Once I closed the door, I put my hand out to her and she gladly grabbed it. We made our way to the front door, slowly, as she looked at all the snow.

"Can we play?" she asked.

"Let's go inside to see grandma and grandpa, first, before we play," I told her and she seemed thrilled with the idea. She then began to tug on my arm to pull me faster into the house.

"Madison! Annabelle!" called my father from the back door. I smiled and let go of Madison's hand. *Thank God, thought she might pull it off.* The little girl ran to her Grandpa. Dad picked her up and held the door open for me. He had obviously just got done shoveling the back walk to the garage when I pulled in the driveway.

"Hello Daddy." I smiled and gave him a hug. As soon as we went inside, Madison was no longer a sleepy little girl. Her attention immediately focused on my parents' cat, Fig. Fig was an old, chubby tabby cat that could care less about the little girl. He was very tolerant. I left Madison alone with Fig and followed my dad. As we walked through the hallway, I noticed all the Christmas boxes had made their way down from the attic. My mom was cleaning dishes when we walked into the kitchen.

"Hey Ma, how are you?" I asked setting Maddy's bag on the kitchen table. I took my coat off and hung it on the back of a chair. "Are we still planning on putting the tree up tomorrow?"

"Of course! I finally got your father *inside* long enough to get the decorations out of the attic!" she said with a grumble. I laughed when my dad rolled his eyes.

"How are you doing today, Annabelle?" my dad asked, changing the subject, as he hung his coat on the hooks by the back door.

I answered with a completely straight face. "I'm great. I dropped off my best friend at the airport who I won't see for three weeks and I have to work until 10:30. I'm just fabulous."

"You're sarcasm is overwhelming, Annabelle. Cheer up for God's sake. Be grateful you're alive and well," my mom commented from her spot in front of sink.

"Yes, yes. I know Ma," I said sitting down at the counter. *Mothers, can't live with them, can't exist without them.*

"Annabelle. You need to get more serious with your life." My mother began her lecture about responsibility. *Here we go...*

"You are always joking around and not taking life seriously. You are graduating college on Monday and then it's out into the real world. I don't want you screwing up your life now. You have to get serious and focus on your future. And what am I hearing about Dolan at the grocery store yesterday? Are you talking to that boy again, Annabelle? You can't ruin your life over some silly boy."

"Ma, I told you last night. Don't worry about him anymore. He's out of my life for good. I promise." I tried to convince her. She shook her head and went on cleaning the dishes. I looked at my dad for any sympathy. He just shook his head and rolled his eyes at her. I laughed and took one of the fresh muffins sitting on the counter. *Just stay out of the line of fire, Annabelle.*

"I saw that, Mark Rockart," Mom called from the sink. I pointed and laughed at him. He rolled his eyes again.

"Stop that! Now get over here and help your wife dry these damn dishes. I'm not the only one that eats around here!" she hollered at him. He slid over to her side and instantly her scowl turned into a smile. She kissed his cheek. I quickly got up and went to find Madison.

"Auntie!" Maddy hollered as I walked into the living room.

"Niece-ee," I mocked her. She had taken off her boots but was still running around in her snow suit. I picked her up and she pushed her hair out of her face. "Aren't you hot in that suit missy?"

"Oh yeah, but we can play outside now. I saw Gama and Gampa." She was so serious. I shook my head and laughed at her.

"Okay, put your boots back on and we will go in the back yard for a half an hour. Okay?"

"OKAY!" she agreed. I set her down and she put her boots on.

Once she was ready to go outside, we walked to the kitchen. I told my parents that we would be in the back yard for a little while and I put my coat on.

"What time do you have to work today, Annabelle?" Mom questioned.

"Two o'clock, why?" I opened the back door and Maddy ran outside.

"What time are you leaving then?"

"Probably around 12:30, what's with the twenty questions?"

"I just want to know, that's all." She turned back to the stove. I looked at my dad and he shrugged. I slid the glass door shut behind me and watched as Maddy ran to the old swing set.

"Push!" she yelled. I laughed and ran out to push her on the swing.

"You are the only three year old I know that plays on the swings when there is snow on the ground."

"What?" she asked confused.

"Don't you remember making a snowman with me last year?" I asked her. She shook her head no. "Oh, well. We are going to have to change that, now aren't we?"

I picked her up off the swing and took her to the middle of the yard. I explained that we needed to clear a big spot in the middle of the yard for the snowman. She eagerly dug a hole in the snow and then smoothed it out with her hands. *Wow, that was fast.*

"Good job!" I high fived her. "Now we have to roll a big ball of snow to start the bottom of the snow man." I picked up a handful of snow and formed a ball out of it.

"That's too small, Auntie." She giggled.

"I know. We have to roll this to make a bigger one." I set it down on the ground and started to roll it around in the snow.

"You look silly." She giggled again from her spot in the snow. I stuck my tongue out at her and continued rolling the snow. Within a few minutes the snow ball had grown into a perfect base of the snowman. I rolled it to the spot that Madison had cleared.

"Okay, now we have to pack snow around the base of the snowman so it doesn't roll away, okay?" I told her.

We continued making the snowman that Madison soon named Bill. When we finished the body of Bill the snowman, Madison found two long sticks to use as his arms.

"He needs a face," she commented. So we went inside to find supplies to make Bill more snowman-like. *Wonder what time it is.*

"Okay, we need a hat, scarf, a carrot stick and some buttons for his eyes," I explained to Madison confidently. I grabbed her hand and we headed toward the house.

"Gampa!" she hollered as we walked inside the house. Dad came into the kitchen from his office in a hurry.

"What? What's wrong?"

"Bill needs a scarf!" she said with a little smile. I laughed at my dad's reaction when he realized there was no emergency. He shook his head and picked her up. He took her to the set of hooks by the back door and said she can use anything on them for Bill.

While she decided which hat to pick, I grabbed a carrot stick from the refrigerator and some buttons from mom's sewing cabinet. I glanced up at the clock and saw that it was already noon.

"All set?" I asked hoping that I would be able to finish Bill before I had to leave. She nodded with her hands full of things to put on Bill.

I followed her outside to where Bill was. She dumped all her things on the ground and turned to me.

"Carrot?" she asked. I handed her the carrot stick. She stood on her tip toes to try and put the carrot on Bill's face. She tried twice, but couldn't reach his head. She only stood about three feet tall; Bill the Snowman stood about five feet tall. I smiled, took the carrot from her and placed it on Bill's face. We finished putting Bill together. Madison was so happy when we were done. *She is so easily amused.*

"I have to go get Gama and Gampa!" she said running towards the house. I laughed and ran after her.

Once I was there, Maddy was already pulling the sliding glass door open.

"It's one o'clock, Annabelle," my mom commented as we walked inside.

"Shoot. Maddy honey, Auntie has to go," I called to her. She turned around to me and pouted. I walked out to her and held my arms out to give her a hug. She frowned.

"Why do you have to go?" she questioned. *Look at that face.*

"Auntie has to go to work, honey." I knelt down to her level. She sniffed a little and gave me a hug.

"Will you come back?" she questioned.

"You will be sleeping when I get out of work," I admitted to her. "But I will see you tomorrow, okay? We will all meet here to put up the big Christmas tree."

"Promise?"

"I promise."

She put her arms around my neck and I picked her up to take her inside. I set her on the counter to take off her snow suit for my parents. While I unzipped her princess suit, she played with my necklace. It was a common thing for her to play with it.

"Can I wear it?" Madison asked curiously. I smiled at her. I put my hand on the charm of my necklace. It was a silver heart that my parents had bought me when I was four. It was a good luck charm that I had worn every day since I received it. *Good luck.... It's really working for you...*

"That's my good luck charm; you wouldn't want to take my luck from me, would you?" I told the little girl. She pouted but shook her head.

"I'll tell you what, tomorrow when we put up the big tree, you can wear it ALL day long, okay?" Madison nodded. I kissed her forehead, said goodbye, and quickly went to my car. I glanced at the clock, pulling out of my parents' driveway, 1:15.

Finally, I arrived home and *look at the time.* It was 1:30. I ran through my apartment while I took off my clothes. I quickly jumped in the shower and turned the water on.

Hot, hot, hot. I showered in record time and was out in five minutes. I wrapped a towel around my body and walked into my bedroom. I looked at the clock. If I didn't leave within fifteen minutes, I would be late for work. I needed to eat something to hold me over until my lunch break. I ran into the kitchen slapped a sandwich together and went to my room while taking off my towel.

Good thing you live alone. I hurried and picked out my clothes with my sandwich hanging out of my mouth. While I put my pants on I picked up my phone and threw it in my pocket and grabbed my shirt.

I hurried to the bathroom and plugged in my hair dryer. I ran the brush through my hair, cursing my thick hair. After two minutes and half-dry hair, I quit trying. I looked up at the clock 1:47.

"Damn it." I slipped on my over shirt and stopped in front of the mirror for one last check: brown polo shirt, long sleeved white turtle neck underneath, brown khaki pants and a pair of brown tennis shoes.

"Name tag! Where's my name tag?" I rummaged through my bag and finally found it near the bottom. I clipped it to my shirt and was out the door. I rushed down the stairs; *you're going to fall if you don't slow down.* At the last set, my shoes caught on the tread of the stairs. I put my arms out in front of me to catch myself on the railing. Instead, a guy appeared, out of thin air, and caught me.

35

"Whoa, careful." He was tall, maybe six foot, average body type, dirty blonde hair and a magical white smile. His eyes were bright blue and they stared back at me with concern. He must have been right around my age, possibly younger. He was like a character from a movie, perfectly built but not too bulky and incredibly soft features, I snapped back to reality.

"I'm sorry. I should have watched where I was going." I realized I was still holding onto his arms and I quickly removed my hands. I smiled up at him and he laughed a little.

"I'm Lucas." He put his hand out.

"I'm Annabelle." I gave him a quick hand shake and looked at his watch. *You'll be late.* "I'm sorry to hit and run, but I really am going to be late for work," I said and walked past him.

"Bye, be careful."

I waved back as I left the building. I ran as fast, and as carefully as I could, across the icy parking lot to my car. I jumped in and turned the key in the ignition. I looked at the clock, 1:54pm. *As long as you do get stopped by any stop lights, stop signs or any other delays, yeah, you can get there.*

I drove to work in such a hurry, there were a few lights that I don't even remember going through. *Hope they weren't red.*

"Rockart, just on time," Ronnie said as I punched the clock exactly at two. I turned around and stuck my tongue out at him.

"Yeah, yeah," I joked. He blushed and I patted him on the shoulder. "No worries Ronald. Your fiancé was put safely on a plane. She should be with her Granny right now, in the place she loves most. Be happy for her."

"I am happy for her. Just wish the Meyers could have given me the time off. But no, Dolan their amazing son had to go and quit." Ronnie's sarcasm was obviously forced.

"Dolan actually quit?" *Wasn't expecting that one...*

"Yeah, this morning, that's why I had to come in and open." Ronnie yawned. "Didn't Billy tell you that?"

"No, she just said that you were covering his shift." I put my hideous red and green plaid apron around my neck and tied the back closed. "I can't wait until Christmas is over so we don't have to wear these ugly aprons."

"You're telling me. I'm a guy; I shouldn't even be wearing a damn apron." Ronnie sighed, leaning on the counter.

"How busy have we been?"

"For a Saturday, not bad." Ronnie nodded at the few people around the aisles. "Pretty much like this all day."

"Hopefully it will stay that way. I'm in no way ready for a busy day." I leaned on the counter next to him. He was picking at one of the muffins from the bakery next door.

"Billy called from the plane earlier. Her flight took off right as scheduled and she said she will be writing to the air line when she gets home. Something about the cost for bringing an animal on board with her, I don't know. She sure is something."

"That's typical Billy-Jean, always finding *someone* to write to about *something* that needs fixing. You'll have your hands full with her." I took a hunk of the muffin in his hands and went around the counter. "I'm going to check some inventory and straighten the aisles a little before the boss gets in."

The day went by pretty quickly. Customers seemed to come and go without lingering too long. It was 5:15, about time for my break, and it seemed like all 2,000 citizens of Fort Kent were in our store.

"How typical is this?" I asked Ronnie from behind my register. We both had at least ten people in our lines.

"What's that?" he questioned while giving a woman her change with a fake, extremely cheesy smile.

"It's time for my break and we're busy." I sighed and continued ringing out customers. Ronnie just chuckled.

"Annabelle, I will finish off your line of customers. Go on break," Matt Meyer said from behind me. *Definitely wasn't expecting that one.* I turned and looked at him questioningly.

"Thanks… Matt." I was taken aback by his politeness. He normally never worked a register, let alone to take over for someone's lunch break.

"Just be back within the hour, okay?" He smiled and turned to the customers. I looked up at the clock, 5:17. *What's gotten into him? Dolan? Who knows?* Who cares? I looked at Ronnie, whose face was completely shocked. He leaned over to me.

"Maybe you should break up with Dolan more often," he joked. I hit him in the back playfully.

"I'll be back… within the hour," I gloated sarcastically and left the store.

The setting sun sparkled on the wet snow and the temperature might have actually gone above freezing, a degree. The snow was melting and where the patches of ice once lay, now formed giant puddles. I hopped through the mess of slush and dirty snow to the diner across the street. Once I ordered my meal, I actually sat down to enjoy it.

"Annabelle, won't Meyer have your neck for actually enjoying your meal and taking longer than fifteen minutes?" Jolene, the waitress, asked from behind the counter.

"No, for some reason today, Jolene, Matt gave me almost an entire hour for break." I took a bite of my beef stew.

"Really? Did someone in their family die?" Jolene laughed, holding her chest. I smiled and shook my head no, mouth full of stew. "That's never happened since they opened that damn bookstore. He and Misses have never given any worker more than 20 minutes for a break."

"Oh, well in that case, I must be a saint."

"No, just lucky." She paused and looked past me at something. "Very lucky." She smiled, winked and walked down to the other end of the counter. I looked up to see a new familiar face sit down next to me.

"Fancy meeting you here." Lucas smiled sweetly.

"Are you following me?" I joked. He laughed and set down his bowl of soup.

"How did you find me out?" he questioned. I laughed at his sarcasm. He smiled awkwardly and stirred his soup.

"I've actually never seen you around here before? Did you just move here?" I asked taking another bite of my food.

"Umm, I guess you could say that." He played with his food. "So what brings you to this little diner on a snowy winter day like today?" he questioned, quickly changing the subject.

"Break, I normally don't stay and eat here though," I admitted, laughing silently to myself. "So what made you move to a place like Fort Kent? Most people don't like the cold."

"Well, it wasn't really my decision. My-" His phone cut him off and he looked at the screen on the front of his phone.

"You can answer it if you need to," I told him.

"No," he said putting the phone back in his pocket. I noticed his hand was shaking slightly. "It wasn't important." He looked around, paranoid. He turned to me, stopped himself from saying anything and shook his head.

"What?" I laughed. He was sweating. "Are you okay?"

Instead of answering, he stood up and walked to Jolene, gave her a hand full of money and whispered something to her and left. *You make a great first and second impression, Annabelle.* I sighed and finished off my coffee. I got my money out of the pocket of my apron and walked towards Jolene.

"Who hit you with the lucky stick today?" she questioned.

"What do you mean?" I handed her a twenty dollar bill.

"No need honey. That boy you were sweet talking paid for your meal." She smiled. "Who is he? I've never seen him before."

"He did what? I just met him this morning." I thought back to the pathetic first impression I left on him by falling down the stairs, into his arms. "H-he really paid for my food?" I was shocked. *Maybe you made a really good second impression.*

"Sure did." She winked. I shook my head at her.

"See you later, Jolene." I sighed and left the building.

I couldn't grasp how fast that happened. *You just met him.* I know. As I reached the road, my phone vibrated in my pocket.

"Billy! How are you? Make it to your Granny's house?" I asked her. The sun had started to disappear behind the horizon and clouds crept into the sky.

"Hey Anna, yep, Granny met me at the airport, we went out to lunch and we got back to her place about two and a half hours ago. How's work going?"

"Good, busy. But guess what?"

"What's that?"

"Mr. Meyer gave me an hour break."

"No way! What's his deal?" she questioned sounding just as shocked as Jolene was.

"I have no clue but I think Dolan has something to do with it. He quit."

"I know, Ronnie told me this morning."

"And why didn't you tell me?"

"I'm sorry; it slipped my mind when I saw your arm Anna."
Silence

"Oh hey, you wouldn't guess what else happened to me?" I asked breaking the silence.

"It better be something good."

"I think a have a stalker." I giggled jokingly. I crossed the road once the traffic disappeared.

"No way, who?" She immediately started the questions.

"I've never seen him before. I just ran into him this morning." I laughed thinking about the literal sense of that statement. "And at lunch today at Joe's Diner, he showed up and we talked for a little bit. He started to get really nervous for some reason, got up, paid for my food and left."

"Hmm, a mystery man, nice Anna. I'm gone a few hours and you've already found new source of entertainment." She sighed.

"Nothing could replace the entertainment you provide for me Billy." I heard her laughter over the phone. I felt a snow flake hit my face.

"You better tell me if you see him again today," she demanded.

"I'll call you when I get off work," I promised her.

"Okay, good. I want to get all the details of your day too."

"Because my life is that exciting."

She laughed. "Well, I'm going to go out to dinner with Granny and some of my cousins. Have fun at work and tell Ronnie that I love him."

"Do I have to?" I joked, and she laughed. "Bye Bills."

"Bye Ann, don't forget to call me!"

"I promise. No worries, Bills." We hung up the phone together and I went back to work.

I walked into the bookstore and saw that the number people had decreased significantly. *Thank God.*

"How was your hour long break?" Ronnie questioned from behind his register as I punched in. I smiled and fixed my windblown hair in the window.

"Fabulous, Billy said she loves you." I pretended to gag. He rolled his eyes and turned around to check out another customer.

"So where's the boss?" I questioned not seeing either Mr. or Mrs. Meyer anywhere. *Anywhere but here would be nice.*

"Mr. Meyer went home about a half an hour into your break; right after the crowd died down. Mrs. Meyer was in the back of the store with a customer last time I saw her."

We stood around the counter for a while, taking the few customers that came every once and a while. I was fidgeting with a pen, lost in thought. I was doodling on a note pad next to the register when I drew two hearts on the back of my left hand.

"Why are you always doing that?" Ronnie asked.

"Huh?" I looked up at him. He pointed at my hand. "Oh, I don't know. It's something I've done all my life. Boredom?"

"You are a strange woman, Annabelle." Ronnie commented as another customer approached his register.

Standing at my register, I noticed a new book sitting on the counter and picked it up.

Poems for the Spiritual, I read to myself. I looked up and didn't see any customers waiting so I opened to the middle of the book to see what was inside. The first poem I read was full of a bunch of, *Hallelujahs* and *Lord* this and that. *No thanks.* I flipped to the next page to find a new chapter: *Guidance.* The first poem caught my attention:

When the snow falls, think of me...
When the snow touches your cheek,
think of me kissing your skin.
When the snow blankets the ground,
think of me making snow angels to watch over you.
When the snow sends a shiver through your body,
think of me warming you up with a hug.
When the snow ends,

know that it will always return in a few months.
When the snow falls,
know that I will always be with you.

Deep, very deep, I like it. *It's like it understands you.* I sighed and put the book down. No more mind tricks please. I looked at the clock, 7:30. *Jesus, it's been almost an hour, where's Nancy?*

"I'm going to see if Nancy needs any help with stocking shelves while we're slow," I told Ronnie, walking to the back of the store.

I didn't see her with any of the three customers that were in the back aisle of the store, so I assumed she was in the stock room. I opened the door to see Mrs. Meyer sitting on a box crying.

"Oh sorry." I quickly turned to leave.

"No, no. You're fine Annabelle. I actually need your help with something if you don't mind," she said, wiped her face and stood up, *quick recovery.*

"No, I don't mind. That's what you pay me for, right?" I joked, hoping that she wouldn't spill her emotions to me.

Nancy explained what she needed me to help her with and then she got up to go to her office in the back of the stock room. She turned to me and began to say something, but quickly stopped. She turned again to leave and repeated the same move.

"I'm sorry," she told me with a look of sympathy.

"For what?" I asked, knowing she was referring to Dolan.

"Dolan isn't who he used to be and I'm sorry for the way he's treated you." *Did she know about last night?*

"It's not your fault; you don't need to apologize for him," I explained, picking up a box and turning to leave.

"No, I suppose not…" she admitted quietly. She looked down and twiddled her fingers slightly. "Maybe his father has been the bad influence…"

"Matt? No. It's neither of-"

"No, not Matt."

"What?" I stared at her curiously. *Matt's not his father?*

"Matt isn't Dolan's real father."

"He is my second husband and Dolan's step father. He has the last name Meyer because I married Matt when Dolan was two years old and Matt adopted him. I divorced Dolan's real father, Hector Martin, when Dolan was only five months old.

"Dolan found out that Matt wasn't his real father when he was about eleven years old. Actually, he met Hector on his eleventh birthday. I never wanted Hector in his life, that's why I kept Dolan away from him. He isn't a nice person." She started to cry again.

I stood in the doorway, still holding the box, not sure what I should say to her confession. I didn't say anything and she continued telling me her life history.

"I never understood why Dolan stayed close to Hector after he was put in prison for four years." *Prison, who is this guy?* "Dolan just seemed so angry at me for never telling him about Hector while he grew up. As time went on, Dolan seemed to be getting angrier and angrier with me." She looked down at her hands again, and then quickly looked up at me.

"But then, then he met you, sweet Annabelle Rockart. Oh, you were such a good influence in his life. You have no idea how much you changed him." She smiled at me. I was taken aback by her compliment.

"But then he changed again, last summer, when Hector was released from prison. Dolan went back to being mysterious. He would be gone at odd hours each night, never spoke to me the same. Matt and I didn't know what we were doing wrong until we realized that Hector was out.

"I knew that we would lose him for good when you broke up with him last week." She let a few more tears fall. "But I don't blame you for letting him go Annabelle. Dolan changed. He isn't the same young man I raised and I am so, so sorry for the way he treated you."

"Please, please don't apologize for his mistakes. I know it isn't your fault. Dolan did change and we grew apart. I don't blame you, not at all," I told her sincerely. *What a basket case.*

I understood now why Dolan had never expressed as much respect for Matt as a normal son would. Matt wasn't his real father. *Dolan should have told you...* Why didn't he?

Nancy and I stood awkwardly for a minute or two, when she smiled at me. I smiled back.

"Well, I'd better go put these books out and make sure Ronnie isn't getting swamped." I turned quickly before she could say anymore. I walked to the aisle where the case of books was going to be put and set the box down.

Before I began my work, I sent a quick text to Billy.

So Nancy just told me that matt isn't Dolan's dad. He has a dad who just got out of jail. Glad I got out of that mess. :) love you Bills.

Sliding my phone back into my pocket, I started the things Nancy wanted me to do. I knelt down and began putting the books neatly on the shelf. I got so involved with straightening all the books down this aisle; I didn't notice what time it was. Once I was on my third aisle, I decided to just continue through each aisle of the whole store.

"Annabelle!" Ronnie hollered from the front of the store. "Its 8:30, I'm getting out of here."

"Okay, put the bell on the counter for me. I'm going to finish these last two aisles and then I'll be up there for the night," I yelled back to him.

"Okay! Good night Annabelle! See you in the morning!" Ronnie said and I heard the bell on the door jingle as he left the store.

Hopefully you can drag these two last aisles out for another hour so you won't have stand up at that damn counter for two hours until closing. Hopefully…

I continued on my merry way, humming to the Christmas music playing through the store and straightening the books. I heard the bell on the door jingle. I was on the last aisle. I quickly finished and went to the front of the store. I looked up at the clock, ten o'clock. *Thank you Jesus, half an hour.* I saw an older woman, maybe in her forties, looking at the poem book I was reading earlier.

"It's a good book," I commented coming around the counter to stand in front of her. She looked up at me and I smiled. She had dark brown hair, tied back in a messy pony tail. Her clothes were too big and she looked tired and worn out. *Maybe she had a bad day at work?*

"I read a little bit of it earlier and even if you are not religious, it's very insightful," I added. She shook her head, and set the book down.

"I don't believe in God," she grumbled.

"Oh, okay." I really didn't have anything to say to that. She glanced around the front counter and shook her head at each book on display. *Hey lady, you do know there's a whole store behind you,*

44

right? I leaned against the counter and twisted my hair around my finger. I looked up at the clock. *10:15, come on lady.* She shook her head one more time and looked up at me.

"Don't you have anything good?" she grumbled again. *Don't you have any manners?*

"Well that depends on what you're looking for. Do you like action, romance, DIY, series books." *You can stop me at any time now...*

"Oh never mind." She huffed and walked out the door. I shook my head and looked up at the clock, 10:25. *Good enough.* I closed up my register. I pulled the apron over my head and hung it on the hook with the rest of them. I punched the time clock at exactly 10:30 and smiled to myself.

"You got through it, Annabelle," I told myself out loud. I went to the door, locked it with the set of store keys.

I turned around to see that my car wasn't the only car left in the parking lot. A blue truck sat only three spots closer to the store than my car. The street light in front of the store was flickering, as usual, and the wind chill had dropped back below zero. The once dirty puddles of water had turned back into deathly icy traps once again. *Looks like a scene from a horror movie, be careful.*

I fished for my keys in my pocket. I finally found them and I made my way to my car, slowly. Right as I was close enough to touch my car, the passenger window on the truck parked near mine rolled down.

Shit, shit, shit. Just keep walking, look straight forward... I was in no mood to deal with anyone; especially those lurking in dark parking lots. *You're in Fort Kent, Maine, what could happen? They steal your bus pass?*

"Annabelle," a male voice called from inside the cab of the truck. *He knows your name.* I turned to the window and was happily surprised to see that it was just Lucas.

"Hello Lucas." I smiled, unlocking my car. "You know, if you were a creepy old man, I would think you were going to rape me or something," I joked. But Lucas didn't laugh, he just smiled nervously. "It was a joke."

"Yeah, I know." He laughed nervously. I stood quietly, while he looked around, acting paranoid like earlier today.

"Is there something I can help you with?" I asked, wanting desperately to get into my car, feeling slightly uncomfortable. *You should have worn a coat.*

"Actually," he started and turned off his car. He proceeded to get out. *This kid is way too odd for you, get out of here.* He came around the truck to face me. "I, umm, wondered if you knew how to, umm, get to the nearest, umm..."

"The nearest what? Gas station, grocery store, what?" I tried to help him. My fingers were so cold; I shoved my hands in my pants pockets and felt my body shiver.

"I can't do this," Lucas said, practically running back to the other side of his truck.

"Please Annabelle. Just get into your car and go home."

Okay, my vote is to do what he says and get the hell out of here. I didn't understand what was wrong with him. He was acting like someone was looking for him. Granted, I just met him this morning, but normal people do not act like this. I looked back at him one last time, nothing. He just looked back at me; almost to tears he was so anxious.

"Okay, okay, I'll leave." I shrugged my shoulders. Opening my car door, I got my keys out again and shuffled through them to find my car key. By now, I was freezing and my hands were shaking. *Gloves would be nice too.*

As I started the car, I looked up to see the same lady from the store earlier, standing in front of me. "Oh my God, you scared me." I told her through the glass, laughing slightly. She stared at me, not saying a word. She had a psychotic glare in her eyes. I stared back at her, motionless and fixated by her look of pure evil.

"Annabelle, leave!" Lucas said coming from behind his truck; I looked at him.

I turned my head and the old lady was now holding a baseball bat. Her enraged grip on the bat was so tight, her knuckles were white. *No, the real question is, what is* she *going to do to you?*

"Whoa, whoa, what the hell are you doing?" I impulsively spoke aloud, putting my hands up, like she was holding a gun to my face. She smiled strangely at me and lifted the bat over her head. With all of the strength she had in her, she smashed the bat through my windshield.

46

"What the hell?" I yelled at her. A shower of shattered glass surrounded me as I turned the car off. Leaving the keys in the seat, I got out of the car.

"No. We can't do this," Lucas said from behind me. *Did he just say we? What the hell is going on?* I went to turn to face him, but she laughed sadistically and I couldn't take my eyes off her, in fear of what she would do.

"You are such a coward, what would your father say? If you won't do it, then I will."

"Father? Wait, is this your mother?" I questioned him, keeping my eyes on the bat as she smashed another window on the passenger side of my car. She smiled evilly and I saw Lucas out of the corner of my eye. He was walking forward, towards her, in the same fashion that a hunter would approach his unsuspecting victim. Lucas put his arm out in front of me and brought my body behind him.

"Janis, don't do this. She didn't do anything wrong. Hector is just a foolish cynical man who doesn't know right from wrong. We don't have to listen to him," Lucas pleaded. *Hector,* Hector? *What the hell is going on?*

"No, the woman will pay for what she did to my life." Janis sounded completely crazed. I knew I needed to act, so I moved back, out of Lucas's grip. As I stepped back, I heard the ice crack beneath my steps. *Shit, you ruined that exit.*

Lucas pulled me into his arms and took a blow from Janis's bat. *What the hell is up with this guy?* I immediately resisted his grip around my shoulders, a knee-jerk reaction, and pushed myself out of his arms giving him a hard smack across the face.

"Don't Touch Me!" I screamed in his face. I turned around and realized that I was standing right in front of the loaded cannon. She swung the bat as I bent out of the way. Her bat crashed into my driver's door and shattered the window. The door slammed closed. I stood up. That's when I felt the bat strike across the middle of my back and all my oxygen escaped my lips. My body crashed to the ground and I shut my eyes, pulling my knees to my chest. *Great, what good is the fetal position going to do for you?*

I felt someone grab my left ankle, and I woke from my trance. I kicked as hard as I could and heard Janis tumble back onto the ice. I struggled to get to my feet, sliding around on the ice, when I felt a strong arm lift me up. I looked up to see Lucas holding me up.

"Get the hell away from me!" I screamed at him. I turned around to get into my car when I saw Janis get back up off the icy ground. She shook her head "no" at me.

"Bad girl, you shouldn't fight me, dear. Best save your strength for later." She giggled wildly, *later?*

I quickly went for my car door and realized it automatically locked the door. I reached through the broken window for my keys on the seat. They were gone. I looked up at Janis. She grinned and dangled my keys in the air.

"Looking for these, honey?" Her voice sent chills done my spine. *What kind of luck is that?* I stood in the middle, between Janis and Lucas. I looked at Janis, who stood with bat in hand and then to Lucas, who actually looked concerned for my well being.

"What do you want? Do you want money? I can give you money," I asked frantically empting my pockets on the ground. Change, my cell phone, and name tag fell to the frozen solid ground. When my cell phone hit the ground, it broke into several pieces and shattered across the ground.

"No, honey, I want you," Janis confessed, she lifted the baseball bat at me again and I ducked out of the way and the icy surface caused me to fall onto the ground. My head slammed into the hard, cold ground and I lay as still as I could.

I pretended to black out momentarily and before I reopened my eyes I heard Lucas and Janis scramble around me. I lifted my hand to the back of my head. When I felt the warmth of my own blood, I brought my hand forward to see the blood on my palm.

"Pick her up and throw her in your truck," Janis demanded.

"Janis, I can't do this. I don't want to do this," Lucas pleaded with her.

"Your father was right; you can't handle this life style. You don't deserve the last name Martin." Janis sounded disappointed. *Hector Martin?* What was going on?

She grumbled and then added, "Out of my way! I'll pick her up myself; she's just a little shit. No more than 100 pounds." I felt her grab my right arm and leg. The pain that exploded through my arm, added to the previous injury to it, and made my eyes shoot open and I thrashed around in her grip.

"God damn you, girl, hold still." Janis picked me up like I was nothing. She slammed my body against the truck and pressed her

48

weight against me. I gasped for air, trying catch the breath that was just stolen from my lips. *Stay calm. She'll let go.*

"Janis! Stop it. You're going to kill her! You are twice her size," Lucas said putting his hand on Janis's arm. She quickly removed it and demanded that he get in the driver's side of the truck. He glared back at her. I watched as Janis reached into the pocket of her coat. I heard the click of a pocket knife open. Suddenly, a cold, metal, blade rested on my neck. I was stunned in her grip; fear claimed me.

Janis shoved the knife into her pocket; Lucas stood in front of her, ready to strike. As Lucas took a step forward, Janis pulled another trick from her pocket. The gun stopped him in his tracks. He stopped to look at me, I could see the fear in his eyes and like a cowardly dog, he obeyed Janis like she was his abusive owner.

"You, darling, will get to enjoy the fabulous ride to our destination in the back of the truck." She smiled wildly; shoving the gun into her pocket and she lifted my body like a rag doll. She tossed my tiny frame over the side of the truck. I landed hard in the rusty bed of the truck. I could feel the tiny pieces of chipping, rusting paint splinter through my clothes and dig into my skin. I tried to sit up, but Janis was already in the back of the truck with me.

"Why are you doing this to me?" I pleaded with her, my eyes streaming with tears.

"Now, now, we don't want you trying to get away, do we?" She pushed herself on top of me, pinning me to the rough surface of the bed. She placed her hand on one side of my face, rubbed her thumb along my cheek bone and leaned down close to my face and whispered, "Good night sweetheart." As she whispered that, she grabbed a handful of my hair and slammed my head into the side of the truck. The darkness surrounded me.

Wake up Annabelle. You're not dead. Wake up.

My mind spun and my thoughts hit me all at once. Where am I? Who is here with me? Who knows I'm here? Why Am I here? How long have I been unconscious? What time is it? What *day* is it? *Whoa, whoa, whoa, slow down Annabelle. Okay, one question at a time.*

Where am I? *As far as I can tell, in a lot of trouble...* I opened my eyes slowly and tried to focus my vision. I was sitting on the floor in the corner of a dark room with dampened, wooden walls. The ceiling was constructed of wooden rafters, splintered and falling apart. Several holes were scattered across the ceiling where roof tiles were missing, producing the tiniest bit of light. It was actually the only source of light in the entire place.

But the next question, who is here with you? I looked around the room as the question sank in. My heart raced inside my chest. Where is Lucas? *Where are Janis and her bat?* My breathing quickened as I thought about the brutal blows to my body... *and more tears...* I didn't understand why I was here, or where *here* even was. All I knew was that it couldn't be a good place to stay. How long had I been unconscious? Is today only Sunday? Maybe I just slept through the night. *Yeah, it's probably only been one night.*

I shivered slightly, *no heat.* I swallowed hard and realized how thirsty I was. My throat was dry, my mouth felt like I had been eating cardboard and my stomach rumbled with hunger. I straightened my legs in front of me, checking all the damages from last night.

My pockets were empty, *thanks to your wonderful display of giving.* I remembered emptying them onto the ground in hopes that they only wanted money. I also remembered the fact that my cell phone, *which is now in pieces,* would be of no assistance to me now. My brown tennis shoes were soaked, dripping slightly, mostly likely from the snowy conditions which begged for attention on the other side of the wooden walls of the tiny room; a cold draft danced around my body. The left leg of my pants was ripped up the side slightly, exposing a long, thin cut up my leg. I couldn't remember where I had gotten it from, but I could only imagine what might have happened while I was unconscious. *Don't even think about that.* My stomach lurched forward and the bile crept into my throat. I swallowed hard to force it back down.

I grabbed a hold of my necklace, twirling it nervously. *Some good luck charm…*

Across the room, opposite of where I sat, was an old sink. It looked as though it hadn't been cleaned since it was made in the 1920's. It was big, basin style, sitting lower than most sinks, might have even been white at one point in time. It had to be only a foot off the ground. Hanging on the wall above the sink was a broken mirror that looked as old as the sink, possibly older. I flinched when I saw a bug crawl up the side of it. *Gross.*

To my left was an old iron framed cot, covered with a dirty sheet that also could have been white once in its existence. The sheet was covering a mattress that looked to be about two inches tall and barely big enough to hold even my small body. Near the sink sat an old wooden chair.

I sighed heavily and pain settled into my skull. My head pounded and I pulled my hands up to cover my eyes. Tears ran freely down my cheeks. I gently brushed my fingers along the left side of my face. The sensitive area burned under the tender graze from my finger tips. I winced when they hit an obvious wound. I felt the dried blood under my finger tips. Tears continued streaming down my face. *You're still alive.*

I crossed my arms and ran my hands up and down, trying to keep myself warm. I braced myself against the wall and tried to stand up. I slowly gained altitude, stumbled slightly, catching myself on the sad excuse for a bed. I sat down, slowly, hoping the cot wouldn't break. It was sturdier and much larger than I expected, probably about the same measurements as a full size mattress.

My body throbbed. *Stop thinking about the pain and find a way out.* I looked around the room and took everything in. Down the wall from the corner I was sitting in was a door. I took a deep breath and stood up slowly. Dizziness struck and I reached out for the wall to brace myself. Using the wall, I made my way to the door. The room spun more and more with each step I took. I stopped and closed my eyes, trying to focus my head.

You can do it Annabelle. Focus on getting out, not the pain. I opened my eyes and started for the door again. I kept my eyes focused on the door and put the pain out of my mind. I finally reached for the door handle. It wasn't a normal door knob; it was more like a bar, nailed to an old barn door. I pulled on the door, nothing. I pushed on the door, nothing.

Panic set in again. I jerked the door as hard as I could. It still didn't budge. I pushed with my entire body to see if I could get it to budge, nothing.

I started to pound on the door. "HELP!" I tried to yell, but my voice was weak, scratchy and barely audible. I cleared my throat. I used all the strength I could find and shook the door as hard as I could.

"ANYONE! PLEASE HELP ME!" I pounded the door with my fists. I felt the tears hit my eyes as the realization set in that no one was there.

"PLEASE! HELP ME!" I shook the door harder this time. I opened my hand and hit the door with the palm of my hand creating a loud, slapping noise. I continued to pound, punch, slap and struggle with the door. *You're wasting your energy.* The energy that I had used banging on the door caught up with me and I felt my knees buckle. I hit the door pathetically one more time and whispered, too exhausted to try. "Please…. Anyone… help me." I fell to the cold, wet floor and my eyelids started to give in to fatigue and I started to fall asleep.

"What if she wakes up?" a deep voice questioned; a male's voice.

"I'll take care of it, nothing you need to worry about," another voice answered, this time it sounded like a female.

"Every time I leave you alone you fail me. How am I supposed to trust you when you never follow through with my demands?" the first voice spoke again.

There was silence, and then a loud noise rang through the air, a slapping sound.

"You have a lot of things to learn, son. When she wakes, I will teach her a lesson. Leave."

I started to wake up when I felt something drip on my face. I turned my head and opened my eyes to see darkness. The sun had gone down and the daylight was no longer peaking through the decaying ceiling. I felt something drip on my cheek again. I quickly realized that the roof was leaking and what I was feeling was water dripping on my face. I tried to move out of the inconsistent stream of water when I realized that I had been tied up. Someone had returned because I was no longer lying on the floor by the locked door. My hands were tied to either side of the iron framed bed in the corner of the room. My legs were tied together and to the foot frame of the bed. *You can panic, now.*

I started to struggle frantically with my new obstacle. I pulled as hard as I could on the ropes around my arms and feet. The energy I had wasted on the door was gone; I was drained of all strength. I could feel the tears burn my eyes. The daylight that had once filled my life had been taken away from me. This dark room had successfully taken the light out of my world. That's when I heard it; soft, deep toned, laughter coming from the other side of the room. I started to fight the restraints again, whimpering slightly and fearful for my life at this point. I was blinded by complete darkness and I didn't know who was here with me.

"Who are you?" I questioned, trying to hide my fear with anger. The laughing continued. "What do you want with me?"

"You shouldn't struggle. Nothing can help you now." It was a male's voice talking to me. The same, male voice from my dream, *or was it even a dream?* I tried my hardest to focus in the darkness, nothing. The floor creaked, the sound moved closer to my involuntary position on the bed. I was certain whoever was in the room with me could clearly hear my heart pound in my chest.

"You must be scared." He pointed out bluntly. The tears streamed silently down my face.

"Please, don't hurt me. I'll do whatever you want. Just don't hurt me," I pleaded with my invisible captor. The laughter was closer and more cheerful.

"Why would I hurt you?" he questioned.

"Why did you bring me here? What did I do?" I was on the verge of hysteria.

"What did you do?".

"Please, tell me why you brought me here." I pleaded.

"I brought you here." He paused, his footsteps moved closer to the bed. "To play."

"Play?" *What is this guy talking about?* "Who are you?"

"I am Hector Martin."

"Martin? Hector Martin?" My mind struggled to remember what Nancy Meyer told me at the bookstore.

"What?" I stared at her curiously. Matt's not his father?

"Matt isn't Dolan's real father. He is my second husband and Dolan's step father. He has the last name Meyer because I married

Matt when Dolan was two years old and Matt adopted him. I divorced Dolan's real father, Hector Martin, when Dolan was only five months old.

"Dolan found out that Matt wasn't his real father when he was about eleven years old. Actually, he met Hector on his eleventh birthday. I never wanted Hector in his life, that's why I kept Dolan away from him. He isn't a nice person." She started to cry again.

I could see why she was so concerned with Dolan spending time with this man.

"Allie Rockart is your sister in-law, correct?" Hector's question startled me out of my train of thought.

"A-Allie? What does she have to do with me? Why did you bring me here? What did I do?" My fear had gotten the best of me. I was weeping audibly now.

"She talked so fondly of you; she loves you like a sister. I thought I would see what is so special about you," he admitted. *This guy is insane.*

His footsteps moved closer and he stopped. I held my breath, trying to brace myself for whatever his next move would be. I felt his hot breath on my cheek. *Smells like a bottle of whiskey.* He ran his hand along my cheek.

"Such a pretty little girl," he whispered into my ear, I tensed my entire body. "My my, no need to get all tensed up sweetie."

I whimpered under my breath as he ran his hand down my body. I cried out loud when he dug his nails into my side.

"Not much insulation on those little bones of yours, is there?" he questioned, pinching and poking at my body. "You must be quite cold."

I shivered, too frightened to answer. All I could do was wait and expect something horrible to happen. *More horrible than being kidnapped, beaten, and tied up?*

"Not going to answer?" He sounded disappointed. He put his hand over my mouth and squeezed my cheeks together forcefully. "You should really answer when you're asked a question." He moved his other hand off my body. "It's the polite thing to do."

I could only rely on my sense of hearing to get an idea of what was going on around me. It was hard to tell exactly what he was doing but, from what I heard, he had his free hand in his jacket pocket, digging for something. I could feel the bruises settle in as he continued squeezing my face.

"Impolite people should be taught a lesson," he stated plainly. That is when I felt a cold, clearly metal object glide smoothly across my cheek; *A knife.* He had slid the side of a knife down my face.

"Please, don't hurt me," I whispered, my voice cracking through the fear.

"Oh, now you can speak."

"Please…" I begged.

"It's too late."

"No, no. Please!" I panicked, struggling under his grip on my face. *Damn darkness!*

"Such worry." He played the knife across my chest, never actually puncturing my skin, just my shirt. I held my breath.

"Please," I whispered.

That was when I felt him push the knife too far. I let out a piercing scream as he dragged the knife superficially down my chest. Not deep enough to kill, but enough to make me bleed. After dragging the knife down my skin, he suddenly stopped. I continued to cry out loud, my body shuddering.

He went silent and removed his hand from my face, actually cutting my hands down from the iron frame. I stopped shaking, too stunned to move. I waited for something worse to happen, but when the room remained still, I was confused as to what his next move would be.

"Until our next lesson," he stated, and I heard his footsteps walk away from the bed. I could hear the jingling of keys and the door unlocked. When he opened the door, his shadow in the moonlight was cast across the room. He stood tall, dark hair, and had a beard. He looked back at me, laughed and closed the door behind him. I could hear the jingle of his keys and he locked the door. I was alone in the dark once again.

My mind went wild, *why did he untie you?* Why was he holding me hostage because of Allie? *When will he return again?* Why me?

I rolled to my side, wrapping my arms around my body tightly. I let tears stream down my face as my new wound burned. With a shaking hand, I felt the gash. The cut in my shirt was straight down the middle and the flesh wound had to be at least four inches long, *not too deep.* The bleeding was a steady flow, *but controllable.* I needed something to hold on it, *keep pressure on it.* I sat up slowly.

I remembered that the bed I was lying on had a sheet on it. I squinted, looking down at the torn and grimy sheet. I saw a piece on the corner that was practically hanging by a thread. I reached for the corner and ripped off a good size piece of fabric. I placed it on my chest. At first, the sticky wound stung, sending dull pain through my body, and I cried softly. *Remember to breathe.*

I curled up on my side, facing the wall. I couldn't remember the last time I felt so alone, depressed or scared. I brought my knees to my exposed, bleeding chest and wrapped my tiny frame in my arms. I put my chin to my knees and cried quietly. *Why does he want you and not Allie?* I wouldn't want Allie to go through this either. *It's better than you enduring the pain for something that she did.*

"Stop it." I pushed the negative thoughts from my head. I stared at the wall of darkness in front of me. I closed my eyes to try and fall asleep. I would much rather have nightmares about my pathetic life than live in reality right now. I felt for the necklace that rested around my neck. I clung to it like a life source. *This is bad, very bad. No time for luck...*

I couldn't help but fall asleep; my body was fatigued from the day's involuntary events. Pointless dreams and nightmares took over my mind.

A loud noise from outside shook me awake. I sat straight up in the bed. Fear that Hector had returned to teach me another "lesson" thundered through my body. I shook in silence, waiting for the door to swing open to reveal my shadowed captor.

That's when I heard another noise outside. *Could it be an animal?* It sounded like a passing mountain lion or grizzly bear. If I was anywhere near home, those animals were pretty common. I strained my ears, waiting for the sound to repeat itself.

There it is again. This time it was a much louder, grumbling noise. *Grizzly bear...* No, it didn't sound like a bear. *Mountain lion...*

"That was human," I said out loud, I kept my arms wrapped tightly around my body and I stood up. "Hello?" I called out in a whisper. Silence, *it's just a bear Annabelle.*

"Hello?" I repeated louder. Still, no reply, but the sound continued to grow closer. I walked to the door and pressed my ear to it, listening for another sound. I knocked on the door softly, knowing someone was there. A small tap on the other side of the door confirmed my guess.

"Hello? Please, help me. I've been kidnapped and I'm bleeding. Please." *Careful, you don't know who it could be on that other side.*

Still, no reply and I sighed heavily, feeling the tears run routinely down my cheeks. I turned to walk from the door when I heard a low sound. I couldn't make out who said what, but I knew there was a person on the other side of the door. I knew I wasn't alone.

"Is someone there? Please, help me." I pleaded, placing my ear back to the door. "Hello?"

"Annabelle?" a voice whispered.

"Yes! Yes, who is this? Please, help me out of here." I was fervent too soon, *for all you know, that is Hector returning to finish his "lesson."* I waited silently, holding my breath. My pulse rang and pounded at my skull; it was the only sound that filled my ears.

A draft snuck under the door, the cold air bit at my face, sending a shiver down my spine. I trembled silently, wrapping my arms around my chest. I turned, back to the door and leaned against it. I felt the tears storm through me, shaking my body violently.

I feared the worst was yet to come and I let my body slide down the door. I sat in front my locked barrier to the outside world. Now, I am alone, I am a victim, and I am a hostage for reasons that I have no control over. *Alone again...*

I struggled to keep my eyes open, feeling the pain in my chest take over my mind. I was in a situation far beyond anything I could have imagined. I had no one to turn to, no shoulder to cry on. Instead I was left, *maybe even left for dead,* alone in an old cabin, with no way out.

Consciousness is a curse that only those who suffer through it can understand.

Day Three- December 16th

I felt a familiar drip hit my face. This would be the second morning that the dripping ceiling had startled me awake. This was the morning of my third day, alone, without any visits from Hector since his first "lesson" on my first day here. Day two was uneventful; I spent most of it lying in bed, curled up in a ball, basically licking my wounds like an abandoned puppy. I was hungry, my stomach begged for nourishment, rumbling consistently through the day. The night came quickly and the darkness filtered into my poor excuse for a shelter, taking over my mind-numbing day.

Maybe today will be different. Today could be different, yes, but hopefully in a positive way. I didn't know how, but I needed to find some source of water. The old sink in the corner of the room, inconveniently, didn't work.

I sat up in bed; vulnerability had taken over my body. My head spun momentarily. My head injury was scabbed over but it had become a quick routine when I sat up to wait for the dizziness to subside before I would actually get on my feet. The laceration down my chest had scabbed over, leaving my chest feeling tight and stiff. *At least you're alive…*

Halfheartedly, I moved to the door. I put my hands on either side of the cracked wood and pressed my face to a tiny hole in the door. I looked around at the snow covered hills, wishing to get a taste of the cold, wet snow.

I moved around the room, slowly. I needed to keep moving around the room, as much as I could. I couldn't afford to lose any of my muscle by lying in bed day after day. I had no clue what was planned for me, how long I would be wherever I was, or even when I would see or hear another human again.

Hours went by as I paced around the room, stopping to sit throughout the day. Time is often taken for granted. People beg for more time in their day to complete usual things like work, school and their social lives. Then, when you have time in abundance, you don't need or even want it. Right then, I wanted the hours to fly by.

I stopped to look out the door again. Peering around to see what landmarks could give me an idea of where I was. The trees surrounding the shelter were thick and covered in at least two feet of snow. *Just like most of Maine was this time of year…*

I knew that I needed to find water to drink. I walked to the bed and sat down. Struggling to gain any bit of spit in my mouth to swallow, I sighed and gave up trying. I leaned down and returned to my fetal position that I spent most of the day before in. My eyes fell on the two hearts drawn on the back of my hand. The pen had begun to fade, but the shapes were easy to see. I closed my eyes, trying to think of happier things.

The stream of water drained from the ceiling near my head. I looked up at the dimming ceiling, as the water dripped little by little down from the partially melting snow.

Are you thinking what I'm thinking?

That's disgusting, no.

What other options do you have?

I don't know what's on that ceiling. That water is probably contaminated.

Annabelle, its water! Do you have any better ideas?

I sighed heavily and turned on my side, trying to avoid the growing voice in my head.

This is childish...

I shook my head,

"No, I can't."

Annabelle...

"No."

Look at where you are. What else is going to help you?

"I can wait."

Annabelle! If you don't drink something, you'll be dead before anyone has a chance to find you.

I froze at the thought of death. I could actually die here, alone. I had never imagined all the people I could be leaving behind if I were to die here, if I were to give up... Thoughts raced through my mind and I started to cry, yet again. *Annabelle, just drink it. For all the people that want you home, do it for them.*

I turned my head back to look at the leaking ceiling. *Just do it. It's not going to hurt you.* I took a deep breath and moved myself under the water. It flowed into my open mouth. The water dripped gradually into my dehydrated throat. When the cold, wet melted snow poured into my mouth, a sense of relief came over my body. I was thankful to give my body the water it needed. As the water dripped from the dirty ceiling, into my eager mouth, I heard something outside.

I sat up slowly, waiting to hear the noise again. *It's only been three days; you can't be going crazy yet...*

I sat, holding my breath, straining my ears to hear the shuffling outside the door. A familiar jingle of clanging metal rang from outside the door; I braced my body, tensing all my muscles. I didn't know what to do. *There's nothing you can do, just sit and wait patiently.* Patiently? How can I be patient when there is a man arriving to cause me pain, again?

I stood quietly from the bed and flat footedly walked around the bed and sat down in the corner. This was the first view I had of the room my first day here. I woke up in this corner and it was the only place where I could see every inch of the room.

Hector unlocked the door, exposing the sun as it set on the horizon, walked into the room. He shut the door tightly behind himself.

"Feeling any better?" he questioned.

I sat in my corner, motionless and silent. He shook his head and clicked his teeth. He set a bag down on the ground and approached me. "Still not being very polite. Even after our first lesson." He stood on the opposite side of the bed from where I sat. I kept my eyes glued on him because I didn't want to be taken by surprise. He smiled, sat down and patted the bed.

"Why don't you come here and sit with me?" he asked. I sat still, my glare stuck on his face. He shook his head again and got up from the bed. He made his way around the bed to the side where I was sitting. He towered over my petite frame, casting an evening shadow across my face. The dark corner seemed to grow tinier and darker with each step he took. He stopped once his feet hit my legs. He crouched down, his face only a few inches away from mine, and whispered, "Why so edgy little miss?"

I held my breath in hope to avoid his whiskey scented exhale. I stayed still, keeping quiet and trying to remain tolerant. My mind soared with ideas and images of what could happen next. As soon as they entered my mind, I pushed them back out.

He once again grabbed hold of my face, pulling me to my feet. His face, remained inches from mine and he didn't stop pulling until his lips touched my ear.

"Still not talking?" His words were harsh and raspy. He pressed my body up against the wall and pushed his weight against mine. "I thought we had been through the polite lesson already. Making me repeat a lesson is a very." He paused, pulling my head back roughly to look into my eyes. "Very bad idea."

I whimpered as he threw my head back against the wall. He stepped back, letting my body fall to the ground. I remained still on the ground, waiting for the blurry vision to dissipate. The room spun as he grabbed my arm and pulled me onto the bed.

"A lesson repeated is a lesson wasted," he informed me, walking across the room to his bag. I stayed on the bed, recovering from the blows to my body. *Get up, fight back.* I struggled to my feet, pressing my hands to my head. Hector turned around with rope in his hands. His look changed from anger to furious in a flash. He lunged towards me. I ducked down, *not fast enough.* His weight hit me like a ton of bricks. The air escaped my lips and my body fell limp. *Don't give up, Annabelle.*

"Not as strong as you think, are you?" he questioned arrogantly and stood up. I had started to lose consciousness when I felt him grab my arms. He forcefully tied my hands together and then to the bed. I pulled on my hands absently when he started to tie my feet together. *Fight back Annabelle.* My strength was almost nonexistent, but I wrestled in the ropes. I started to kick my legs, while he was still tying them together, as hard as I could. He began to fight to hold my legs still. I gave one last effort to shove him off of me. *Bingo,* I kicked him square in the face. He stumbled back away from the bed, his nose visibly broken. *You got him!*

I watched as he wiped his bleeding face and looked down at his hands. It slowly sunk in that I had just woken the sleeping beast. *Stupid... stupid...* Stupid... He repeated his wiping sequence once or twice before his glare met my eyes. *Shit...*

"You are a very stupid girl." His voice was threatening. He unzipped his jacket and used his shirt to wipe off his face. Once he zipped his coat up again, he came towards the bed.

He grabbed my tied arms, pushing them down to the bed. His face resumed its position a few inches away from my face. He growled out the words, "You haven't even begun to see what I can do to you."

He shoved his hand in his pockets and pulled out a small silver object. He opened it to reveal the same small knife that caused my injuries the other night. I tightly shut my eyes, preparing myself for him to repeat the same superficial wound down my chest. Instead he cut my hands free.

"Get up," he demanded. I looked at him in alarm. "Did I stutter? I said-" He grabbed my hair and pulled me to my feet "-GET UP!"

I caught my balance on the wall and turned to face him. His eyes were on fire and his breaths were deep and labored. He approached me, putting his hands on the wall, one on each side of my head. He leaned forward and whispered, "Want to fight back? I'll show you how to fight."

He connected his right hand on the right side of my face and pushed my weak body to the ground. "Lesson two, fighting." He laughed hysterically as my body hit the hard surface of the floor. My head bounced on contact and I rolled to my back, crying out in pain. He towered over me, casting a dark shadow on my face. He grabbed the front of my ruined shirt and pulled my body up to meet his eyes.

"What? Now you don't want to fight back." His tone was livid and wild. He held my shirt for a moment, growling and breathing heavily in my face. I could see the wheels turning in his head, trying to figure out what demented action he could do to me next. He glared into my eyes, burning fear into my brain.

"You aren't that smart, are you little girl?" *Think of a new question already...*

"Smarter than you," slipped from my lips faster than I could think about the right thing to say. Regret burned into my cheeks and I felt the fear drain into my chest.

He held his breath, letting the anger fill his veins and I could hear his heart pound in his chest. He dropped me to the floor. I fell limp to the ground, frozen with anxiety. *Good job, Annabelle. You did it this time.* The voice in my head tormented my mind. I shook my head and woke from my trance.

Hector stood above me, arms stiff, fists tight, teeth clenched, breaths heavy and livid. I crawled backwards, toward the wall, away from Hector. He watched as I moved away from him. He stood motionless, deep in concentration.

By the time my back was against the wall, the light in the room was quickly fading. The look of concentration on his face turned to an absent stare, similar to the stare he had given me, right before he took a knife to my chest two days ago. *This is it...*

He approached me, staring distractedly at my face. Once his feet touched my legs, he bent down and grabbed my shoulders, roughly pulling me to my feet. With his grip still firm on my shoulders, he slammed my body into the wall. Once again the air escaped my lips and I didn't dare fight back. His grip moved from my shoulders to my wrists. He twisted my body around, putting my face to the wall. His hold on my tiny arms tightened and he threw me across the floor forcefully. I rolled, landing at the other side of the room, my body defeated and disheveled. Face down; I lay helplessly on the floor, waiting for fate to show its ugly face. *Death isn't your fate, not yet.* I couldn't move, fighting back was not the answer for me.

"Not so witty now, are you?" he teased, lifting my head by my hair. "Another lesson wasted on a pathetic little girl." He spat in my face and turned to retrieve his bag.

The darkness had almost consumed the entire room when Hector returned to my side. He knelt down next to me and whispered, "Until our next lesson," *Repetitive...*

The rattle of the keys rang loudly in my head. The door was unlocked, opened, shut and relocked all in a matter of a minute. A minute in which, my mind stood still, paralyzed by the pain in my body.

I rolled to my back slowly, gazing towards the ceiling. My body was weak, defeated and screaming in pain. My head rolled to the side, my eyes involuntarily closed, leaving me in complete darkness. I lay, quietly, and waited for anything different to happen. All I could do was wait and hope to God that this would all be over soon. I wanted so desperately for it all to be over.

I stayed motionless for what seemed like eternity until I heard something outside. Hopeful, I turned to the wall, knocked as hard as I could. A sound like a soft whisper on the other side of the wall could be heard.

"Hello?" I called out in a tired, distraught tone. My tears had just begun to subside.

Is your visitor back, Annabelle? The voice ridiculed.

"Annabelle?" the soft whisper questioned. My heart stopped.

"Please, help me," I cried out softly. *You are hearing things again Annabelle. No one is out there.*

"Don't give up, Annabelle," the whisperer encouraged.

"Please, don't go. He'll come back."

"I'll come back again." The whisperer promised.

"No, stay, please!" I called out.

Silence hit me. I cried hysterically and without any energy left to spare, I absentmindedly pounded at the wall. I continued my useless actions until the darkness consumed my body and mind.

"Please… don't go…" I whispered, surrendering to oblivion, I fell asleep.

Dreams filled my brain with nonsense, sending my body in fits of fear and rage. I tossed and turned through the night, leaving my body exhausted and injured in the early morning.

Day Four – December 17th

I woke to a beam of bright light blinding me through the broken shelter walls. I sat up against the wall and felt my brain pound against my skull, begging for relief. *Food…* It had been almost four days since I had eaten anything. The dirty water would only hold me over for a few more days without food.

A new noise came from outside my cage walls. *Humming… it's a woman.* My mind was not imagining this. I heard the humming as it approached the door of the shelter. I sat motionless, bewildered by my suffering. Speechless…

My heart pounded when I heard a frighteningly familiar jingle of keys outside the door. *Janis…* The door opened, exposing the darkened room to a light source greater than it's ever known; sunlight. I covered my eyes, guarding them from their once familiar love of light.

Janis sulked into the room, toting a large bag with her. She glanced at me as she passed through the threshold, slamming the door behind her. My eyes readjusted to my gloomy quarters and I watched her throw her bag onto the bed. She turned to me, taking a seat in the old wooden chair.

"Girl," she addressed me like I was a prisoner. *You are a prisoner.*

I stared at her, waiting to see what she had planned for me. Compared to Hector's lessons, just about anything would be a relief.

When I didn't answer her, she shook her head, sighing heavily and dug through her bag. She continued her search for something in her bag and then stopped, looking down at me. "Why are you so gloomy? This all could be much worse, you know. At least you're not outside in that weather." She looked around the room. My insides boiled with anger. *Bitch...*

"It's disgusting here. I wanted to keep you tied up outside our house, but Hector insisted on this place." She glared at me. "Now we have to drive to get here, constantly carrying around bags of supplies and tools. It's a waste of time." She looked back down at her bag. I was holding myself back, trying to remember that I was weak and I couldn't defend myself. "Hector was right, you are rude."

"I'm not rude to people who respect me," slipped from my lips and I kept my stare on Janis. She laughed and finally pulled a bowl out of her bag.

"Respect, is that what you want?" She laughed, grabbing another package from the oversized bag. "Don't hold your breath for that one. I don't even get that from Hector. But, I've learned to live with that." She laughed quietly.

She had a very strange demeanor to her. She was content with my abduction, obviously just as crazy as Hector, and completely confident in their deranged relationship. She was taller, wild light brown hair. Her clothes were dirty, smelling of cigarette smoke and alcohol. She acted like the crazy woman no one ever enjoyed to be around. The woman who would sit on her porch with twelve of her twenty cats, staring down the neighborhood children as they passed her yard and who would drop cans in the grocery store to get a discount. *Moocher ...*

We sat in silence for a short while. I kept my curious eyes on her as she fidgeted with something in her lap. To my surprise she got up from her seat suddenly and approached me. I brought my legs to my chest and tensed up.

"Relax, it's just potatoes." She dropped the container in my lap. *She's feeding you?*

"What?" I questioned, confused.

"Food," she nonchalantly pronounced. "Eat it."

"Why are you feeding me?"

"Because you have to eat," she explained taking her seat in the chair once again. "We don't want you dead."

I stared at her, bewildered. She laughed and looked down at a book she had pulled out of her bag. Silence filled the room once again.

I looked down at the bowl. I furrowed my eyebrows together and opened the lid. It was a bowl of mashed potatoes. *No source of energy there...* The buttery scent captured my nose like a trap and my mouth watered on cue. The spit that I had so desperately tried to retrieve earlier this week coated my mouth. *Nothing to eat with...*

"Do you have silverware?" It was a shot in the dark to even waste my breath to ask. She looked up at me and laughed. She lifted her hand to her mouth once or twice, motioning for me to use my hands. *See? You're a prisoner.*

She rolled her eyes and continued reading. *Now you're being baby-sat.* I sighed and looked at my fingers. My hands were worn, dirty and bloodied. I tried to wipe them off on my pants, getting them as clean as I could. I took two fingers and scooped the potatoes into my mouth. The cold, salty, buttered mass of starch hit my throat like a ton of bricks. My throat was dry and rigid, making swallowing a difficult experience. The soft, fluffy potatoes felt like sandpaper sliding down my throat. I winced as they slowly fell into my empty stomach. The sensation made me gag, making a revolting noise. Janis looked up at me and gave me a dirty look. She slammed her book down and walked to me. She knelt down and snatched the bowl from me.

"What? Are you too prissy to eat a bowl of smashed potatoes with your fingers?" She assumed I was rejecting the food. "At least we're feeding you!" she screamed. She turned to walk away with the bowl and muttered, "Ungrateful little bitch."

"Ungrateful?" I questioned back, feeling the anger burst through my mouth. *Wrong thing to say lady...* How could she call me ungrateful? How can someone who was taken unwillingly, beaten and left alone in the cold be considered ungrateful?

Janis whipped around and glared at me in disbelief. I knew that I was walking the line of danger, but something about calling a victim of kidnap, ungrateful, hit a nerve inside me.

"Ungrateful little bitch?" I gained a small voice back. "I didn't ask for any of this."

Janis stared in amusement. She returned to my side, kneeling back down and dropping the bowl into my hands. She gave me a fake smile, patting my face.

"Then stop fussing. Listen, I know what my husband has done to you. You don't have strength, don't make me force you. No more gagging, no more talking. Just eat." She sounded like a fed up, strict, deranged mother telling her child to clean their plate. She gave me a rough smack across the face and returned to her book.

The slap burned in my cheek. I held back reaction tears and looked down at the bowl of razor mashed potatoes. I forced myself to continue eating. Silently suffering through the entire bowl, I finished them. I set the bowl on the floor near me. I sat still for a few minutes. I shifted my body, pulling my knees to my chest and wrapping my arms around them. *Now what?*

I looked up to see Janis curiously gazing at me. I suddenly felt a cold sweat drip from my brow. I started shivering involuntarily. Nausea set in my stomach like a rock. I took a deep breath, realizing that something was wrong. I realized what had just happened. *What is she going to do now?*

"How are you feeling?" she asked.

"What-did-you-give-me…" I trailed off, slurring my words together. She smiled confidently and started to pack her things away. I felt the urge to vomit. I grabbed my stomach, feeling my shoulder muscles tense and my body convulse forward. I let out a cry of pain and my breaths were rigid and broken. I struggled to catch my breath, dry heaving slightly.

"Don't fight it," Janis commented, taking the bowl from the floor beside me. She giggled nervously and shoved the bowl into her bag. I looked up at her as the room danced around me. Unable to distinguish which direction was up or down, I struggled to sit up.

My body twitched and shook furiously. I felt the newly ingested food make its way back up to my mouth. I bent over and vomited violently on the floor next to me. I felt my insides twist and knot. My eyes begged to close and I did nothing to stop them. I fell to the floor, limp.

"Good night, Princess," Janis whispered into my ear and she left my side. I opened my eyes, and watched as she left, locking the door behind her. *Fight back, Annabelle.* I fell into an unconscious state.

Later, it was dark when I opened my eyes again. I blinked quickly to adjust my eyes to the familiar darkness. I got to my knees and began to slowly crawl to the bed. I lifted my shattered body onto the thin mattress and tried to get comfortable. The pain raged on, wreaking havoc on my body.

I breathed heavily, trying to control the urges to vomit and involuntarily cried out. My tears were slowly falling and I knew that night would be long. *Fight back, Annabelle.*

I took another rigid breath and fought to regain control of my body. The pain dug into my sides like a dagger, forcing me to dig my nails in the palms of my hands. The old blood stains on the sheet were met with fresh spots of crimson from my hands. *Fight back.*

"I'm trying!" I cried out painfully. My voice was weak and irritated. I curled my body into the fetal position once again. I brought my knees to my chin and began to rock back and forth. I began to loudly cry out in pain. I held my necklace tight in my palm. *It can't change your situation...*

"Make it stop, make it go away." Continuing to rock myself into unconsciousness, I repeated the same sentence, over and over until I was pushed into a dreamless sleep.

Day Six- December 19th

Annabelle… Annabelle?

Wake-up darling, it's time for you to get up.

Annabelle? Please, don't make me ask you again.

The motherly tone hit my ears in a piercing wall of pain. My head pounded, like someone was squeezing my skull. My stomach muscles were tight and aching from the several hours of dry heaving I had gone through the night before. I opened my eyes to see a blurry surrounding. I quickly closed them when I realized I was still in hell. Unfortunately, I had not died and gone to better place.

Annabelle, stop fooling around. Get up! A familiar voice echoed through my skull. I groaned out loud, letting my voice fill the room.

Annabelle. The voice echoed again. *Annabelle, you're wasting time.* It ridiculed. *You are going to be late. Time is wasting away while you lay there.*

"Stop it," I begged, my voice raspy and broken.

Annabelle, you must be a lazy child to be lying in bed so late in the day.

"Leave me alone," I absently answered the imaginary voice in my head.

But you are wasting away the daylight. Isn't that what you love, daylight?

"Not anymore, daylight means lessons and with darkness comes sleep. When I sleep, I don't hurt anymore." I wasn't even sure I was actually speaking out loud. I continued to answer the false voice, begging it to leave me alone and let me sleep.

Sleeping only covers your pain; you must face your pain.

I didn't know what day it was, let alone care what time of day it was. I had been awake for four days, on and off, that I could remember. Whether or not that meant I had been here for four days or not, I wasn't completely sure of.

"I can't…" I trailed off into another dreamless sleep.

"She will just have to wake up," a female spoke roughly.

"I must warn you, she is a very bad student. Barely listens to anything I tell her…" the male's voice was angry and annoyed.

I opened my eyes to see the door swing open, *Lesson…* Time to suffer through another pointless day of survival…

"Get up." A bellowing male voice came from the doorway. I stayed still, my body aching from the toxic day I had already encountered. I refused to succumb to their wishes, not after the treatment they had given me. They didn't deserve my respect.

"Up Girl," an angry female's voice rang through the room.

I slowly rolled to my back, feeling all my muscles stretch and bend painfully as though they might split into pieces. The pain ripped through my body and I let out a small moan, squeezing my eyes closed, letting the tears fall from my eyes. *Bad idea...*

My tiny slip of noise was cause for a smack across the face and a violent nudge in the side to get me sitting up. I put my hand to my face and opened my eyes to see Hector staring back at me. His nose, still obviously broken, was covered in a white bandage.

"Respect will get you places that you have never imagined," he said simply. I stared at him like he was growing another head. *What was he getting at?* I was in a haze. The room swayed back and forth, blurring the edges of my range of view.

"You haven't learned very much in the time that you have been here," Janis commented.

"Right, and you have been here, how long?" he questioned me. I tried to count in my head...

"Today is your sixth day. I have been here a few of those days, only to receive a broken nose. Janis was also here two days ago to feed you." Hector turned to Janis and smiled. "She tells me that you weren't a very nice girl. You will respect her authority and appreciate her kind thought to feed you."

That was two days ago? Did I sleep through the day yesterday? *Must have...*

"Why didn't you respect her? Did she or did she not come all the way here to feed you?"

I sat quietly, trying to focus my hazy vision. I couldn't answer the question without offending their ridiculous idea of being polite or respect.

"Well, are you going to answer?" Janis asked forcefully. I just looked up at her and shook my head, no, as if it *weren't* a life or death situation. *The sooner death comes, the sooner the darkness will consume your existence.*

"Can we just quit the small talk and get this over with already?" Janis begged Hector. He glared at her and pulled her by the

70

wrist closer to him. He whispered loudly into her ear and let her go. I held my necklace tightly as they spoke in the corner. She quietly rubbed her wrist and became a silent object in the background.

"Well, looks like another lesson wasted on you," he announced grabbing my left arm roughly, pulling me to my feet. The strength in my legs was nonexistent and I felt my knees buckle from underneath me and I fell to the ground. Hector stared down at me, disgusted. *The time will come sooner or later... sooner is preferred.*

"Hector, can I do it now?" Janis begged annoyingly. He rolled his eyes.

Reaching down for my arms, he yanked my body upwards, forcing me to my feet. My stance was abnormally weak and unstable. I watched as he backed away and whispered something into her ear. His focus then turned back to me and he smiled strangely. Janis seemed eager with a wicked smile on her face.

"This lesson is not for you. But instead, Janis will be the student, I, the teacher, and you, the opponent." His smile turned into an evil grin and his stare went blank, whispering once again into his accomplice's ear.

I watched curiously as they both turned to face me. Janis looked concentrated, ready to pounce. *As if you are a threat...*

"One at a time, don't be afraid to really put your weight into it," Hector encouraged. Janis nodded silently, raising her fists. *Annabelle, you are the punching bag.*

Before I had time to think, her fist crashed into the side of my face. The blow to my weakened body and disoriented mind caught me off guard and I stumbled to my knees. I clenched my teeth, slowly reaching my hand to my face. My cheek burned, and I could feel the bruising begin under my finger tips.

"Not bad, not bad. This time, swing your arm in a more upward motion." Hector coached as he approached me once more. He glared down at me while he hoisted my body back to its feet. My body swayed backwards, causing me to lose my balance and fall into the wall behind me. Luckily, I caught myself from crashing to the ground and regained stability. I closed my eyes briefly, waiting for the fatigue to pass.

I opened my eyes slowly to see yet another fist fly into my face, this time my chin was the first to be impacted. My head jerked backwards, but I kept myself standing by bracing myself on the wall. I felt the warm rush of fluid to my mouth. I could taste the metallic flavor of my own blood in my mouth, and realized I had bitten my tongue.

"Great job, one more thing, when you punch someone, to really get them good, you have to follow through with your impact. Don't stop short." His little talks to Janis before she struck my face with her bare fists sounded like a pep talk before a high school baseball game. *And you are the ball...*

Janis's beastly disposition scared me. She was four times the size of my tiny frame. Her fists were like boulders crashing into my face. She nodded eagerly and braced herself to throw another punch at me. I started to move out of the way and as soon as she saw a hint of movement, her fist was flying. She hit my chin first, again, this time sending my head backwards into the wall behind me. I slid to the ground, grasping my head in my hands. I screamed in pain, wishing for it to be over.

I cried loudly, "Why are you doing this to me?"

The silence was piercing. I held my breath, waiting for yet another blow. But instead I looked up to see both Hector and Janis staring at me.

"Don't you get it?" Janis questioned. I let tears silently fall from my eyes.

"You have no meaning to us," Hector blatantly pointed out.

"We are only after the sorrow of your friend Allie. We want her to suffer the way me and my family had to while Hector was away," Janis replied in a distant, cold voice. "I want her to miss someone as much as I missed my husband. And you are much weaker than her husband. He would have been our first choice if he weren't so damn big."

"But I-I didn't do... I did nothing wrong," I stammered.

She laughed into my face, pulling me up to my feet by the pieces of my shirt and spat into my face. "You exist, darling."

"Janis, my dear, put the girl down and let's go home. That snow storm will be approaching by now." Hector said. She let go of my shirt, letting me fall to the ground. I groaned in pain, feeling the broken wood underneath my legs, splinter into my skin. They turned to leave, both Janis and Hector with devilish grins, plastered onto their faces.

"At least I have a family worth missing." I let the words slip from my lips faster than the thought processed in my brain. *Of all the possible times,* now *you choose to be witty.*

Janis shot me a look that could kill. She took one step towards me, pulling my head inches away from hers. "You *don't* want to say that…"

Her words were more of a promise than a statement. She glared into my eyes like she was trying to burn a hole into my skull. She took the handle full of my hair that was in her hand and pushed my face into the floor. *More splinters…*

"Janis! Now," Hector growled from the door way. As he unlocked the door, I felt the bone chilling gust of wind escape into the room. *Tonight will be a long night…*

"Next time, you will understand how serious I really am about my family." Janis promised into my ear. She roughly let go of my hair, giving my head one last jolt. I closed my eyes for what seemed like only a few minutes.

When I reopened them, it was pitch-dark. I had to have fallen asleep for a while; it was still daylight when I had closed my eyes. The darkness surrounded my mind and body. The warmth it created in my mind was everything that the light had never offered for me. I searched the room for a hint of light to guide me to the bed. *Nothing…*

I heard a noise from outside. *Is it your visitor Annabelle?*

"Hello?" I whispered. The wind blew angrily outside the pathetic walls. I heard the shuffle of a coat outside the paper thin barrier between me and freedom. I rolled slowly to my side and crawled to the edge of the room. I put my hand on the wall like I expected that person to feel my touch. "Hello?" I repeated.

"Annabelle, how are you?" my visitor asked. *A new question today…* I heard more than a hint of concern in their voice. Their voice was filled with regret and sorrow.

"I'm not okay. I need your help, please. Don't leave me. They'll come back, they'll come back to kill me." I pleaded, my voice cracked as I started to cry, realizing the state of emergency I was truly in.

"I'm trying." My visitor paused. "I'll come back."

"Just stay with me," I cried out, "I don't want to be alone anymore. I can't survive alone." The excitement of my outburst caused a deafening pain in my skull. I cried out in pain.

73

"Please, give me one more day," they bargained.

"I don't know if I can make it one more day..." I trailed off, slowly succumbing to the peaceful, darkness once more.

"Please, just one more day Annabelle, I will come back for you."

I couldn't find my voice, my eye lids became heavy.

"Annabelle?"

My mind was screaming for my visitor to stay, but nothing come out of my mouth. I moaned.

"Please, don't give up, not yet."

That was the last thing I heard my savior say before I slipped into yet another dreamless, restless slumber.

Day Seven- December 20th

The pain surged through my head; my hearing was muffled, like I had been standing in front of the speakers at a metal concert. I squeezed my eyes shut in hope to focus my vision. I eagerly opened them again to find a less foggy surrounding. The night of sleep was pointless. A few hours of restless sleep was hardly considered a reenergizing slumber.

I brought my hand to my face, feeling the raw spot on my cheek that had been rubbed on the sandpaper floor. The swelling of my eye was obvious, throbbing and pounding. I sat up slowly, realizing the severity of my injuries. The metallic taste in my mouth lingered and I felt my bruised and swollen bottom lip. I sighed and lifted my broken body off the ground. I struggled to the sink, holding myself up on the sides of the useless piece of ceramic. I felt my stomach groan in hunger. I put my hand on my face, looking into the broken mirror on the wall. This was the first time I had taken the time to look at myself in a mirror in six days.

The broken pieces of reflective material didn't show me the person I once knew. Instead, I saw a battered, broken, and beaten woman. My hair hung in my face, tangled and dirty. I pushed my hair out of the way to see my eyes. My once bright, eager, strong blue eyes were swollen, red and lifeless. The right side of my face was covered in new dark, purple bruises and yellowing old bruises. My left cheek was cut open, causing a bloody trail down the side of my neck. Tears burned my eyes and I didn't recognize the person staring back at me. *Annabelle is missing...*

I let tears fall down my face and I bent down to tear off a piece of my already ripped pants. It was a struggle to rip the fabric across the seam, but I finally got a small, portion off to clean my wounds.

The reflection of the sunlight on the snow had changed the lighting of room considerably. The daylight was brighter than the past days, a factor of more snow I assumed. I heard the familiar drip of water onto the mattress; an effect from the bright sunlight, I assumed. I stumbled to the bed, holding myself up on the iron head frame while I let the steady stream of water run into my mouth. This intensified the metallic taste of my own blood in my mouth. I rinsed my mouth with the melted snow and spit it out, not really caring where it went. I bent back down under the stream and took a drink of the water. It was a welcome feeling that ran down my throat. I was glad to get any bit of liquid in my dry mouth and throat.

As soon as I finished taking a well deserved drink, I let the stream of water saturate the piece of material I had ripped from my pant leg. I turned, returning to the mirror and leaned slightly over the sink to use the mirror to clean my facial wound. I winced as the rough, obviously dirty material touched my face. I slowly rubbed off the dried blood; carefully avoiding the fresh scab to prevent reopening the wound.

Once I finished cleaning my face, I looked down at my chest in the reflection. The rip in my shirt covered the laceration down the middle of my chest. I moved the flap of fabric out of the way to look at the damage. The scab was hard, stiff and restricting. But the area around the cut itself didn't show any sign of infection. *One good thing out of... how many bad?*

I placed the dirtied piece of material into the sink. As I looked up into the mirror one last time, something on the wall caught my eye. A portion of the deteriorating wall, about the size of a small window, maybe two feet by two feet, was waving in the wind. *You're going to escape through that?*

Suddenly, my previously weakened body was strengthened by adrenaline. I looked around the room and remembered the wooden chair. I staggered back to the other side of the room and leaned down on the chair, grabbing it with both hands. I tried, first, to pick it up and carry the lightweight chair to my new escape hole. *You are too weak.*

As soon as my arms felt the weight of the chair, my body collapsed into the chair, face first. I yelled out in a frustration. My muscles had been misused and mistreated in the past six days. Even something as simple as an old dining room chair was the weight of a full grown human being. I grunted and caught my breath. I got down on my knees with the chair in front of me and pushed it forward. I closed my eyes, feeling as though the crawl, a few feet across the room, was a long distance sprint.

Once the chair hit the sink, I knew I had made it. The short distance exhausted my damaged body. I turned off of my knees and sat down on the floor, resting my head on the seat of the chair. I couldn't catch my breath, gasping desperately for a fresh breath of air. *Go to sleep, Annabelle...*

"No..." I whispered. I started to close my eyes, inhaling slowly. I felt my head spin in a strange subconscious state. My hands shook as I took my face in them, rubbing my eyes slowly. *Go to sleep, Annabelle...* My arms fell limply to my sides as my body slid to the ground.

I lied on the ground, helplessly, pathetically falling asleep after finding my only chance of escape from my hell on earth. *The darkness is welcoming...*

"Go to sleep, Annabelle." The familiar voice sounded just as tired as I felt.

"Bills, I'm totally awake. I can't sleep." I complained, not wanting to be suppressed by darkness yet.

It was a memory from high school, senior year, sleeping over at Billy Jean's house on a weekend. It had to be about 3 in the morning and Billy had been desperately begging me to sleep for the last hour.

"Why do you hate sleeping so much?" She asked me for the millionth time during our friendship. "It's such a rejuvenating experience every night, how could you hate it?"

"Billy Jean, you know why." I sulked, pulling the blankets closer to my chin.

"Just explain it to me." She sighed with a yawn. I knew full well what she was trying to get me to do.

"You only want me to tell you again so I put myself to sleep like the last time," I pointed out.

"No, I really want to know..." she trailed off, resting her head deeper into her pillow.

I looked over at my soon to be sleeping friend. "I hate the dark."

"Mmhmm..." she subconsciously answered my statement. I smiled.

"It's not a fear or from a tragic experience, I just HATE the dark. Sleep is a dark, lifeless routine that every human has to succumb to each night. I don't like the idea of wasting away, precious hours of my life, sleeping in a dreamless world, where nothing can be accomplished."

"Right..." Billy added, completely obliviously.

"I much prefer daylight. The light has so much more to offer than darkness does. During the day for one thing, you can see. You always hear of people getting kidnapped at night, lost in the darkness. You don't hear the statement, lost in the light, very often. The light offers a certain happiness that nighttime cannot."

Drip, drip, drip... I opened my eyes to a familiar drip on my hand. This time, however, a new hole in the roof of my pathetic shelter was the cause. I glanced around the room to realize what had just happened. *You fell asleep, while trying to escape.*

I looked up to the ceiling. The hole was still there, not a figment of my imagination fooling me. I had a chance to escape. The light coming through the hole warned that I didn't have much daylight left today. *You could wait until morning...*

"No way, I'm not taking that chance." I growled to myself. I squeezed the necklace around my neck for any bit of luck. *You'll need more than that.*

I pushed myself onto my knees once again, grunting in fatigue. I lifted my body onto the chair, looking up once more at the hole in the wall, the piece of wood waved back at me in the wind. I took a deep breath and lifted one foot onto the seat of the chair. I braced myself on the wall, hoping to God that the wall would just collapse under my weight to avoid climbing.

Holding onto the broken wall with both hands, I brought my second foot to the platform of the chair. My limbs shook, like a tree in the wind, I swayed back and forth. I looked up to the hole and realized I was looking outside of my tiny shack.

Trees, trees and more trees is all I could see. The snow was deep, covering every inch of ground in sight. I couldn't tell where I was exactly but something about the untouched snow told me that I wasn't close to civilization.

I looked back down at my feet to see what I could step on next to give myself a boost. I noticed a slight ledge on the top of sink that could be at least another foot taller than the chair I was standing on.

While I lifted my foot to the ledge, I heard it. *Jingling keys…*

"Shit," I told myself. *Jump out now and risk another injury, stay where you are and give away the only escape you have?* I began to panic, still holding onto the ledge of the hole in the wall.

I scrambled to think of which idea was better. *Jump, Annabelle.* The idea sounded logical. The snow was deep and soft; it could help keep my fall quiet and less painful. I needed out, *you need help.*

I gathered all the strength I could find inside of me and I lifted my body onto the ledge of the sink. I took a deep breath, and prepared myself for one last push. As I pushed myself up, towards the opening to freedom, the door to my tiny hell opened.

- 8 - Annabelle: No One Deserves To Be Alone

"SHE'S ESCAPING!" hollered Janis as she entered in front of Hector. *You're dead now, Annabelle.*

"Grab her!" Hector hollered after he realized the meaning of his wife's scream.

The adrenaline that had overwhelmed my body gave me the strength to push free of the tiny hole in the wall. I fell into a deep, cold, wet pile of snow. The soft, white snow was a welcoming feeling. I was surrounded by gentleness. Like a mother's touch on a baby's face, caressing each part of my weakened body. I remained still, waiting to hear their next move. I couldn't hear anything or anyone. I realized my welcoming pile of snow was also impairing my hearing, blocking all outside noise.

I decided I needed to get out of my newly found comfort. I slowly lifted myself out of the hole I had made, feeling no new injuries. I lifted my head out of the deep snow to see no one around me. The snow left a wet coating on my clothing, weighing my body down. *You're not strong enough.*

"Annabelle?" a strangely familiar voice questioned from behind me sounding shocked to see me. I whirled around, wondering who would be here, calling me by my first name.

I struggled to keep my balance, feeling unstable my fatigued body quiver. I focused my vision on a person, standing a few feet in front of me, dressed in a snow suit, carrying a back pack; a hammer perched in his grip. *You know who that is…*

"Lucas?" I questioned. I should have realized he would show up to help his parents sooner or later. *He's one of them…*

"How did you get out?" He seemed dumbfounded, completely uncaring that I had actually escaped.

"She has to be around here." Janis's voice came from the front of the small shelter. I felt the hair on the back of my neck stand up nervously.

"I have to get away," I whispered quietly. I took a few steps forward in the deep snow. The snow consumed my weak legs and I fell forward. Lucas dropped the hammer and caught my fall with a gentle grip around my shoulders. I looked up at him curiously, wondering why he was being so gentle with me.

"Lucas!" Hector called rounding the corner, "good, you caught her!"

"Hector? Did you get her?" Janis questioned rounding the corner a few minutes after Hector had. She stopped when she saw her son. "Lucas, what are you doing out here? We told you we didn't need your help." *He isn't with them?*

"Janis! He caught the damn girl. Don't scold him for helping!" Hector yelled. Her head dropped cowardly. Hector turned his attention back to Lucas who was still holding my shoulders, gently supporting my body. "Bring the bitch back inside."

Hector turned around, grabbing Janis's arm and dragged her along with him to the front of the building. Lucas stood silently, letting go of my shoulders. I felt suddenly faint, feeling the ground move underneath me. My surroundings danced. I closed my eyes slightly, letting the strength I had left drain from my body. I began to collapse when Lucas caught my shoulders again.

"Annabelle, don't give up yet," he encouraged. *Familiar ...*

"What did you say?" I opened my eyes and looked up at him tiredly.

"Don't give up yet," he repeated, emotion filling his voice. *Very familiar...*

"You..." I started but paused to think about the similarities. *He couldn't be...*

He didn't say anything to me, just looked into my eyes. *It couldn't be the same person...*

"You were the person who-"

"SON! What is taking you so long?" Hector hollered from inside the pathetic building.

"Coming!" Lucas yelled back, turning to me and without any warning he lifted me off the ground. I was surprised how effortlessly he tossed me over his shoulder. "Just go along with me."

He carried me over his shoulder, my hair hung loosely into my face and the blood rushed to my head. I closed my eyes with the strange pressure that overwhelmed my skull.

As we rounded the corner, the wind hit my frozen body like a ton of bricks. My body shook violently and I shivered reluctantly. The pain in my head worsened and I felt the tears burn my eyes.

"What took you so long?" Hector asked when we entered the room.

"She put up a fight." Lucas paused, taking a deep breath. "I had to teach her a lesson."

What is he getting at?

"*You* taught her a lesson?" Janis questioned sounding both shocked and appalled.

"Yes." Lucas began to pull me off his shoulder. "It was pretty easy. She passed out pretty quickly." He dropped his bag onto the floor with a thud. His grip remained gentle but he roughly set me onto the bed. Pain ran through my body in its familiar path of destruction. I opened my eyes slightly to see him lean down to pick up his bag again.

Our eyes met and I wanted to scream out in anger for setting me down so roughly but instead he whispered, "Keep quiet." He stood back up with his bag and I reclosed my eyes.

"What should we do with her now?" Janis questioned. "We can't leave her alone now; she'll escape again when she wakes."

"Yes..." Hector's voice was concentrated, "She cannot be left to escape. That hole can be fixed but I don't have the right materials with me."

"I'm not staying here. I refuse to be left alone with her." Janis protested without anyone even suggesting that scenario.

"No, of course not darling," Hector agreed. The room fell silent again. Minutes passed and I desperately wanted to open my eyes to see what was going on.

"Lucas will be staying tonight to keep an eye on the girl." Hector finally spoke, sounding annoyed and bored. *Baby sitter...*

The room filled with silence once again. I begged for a hint of Lucas's reaction, but the sudden sound of movement startled me. As the door slammed, I reminded myself to stay still...*play dead.* The familiar sound of keys jingled and the screaming silence filled my ears. I couldn't open my eyes, fearful of who was still in the room with me.

I waited quietly, knowing someone was still in the room. I opened my eyes to see the sunlight was completely gone. I sat up slowly, not hearing any sound anywhere around my bed. *Maybe you are alone...*

I stood up from the bed, feeling my way across the room. I felt the cool ceramic of the sink. I felt around for the wooden chair. It was in the same place that I had left it. I felt my head pound with the same adrenaline that had pushed me through the hole earlier. *Someone is just going to catch you again...*

"I have to get out." I reminded myself with a hint of worry in my voice. With a shaking hand, I grabbed the back of the chair and the side of the sink and lifted myself onto the seat of the chair once more. I stood holding the wall on either side of the corner. I put my foot on the same ledge of the sink and took a deep breath.

You can't do it.

"I have to. There's no other way to survive."

You can't do it.

"Yes, I can."

A familiar noise rang in my ear, jingling keys. I felt the hair on my neck stand on end and my body shook in fear. *You are just going to get caught.*

"Not this time." I encouraged myself taking one more deep breath. Just as the door opened and I pushed myself up to the hole, the chair made a terrible groaning noise and tipped backwards, crashing to the ground. Before I was completely off the sink, I lost my footing on the ledge and slipped off. I dangled from the opening in the wall, splinters of wood dug into the palms of my hands. I growled in pain, letting go of the wall. My body fell crashing to the ground. My head slammed into the corner of the sink and darkness consumed my mind.

A feeling of weightlessness surrounded me. When I reopened my eyes, I saw darkness. I was tied to the wooden chair. Suddenly, a light shined brightly into my face as if I was being interrogated. Janis and Hector appeared from the darkness.

"If you aren't polite to others, don't expect others to be polite to you," Janis reminded me, circling around my chair, giving my face a rough pat.

"If you don't fight back, you will lose." Hector screamed into my face suddenly. I jumped slightly, restricted by the tightly bound ropes.

"Weren't you taught to respect your elders?" Hector put his hand around my neck and put his face near mine. "When we are done with you, you will beg for death on your hands and knees."

His grip around my neck tightened and I began to struggle. His face was happy, psychotically happy. I gasped for air, wishing for it all just to be over with. *Death...*

Suddenly my arms and legs were free and I was thrashing around in bed. The pain in my chest and burning my lungs told me that

I was still alive. A pair of hands grabbed my arms, holding me down. I began to cry, screaming in fear.

"Don't touch me!" My voice was raspy and broken. "PLEASE! Just leave me alone! I didn't do anything to you!"

"Annabelle!" This voice wasn't angry.

"No, leave me alone!" I tried to resist their grip on my arms but I was too weak. They easily dominated me and held my body down to the mattress.

"Annabelle! Please, I won't hurt you," The voice said sternly, still holding down my struggling body. I looked up to see Lucas looking down at me. I gave up struggling and started to cry. He sat down on the edge of the bed, letting go of my arms once I stopped trying to get up. The room was dimly lit by a flash light sitting on the floor. I sat up in the bed. *Calm down... don't waste your energy.*

"Why is this happening to me?" I cried out, loudly. I looked at him, "What did I do wrong?" I stared at him, letting tears stream down my face. He reached out, but I flinched away from his hand. "Please, just leave me alone."

My body shook, my clothes were still soaked from the snow and my hair was frozen to my face. I curled my knees into my chest and tightly squeezed my eyes shut. I wrapped my arms around my body, rubbing my hands up and down my arms. I could feel the cold metal chain around my neck. I put my right hand on my necklace and continued rubbing my legs with my left.

Lucas looked away from me, and slowly got up from the bed. He started to walk towards the door and realization hit me. *You will be alone...*

"No, wait!" I yelled, closing my eyes. I rocked myself back and forth. "I don't want to be alone." I continued to cry, sobbing uncontrollably.

"Annabelle, I'm not going to hurt you." His voice was stern and full of certainty.

I opened my eyes to look at him. His face was barely visible in the darkened room. His blue eyes glowed back at mine, sending a wave of heat over my body. I had never seen such blue eyes. *It's a trick, Annabelle.*

"How do I know that?"

"I'm not like my parents," he admitted sitting down in the chair that had been moved near the side of the bed, "I'm locked in with you."

"Why didn't you stop them?" I whispered.

"I didn't know how." His head dropped down, cowardly. He fidgeted in his bag.

"Why don't you help me out now?" I questioned him sobbingly.

"I don't have the keys." Lucas looked down at his hands. The way he said it made me think he felt imprisoned as well. The sense of unity confused me.

"The hole…" I said in a plain confidence.

"You're not strong enough," His words hit me. *He's right. You're weak,* "please rest."

I watched his silhouette move around in the dark. He paced back and forth. He ran his hands roughly through his hair.

"I don't know what to do." He nearly yelled at me. "Ok?"

Silence followed his outburst. I watched as he pulled something from his bag and stood up, towering over me.

"Please, don't hurt me." I cried out, confidence melting away with my tears. I quickly put my hands over my face and closed my eyes. I tensed my body, waiting for the lesson to begin. *Told you it was a trick…*

"Annabelle…"

"Please…" I whimpered.

"Annabelle, I'm not going to hurt you," he reminded me with a sad tone.

I felt something touch my body. First it covered my legs, then my torso, then my shoulders. I opened my eyes to see Lucas sit back down in the wooden chair. I moved my hands away from my face and felt the soft, warm blanket that covered my body. I pulled it closer, tucking it under my chin. My body shivered eagerly, waiting for the warmth of the thick blanket to take effect on my body. I closed my eyes again, squeezing the blanket tightly.

"I'm not going to hurt you, Annabelle," Lucas repeated softly. *Tricks…*

I opened my eyes again to look at him. He held something that I couldn't really make out in the dark. He lifted his hand, slowly and gently he placed it on my arm. His body heat radiated through the blanket onto my arm. My eyes looked down at his hand, then back up at his face. I could see the corners of his mouth curl upwards. It wasn't the same sadistic smile I had received from his parents, but instead it was a warm, caring smile.

"I don't know why you lied to your parents or why you are treating me so kindly," I began. Lucas sat down on the edge of the bed once more, I looked up at him, tears streaming down my face and I said, "But I don't want to be alone."

"I'm not going anywhere tonight. I promise," he told me moving closer, pushing the hair out of my face. I didn't do anything to stop him. He tucked the pieces of hair behind my ears and touched my forehead gently. I winced slightly at his touch and he pointed out, "That needs to be cleaned." *Tricks...*

I nodded absently, not certain I knew what I was doing. Could I really trust the son of my captor? *No... you shouldn't trust him at all...* But I wanted him to stay; he is gentle with my broken body. I needed human contact.

He grabbed a small white box that read FIRST AID KIT in blue on the front. He set the box on the bed beside me and opened it. I watched him as he touched everything so smoothly, like every piece was made of glass. His movements reminded me of snow fall; free, uncontrolled, and graceful. He pulled out a small bottle of peroxide and a handful of cotton balls.

"Do I need to sit up?" I asked quietly.

"No." He smiled.

He looked down at my face and gently touched the cotton ball to my forehead. The burn of the peroxide seemed like a small pain compared to what I had been through in the past week. *Has it really been a week?*

"What day is it?" I asked curiously filling the silence as he cleaned my wound. He looked into my eyes, smiling at my curiosity. He pulled his sleeve up to look at his watch.

"It's December 21st, 2:34am."

"Day eight..." I whispered, thinking out loud. His smiled faded quickly and he continued cleaning my injuries silently. I ran my finger tips along the palms of my hands. They were torn up, bloodied and scarred. I flexed my fingers, opening and closing my hands a few times. I cringed at the sore stiffness the scabs created. Lucas looked down at my hands and sighed. "I have never been-"

85

"Don't worry about it. Just rest, I'll take care of you." Lucas spoke as if we had known each other forever. He took my hands gently into his own and surveyed the wounds. His thumb lingered over the fading hearts on the back of my left hand. My eyes found his; his face was soft, controlled by empathy. He grabbed another handful of supplies from the box.

I wasn't quite sure how to take his voluntary kindness, in our awkward situation. How could someone so kind come from two people who held such hate in their hearts? He was so gentle and they were the farthest thing from gentle.

Tricks, the voice in my head repeated. *Poor, little, Annabelle, you've always been so naïve.*

I looked up at his face as he worked on my hands. His face was kind and his expression was concentrated. He didn't resemble either of his parents. His eyes were a gentle blue, normally compassionate, now they were filled with exhaustion. His dirty blonde hair hung loosely around his eyes and a small hint of facial hair rested on his chin. There was a mystery behind his eyes that I desperately wanted to know the secret to. I didn't know what it was about him but something told me that he wasn't like his parents. Something told me that he was telling me the truth. *Tricks...*

Curiosity struck me. "You were the person outside every night when your parents left, weren't you?"

Lucas looked into my eyes. "I was here every night." He looked back down to my hands and didn't say another word. I watched him wrap my left hand in gauze. He tucked in the end of the roll and did the same to my right hand. When he was finished I looked back up at his face.

"Why?" It was the only thing I could think of at the moment. He stared back at me, not saying a word. I quickly looked away from his eyes. Starting to cry, I felt so helpless and wounded. This was the first real conversation I'd had in eight days and I didn't know how to put my feelings into sentence form. I cried quietly, covering my face with my hands.

Lucas put his hand under my chin and tilted my face to look at him. He wiped my tears away with a soft touch of his thumb. He looked into my eyes and said, "No one deserves to be alone."

Those words left his lips and hit my ears like a tidal wave. I felt my emotions spill out of my eyes, tears streaming down either side of my face. I just looked at him and cried. I couldn't believe what he said. I was in hell. There couldn't possibly be anyone who remotely cared for my well being here. *Then why hasn't he helped you escape?*

"Why haven't you tried to help my get out each night you've been here?"

Lucas looked back at me, defeat crossed his face.

"I don't have keys and the hole in the wall was my doing." Lucas remained still. "I didn't think you'd be-" He clenched his fists.

I had prayed and begged for help multiple times in the past eight days. Now that help is sitting in front of me, I didn't know how to accept it. I opened my mouth to say something to him but I couldn't speak; words held no meaning close to the feelings I felt at that moment.

"Don't say anything. Please, just rest," Lucas encouraged.

Lucas pulled a pair of gloves from his pocket and handed them to me. I slipped the thick wool gloves over my frozen hands. Shivering slightly, he tucked the blanket under my chin. He held onto the ends of the blanket for a minute and looked into my eyes. "I'm not going to leave you." He brushed my cheek with his thumb once more and let go of the blanket. I held onto the blanket, pulling it closer to my body. The flat surface of the bed left little room to make my head comfortable. Lucas noticed my fidgeting.

"Here, use this," Lucas said taking off his coat and sliding it under my head. I didn't protest. I looked up at Lucas, watching him pull out another blanket from the bag and placing it around his own shoulders. He looked back at me, smiling sweetly. "I'm not going anywhere."

I closed my eyes feeling safe for the first time in eight days. *Don't get used to it.*

Day Eight- December 21st

  I woke up to a familiar drip on the side of my face. The sun beat down on my face; I opened my eyes and looked around. Forgetting exactly where I was, I sat up quickly. *Too quickly...*

  The pain in my head forced me to cry out in pain. The pain was deep, throbbing and constant. I pulled my hands to my face to shield my eyes from the light. I felt the gauze on my hand and the events of last night played out in my mind.

  "Are you okay?" The sudden voice scared me out of bed. I jumped up with my back against the wall. I felt my breaths quicken and my heart pound in my chest. I saw Lucas standing in front of me, a startled look on his face.

  Once I realized I overreacted, the adrenaline wore off and my body screamed to lie back down. I put my hand on my chest and tried to calm down. My knees shook and I felt my legs give in to exhaustion. I put my hands out to catch myself on the bed frame but Lucas grabbed me first. He lifted me up and set me down on the bed.

  "I'm sorry. I didn't mean to scare you. You sat up in bed so suddenly I didn't know if you were dreaming again."

  I couldn't catch my breath and I felt my chest ache. My breaths were fast and shallow. My throat was sore from the lack of water and my chest burned in pain.

  "Calm down, Annabelle. It's okay." Lucas put his hand in mine and brushed my hair out of my face. He rubbed my arms softly, trying his best to calm me down. I coughed slightly, feeling the urge to vomit. I pushed his hand out of the way and leaned over the bed. My body convulsed pushing the stomach bile into my mouth. I vomited on the floor near Lucas's shoes. He held my hair back as if this was a usual occurrence for him.

  I wiped my face off and rolled onto my back. I slowed my breathing to a regular pace. I closed my eyes and put my hands over them. I took a deep breath and felt the familiar drip on my arm. I opened my eyes again to see the familiar stream of water. Without caring if Lucas was watching me, I turned my face to catch the water in my mouth.

  "What are you doing?" Lucas asked surprised. I let the water run down my throat and then turned my head to look at him.

"What other choices do I have? This has been my only source of water for the past eight days," I admitted shyly. *Let's see him put up with the shit you've had to deal with this week.*

"Here," Lucas said grabbing a bottle of water out of his bag. I took the bottle with a shaking hand. I opened the lid slowly; the bottle shook in my unsteady grip. I brought the plastic container to my lips and took a drink. *Clean water tastes like heaven compared to melted snow draining from a condemned building.*

Lucas watched me curiously as I drank the water eagerly. I brought the bottle away from my lips and gasped for air.

"My parents have fed you, haven't they?" he questioned, clueless. I looked at him, lips parted and my eyes wide.

"No," escaped from my lips. "Your mother drugged me the only time they actually brought me any food." I shivered thinking of that horrible night.

Lucas sat, speechless. He looked appalled and quickly grabbed his bag. He dug around inside and pulled out another small bag; a small cooler. He unzipped it and pulled a sandwich out. *Tricks...*

"You need this more than I do." Lucas handed me the sandwich. I took it from him and didn't object or even question what was between the two slices of bread. I opened the baggie and pulled out the sandwich, feeling the soft white bread on my finger tips. I took a bite of the sandwich, chewed and slowly swallowed the small bite. I sat for a minute waiting for the small amount of food to reach my begging stomach. *Wait for the poison to settle in...*

I waited for any symptoms of poison. Nothing happened. I took a second bite not caring at all about what the sandwich contained. Third bite, fourth bite... last bite, I never stopped to think about the flavor of the sandwich. All I knew was that my body was finally getting some type of nutrients.

"I'm sorry I don't have anymore," Lucas said quietly. I looked up at him and thought about his words. I studied his face, wrinkling my brow slightly. He was genuinely sorry for not giving me a feast right then and there. *Tricks...*

"Why are you being so nice to me?" I asked the only thing that came to my mind. He smiled, laughed slightly.

"I thought we were past this." He paused, waiting for any reaction to appear on my face, nothing. "Annabelle, I am not like either of my parents. I am not sadistic and devious like my mother and

I am not evil or violent like my father. No one deserves to be alone, especially in the care of my parents."

"How old are you?" I asked curiously.

"21, why?"

"You were alone for 21 years, in the care of your parents. Who was there for you?"

Lucas stared back at me. The question had obviously hit home. He stood up and walked away from the bed. There were no windows to look out but instead he looked out one of the cracks in the wall. He stood silently for an awkward few minutes. I wrapped the blanket around my shoulders, feeling a bit nauseated. I rested my head on the coat Lucas had so willing given me to use as a pillow. *Look at how you repaid him, insulting his motives.* I didn't insult his motives, just asked who was there for him as a child. How is that insulting? *Look at him, he's obviously insulted.* I looked up at him. He did look upset.

"Lucas?" my voice cracked, sounding a bit forced. He returned to my side.

"What?" he questioned, tucking the blanket in around my small body.

"Did I upset you?" I asked curiously. He sat down on the side of the bed, putting his hands in his lap. He looked into my eyes and all I saw was pain. "I didn't mean to upset you."

"No, you didn't upset me," he admitted looking away from my eyes. I watched him closely; I believe I saw a hint of a tear in the corner of his eye. I placed my hand on his and caught his attention. He looked at me, his eyes glazed over with tears. I wasn't quite sure what made him start crying, but I hoped he would tell me.

"Then why are you crying?"

"Until you reminded me, I had forgotten about her." He focused on our tangled hands.

"Who?" I was curious who this woman was.

"My grandmother, Mable is what I called her." He smiled slightly, tracing the gloves on my hand with his fingers. I waited for him to continue. He lifted his hand to the collar of his shirt. Pulling on the silver chain, he revealed a small charm on the end of it. "She was my mother's mother. She was the only person there for me as long as I can remember. She kept my father from hurting me until…"

"Until?"

"My father was put in jail June of 2003, Mable died that December. My mother didn't even go to her funeral. I was the only person in my immediate family that attended. I have never felt more alone than I did standing at her grave side."

I watched him as he let a few tears fall from his eyes. I gave his hand a gentle squeeze and he looked at me. He had a mystery in his eyes that was desperately fighting to free itself. Pulling on the chain, the necklace fell into his hand. He handed me the small charm. I tried to focus on the small engraved words on the back. It read, *Luke, you are my world.* I smiled at the simple inscription.

"What happened while your father was in jail? When it was just you and your mother?" I questioned curiously.

"Nothing, literally nothing; I never spoke to my mother, she never attempted to speak to me. She was depressed because the two people she loved most were out of reach. Her mother was dead and her husband was in jail."

"Why was your father put in jail?"

"Well I don't remember much of that night. I do remember my mother and my father fighting about something. He was very angry at something I had done or said." Lucas focused on our hands once more, his look was completely blank. "He beat me with a metal shovel. I remember a female police officer telling me that I would be all right."

"Allie…" I said quietly.

"Yes, sadly that is the reason my father is after you; to get to her. He believes that since 'She is such a hero to complete strangers that she will heroically find you. Then he will take his revenge on her for putting her nose in other people's personal lives'…" His voice trailed off imitating his father.

"Allie wouldn't look for me alone; she would be out of her mind if she did." I defended.

"I know that, Hector on the other hand docsn't bclicvc she is. Hector, himself, is out of his mind. He has been since I can remember."

I handed him the necklace, watching him as he clasped it around his neck, tucking it into his shirt. My hand found the chain that sat on my chest. Squeezing the charm tightly, I understood the connection he had with the delicate piece of metal around his neck.

We sat silently, still holding hands. Comfortable, I began to fall asleep as he continued to trace the outline of the glove. My eyes closed and I knew I would be fast asleep soon. His hand moved to my cheek and rubbed his thumb over my cheek bone. I opened my eyes to see him lean over the bed and give my forehead a gentle kiss. When he went to sit back down, he was surprised to see my eyes looking back to him. He opened his mouth to say something but he stumbled over a few senseless syllables. I reached for his other hand.

"Why are you being so kind? I understand that you are not like your parents, but why me?" I tried to make sense of the situation in my head.

"Annabelle, nothing about this situation is easy or even remotely normal, but I feel compelled to finally do the right thing. I feel like I need to change a situation that I should have prevented." Lucas's voice was low, slightly ashamed.

"You can't blame yourself for your father's insanity, Lucas," I pointed out. *Sure he can...*

"No, I can't." He paused. "But I should have stopped Janis from taking you. You should have never been put in this situation."

I watched his face as he struggled with his feelings. I felt sorry for him. *For him? What about you?*

"I can't blame you; I don't blame you for this." I spoke softly, feeling nauseated.

"You should. Don't be so kind to me, I don't deserve it."

I closed my eyes with the pain that passed through my skull.

"I'm sorry. You should rest. Don't worry about me." He squeezed my hand gently, turning to get up and to let me sleep. Before he was able to get up, I kept my weak grip on his hand. He turned towards me and gave me a curious look.

"Stay with me, please," I stated, never making a question out of my words. He squinted slightly, hesitation hung in the air.

"Are you sure?" he asked. I nodded.

"Sit here." I patted the spot by the head board gently. *Bad idea...He is the enemy.*

He moved to the spot I had pointed out and leaned his back against the head board with his feet straight out in front of him. I rested my head on the jacket he had given to me previously for a pillow. I closed my eyes and took a deep breath. I could feel the warmth radiated from his body. I moved closer, pulling the blanket around my body tightly. *You're lying with the enemy Annabelle.*

I pulled the jacket out from underneath my head and placed it on his leg. I lifted my head and rested it on the newly arranged jacket. He didn't move; his body was tense. I draped my arm over his legs and nuzzled my face in the wool blanket. I felt his body relax slightly and he placed his arm over my back, rubbing it slowly. The soft, slow repetitive motions of his hand on my back quickly relaxed my sore body and closed my eyes again. My hand found my necklace and I wrapped my finger around the charm. *You should be ashamed of yourself.*

I drifted in and out of sleep for the next few hours. Pain seemed to creep into my pleasant dreams and the nightmares filled my head with pictures of death and torture. Sadly enough, the darkness was the best place for me to be now. The daylight only meant one thing, more pain. But then I remembered the man I so desperately clung to during my hours of tragic slumber. The daylight had once again brought me something to hold close; something to look forward to when I opened my eyes to the let the light back into my existence. *You're too kind, Annabelle, naive...*

There was something about the man that held onto my tiny broken body so gently. He wasn't like his parents. He wasn't like my previous male companions. His touch was kind, his words were thoughtful and his eyes were sincere. I wasn't afraid of him. I didn't want him to leave. I needed him to stay with me. He was my strength. *He is your enemy. He will hurt you, just like all the others did. He isn't any different. You are foolish; you will fall for the wrong person, again.*

No, I know he is sincere. He won't hurt me. He is only here to help me. *You're wrong! He will hurt you. He is just like the rest of them. He will leave you.*

No, he told me he wasn't going anywhere. He will help me get out. He is my way out. *You will die here, Annabelle. This is the bed you will die in, alone.*

"No!" My dreams escaped through my lips and I tried to catch my rapid breaths.

"Annabelle." His voice was soft and his hands held onto either side of my face. I opened my eyes, newly formed tears escaped into the daylight. I looked into his brilliant blue eyes and didn't want to look away.

"It's okay," he reminded me, pulling me closer to his chest. His hand brushed my hair from my eyes and he cradled my body, rocking slightly. "I'm right here, Annie."

His voice brought me back to reality. I had never let anyone call me Annie. But the way he said my name, how he used it instead of calling me girl or bitch; I was positive he was being truthful. I buried my face into his chest. I cried out loud, trying to shake off the tremors that consumed my body.

"Don't leave me, please…" I whispered to Lucas through my tears.

He pulled my body away from him and looked into my eyes. "I'm not going anywhere." His thumbs brushed my cheeks and he wiped away my tears. "I'm right here."

He brought me back into his chest and wrapped his arms around my body. He recovered my blanket and wrapped it around my shoulders. He cradled my body in his arms. I clung to his shirt with the strongest grip my weak body could manage.

The comfort I felt in his arms was the kind of comfort an infant begs their mother for with each growing day. His protection only made me hold him closer. My body and soul begged to be close to him. My mind fought with me each step of the way. Something about this man made me complete. I felt safe.

That is your emotions speaking. Use your head, naïve Annabelle.

He isn't bad. He means well.

He is the enemy…

No, Lucas is not my enemy. Fighting with my new thoughts exhausted me.

"I just want this all to be over," I mumbled.

He never said a word. He continued to rock me back and forth until I began to fall asleep again. My eyelids were heavy and my breaths were deep and slow. I began to lose consciousness when I heard a faint noise outside. The noise rang in my head like a lyric to a song that you can't quite put your finger on.

I opened my eyes, waiting silently for the noise to repeat itself. The familiar sound burned my ears. *Jingle, jingle, jingle…*keys.

"Lucas," I whispered anxiously sitting up on. "That noise."

"Relax." He tried to calm me when the noise obviously hit his ears.

He moved my body off of his lap and onto the bed smoothly. He stood and walked towards the wall closest to the door. He peered through the crack in the wall. He stood for a moment, obviously looking around for the source of the noise. Once he realized the source, he punched the wall with a low growl. He spun around quickly.

"Lay down in bed, pretend you're sleeping. Don't make any sound," Lucas demanded. He hurried around the room gathering the empty water bottle and first aid kit from the floor and shoved them into his bag. He walked over to me as I moved under the blanket, lying down like he told me too. He took the blanket from the floor and took his jacket and put it on.

"Please forgive me. I will give it back as soon as I can." He removed the blanket from my body. "I'm so sorry, Annie."

The cold air hit my body and I shivered. I tucked my arms into my chest and rolled to face the wall opposite the door. My limbs quickly became numb in the bitter cold air.

He's been lying to you.

"Annabelle." He walked around the side of the bed and knelt in front of me. "Ignore anything I say to or about you. I have to keep this act up if I want any chance to help you." *He's a good liar.*

I looked at him with tears in my eyes. "I'm scared," I admitted. *You should be scared of him.* He put his hand on my cheek.

"I know you are. I am too." he leaned forward to kiss my forehead. Taking a final look into his blue eyes, the fire to help me was stifled by fear. I closed my eyes and let a few tears slide down my cheek.

"Try to stay still," he reminded me and then he left my side. I stayed facing the wall and I heard him sit down in the wooden chair. Within a few minutes, Hector and Janis would be entering the room to inflict pain or humiliation on me.

I waited silently as the jingle of the keys approached the door. I heard the door unlock and felt the cold wind as the door whipped open, bouncing off the wall behind it. I tried my best to remain still, not shivering in the brisk wind.

"She looks dead," Janis commented.

"She's been like that for a while." Lucas commented, "Gave her a lesson of my own."

"Really?" Hector's voice was astonished and proud.

"Yes, she mouthed off. So I showed her what happens when she disrespects." Lucas's voice was flat and emotionless. *He's a good actor.*

"Good job son." Hector audibly patted his son on the back. "Now let's fix up this hole so the bitch doesn't try to escape again."

I stayed as still as possible, trying my best to hear what was going on around me. Within a few minutes, the sound of a drill hit my ears. It continued for another ten minutes as they were clearly closing off the only exit to my hell. *Some help he is.*

After the noise of the drill silenced itself, the noise of footsteps rang in my ears. They approached my bed and my body tensed.

"I was hoping to have a little fun tonight." Hector's voice sounded hopefully evil. I tried to contain my anxiety the best I could. My fingers grabbed hold of my shirt and I held on for dear life. "Are you sure she's breathing, Lucas?"

"Last time I checked, yeah." Lucas's familiar voice seemed as though he was standing right next to his father.

"We should make sure." Hector's voice was not concerned, but annoyed. Before I knew what hit me I was being pulled off the bed by my shoulders. Hector pushed my body up against the wall and squeezed my arms tightly. I cried out in pain.

Lucas's voice remained emotionless, "I told you I already-"

"Hush!" his mother hissed.

"I know. I was just making sure she wasn't dead." He pulled my head back roughly to force me to look at him. I glared at him and he shoved my body to the ground. "Not yet, at least."

My arms throbbed from his death grip. I pulled my knees into my chest and closed my eyes, not making a sound. Tears fell silently from my eyes.

"Come on, let's go home." Hector's voice was dead and quiet.

"You probably want a shower and some real food, Lucas." Janis spoke to her son.

"Shouldn't I stay here to keep watch?" Lucas questioned.

"No need anymore. How could she possibly escape now?" Hector chuckled at his son.

I opened my eyes to see Hector and Janis turn to leave. Lucas was looking down at me helplessly. My eyes begged for him to stay.

"Lucas? Are you coming dear?" Janis called from outside the small shelter.

"Yeah, I am just getting my bag." His voice echoed.

Tears trickled from my eyes as he picked up his bag and he turned to leave. Once he reached the door, he dropped something on the floor. He turned his head one last time and mouthed the words, "I'll come back for you." His eyes lingered on mine for a few seconds, burning their place in my mind.

With that the door slammed, bringing me from my thoughts, and the jingling keys locked the door once more. My eyes dropped to the object he left on the floor. It was fabric, but not a blanket. I picked myself up and crawled across the floor to the heap of material on the floor. I reached out for it and realized he had left a shirt behind. As I lifted the shirt, something fell out of the fabric. A water bottle dropped into my lap.

I focused on the shirt. It was a thick, long sleeved shirt. I put my arms in the sleeves and slowly lifted them above my head to finish putting it on. The pain was unbelievable. I cried out loudly and buckled over in pain.

After a minute or so, I took a deep breath and regained my willpower. I held my breath and repeated the same movement. The same stabbing sensation hit my shoulders with a deafening pain. I worked through the torture and shoved the shirt over my head. I let my arms fall to my sides and curled up on the floor trying to let the nausea subside.

He isn't going to come back to help you. When he comes back, he will only hurt you. You are such a naive little girl, Annabelle.

I closed my eyes and tried to ignore the voice in my head.

He will hurt you. He is the enemy.

I wrapped my arms around my body and rocked my body back and forth.

You will only hurt yourself more by getting close to him. He is the enemy.

"No..."

The voice continued its ridicule until the darkness took over. When the darkness did finally take over, I fell into a deep sleep. His eyes burned into my memory. I found my temporary peace in the darkness.

- 10 - Annabelle: Hell, Sweet Hell

<u>Day Nine- December 22nd</u>

My ninth day went slow. I stayed on the floor for most of the day, not wanting to upset my sore body. I woke up feeling sore and misplaced.

Yesterday ended abruptly. It started peaceful and turned into just another one of my days here in hell. Lucas had kept me warm, fed, and happy while he stayed with me. *Don't fall for the enemy.*

He wasn't my enemy. I didn't care who his parents were while he held me. It never crossed my mind how we met when he looked into my eyes. He was true, sincere and definitely not my enemy. Lucas had shown me a level of compassion that not even my best friend could own up to. He was there for me when I needed someone the most.

With thoughts of Lucas, I was surrounded by his scent. I tucked my face into the collar of the shirt he had left for me. My arms were tucked underneath the fabric, my grip clung the cold metal of the charm that hung from my neck.

Drifting in and out of a slumber-like daze, I could have easily mistaken it for sleep. I never once moved from my spot on the floor, fearing the pain that would come with movement.

He won't come back for you. He is going to leave you here, all alone. He doesn't care for you. He never will.

I opened my eyes to look around the room. It was a dirty, dark, damp room with no point of existence except to ruin my life. I felt the soreness in my arms and remembered what had happened last night. I lifted the sleeve of my new shirt and sure enough, dark bruises in the shapes of hand prints marked my arms, up and down.

A noise from outside the door made me sit up quickly. It got louder, telling me something was approaching the door. *No jingle...* No jingle.

I heard the lock on the outside of the door rattle against the wood of the door. Someone was trying to get in. *Why would someone break into a broken down building?* Maybe it is someone trying to find me. My heart lifted with the idea that someone might be trying to rescue me. *What if Hector got drunk and left the keys at home?* Instantly, the blood drained from my face with the prospect of it just being one of my captors.

98

"ANNABELLE!" A male's voice rang through the wooden door. I recognized this voice. *Who is it?* I wasn't sure who it was, but they sounded concerned. I stood gingerly from my spot on the floor. My legs shook underneath my body as I took a step towards the door.

"Annabelle? Are you in there?" The voice became quieter, still sounding concerned.

"Yes," I whispered, my voice was weak and defeated.

I listened to the silence, waiting desperately for the man to cheer for joy or maybe even respond. Nothing happened. Not a sound could be heard. I shivered in the cold air. There was a distinct icy draft coming from underneath the door.

"Hello?" I crept slowly towards the door. "Can you help me?" Desperation filled my voice and tears burned my eyes.

When I was merely a few feet away from the door, it swung open revealing one person I never expected to see.

"Dolan…" escaped my lips like a breath of air. I quickly put pieces together. His biological father was the reason I was in this hell. *Of course he would join them…*

"Annabelle." He smiled walking towards me and embracing my small body. His arms around my body felt forced and unwelcomed. The pain in my arms made me yell out in pain and he didn't let go.

"Dolan, you're hurting me." I cried softly.

"I'm so glad I found you." He acted as though I never spoke. He put his hands on my shoulders and held me out in front of him to take a look at me. His hand placement on my arms was identical to the hand prints left by none other than his own father.

"Please, Dolan, you're hurting me." I whined, trying to push his arms away from mine.

"You look like hell. What have you been doing?" His breath hit my face. *Someone's been drinking.*

"Let go of me." My voice fell dead. I knew this was not a desperate attempt to save me. He was here as one of them, as one of the Martins. He has never cared about me and never will.

"I'm here for you though." His voice was falsely innocent. His crooked smile quickly turned into a devilish scorn.

"No…" I whispered. I gathered myself and stopped my tears. I couldn't let him see my pain. Not him.

"Bell, you don't know what you're talking about. You are obviously tired." He tried to convince me. *Tired… try exhausted beyond the point of return.*

He roughly moved my body to sit on the bed. He grabbed the wooden chair from near the sink and set it down in front of me. He sat down on the chair, facing me. The room was rapidly losing light and I could just barely make out Dolan's erratic features.

"You need to relax… You're so tense." Dolan rubbed my shoulders roughly, acting as though he was giving me a massage. I shrugged his hand off my shoulders. He frowned at me. "You used to love getting a massage. What happened?"

"Being kidnapped can change a person," I retorted. He chuckled loudly. Dolan's demeanor changed. He glared at me.

"You have it easy Miss Rockart. Way too easy for my liking." Dolan looked around the dirty, moldy room. "My father, his wife or that pussy of a boy they like to call their son could never give you the treatment you deserve. Look, you've even got a pair of gloves!"

Dolan stepped towards me, grabbing the gloves off my hands. He moved so quickly I never had time to react. Before I know what hit me, Dolan was on top of me tying my hands together, similar to the way his father did, but not attaching the rope to the bed frame. *Mistake number one…*

"What do you want?" I cried out completely taken by surprise.

"You," he said angrily. He grabbed the rope in one hand and pushed my arms above my head. He savagely kissed my neck and used his free hand to begin to unbutton my pants. I struggled against his weight, my legs thrashing around underneath him. He pulled them apart, putting his legs on either of mine. The weight of his body pushed my body farther into the pathetic excuse for a mattress.

"No, please! You can't do this. Not this." I pleaded with him.

"I've waited much too long and much too patiently." Dolan's voice was muffled by the skin on my neck. He bit down violently on my neck, sending pain shooting through my neck. I growled out in pain.

That's when he slapped me across the face. "Shut your mouth," he demanded me. Still with the rope in his left hand, he successfully unbuttoned my pants and had begun to pull them down. I began to cry, letting my tears run freely down my cheeks. He roughly pulled my legs apart, taking his time groping and prodding at my innocent body.

Exhausted, completely pinned down, and blindly crying wasn't exactly how I imagined my first time. *Rape isn't how anyone imagines their first time, Annabelle.*

"Please, don't do this," I begged Dolan. He wasn't listening. Instead, he was struggling with his own pants. He couldn't seem to get them undone while still holding onto my arms. He was completely concentrated on unzipping his own pants that he moved his left leg enough that I could free my own leg. *Mistake number two...*

I took the opportunity to kick him as hard as I could in the groin. *Success...*

Dolan groaned in pain. He rolled off of me and onto the other side of the mattress. I rolled off my side of the bed quickly and stood against the wall. I was weeping loudly as I tried to pull my own pants up and realized I needed to untie my hands. *Mistake number three... You have a way to escape.* Open door...

"What the fuck do you think you're doing?" Dolan's voice grumbled into the mattress. He regained his composure and stood up on the other side of the bed, opposite of me. He glared at me, *if looks could kill...*

He jumped onto the bed in my direction. I tried to run around the bed with my pants around my knees but he grabbed my hair as I ran past. The force of his grip pulled my body back and he dropped me to the ground. I fell onto my back, feeling the air explode from my lips. I gasped for air as he grabbed the front of my shirt to lift me off the ground.

"You think it's that easy?" He questioned into my ear. "You really think I'm going to let that slide?"

"Fuck you, Dolan." My nerves were shot. I was livid. *Watch yourself, Annabelle.*

"Is that a promise?" He sneered.

I pulled my arms up to punch him in the face but he grabbed the rope and threw me to the ground. This time, I fell to the hard floor face first. I quickly tasted my own blood in my mouth. I spit the blood out, revolted by the taste and rolled to my back. My adrenaline was pumping and I got to my feet. Using all of my strength, I charged at him. Catching him off guard, we went tumbling to the ground. His head slammed into the metal frame of the bed and was instantly knocked out, on top of me. *How convenient...*

His weight on my tiny, weak frame was almost unbearable. I tried to roll him one way or the other, but I was too weak. I gasped for air, trying my hardest to stay conscious. I was suffocating. *This is the end for you.*

"Why the hell is this door open?" The voice rang in my mind. *Janis...* "What the hell? Lucas, get in here, now!"

"What?" His voice was annoyed and distant. I began to close my eyes, my oxygen level was depleting quickly.

"Get him off her! I can't have her die while I'm in charge. Hector will kill me!" As soon as Janis's selfish comment hit my ears, Dolan's limp body was being hoisted off me. I gasped for air. It burned through my lungs. I rolled to my side and began to crawl away into the corner. I let tears fall from my eyes as I fell to the floor after reaching the corner of the room, behind the bed. I sat silently and watched as things happened around me. My cheeks burned with embarrassment, fear and anger. My pants still hung around my knees and my hands remained tied in front of me.

"Dolan, wake up! Why the hell are you here?" Janis said as she smacked him across the face a few times. I looked up at Lucas; his eyes were watching me closely. Feeling humiliated, I curled my face into my knees. Bringing me from my thoughts, Dolan groaned at Janis, sitting up quickly when he was conscious.

"What?" He asked, holding his head. A trail of blood trickled down the side of his face from a small cut on his forehead.

"Why are you here? You're father told you to stay away until he said it was time." Janis was angry.

"Whatever. None of you know what the hell your doing. She is fine." Dolan got to his feet and walked in my direction. "If I were in charge, she wouldn't be able to lift a finger." He towered over me. I braced myself, my breathing increased. *He's going to let you have it now...*

"He wants her alive. Don't do anything Daddy would disapprove of." Lucas ridiculed Dolan. Dolan turned his head towards Lucas and glared. They stood, both ready to fight, staring at one another for a minute or two.

"I have no choice but to leave you hear to watch her again, Lucas. In case this idiot comes back." Janis shook her head and left the room muttering, "Hector's going to kill us all."

With his eyes still focused on Lucas, Dolan lifted his leg and kicked me straight in the chest. I had no time to react. I slumped down to the ground, my head resting on the rotten floor.

"Dolan, let's go!" Janis yelled from outside the door. Dolan smiled at Lucas and walked towards the door. As he passed his younger brother, he gave him a pat on the cheek.

"Good luck with the little whore; she's not an easy catch." Dolan laughed back at me, left the room and slammed the door behind him. I heard the keys jingle and the door was locked. My eyelids began to droop and my thoughts began to diminish. Footsteps approached and I didn't care to look up.

"I'm so sorry, Annie. I should have never left you." Lucas's voice sounded close to tears. He immediately dug through his bag. I felt his gentle hands cut the rope from my raw wrists. I unconsciously pulled my pants back to their rightful position. I closed my eyes in exhaustion and waited for the darkness to take over. I needed the darkness to take over. The pain in my chest was unbearable. I felt him lift me off the ground and set me gently onto the bed.

I wanted to succumb to the pain and let everything end. *Just close your eyes and let time do its job.*

"Annabelle?" Lucas called.

"I'm so tired," I whispered almost inaudible to even my ears.

"I know, just let me look at your mouth for a minute. You're bleeding," he pointed out. *Like she didn't know that already... this guy is a real genius...*

"I just want to sleep." I whimpered.

"You're bleeding. Let me help you." He was talking to me like a child. *You aren't a child, are you Annabelle?* No. He reached down to pick my head up in his hands and I jerked away from his grip.

"Don't touch me! Why did you leave me?" I yelled at him. He recoiled and stood stunned, starring back at me. I rolled over on my side and faced away from him. My chest pounded with pain and regret. *You shouldn't have yelled at him.*

I squeezed my eyes closed and clenched my teeth together. I brought my hands to my head and rocked my body back and forth.

Annabelle, you shouldn't have yelled at him. He was only trying to help.

I shook my head and tried desperately to suppress the voice in my head.

I'm not just a voice, I am you. Reminding you what a horrible person you truly are.

"No…" I whined. I shook my head again.

Yes, Annabelle. I'm the thoughts that you wish you could say.

"No, you're not." I spoke louder this time. I struggled with myself and my thoughts.

Annabelle, I am you. I am what you will be after you die; a thought, a memory, and a whisper. I am your existence. You can't deny my voice, for it is your own.

"No, you are not me…" I rolled over and turned to Lucas. "Make it stop, please. Make the voice go away." I whined holding my arms out to him.

He looked at me helplessly. He moved closer to me, wrapping his arms around my increasingly smaller body. He took a seat on the mattress next to me and wrapped a blanket around my shoulders. He brought my legs up, closer to him and held me in a cradled position. The blanket was completely wrapped around my body and I cried heavily into Lucas's chest.

"It's okay. I'm right here," he whispered into my hair. He softly brushed my matted hair away from my eyes. He looked down at me and I looked up at him. I had reached my breaking point. I felt like I was losing my mind. Something about his touch and his voice calmed me, the voice was gone.

"Don't leave me, Lucas. I need you," I told him hysterically. Tears slipped down my cheeks and he caught each one with his thumb.

"I'm not going anywhere." He held me closer. "I promise."

I clung to his shirt like it was my life source. I didn't want to be alone. I couldn't afford to be alone. I was losing my mind with each moment I spent alone.

My thoughts were jumbled and the room spun each time I opened my eyes. I rested my head on Lucas's chest and he kept his arms wrapped tightly around me. I began to fall into a strange slumber. With each breath, my eyes got heavier and with each minute, my thoughts become more cluttered.

After what felt like hours later I woke up to a warm sensation on my face. I slowly opened my eyes to see the sun shining brightly above me. I looked around the room to see that the building around me had vanished and I was sitting on a luxurious bed in the middle of the snowy woods. The snow was cold and falling freely around me. With each flake that fell, the sunlight cast a blinding light into my line of sight.

"What did you do Annabelle?" The voice startled me. I looked around, no one was there.

"W-who's there?" I called out.

No one answered. I stood up from the bed and realized that I was completely untouched. Not a single bruise or scratch appeared on my body. I felt energized and completely nourished. I looked around the area where I stood. The woods looked nothing like I was used to. The trees were short and stubby. The leaves were replaced with pine needles and sharp thorns. The snow covered everything around me except the bed. The air was warm, like a spring breeze, yet the snow, each flake was cold and wet, continued to fall.

"Annabelle, why did you do it?" It was a female's voice. It was projected as if from a speaker. I spun around again, searching for a source. Nothing... no one...

"Who are you?" I questioned, "What did I do?"

"Why did you hurt someone who sacrificed so much for you?" the voice ridiculed. I spun around again.

"What are you talking about?" I yelled.

"Lucas. Why did you hurt him?" I spun around again. The bed came into my range of sight and something caught my eye. I turned to get a closer look and realized there was a person lying in the bed. I walked closer and when I reached the bed I saw that it was Lucas lying face down in the bed. My heart stopped when I realized that there was blood stains on the blanket. I reached out with a shaking hand to turn him over. When I did I brought my hands to my face in utter shock. The sight was horrendous. Lucas was lying lifeless in the bed with multiple stab wounds to his chest and abdomen. I looked down at my hands; they were covered in blood, none of it was mine. I gasped, backing away from the bed.

"No..." I whispered breathlessly.

"Yes, Annabelle." The voice echoed around me.

"Why? Who?" I babbled, tears streaming down my cheeks.

"You should know the answer to that question."

"Why would I know?" I stared at Lucas's lifeless body.

"You did this."

"No..."

"Yes, you did. Why did you do this Annabelle? He was so good to you. He went against everything he knew to help you. He risked his life to save you. How could you do this to him?"

"No... I-I didn't... I would never." The area around me was silent. I stood silently staring at the only person who had ever put their life on the line for me, lying dead.

"No...NO!" I screamed out. I ran to him and wrapped my arms around his cold body. "No, you can't leave me. No, please don't go." I put my head down on his chest and cried out, "I'm so sorry! Please don't go."

"Annabelle?" His voice called to me. I shook my head into his chest and squeezed my eyes shut.

"No, don't go."

"Annie, I'm right here. Open your eyes." I felt his warm hands touch my face. "I'm right in front of you. Open your eyes."

I opened my eyes slowly and saw the gleam of his eyes in the darkness. I reached out and put my hand on his cheek. *It was a dream...*

"It was so real. I was so scared." I cried.

"It's okay. You're awake now. Calm down," he said putting his hand on the back of my head and I rested on his chest. "You're okay."

He rocked me slowly and I kept my eyes open, looking around the room. He had set a flash light on the floor near the bed and it casted a warm glow in the room. I took a sharp breath in and began to cough. I sat up and continued to cough. I buckled forward, unable to catch my breath. I brought my hand to my mouth and tried to stop myself from coughing. Lucas put his hand on my back and rubbed it slowly. When I pulled my hand away I saw blood. I looked up at Lucas and he looked at my hand helplessly. He quickly set me down on the bed and grabbed his first aid kit.

"Annabelle, can clean the cuts on your face? You have a lot of dried blood on your face." He pointed out, changing the subject quickly. I sat up slowly, nodding aimlessly. We exchanged looks, both understanding the severity of my condition without a word spoken.

Lucas pulled the chair in front of where I sat on the bed and sat down facing me. *What does this remind you of?*

"Please... don't sit like that." I felt tears form in my eyes as the memory of my recent molestation raced into my head.

"What?" he questioned quietly.

"Just don't sit there!" I yelled at him. I brought my hand to my throat and cried out in pain. My throat was on fire.

"What's wrong? What happened?" He stood up, sitting on the bed next to me.

"Water..." I requested; my voice coarse.

"I can't understand you." He held my hand helplessly clueless to my request.

"Water, please. I need a drink," I whispered quietly. This time my request was heard and he quickly grabbed the water bottle from the floor and unscrewed the lid. He put the bottle to my lips and helped me take a drink. It slid down my throat smoothly. I continued to drink until I needed to breathe. I pushed the bottle away from my lips and gasped for air. The pain subsided momentarily.

"Don't sit there, please." I felt the pain in my chest as I thought back to earlier that day.

"I'm sorry." He gently took my face in his hands. He slowly began to wipe my face with a damp cloth. As soon as he had gotten all of the dried blood, his curiosity got the best of him. "Annabelle, why did it bother you so much when I sat there?"

My head dropped and I looked down at my hands. I twisted my fingers together and never looked up from my hands when I whispered, "Dolan."

"What happened?" he asked quietly.

I didn't answer and kept my head down. The tears burned behind my eyes with the thought. I felt my body shake and I knew Lucas could tell I was crying. He placed his hand on my chin and lifted my face up to look at him.

"What did he do to you, Annabelle?" He was genuinely concerned. The tears spilled from my eyes and let out a small whine.

"Please, don't make me say it." I cried softly.

"He didn't... rape you, did he?" His voice was low and calm.

I shook my head, "But that was his intension." I whispered and looked up at Lucas to see his reaction. Lucas's jaw clenched and his hands turned to tight fists, causing his knuckles to turn white. Our eyes met and I cried harder. His features softened instantly when he saw my reaction.

"I'm so sorry, Annie." He pulled me closer to him and rocked me slowly. "I should have never left you alone. I'm so stupid."

"I don't know what I did to deserve this, Lucas." I sobbed. "What did I do?"

"Nothing, you've done absolutely nothing, Annie." His voice was regretful and cynical.

He held me close to his chest until I stopped crying. He knelt down in front of me and looked into my eyes.

"Annie, if I have to risk my own life, I will do everything in my power to keep you safe. I'm never going to leave you alone again." His eyes glistened with tears. I looked down at him and it was my turn to return a favor. I lifted my bandaged hand and ran my thumb along his cheek bone, wiping his tears away.

"Don't make promises you can't keep, Lucas," I told him sadly. His eyes lost their fire and he stared sadly back at me. "But I trust you."

A smile crept across his face and he pulled me into his arms, hugging me tightly. His touch was never too much for me. He remained gentle and pulled me away from him and looked into my eyes once again. Our eyes melted into each other and I felt my heart flip in my chest. For a split second, my pain was gone. I moved instinctively forward and placed my lips on his. Nothing could be sweeter in this hell.

Day 10- December 23rd

Lucas ran his hand gently down my cheek. I opened my eyes slowly and looked up at him. He smiled sweetly. Lucas slipped his arm under my back and helped me sit up. I leaned, fatigued, against the frame of the head board. "How are you feeling?"

I shook my head at him. I felt much too weak to even speak. All my injuries were adding up. My throat felt like sand paper when I swallowed. My breaths were shallow and wheezy. I knew if I didn't get medical attention soon I could die of pneumonia or something much worse. I coughed reluctantly and Lucas looked at me.

He looked over at his small white box of medical supplies and sighed. I watched him look through his supplies once or twice that morning, like the numbers would change if he checked again.

"You're running out, aren't you?" I asked. His eyes didn't meet mine. He closed the nearly empty box and stuffed it into his bag. He stood up from the edge of the bed and paced the length of the room once or twice before throwing a punch at the door. He turned quickly and kicked the wall beside the sink. The wooden walls didn't budge. After throwing an angry tantrum, he turned to look at me, his face defeated and exhausted.

"Lucas, we both know there is no way out." I paused, looking up at him weakly, "Please, come and sit with me."

"You are sick, getting sicker each day. I can't pretend that this will be over soon. I don't know how or when, but I'm going to get you out of here." He looked at me, "and not in a body bag."

His words shook my body. Death, never something I liked to dwell on. *But the way things are looking for you Annabelle, maybe you should consider it.* I couldn't let myself think about dying. I couldn't stand the thought of never seeing my family or friends again. The thought of never eating a real meal again or even drinking a warm cup of coffee, all were mere memories to me. I wanted to experience a hot shower and relaxing on the couch watching black and white reruns with Billy-Jean or cartoons with Madison.

Death was simply not an option for a 22 year old woman. *Until now...* My thoughts brought tears to my eyes and I pulled the blanket closer to my chin. Lucas watched me closely and sat down on the edge of the bed once more. He quickly wiped my tears as they began to fall from my tired eyes. His free hand found my hand and he entangled his fingers with mine. I watched his face turn from worry to a soft smile when my tears began to subside.

"I'm sorry. I shouldn't have said that," he whispered, moving my hair from my face. I sniffed and nodded. My eyes begged for darkness.

"Can I sleep now?" I asked, wanting to rest my tired body.

"Of course." Lucas helped me lie back down and he tucked the heavy blanket around my body. Once I was completely encased in the blanket, he sat down beside me, placing his hand on my back. He gently rubbed his hand down my spine and back up to my skull. His touch was smooth and tender. He leaned down and kissed my cheek as I quickly fell to sleep.

> *When you sleep with the enemy,*
> *the enemy will strike.*
> *When you mess with the enemy,*
> *the enemy will strike.*
> *When you fight the enemy,*
> *the enemy will strike.*
> *But if you ignore the enemy,*
> *the enemy will surrender.*

Day 11- Christmas Eve

"Annabelle, please! Wake up." Lucas sounded hurried and scared. His hands were on either side of my head, softly rubbing my cheeks. When I opened my eyes, I realized that there were tears streaming down my cheeks and I had my arms clung to Lucas, my nails digging into his arms. I panicked and let go of his arms. No harm done, but my heart raced and my head spun.

"What happened?" I whispered; my voice was nearly gone. The pain worsened.

"You started crying in your sleep. When I tried to wake you up, you acted like I was hurting you. Did I hurt you Annie?"

"No, I don't know why that happened." I forced my voice to speak. It was quiet and raspy. I put my hand to my throat and coughed. I cried out in pain.

"Water?" Lucas sat on the edge of the bed, with a bottle of water in his hands. I nodded and he brought the bottle to my lips.

Sandpaper had made a permanent home in my throat, causing terrible pain each time I swallowed anything, even my own spit. We sat in silence for a few minutes until I realized that it was about time for their return... *they are his family.*

"They'll come today, won't they?" I asked blankly.

"More than likely." He didn't look at me. I heard his nerves in his voice.

"Will you leave with them this time?" *He'll always leave you behind.*

"No. I need to be here for you. I will not leave without you."

"How can you choose?"

"I just will."

"Lucas-"

"Annie, please. Try to trust me." He looked deeply into my eyes and he sat his hand on top of my hands. "I will do everything in my power to get you out of here tonight."

"Please, don't promise," I begged, closing my eyes sadly.

"No promises, just know that I will not leave by choice unless I have you with me." His eyes burned into mine. His blue eyes were on fire, showing his passion for my safety and his will to keep me alive. He leaned forward and pressed his lips to mine.

A strange feeling spilled out of my veins. It was like my body was floating, a sense of complete tranquility. I let all my muscles relax; my breaths were taken from my lips, willingly and knowingly. I felt my heart smile with the warmth of his breath on my cold skin. His hands enveloped my face, brushing his finger tips on my cheeks.

"How did this happen?" I thought out loud.

"What?" Lucas questioned.

"This." I held up our tangled hands. "How did we get like this?"

Lucas remained focused on our hands. He never spoke a word. Instead we both sat, silently pondering my question. I shivered, not from the cold, but from that strange feeling that sat in the pit of my stomach. It wasn't bad, but it felt wrong, *because he is the enemy.*

No, because I knew it wouldn't last... I wouldn't last long enough to see this feeling through. I would be long gone before this feeling would have a chance to see the light of day. I would be in a different place with this feeling still lingering within me. *Death* would ruin this feeling's chance for survival.

"You know—" I paused. He looked up at my face. "I haven't let anyone call me Annie in years. Not until it came out of your mouth. It's never sounded better."

Lucas smiled widely and he leaned over to kiss me. Silent tears fell from my eyes as my lips lingered around his. He felt the tears fall and pulled his lips away and looked into my glistening eyes. I looked back at him sadly, our faces only inches apart.

"What?" He whispered; his warm breath touched my face.

"I don't want this to end." I whispered. "I don't want *me* to end, Lucas." Tears fell freely from my eyes as he gazed into my soul.

"You are not going to die, Annie. You are strong and I will get you home." His own tears suffocated his passionate words, making them broken and soft. Our foreheads met and he held onto my face. He kissed my nose, my cheeks and my lips multiple times before he pulled away and looked at me again. He moved closer and he slid his hands under the blanket, wrapping them around my waist. Gently, Lucas lifted my small frame into his lap and cradled me in his arms. I tucked my chin into his neck and kissed his neck softly. With tears still sitting on the edge of my eye lids, I wrapped my arms around his neck, holding on as tight as my weak muscles could handle.

"Please, don't give up, Annie. You're not alone, I'm here." His breath on my neck warmed my senses and I closed my eyes and took in each touch, each word.

"I don't want to die, Lucas. I don't want to die," I begged him as I clung to his neck. He held onto me tighter and I felt his tears on my neck.

"I know you don't, Annie. I won't let you."

"Please, don't leave me, Lucas. I need you here. I need you with me," I confessed.

"I know. I know you do Annie. I want to be here with you."

I pulled away from his neck and looked at his face. His cheeks were wet and his eyes were soft. All of my feelings melted at the sight of his eyes. He was here; going against everything he had been taught. Here I was with the man whose parents kidnapped me, wrapped in his arms. He was in my arms, I was in his. We had been brought together by the worst means possible, but we were still together.

"I think I love you." His eyes glowed.

"Well, isn't this touching?" the voice filled the room with a dark presence. While Lucas and I were confessing our feelings, we missed the jingling of the keys and the fact that Hector and Dolan were now standing in the doorway. *It's the plan... they want to have a reason to hurt you more. He's in on it.*

My back was to the door, I froze. Lucas was facing the door and his eyes shot to mine immediately. He stared into my eyes as if he was trying to communicate telepathically. His eyes were filled with fire.

"Get up, now." Hector's voice was annoyed. He walked closer to the bed as Lucas moved me off of his lap and onto the bed next to him. Before getting up from the bed, he pulled the blanket around my shoulders and leaned forward to kiss my forehead.

As soon as his lips touched my skin, Hector shot into action. He ripped Lucas away from the bed, throwing him across the room without an effort or thought.

"How dare you touch that filth? What is going through your mind, son?" Hector hovered over Lucas. Lucas stood from the spot where he landed, seemingly unharmed. He ignored Hector's questions and stood silently, staring into oblivion.

"Dad asked you a question, little brother. You'd better answer it," Dolan taunted from behind Hector. He fidgeted like he was waiting for his father to give him the go ahead. Hector walked closer to Lucas; they stood at the same height. Their faces stood only inches apart and Lucas glared back at his father, never saying a word.

Bad idea, Lucas, bad idea, I thought to myself. Hector stood, smiling at Lucas. It was the same sadistic smile that I received from Hector my first day here.

"Not speaking, huh?" Hector spoke angrily and illogically. Hector turned to Dolan and nodded. That is when Dolan turned to me and smiled. He reached for my arm and pulled me from the bed.

"Leave her alone." Lucas lunged for Dolan but was stopped by Hector's arm around his neck. Hector bent his knee into Lucas's stomach and brought Lucas to the ground by his neck. As Lucas struggled in Hector's grasp, Dolan stood with my arm in his tight grip, waiting for the next instruction from his father. I barely felt the pain in my arm because I was so focused on Lucas and Hector as they wrestled to the floor.

"Give up son, there's no sense in fighting. Lost loyalty to your own father is worth a punishment. You should know by now that I always win." Hector's voice was loud and stressed. He was out of breath from wrestling with his son. Lucas remained quiet with Hector's arm still wrapped around his neck. I held my breath as I watched my only companion here in hell get taken down by the devil himself. Lucas stole a look at me and for the first time I saw hate in his eyes. Not towards me, but towards his father and his half brother who held me captive.

Without even realizing my actions, I had begun walking towards Lucas. Dolan, who was distracted by the live action wrestling match going on in front of him, didn't notice my movements at first. When he did realize, he used his other arm to bring my body slamming into his. With one arm wrapped around my chest and the other still gripped to my arm, he jerked my body backward so that I would look at him.

"I wouldn't do that, Bell. Who knows what could happen next?" he warned with a mad smile. I ignored his comment and looked back to Lucas who was now pinned, face down, underneath Hector. Hector had released his grip from Lucas's neck and had moved to tying Lucas's hands together behind his back.

"Please let her go," Lucas begged to the floor. Hector stood, laughed aloud and gave his youngest son a hard kick to the side. For the first time, I saw Lucas close his eyes in pain.

Hector knelt down to his son's face and whispered loudly, "This is a Lesson of Loyalty, son." Hector then lifted his youngest son to his feet by a handful of hair. Without a thought or concern, Hector pushed Lucas into the wall. Lucas was obviously still in pain from the kick to his side. He was bent forward, hands tied behind his back, not looking up at his father. Hector slapped Lucas across the face.

"Look at me when I am talking to you." His fury shook the small shelter's walls.

Lucas didn't look up. *Bad idea, Lucas,* bad idea....

Hector, obviously insulted, took hold of Lucas's neck and pinned him to the wall. Lucas stood, blank faced for the first few seconds. But suddenly I could hear his struggle for air. I watched in horror as Hector squeezed the life out of his own son.

"Leave him alone!" I yelled, completely oblivious to my actions. Dolan slapped me across the face and I flinched and closed my eyes. Dolan threw my body to the ground, as if discarding trash. I fell to my hands and knees, feeling the pain shoot through my already aching body once again.

"Have fun, Bell. Tomorrow will be an exciting day," Dolan taunted.

"Go to hell Dolan." I growled, knowing I would pay for my words. Dolan smirked and with that, he kicked me to the ground. Falling off my hands and knees, pain splintered into my palms. He rolled me over. I looked up at him from my back. He put one leg on either side of my body and bent down over me. He pulled my shirt toward him; bringing my shoulders up off the ground. He brought his mouth to my ear and whispered, "Save up your energy for tomorrow, you're going to need it." He kissed my cheek with his disgustingly wet lips and proceeded to slam my body into the ground. When my head reached the ground, I immediately closed my eyes in pain. When he let go of my shirt, I stayed still, acting as though he knocked me out. I needed to avoid anymore blows to my fragile body.

I remained as still as possible while I listened for the door to close and the sounds to end. I waited while they continued to shuffle around the room, sounding as though they were gathering all of Lucas's things, possibly even Lucas. *He will leave you... Just like he said he wouldn't.*

My chest was heavy and the pain in my head throbbed. This pain wasn't anything new to me anymore though. I had grown much too close to pain, like it was an annoying roommate. I was an expert at numbing the pain and forgetting to live. I had gone passed my point of no return and there was nothing left to gain. Pain was my new best friend.

"If he wants to stay with the bitch so bad, let him." Dolan's voice was vindictive and haunting. With those words, I heard laughter and the door slam. I remained still until I was sure they were gone.

After about five minutes, I opened my eyes slowly. The sun had nearly set and the light in the room was dim. I turned my head slowly to get a view of the room. I could see Lucas lying, motionless on the other side of the bed.

"Lucas..." I called out, in a loud whisper. No response. "Luke..." my voice was slightly louder, but still no movement. I felt worry flush my cheeks and panic struck my heart. I knew I had to make my way to him.

I rolled onto my stomach and waited for the blood to rush back to my head. When I could see clearly once again, I got to my hands and knees. I slowly crawled to Lucas's motionless body. As I got closer, I could see his breath in the cold air. Relieved, I felt my heartbeat slowly return to normal.

When I reached his body, I first examined the ropes on his wrists. They were tight but poorly tied. I sat down next to him and looked at my hands. The old injuries to my palms had been reopened and new splinters had made themselves at home. I sighed and shook my head. *You can't seriously be considering hurting yourself more to help him… Annabelle, what has gotten into you?*

"Shut up!" I growled. I continued to untie Lucas's hands. The rope was quickly soaked with my own blood. I gritted my teeth and finished through the pain. Once his hands were untied, I tried my hardest to roll him to his back. However, my current state was much too weak to even move myself around, let alone another person.

"Luke," I whispered completely drained. I felt myself begin to fade. My eyes were heavy and my chest pounded. He didn't respond. Feeling like I was lifting one hundred pounds, I lifted my arm to his shoulder and shook him. "Luke, wake up." His eyes opened and he looked up at me. I gave him a weak, but genuine smile. I leaned against the bed, out of breath.

"Annie." He sat up, obviously in pain. He reached out for me and pulled me into his chest. Once my head reached his chest, I closed my eyes. I immediately began to surrender to the darkness.

Opening my eyes, I looked up at him. He smiled at me strangely, "You called me Luke. No one has called me Luke since Mable died." He kissed my forehead. I returned the smile only to feel my body ache at the tiny movement of my lips.

"I'm sorry, Lucas," I whispered.

"Why are you sorry, Annie? There is nothing for you to be sorry for. None of this is your fault." Lucas pulled me closer to his body, snuggling his chin into my neck.

"I can't do this anymore; I don't want to fight anymore." My voice was soft and painful as I closed my eyes.

"No, don't say that." Lucas pulled me away from his chest and rested my head on his arm. "Annabelle, open your eyes. Please, look at me." I opened my eyes slightly to look up at him. *He doesn't want to let you die; he's keeping you alive for them to torture you.*

"I don't want to struggle anymore. Just let me go, Lucas. I'm where I want to be." I smiled at him. He wasn't fooled.

"No, you are not going to die in my arms. You are not going to die. Not here; not in pain." Lucas kissed my forehead and I felt his tears on my cheeks. I closed my eyes, too weak to find the right words to say. He moved his hand to my face and brushed his fingertips along my cheekbone.

"Annabelle, open your eyes." Lucas's voice was pleading.

I remained blind to reality and kept my eyes closed. The pain would soon go away and I would soon be numb. *Yes, let the darkness do its job. Let the darkness take over.*

"Please, don't give up. I need you here." His voice was broken. He brought my body closer to his face and buried his tears in my neck. I felt his tears stream down my skin and his arms wrap around my body. He began to rock back and forth, kissing my face and neck.

"I love you, Annie," Lucas whispered into my ear.

His words stormed into my brain and my heart stopped. I tried to open my eyes.

There's no going back after you've made the decision to quit.

No, I have to go back. I have to tell Lucas my feelings. I have to tell him I love him.

You have lost the chance; you have already made your decision. You have already given yourself to the darkness.

No, it can't be over. I need more time. I am not done with life; I am not done with Lucas.

You have no choice.

"Annabelle, please."

Please, I have to go back. I have to tell him.

The choice has been made.

I am making another decision, I want to fight.

For the enemy... you want to fight for the enemy. What is so special about this man?

He has been here for me during the worst experience of my life, possibly the end of my existence. I want him to know that I feel the same about him; I want him to know that he's worth the fight. He is why I want to live. He has shown me that even in the worst of times, people care. He was my light in the darkest time of my life. I need him to know that he saved me from my own death wish. I need to live for him.

"I'm sorry, Annabelle." His voice filled my head.

No, please, let me go back to him.

"Annabelle, you can't give up."

I don't want to.

"Annabelle, come back to me."

A sudden breath caught my lips. I inhaled sharply, gasping for any bit of air I could.

"Annie?" Lucas cried harder, "Annie, I thought I lost you." I opened my eyes to look up at him. He stared back into my eyes, smiled and kissed my forehead.

"I'm right here," I told him, with heavy breaths. He put his hand on my face and rubbed his thumb along my cheek. "Lucas, I love you."

His smiled at me and kissed my cheek. I closed my eyes slightly. He hugged me tightly and growled in pain. I opened my eyes to look at him. I was unable to speak.

"My side," he answered my unasked question. He lifted his coat and shirt to reveal a purpling bruise across his rib cage. I ran my fingers across his side. He flinched at my ice cold fingers. My hand recoiled quickly and I looked at him apologetically.

"No, it's all right." He put his shirt back down.

I looked around the room. They had taken everything. Or so I thought until Lucas reached forward and pulled a blanket from underneath the bed.

"I figured they would take my things," Lucas said plainly as if he was reading my mind. He let go of me and stood slowly, holding his side. He walked to the corner of the room, near the sink and knelt down. "That is why I put this in here." He lifted the floor board and removed the little white box and another small bag.

I smiled weakly. *Guess he is pretty smart...*

"Flash light." He removed a bright green light source from the small bag and turned it on, setting it on the floor near the bed. It casted a familiar glow that I had grown to know these past nights.

I rested my head against the wall as I watched Lucas go through his supplies. He finally stood up and walked towards me after a few minutes. He had a bottle of water in his hands that he held to my lips. I took the water willingly. It felt like sandpaper, but I needed water in my dry mouth.

"Thank you," I whispered, barely audible. I closed my eyes once again unable to do anything else.

After a few minutes, I opened my eyes again. Lucas sat across from me, leaning against the bed. His eyes were closed in exhaustion. Ignoring the pain, I turned and crawled to him on my hands and knees.

"Luke," I whispered. His eyes opened and he looked up at me. "Lay down with me." I spoke softly. I stood, trembling. Climbing onto the flimsy bed, Lucas followed me. No more words were spoken that night. He lay down next to me, wrapping his arms around me. The blanket secured around us protectively and we fell asleep.

<u>Day 12 – Christmas Day</u>

I survived the night. I fought through the pain and fatigue and woke to see the sun. I opened my eyes slowly to see the sunlight that bled through the flaws in the shelter walls. The room felt damp and cold as usual, but I was warm. I turned my head to my right to look up at my personal heating system, Lucas. He was lying on his side, facing me, and his arms were wrapped around me protectively.

It was comforting to have some that cared enough about me to risk their own life. But I didn't feel right, asking so much of one person. *He's the only person you have right now.* He was exactly what I wanted, but why did it feel so wrong? *Possibly because his parents kidnapped you 12 days ago and you are just waiting around for death because of them.* He's not like them; I know that for sure now.

"Luke," I spoke, watching as he slowly opened his eyes to look at me. He smiled and ran his hands through my hair. "Thank you."

"I don't need you to thank me. I don't deserve your thanks." His eyes filled with shame and he turned his face away from mine.

"No," I lifted his chin and our eyes met, "You are risking your life to be here with me." I kissed his lips softly. "For that I am thankful. You are keeping me alive longer." I paused feeling tears burn my eyes. "And if I don't make it out of here, I'm so glad I had the chance to know the real you."

"Don't say that," he told me sternly, putting his hands on either side of my face. "You are not going to die here. Don't ever consider death. I'm going to get you out of here."

I let tears fall from my eyes; I smiled through my tears and wrapped my arms around his neck. He wrapped his arms around my waist and put one of his hands on the back of my head. I tucked my face into his neck and cried into his shirt.

"I love you, Lucas. I have never been more certain about something in my life. You are here; going against everything you've been taught."

He smiled and kissed my forehead. I closed my eyes again, feeling suddenly nauseated. I took a deep breath.

"What's wrong?" Lucas questioned. I couldn't help but let out a low laugh. *What isn't wrong?*

"Just nauseous, it will pass." I took another deep breath through my nose and felt my head spin slightly.

"Do you want a drink of water?" he asked, propping himself up on his elbow. I nodded. He reached for the water bottle on the floor and I propped myself up on my elbow as well. He handed me the bottle and helped my shaking hand bring it to my lips. I took a drink and felt the lump in my throat disappear.

I laid my head back down on his chest and felt my eyes beg to close. Lucas placed his hand on my shoulder and rubbed them gently.

"What day is it Lucas?" I asked trying to figure out if my calculations were correct.

"Today is…." He paused, obviously doing the math in his head as well. "Christmas."

My heart dropped, I was missing Christmas with my family. We continued to lie in silence.

"Annie?" His voice was soft and thoughtful.

"Hmm?" I questioned tiredly.

"What's your family like?" He seemed genuinely curious. I smiled and reached for my necklace.

"Well my parents have been married for 32 years. My dad is known throughout Fort Kent for his famous Rockart Triple Chocolate Chip Cookie Crumble Pie, especially around this time of year." I smiled at the thought of my dad in the kitchen making a mess with powdered sugar coating his entire body.

"There is my mom who is a high school biology teacher and is known for her strict ways. Fortunately, she means well and couldn't love me and my brother more. I am their second child. My brother, Evan, is three years older than I am. He is an engineer and is married to Allie, who was just promoted to sheriff on the 10th of December. They have a three year old daughter named Madison who is the love of my life. Her birthday is on the third day of the year." I smiled when I thought of Maddy. Wiping my smile away, my heart was heavy with the promises I had made to her the day I left.

"There is Billy-Jean, my best friend who just got engaged the day before I was…" I trailed off thinking about all the things I was missing right now and would be missing if I didn't get out of here. Tears burned my eyes and I turned my head away from Lucas.

"I'm sorry," he said, sensing my suddenly sad silence. He wrapped his arms around me and let me cry silently.

"I'm missing Christmas with my family. I'm going to miss my niece's fourth birthday and I will probably miss my best friend's wedding." I cried.

"I'm going to get you out of here Annie." Lucas told me filling his voice with confidence.

I looked up at him and he looked back at me. He smiled and wiped the tears from my cheeks. He leaned down and kissed my lips softly. My heart fluttered happily. It felt so right. *Too bad it won't last; nothing like this ever does with you Annabelle.*

I pushed the thought from my mind. I rested my head on his chest again. My eyes closed again as he continued his gentle rubbing on my back.

As I began to drift to sleep, my mind wandered. It wandered to places that I didn't think existed anymore; my future. *What future? You have no future anymore, remember?* No, the determination that Lucas has in his voice gives me hope for my future. Lucas is the reason I still have my future in sight. I graduated college and am becoming a teacher. I have family who cares deeply for me and a best friend who couldn't possibly survive without me as her maid of honor. I laughed quietly to myself. My laughter made Lucas look down at me.

"What?" He smiled, relieved to see me smile.

"Billy Jean will kill me if I'm not there to help her decide whether to get an off the shoulder dress or strapless or which flower to put in the center pieces or who can sit by who at the reception." I laughed again, slightly louder.

"Sounds like a very indecisive friend you have." Lucas smiled, just watching my every move.

"She is…" I paused, lingering on the thought. "That's why I love her."

Lucas watched me quietly until I realized he was staring. I looked at him and squinted my eyes at him. "What?" Giggles slipped through my lips.

"I've never seen you smile like this." He smiled, rubbing his thumb along my cheek. "I like *this* Annie."

I felt the crimson burn in my cheeks and I looked down. He placed his fingers on my chin and lifted my head to look up at him. Our eyes met and I felt a shiver down my spine. "I love you," he whispered.

My heart skipped a beat or two and my head spun in a frenzy of emotions that had blossomed so suddenly. I looked back at him and smiled wide eyed. "I love you, Luke."

I watched his face fall slightly as I said his name. His hand subconsciously touched his necklace. I touched his hand gently.

"Does it bother you?" I paused watching him. "When I call you Luke, do you think of her?"

A genuine smile slipped across his mouth, sending a chill up my spine. He looked down at me and said, "Yes, but without you, I would have forgotten the things she told me and the promises I made to her before she died."

I wrapped my arms around his neck and his hands rested on my waist. I nuzzled my face into his neck and breathed in his scent. It felt right, it felt good. *Remember where you are…* It didn't matter. I was in love with the one person I was never meant to love.

"I know it doesn't mean much, but Merry Christmas, Annabelle." He kissed the top of my head and I kept my arms wrapped tightly around him. I began to fall asleep once again, drifting in and out of consciousness. I opened my eyes to look up at Lucas and smile one more time before I gave in to the darkness.

My dreams had changed. They weren't filled with Hector and Janis torturing me. They held a brighter light than my past dreams had. I lived in the future through my dreams. I saw a family; a father and young son, playing on a swing set in the backyard of a humble home with a mother watching from the porch rubbing her growing stomach. One thing I noticed however, none of these people had faces.

A space to fill as your fate is drawn out. This could possibly be you one day, Annabelle, but it could turn out that this is just another dream of yours, never to be fulfilled.

As the voice in my head pointed out this blunt truth, the picture I watched changed drastically. Suddenly the sunny day turned gray, the home and family vanished from the picture to reveal a snowy cemetery. My parents, Evan, Allie with Maddy in her arms, Billy-Jean, Ronnie all stood around an empty grave.

As I approached them with caution, as if I had screamed aloud, all of their heads snapped in my direction. Tears streaming down each cheek of each person I had ever loved more than myself. They said nothing, all moving to the side as I subconsciously moved towards the freshly dug hole in the frozen ground. A light snow fell from the gloomy sky. I stood at the edge of the grave and turned to look at the faces around me.

As I turned around an unwelcome face appeared. Dolan smiled an evil grin and waved goodbye to me. Before I could even stop to think, he pushed me backwards into the unmarked grave. I reached out for someone to hold onto but everyone had vanished. I fell, screaming into the darkness of the grave. Except when I thought I would hit the bottom, I continued to fall. Helplessly screaming aloud, I reached out from the sides of the earth, digging my nails into the dirt and ripping my flesh.

Day 13- December 26th

"Ahh, you stupid bitch." An angry voice growled into my ear. A sting across my cheek made me open my eyes. *Dolan...*

It took me a minute to realize what was going on. I was tied to the pathetic little bed. And Lucas... Lucas... Where was Lucas?

"Lucas?" escaped from my lips as I struggled to look around the room. I found the answer to my question. Across the room, Lucas sat, tied to a chair, visibly unconscious and bleeding.

"What do you want?" I screamed at Dolan. He laughed.

"Honey, the only thing I want is you." He smiled and turned around to reveal Hector standing behind him. They walked to the corner of the room and whispered inaudibly. I looked up at my hands; they were bound by thick rope to either side of the head frame of the bed. I struggled to see but from what I could tell my feet were in the same predicament. I felt tears burn my eyes. I panicked and looked over at Lucas.

"Lucas..." I whispered, not caring if they could hear me or not.

"No talking!" Hector hollered at me, never looking up or moving from his spot in the corner.

"Luke, please wake up," I begged, tears in my eyes, disregarding what the idiots in the corner told me. *Bad idea...*

"What did I just tell you?" Hector screamed, still not moving from the corner. No threats...*yet.*

"Lucas, wake up!" I screamed, tears streaming down my face.

"You are a stupid bitch," Hector told me, closing the distance between us and slapping me across the face.

"What are you going to do to him?"

"You should be more concerned about your wellbeing." Hector chuckled and looked over at Dolan.

Hector walked to Lucas and shook his shoulders roughly. I watched as Hector violently woke up his youngest son. Lucas opened his eyes, enough for Hector to stop shaking him around. Lucas looked up at his father then around the room in confusion. Once his eyes met mine, instant tears rolled from his eyes. I looked back at him with the same amount of grief and sorrow. *You are losing this battle...*

"Don't hurt her." Lucas growled at his father. Hector laughed out loud and grabbed his son's face.

"And what are you going to do about it?" Hector questioned. Lucas had nothing to say in response. Hector glared down at his youngest son. In a flash, he grabbed Lucas's neck. Before anyone realized what he was doing, Hector pulled at the chain around Lucas's neck. Ripping it from his neck, Hector whispered in a low, malicious tone, "No one loves you, no one ever will."

Hector let go of his face with a jerk, took the necklace and walked away from him. He turned to Dolan and nodded. "I'll be outside."

Hector walked to the door and left the small building, closing the door tightly behind him. I turned my focus to Dolan and watched him move around in front of the bed, slowly, contemplating something. His nerves were completely visible; anxious, shaking hands, and pacing.

"Why don't you just let her go?" Lucas spoke from the corner. "You know this has become a battle between you and me."

My eyes shot to Lucas. *See, he's always been with them.* He was focused on Dolan.

"What are you rambling about?" Dolan's voice was annoyed, much like his father's always was.

"I got the girl." Lucas put his words plainly, but it was a bold statement.

"What? Her?" Dolan pointed at me. Lucas smirked. "You've *gotten* her." Dolan's emphasis on the word gotten stuck in my mind. What was Lucas doing? *Mind tricks...*

"I beat you to the goal, brother." Lucas was much too confident. I tried to think quickly about what Lucas was getting at. Then it hit me. *...sex...*

Dolan's eyes squinted. He looked from Lucas to me. I panicked and felt tears burn in my eyes. What was I supposed to do? *Play dead...*

"Is that true?" Dolan barked in my direction. *Play dead...*

125

I lost my voice. I couldn't find the words in my head to play along. I was choking on my thoughts as they fluttered around my head. I glanced to Lucas whose expression begged for my words just as much as I did. Dolan studied my struggle for words and grinned.

"Liar." Dolan turned back to Lucas. Lucas stared back at Dolan looking angrier than I had ever seen him. Dolan lifted his arm and slapped Lucas across the face. He moved to the side of the chair and lifted his foot onto the side of Lucas's leg. "I don't like liars."

"Then you must really hate yourself." Lucas growled. Dolan became livid and kicked Lucas to the floor, still tied to the chair. I watched as Lucas's head hit the floor, not once but twice and he was still and unconscious. I let out a small whimper as I waited for him to show any kind of movement, but there was nothing.

Dolan turned to me and smiled. He stepped over Lucas and approached the bed. He pulled a metal blade from his pocket. I froze, quickly flashing back to the first night here. He reached out for the front of my shirt, cutting it open down the center to reveal the old shirt that had already been ruined by his father. Pushing the ruined fabric out of the way, he made his way on top of me, crushing my fragile body to the bed. I struggled under his weight and pulled on the ropes tied around my wrists and ankles.

"Don't waste your time Bell, you're too weak," Dolan whispered. He ran his hand slowly down the side of my face, resting his hand under my chin. "You know, I always thought you were a pretty girl, much too prude for your own good, but pretty." He smiled and touched the scaring wound on the side of my face with his fingertips. "The funny thing about all of this is that ring was actually real." His hand moved to my neck, tracing circles on my bare skin. I held my breath, knowing nothing good could come out of this.

"Why are you doing this?" I whispered through my tears.

Dolan smiled down at me, he lowered his face until it was positioned only centimeters away from mine. He stared into my eyes, filling my head with memories of our past and painful forecasts of my immediate future. He laughed at my terrified expression and whispered, "Because I can."

I immediately felt repulsed. Completely nauseated at the thought of what Dolan was about to do to me. *Don't give up...*I knew there was no way out this time. *Why are you letting him win?* He had taken all the precautions to make sure he got what he wanted; me.

He kissed my neck, pushing my hair out of the way, leaving a trail of meaningless kisses down my neck, to my bruised shoulder. When he reached my chest, he pulled on my bra, trying to rip it from my body.

"No, Dolan. Please, don't." I cried, struggling under his grip.

He ignored my cries and after several painful tries, my bra was tossed to the side of the room. He squeezed and groped my breasts, sending mortifying agony through my body. *Don't let him do this to you, Annabelle.*

"Dolan, please, stop." I cried softly, begging for him to stop. He continued his kisses but as he made his way around my chest, he decided to bite my skin. As he bit down on my flesh, I felt a numb sensation begin to take over my body. *Fight for yourself.* It was a feeling of helplessness and of complete disgust. I let my head fall to the side, unwillingly letting Dolan do whatever he wanted with my body. My eyes fell on Lucas, still tied to the chair and his eyes closed. I could only hope that he would be okay.

"Look at me." Dolan grabbed my face and jerked it in his direction. I let a small shriek escape my lips in pain. He slapped me across the face. He placed one of his hands over my mouth and growled, "Shut up. Not a sound."

I struggled under his grip, trying desperately to free myself. He tightened his grip over my mouth and leaned even closer to my face this time. "I would hold still if I were you. If you wiggle around like you are it's just going to make it worse honey."

Dolan then slid his hand into my pants, exploring my pure untouched body. He roughly pushed my pants out of his way, exposing my underwear. Tears fell silently from my eyes as he ripped the only bit of cloth I had left covering my innocence.

The ice cold air hit my body and I shivered involuntarily. He leaned down to my face and removed his hand from my mouth. He roughly kissed my mouth and I held back my vomit. I was so repulsed that I acted on an impulse and bit down on his lip. He sat back and put his hand to his mouth. Once he realized he wasn't bleeding, he slapped me across the face.

"You are a very stupid girl." He laughed and leaned forward on my body. "Very stupid." His repeated words echoed in my head.

The pressure of his body on mine was unbearable. I felt the air in my lungs slowly leave my lips. I tried desperately to inhale any bit

127

of oxygen I could, nothing. I made any noise I could, hoping to wake Lucas up, he was my only hope. *If he is your only hope, good luck.*

Finally, Dolan shifted his weight to his knees that he positioned between my tied legs. I gasped for air. Tears burned my eyes once again. I felt Dolan pushing my pants to my ankles, completely exposing my body. I cried harder as he invaded my body, taking every bit of innocence I had left.

"No, no, no…" I mumbled through my tears. "Dolan, stop, please."

The pain I felt was indescribable. He took no mercy on me and thought nothing of my screams of torture. I cried harder when he pushed my legs farther apart, letting the ropes dig into my ankles.

"Please, Dolan stop," I begged, yelling out in agony.

He looked down at me, his eyes were emotionless. He wasn't going to stop; nothing was going to stop him. Everything had been taken from me, my sanity, my health and now the only bit of self preservation I had left, my virginity. I couldn't concentrate on anything in particular. Everything was a blur, Dolan was in control and I began to succumb to the pain. I let my eyes close slowly.

Once my eyes were closed, Dolan made no effort to make sure I was even still breathing. He took his anger out on me. He continued pulling, pinching and torturing my body. I was nearly unconscious when I heard a new noise. Shuffling on the floor in the direction of where Lucas was. I figured Dolan was too busy to hear this noise.

I slowly opened my eyes to see Lucas smash the chair into Dolan's body. A completely unsuspecting and now unconscious Dolan went limp. His body weight crushed into my body, once again stealing the air from my lungs. My eyes closed and I prayed for relief.

A moment later my prayers were answered. I opened my eyes to see Dolan lying on the floor next to the bed and Lucas rummaging through his half-brother's pockets. Lucas found what he was looking for, the knife. He stumbled over Dolan and cut my legs free from the bed frame. I immediately brought my legs together and curled up.

When Lucas cut my arms free, I reached for my pants and started to pull them up over my broken, naked body. Emotions swarmed my brain as Lucas's hand helped me dress myself; humiliated and violated being the worst. Silent tears fell from my eyes and Lucas sat on the bed next to me. He took off his jacket and wrapped it around my body, pulling me closer. I rested my head on his chest, closing my eyes slightly.

As I closed my eyes, the door swung open and Hector stormed in. "What the hell is taking you so long?" he screamed. He stopped in his tracks when he saw Dolan lying unconscious on the floor with his pants around his ankles. Hector's focus went from his eldest son to his youngest. "What did you do?"

"What I should have done a long time ago, no more of this. Just let her go, let her live her life. She did nothing wrong. Don't blame other people for your stupid mistakes. Let her go home." Lucas's speech made me cling to him tighter. I knew that Hector would retaliate against his son's words. He felt my grip change and held onto me tighter. He was protecting me. My thoughts shot back to my conversation with Billy-Jean the day before I was kidnapped…

"You're so out of it right now. Are you sure you're okay Anna?" Billy-Jean questioned.

"Not at all Billy," I began, feeling Billy's eyes on me. "I don't feel like I'm ever going to find a man to actually treat me like a human being instead of an object to own or use and ruin. I want to find the one guy in the world that would risk everything including his own well being to make me safe and happy."

"Annabelle…" Billy's voice was sympathetic.

"Don't Billy, just leave it alone. I'm fine."

I had actually found that one guy. *He's just going to be taken away like every other guy…* I let tears fall thinking of the sad truth. Lucas was the first guy to ever protect me over himself and I would lose him.

"So that's what you've decided? You are going to choose some girl over your family?" Hector's voice was blank.

"I don't have a family. You are a pathetic excuse for a human being, let alone a father. Just let her go."

Hector thought about his son's words quietly for a few minutes before he nudged Dolan with his foot. Dolan grunted slightly and rolled over. Once he realized where he was, he stood up quickly and pulled his pants up. Hector looked at him, disappointment written all over his face.

"It seems as though your brother wants us to let her go." Hector's words hit Dolan and he smiled.

Dolan, seeming much too happy, questioned, "What should we do?"

"Of course, being family, we should give him what he wants." Hector's words made no sense. Why would they let me go? *Tricks, Annabelle, tricks...*

"What?" Lucas questioned, knowing his father much better than this. "What are you planning?"

"Just what you asked for, we are going to let her go." Hector approached the bed. Dolan went to the other side of the bed, opposite of his father. They each grabbed for my arms, Lucas clung to my waist. Hector caught my right arm but I got my left arm away from Dolan.

"Leave her alone." Lucas struggled to hold onto me. He wasn't as strong as his father because of his exhaustion.

Dolan finally grabbed hold of my arm after elbowing Lucas in his already injured ribs. I cried out in pain as the father and son duo pulled me by my arms away from Lucas and off the bed. Lucas's jacket fell off my shoulders. Lucas struggled to get off the bed, holding his side in pain.

"Where are you going with her?" Lucas stumbled after us.

They pulled my fatigued body outside of the small worthless shelter. My shirt hung open, exposing my body to the brisk evening air. The sunlight was dim, clouds had filled the sky and there was a light snowfall beginning to descend. Hector and Dolan threw me into a pile of snow without a second thought. My clothes were instantly soaked. My body shook violently in the cold. I crawled out of the pile they had thrown me in and found a small patch of shallow snow where a drift had formed, keeping the wind off my body.

I watched as Lucas stumbled from the building. He searched the area for me, unable to see me from where he stood; he walked up to his father and demanded, "Where is she? What did you do?"

"We let her go; just as you asked." Hector smiled, triumphant

With shaking legs, I stood up and held onto a tree near the drift. I took a few steps forward, feeling my legs buckle under my low body weight, I fell to the ground. Lucas immediately focused on me. He walked toward me, gaining speed as he did. Dolan caught his arm as he walked past.

"Let go of me," Lucas threatened.

"We've done what you asked of us, now it's your turn. You owe us a favor." Dolan's voice was authoritative.

"I don't owe you anything." Lucas grunted, pulling away from Dolan's grip. But Dolan kept his grip on Lucas and Hector grabbed his other arm. They began pulling Lucas away.

"Let go of me!" Lucas struggled. "Annie, run! Get as far away as you can!"

I heard his voice and felt his struggle as I watched him being dragged away by his so-called family. I felt tears begin to fall from my swollen eyes. I sat on the ground, trying to gather myself.

I was alone, in a snowy forest, weak and clueless to where I actually was. My heart felt like it had been ripped from my chest. The seemingly empty cavity of my chest ached with the longing for someone to help me. Lucas was gone, ripped away from me. *Get up, listen to him... Get out.*

I gathered myself and held onto the tree once more and stood up. My legs shook under each frantic step I took; blinded by my tears I fell to the ground once more, only a few feet from where I started. The wind picked up and I held my shirt closed around my body.

"Come on, Annabelle." I grunted.

"Yes, Annabelle, come on." The voice came from behind me. I turned around to find Hector standing behind me. He smiled and grabbed a hand full of my hair and pulled me to my feet. Without a word, with my hair still in hand, he walked towards the little shack. One hand on the door, he pushed me back into my hell. Slamming the door behind me, I heard the jingle of the keys and his footsteps fade away.

I crawled to the door, feeling the splinters dig into my knees. I reached the door and stood up. I pounded on the old wood.

"LUCAS!" I screamed, crying loudly. "DON'T LEAVE ME HERE!"

I continued crying, pounding subconsciously on the door. I felt my knees begin to collapse from under me and I walked to the middle of the room. Before I could reach the bed, I fell to the ground.

I sat in the middle of the room, my bleeding knees curled under my chin and my shirt wrapped tightly around my body. My eyes caught sight of Luke's coat lying next to me. Ignoring my fatigue, I reached for the lump of fabric and shoved my arms through the sleeves. I tugged the sides together, wrapping my arms around my

131

body. Luke's scent surrounded me with a painful sorrow. I was alone again. I was sure I would never see Lucas again. I set my head on my knees and cried silently to myself.

I had been violated by my enemy and the only man who had truly ever loved me had been ripped away from me. My light was gone… the darkness crept back into my surroundings.

Day 14- December 27th

 Pain struck my body as I woke up in the middle of my deserted hell. I instantly felt the physical and emotional bruises on my body. Violated couldn't compare to the way I felt. I was alone again, left for dead. But a strange feeling came over me as I opened my eyes to look up at the broken ceiling; determination. For the first time in days I felt the will to live. I wanted freedom now more than I ever had in my entire life.

 I would escape and I would see my family again. I wasn't just optimistic, I was sure of it. My life was only just beginning. I had to live. I had to live for him, for my light.

 With all my injuries, the pain in my chest pounded. Would I ever see him again? *What did his parents do to him after they left?* I shook my head and closed my eyes tightly, pushing the tears from my eyes.

 I wiped my tears with my hands and noticed something out the corner of my eyes. I sat up slowly to see the door swing in the wind. *It's open.*

 Why is it open? I looked around the room, waiting for a Martin to jump out and bring me back to the reality of the situation. *There is no one around.* I reached for the bed frame to pull myself off the ground. My knees pleaded for the floor, barely holding the weight of my thinning body. Without loosening my grip on the bed frame, I stared at the open doorway. Tears burned my eyes as I waited for something or someone to wake me from my dream.

 I took a step forward. Slowly, I made my way to the open door. Once my hands met the door frame, I held on tightly. A biting wind hit my face and instantly froze my tears to my cheeks. The sun had just begun to rise on the horizon.

 In the dim light of the dawn, curiosity struck me and I looked down at the lock. The large metal lock hung from the door, never attached to the building itself. *Good thing Hector doesn't pay attention to detail.* I looked around at the trees and the piles of snow, trying to make a plan in my head. Then I thought briefly about the broken floor board. *Was anything left?*

 I turned to the sink in the corner of the room and walked toward it with a dazed feeling in my head. I knelt down, ignoring the pain in my knees. I lifted the board and found the small white box and small bag that Lucas had hidden. Opening the small white box, my heart sank when I saw the small roll of tape and a few bandages scattered across the bottom of the box. I emptied the box and put the bandages on my hands, damaged from my pathetic attempt to escape last night. I picked at the roll of tape, trying to get a piece of it off. When I finally ripped a long piece off the roll, I tried to tape my shirt together to prevent the wind from hitting my bare skin. After a few attempts, I was satisfied with the makeshift tie on my shirt and put the rest of the tape in my pocket. Luke's coat was torn, the zipper no longer working.

In the small bag, I found the bottle of water. I unscrewed the lid, hoping for any amount of liquid to quench my thirst. There was a few swallows of water to take the dryness out of my throat. I set the bottle aside, having no other use for an empty bottle. I looked inside the bag to find a flashlight. I clicked it on then off. *It works*. I put the small object in my pocket as well, hoping I wouldn't have to depend on anything but daylight. I was in no shape to spend the night outside in the snow. I pushed the thought from my mind and looked in the bag to find nothing else of use.

I sighed and held onto the sink, lifting myself off the ground. The broken mirror showed a stranger. My face was pale, my cheeks had sunk into my face, and dark circles under my eyes were barely visible beneath the bruises and cuts that covered my face. My hair was dirty and knotted; my clothes were torn and stained with dirt and my own blood. I looked down at my body, realizing how much my physical appearance had changed in the past two weeks. I shut my eyes and let a few tears fall. *Stay focused, you need to leave now.*

I pushed myself to the door, gathering all the energy I had inside of me. The wind brushed my skin and my body shook. With a deep breath, I took my first step to freedom. I continued my steps in the direction that the Martins had dragged Lucas yesterday.

Taking a few steps forward, a light caught my eye. Looking down for the source, I realized there was a reflective piece of metal in the snow. Going against everything inside of me, I bent down. Barely reaching it with my fingers, I lifted the small item.

As I pulled it out of the snow, it was followed by a long chain. My heart leapt into my throat as I realized it was Lucas's necklace that Hector had ripped off his neck. I kissed the charm softly and shoved the necklace in my pocket. With the piece of metal safely in my pocket, I prepared myself to continue walking.

The snow was deep in spots and my tennis shoes were soaked immediately. After a few more steps, I held onto the nearest tree to catch my breath. *This is going to be a long trip.*

I blindly made my way through the unfamiliar land. The snow was up to my ankles in places and to my waist in others. The trees seemed to get thicker as I walked. I began to fear that I had gone the wrong way.

I had been walking for what felt like days. *It's only been minutes, Annabelle.* My legs begged for rest. I needed to sit down. I started to become disoriented and felt myself stumble to the ground. I landed on my hands and knees on the ground. This spot of snow was harder than usual. I tiredly looked around the area where I had fallen and realized that the snow had been shoveled. The area to the right of where I fell was a cleared path of patted down snow. My heart skipped a beat. The trees thinned and a visible tree line formed. *Civilization…*

I stood up on my shaking legs. Holding onto the tree next to me, I climbed out of the pile of hardened snow. I felt a shiver run down my spine as I heard footsteps approach from behind me. Frozen, stunned, unable to turn around, I stood waiting for the person to speak. As they got closer to me, I could feel the heat of their body. It was a memorable sense of warmth. *Don't get caught up in it, continue on your way. Ignore them.*

"There you are." The growl nearly caused my heart to stop. The unwelcomed voice sent a painful feeling of hopelessness through my body. My chest cavity felt like it caved in. I didn't have the strength for this. "Where did you think you were going?"

Before I had time to think, my body was thrust to the ground. Snow covered my face, my hands stung with a numb pain. Pressure overwhelmed my chest, his body pressed against mine. As memories filled my mind, he took away my will to live once again. For the third time, Dolan violated my once innocent body. I couldn't move, paralyzed by my weakness and unparalleled sense of despair.

Once he was finished with me, he stood up, put his own clothes back on and turned to walk away as if nothing had happened. "You were never worth the trouble," was the last thing he said to me before he left me alone. *He's leaving you to die…*

Unable to process what had just happened, I felt my head spin. I closed my eyes to collect my thoughts. Numb to the pain, numb to the emotion, and numb to the touch, I stood up. My pants lay torn on the ground. I bent down and picked up the ripped pieces of fabric. Without caring, I put the pants on. The left pant leg was gone, the seam ripped up to my thigh. I wrapped my arms around myself and prepared to continue through the woods to civilization.

With the tree line only a few feet away, I stepped forward. Without knowing there was a hill, I tumbled forward through the trees. I tried to catch myself on the small tree in front of me but I continued to fall onto the path. I screamed in agony as my right hip caught a tree, jerking my leg violently in the wrong direction. A chilling sensation ran down my leg as I landed on my back.

I closed my eyes and grabbed my right hip. Shock struck my body when my hand met an object protruding from my flesh. My eyes shot open and I looked to see a piece of broken wood sticking out of my side. Instant nausea caused me to close my eyes again. I felt the blood trickle from the fresh wound. I felt the silent tears slide down my frozen cheeks. I needed help, now more than ever.

Holding my side, I stood again. Feeling the new pain grow inside of me, I pushed myself forward, stumbling down the path. I needed to find anyone that could help me get back home, to where I belonged. I looked ahead to see blurry figures approaching me. I felt my legs carry me forward, but my mind spun.

They approached, calling out to me, but their words never hit my ears. I fell to my knees, succumbing to the pain, more than likely the loss of blood. I looked down at the side of my shirt to see a blood stain that ran down to my knee. I let go of my side and my arms fell heavy to my sides. Dazing forward, in the hazy distance, the figures were much closer, still speaking their inaudible words.

"Help me." Words slipped through my lips without my mind realizing it.

Giving into the darkness, my body fell to the ground, limp and lifeless. *Determination got the best of us.*

PART TWO

A fresh snowfall over night covered the small town in Maine, ten inches to be exact. All seemed still on this particular Sunday morning. Not a soul in sight. Churches had canceled their Sunday services and stores were closed for the early morning. The children didn't dare play in the frigid cold. Not a single car left a mark on the snow covered roads. The parking lots were deserted, except for a single gray sedan that remained abandoned in the lot of the Meyer Bookstore.

Allie left home for work, unable to get her mind off her driving. "I really hate this." She whispered to herself each time her car slid in the snow covered roads. She navigated through the familiar streets that lead her straight to the Police Station. The normal ten minute drive had turned into at least twenty minutes by the time she reached the station.

"Rockart, I was beginning to think you weren't coming in today." Jeff Michaels, Chief of Police, greeted her as she knocked off her boots on the freshly salted front step of the station.

"Sorry about being late, roads are terrible."

"I know. I'm only kidding Allie." He smiled at her and held the door open for her to step into the small one room, station. Taking her coat off and hanging it on the stinky, weak looking coat rack by the door, Allie looked around the small room. Officer Henry Richardson was sitting at his usual messy desk, eating a healthy portion of eggs and toast. She glanced over at the Chief's desk and watched him sit down and answer the ringing telephone. Allie poured a cup of coffee. She stirred in a packet of sugar and sat down on her neatly organized desk. She took a cautious sip of her coffee and waited for Michaels to end his phone conversation.

"What's wrong, Jeff?" Allie addressed Michaels as he slammed the phone down on the receiver.

Jeff rubbed his face. "Mrs. Meyers called to tell me that her son is missing. Dolan never came home last night and she's concerned his father has something to do with it."

"Matt?" Allie questioned setting her coffee down on her desk.

"No, she mentioned a birth father." Jeff stared out the window for a minute then snapped back to reality. "Allie, I hate to ask this of you, but would you-"

"I'm on it." Allie cut him off before he could finish. "I'll drive over to the Meyers' and talk to Nancy."

"Thank you. If it's still snowing when you're finished, please go home. I'll call if I need you. Today is going to be a slow day."

"Thank you, sir." Allie swallowed the last of her coffee and put her coat back on. She nodded to Richardson and Jeff and left the building.

The wind hit her as she rounded the corner of the police car. She shivered aloud and unlocked her door. Once inside the car she dialed home to tell Evan the plan. She started the car as the phone rang twice.

"Hey sweetie," Evan answered.

"Hello. Good news, Jeff gave me one thing to check out and I'll be home. It shouldn't take me too long. I should be home by ten." She looked at the clock; it was 9:02am.

"That's great. That way you can go with us to Mom and Dad's. Mom's making lunch for us. I've called Annabelle twice, but her phone is going straight to voice mail."

"Evan James! I told you to let the girl sleep in! You know she worked late last night. She probably turned her phone off to sleep in," Allie scolded.

"Okay, Okay, I'll let her sleep." Evan surrendered to his wife with a slight laugh.

"Good I'll be home in a little while." Allie looked up to see a plow drive by. "Oh good, Jim is plowing Market Street now. I'll follow him down to Dufour Street."

"Dufour? What exactly do you have to check out?" Evan's voice was suspicious.

"Don't worry honey; Nancy called Jeff this morning about Dolan. It's nothing. I'll be home in a little while."

"Be careful Allie. I don't like that family."

"Oh hush, I'll be fine. I love you."

"I love you too." Evan spoke softly, giving up his concern. They hung up the phone together and Allie pulled out of the station's parking lot. She drove behind the town's only snow plow, Jim, to the corner of Market and E Main Street.

"Turn left, turn left… please." Allie wished aloud. She watched as the plow turned right down East Main Street instead of left towards Dufour. "Damn it," she muttered, turning down the unplowed road towards her destination. The drive turned into a slow paced parade to Dufour Street. Allie turned right down Dufour to see Nancy Meyers standing in her drive way, pink robe and black boots, arms crossed over her chest. Allie smiled and shook her head at the strange scene in front of her. Silently turning the Jeep's hazard lights on, she pulled to the side of the road in front of the Meyers' home.

"Thank you so much for coming out here on a day like today, Allie." Nancy approached the jeep eagerly. Allied stepped out of the car and closed the door behind her.

"It's no problem at all, Nancy," Allie reassured her.

"It's Dolan; I know his father got to him." Nancy's bottom lip quivered.

"Chief Michaels mentioned a birth father. I never knew that Dolan had a different father, other than Matt that is."

"Of course you wouldn't have. Not many people do. I tried my hardest to keep Hector away from Dolan, ever since he was an infant," Nancy explained. "I left Hector Martin when Dolan was a baby. Hector was an abusive man. I never wanted my son to grow up like that."

The names sent Allie into a flash back. Four and a half years earlier, she arrested Hector Martin; a day she'd rather forget.

"What makes you think that Mr. Martin has anything to do with Dolan's absence?" Allie questioned.

"When Dolan was eleven years old, Hector reentered Dolan's life. Dolan became attached to his father almost immediately. Hector moved back to the area to be close to Dolan. That's when I noticed Dolan's behavior begin to change. He became angry and cold towards both me and Matt. I knew it wouldn't end well. Hector is a very bad man."

"I know that. I've dealt with Hector before." Allie thought back.

"Before Hector was put in jail?" Nancy questioned.

"I put him in jail. He continued his abusive behavior with his new family, Nancy."

Nancy's face went pale; she put her hand to her mouth. "New family?" slipped from her lips. Allie nodded.

"He put his son, other son, in the hospital. You had the right idea to get out of that marriage when you did," Allie reassured Nancy once again. Silent tears fell from Nancy's eyes.

"I know Dolan is with Hector." Nancy choked, "I know Hector has put something in his head. After Hector got out of jail last October, Dolan's behavior has gotten worse. He leaves for work, but never actually goes to work."

"What makes you think he is missing, Nancy?"

"He hasn't been home since yesterday morning, Allie. He quit the bookstore yesterday morning. It's his drastic change in behavior that scares me."

"You don't think he'll come home tonight?" Allie questioned. Nancy's tears began to fall and she shook her head numerous times.

"No." she whispered.

"Okay Nancy, I'm going to write this up and call you in the morning. If Dolan hasn't returned by tomorrow morning, I will make a call to surrounding police stations and make a missing person report. Right now, we have to wait and see if he returns tonight."

Nancy nodded silently. Allie escorted Nancy to the front door and made sure she was okay.

"I'm just a phone call away, Nancy. Don't hesitate to call." Allie smiled

"Thank you, Allie." Nancy returned the smile and said goodbye to Allie. Matt smiled from the door at his wife, who, in a hysterical daze, walked into the house passed him. Matt stepped onto the porch with Allie.

"She's been like this for days. She's stressing over Dolan's relationship with his father," Matt explained.

"Has she ever been to the point of calling the police before?"

"Yes, I've always been able to talk her out of it," Matt told Allic.

"You don't seem worried," Allie pointed out.

"Dolan will come home. He's never been gone for more than two days. If he's not back tonight, then I'll start worrying."

"I will give you a call in the morning."

"Thank you, Allie." Matt shook her hand.

"It's my job, Matt." She smiled and they parted ways. Matt closed the front door behind him.

Allie got back into her Jeep and looked at the time, 9:47am. She sighed. She got out her phone and dialed the station. She took ten minutes to explain the situation to the chief. He seemed slightly interested.

"What do you think the chances are that Dolan will come home tonight?" Jeff questioned Allie.

"Sir, to be honest, I'm not sure. Nancy seemed completely convinced that Hector has gotten to Dolan. With Hector's past, I don't doubt her concern. But Matt makes a good point that Dolan has done this before. It's a hard situation to judge prematurely. I believe this is a case that you would call a wait and see approach. If the morning comes and Dolan is still not home, we should make some phone calls and figure out what steps we can take to make sure that he is safe."

"I knew I made a good decision making you sheriff." Jeff's voice was confident and proud.

"Thank you, sir." Allie smiled to herself, feeling like she had done the right thing. "I am going to be heading home now. I will have my pager on me and if you need me, please call."

"I will be sure to do that. Drive safely, Allie."

They hung up the phone and Allie started the jeep. She turned the emergency lights off and made a u-turn at the end of the road. She made a right hand turn on E Main Street and a left on her street, Pleasant Street. By the time she pulled into her drive way, it was 10:24am. She was happy to see Maddy waiting in the window for her.

As Allie opened her front door, Baby, her overgrown golden retriever puppy, galloped towards her.

"Baby," Allie sternly spoke. Baby halted a few feet from Allie's feet. Allie smiled and reached down to ruffle the dog's hair.

"Mommy, are we going now? Do we get to go see Auntie? Gama and Gampa?" Maddy's excitement made Allie laugh and pick her daughter up.

"We sure are. Mommy has to go change her clothes and you have to change out of your pajamas." Allie carried Madison into the kitchen where Evan was sitting at the table.

"Hi Honey." Allie greeted Evan with a kiss. She set Madison down on a chair.

"Annabelle is still not answering." Evan set the phone down.

"Evan! Stop it. She is sleeping. We will call her later on. I'll go change my clothes and help Maddy get dressed. Once we're done, we'll go to your parent's house. Annabelle will call when she wakes up. Stop worrying." Allie took control.

"I just-"

"Evan, please." He sighed and left the table. Allie shook her head and took Madison's hand. They went upstairs, first to Maddy's room.

"Pick out what you'd like to wear today," Allie said, sitting down on Maddy's bed.

She watched as her daughter bounced to her closet and picked out a pair of jeans. Maddy smiled happily and handed them to her mom. When Allie smiled back, Maddy returned to her closet and searched for a shirt to wear. After a few minutes of searching, she found a pink sweater that Allie had bought for her a couple days ago.

"Perfect, honey," Allie encouraged her three year old. Allie helped her daughter dress herself. Madison was unable to fasten the buttons on her jeans.

"I know what shirt Mommy can wear!" Maddy cheered after she put her pair of pink socks on. She grabbed her mom's hand and led her into the master bedroom closet. Maddy stood on her tip toes to flip the light switch. Allie stood at the door while Maddy looked around at the shirt racks. She smiled proudly and pointed when she found what she was looking for.

"The red one," Maddy pointed out.

"This one?' Allie asked, she held a bright red sweater, similar to the pink sweater that Maddy was wearing. Maddy nodded happily. "Okay sweetheart, go downstairs and make sure Daddy is ready. I will get dressed and be right down." Allie watched Maddy leave the room.

Allie walked to the mirrored dresser in the corner of the room. She unbuttoned her uniform shirt and slipped her arms out of the sleeves. She laid it on the back of the chair and glanced up in the mirror. Her eyes lingered on the scar that sat above her left collar bone. She remembered the day when she received this scar.

"Fort Kent Police!" Allie yelled with her back to the door, gun in hand. No answer at the door. She turned around and nodded to her partner, Henry Richardson. He took the signal and kicked in the door. Allie went into the house with great precaution, gun pointed. She walked into the living room, while Henry went upstairs. Allie found the teenage boy, who made the call to the station about the domestic disturbance, lying on the floor.

"The boy is in here!" Allie got down in front of him and lifted his head to see a gash across his forehead. As soon as she moved his head, he thrashed around and tried to get her away from him.

"Hey, hey, I'm a police officer. My name is Allie. You're okay now." She calmed him down and he looked up at her, fear in his eyes. "Can you walk, honey?" she asked him.

"I d-don't know." His voice was soft and pained.

"Okay, Why don't we sit up first?" she suggested. "What's your name?"

"Lucas." He closed his eyes.

"Hey, Lucas, stay awake buddy. We are going to get you help," Allie said, putting her arm underneath his shoulders and lifting him into the sitting position. He opened his eyes groggily and said nothing to Allie.

She helped him to his feet and together they walked to the front porch. She set him down on front steps as the paramedics pulled into the driveway.

"I'm going to leave you here for just a minute. The paramedics are coming," Allie reassured Lucas. "I have to go find my partner."

Allie ran back into the house, gun in hand. She heard sounds coming from the back of the house and proceeded down the hallway to what appeared to be the kitchen. Once in the kitchen, a man grabbed Allie by the neck and pushed her up against the wall.

"What the hell are you doing in my house?" his voice was deep and raspy. She felt the cold metal of a knife on her neck. Thinking quickly of her training, Allie flipped the man over her shoulder and he landed on the ground. She grabbed his hands and hand cuffed them behind his back.

"Rockart!" Henry yelled.

"Kitchen!" she yelled back. There was a strange pressure in her shoulder as she lifted Hector Martin up off the ground. She stumbled slightly and Hector laughed at her.

"Allie," Henry faced Allie and she turned to him. Shock hit Henry's face immediately and his eyes fell on her shoulder. Allie looked down to see the small pocket knife protruding from her shoulder.

Allie felt the adrenaline drain and pain struck her body. She felt faint and began to fall to the ground.

144

"Allie?" Evan's voice brought Allie from her memory. Tears rested on her eye lids and she quickly continued putting her sweater on, trying not to blink the tears free. Allie turned from the door, waiting for the memory to subside.

"Allie?" Evan repeated, standing behind his wife. His hands, warm and smooth, rubbed down her arms and he pulled her into his arms.

"It was over four years ago, Evan. I shouldn't be like this." Allie let the tears escape her eyes.

"Allie, it was a traumatic situation, for all of us. When I got the call that you were taken to the hospital..." Evan trailed off. "There is nothing to be ashamed of."

"Evan, I learned something today." Allie remembered her conversation with Nancy. Evan watched his wife struggle with her thoughts. She closed her eyes slightly and took a deep breath.

"Evan, Hector Martin is Dolan's birth father."

He looked at her carefully. "Is that bad?" Trying his hardest not to upset her, he waited silently for her answer.

"I'm not sure how I feel about it. I don't know if it is a bad thing, or if it's just ironic. He treated his family, who I now know is his second family, with such disrespect that it makes me wonder if that is where Dolan got his attitude from."

"Don't try and justify that kid's actions. He is a jerk and he never deserved Anna," Evan reminded Allie.

"I know, I know, it's hard not to analyze people. It's part of my job."

"Yes but Dolan isn't worth the analysis." Evan smiled and kissed Allie. "Let's forget about this right now and enjoy today."

"I'll try, but you know how I worry." Allie smiled back. Evan shook his head and left the room. Allie finished putting her clothes on and followed him down the stairs.

"Mommy!" Maddy raced to her mother with her full snow suit on. "I'm ready to leave."

"I see that, honey. Let me get my coat and we will leave." Allie patted her daughter on the head softly. Maddy toddled to her father, limited by the bulk of her suit.

Allie walked to the kitchen and put on her winter coat, slipping a knitted hat over her head and wrapping a scarf around her neck. She grabbed and pair of gloves and shoved them in her pocket. She took a deep breath, trying her hardest to get her thoughts into a better place. Focusing on making today good day, Allie put her feelings aside.

"Ready." Allie smiled as she walked into the living room.

"Let's Go!" Maddy proclaimed, pulling at Evan's coat.

The family of three walked to Evan's truck, after deciding it was the best choice for the hideous weather and climbed in. After Evan buckled Maddy in the booster seat, she excitedly pounded on her seat.

"Gamma and Gampa!" she yelled.

The small family started their slow drive through the snow to Mark and Marie Rockart's house, on the other side of town. When they turned onto E Main Street, the roads were noticeably clearer than theirs, Pleasant Street. Maddy laughed at the funny faces Evan made at her in his rearview mirror. As they passed Market Street, Maddy began to get quieter in the back seat. Allie glanced behind and saw her three year old fast asleep in the backseat.

"It never fails." Allie laughed.

"What?" Evan looked into the rearview mirror and smiled when he realized what Allie meant. Evan grabbed Allie's hand and she smiled sweetly. They sat quietly, listening to the soft Christmas music play on the radio. They waved to Jim in the plow as he finished up the Meyer Bookstore parking lot. Little did they know, as they passed, the plow was hiding a gray sedan now buried in a pile of snow.

Arriving at Marie and Mark Rockart's home on 410 Park Avenue, Madison began to stir in the back seat. She stretched her short arms out around her booster seat's straps and yawned loudly.

"Gamma and Gampa?" She smiled.

"Yes, dear," Evan answered, pulling into the drive of his childhood home. They were greeted by Mark Rockart, suited up from head to toe in snow gear, shoveling the nearly clear drive way.

"Your father needs a hobby," Allie joked.

"This is his hobby, honey," Evan reminded her, putting the truck in park.

The small family of three unloaded from the truck and they greeted Mark Rockart with hugs and kisses. Mark lifted his granddaughter up off the ground.

"Gampa! Can we visit Bill?"

"Of course we can, right after we eat lunch." He promised, setting her down on the ground. "Grandma is cooking right now."

146

"Okay!" She grabbed Allie's hand and tugged her forward. "Bill is waiting." Maddy pulled her parents into the house.

They walked into the warm home, shedding their layers as they did. Once all four of them had shed their coats, hats, and gloves, they followed the scent of fresh bread and homemade chicken soup.

"Good morning, Ma." Evan kissed his mother on the forehead. Allie followed with Madison running closely behind.

"Hello, Marie." Allie hugged her mother-in-law. Maddy tugged on her grandmother's shirt and Marie looked down.

"Would you like to help Grandma finish the soup?" She asked the young girl. Maddy clapped happily. Marie lifted her granddaughter to the counter near the stove top. This was a common sight to see in the Rockart's kitchen. Marie helped Maddy stir the big pot of steaming soup.

Allie smiled as she watched her daughter happily help her mother-in-law. Evan and his father snuck into the living room to get the tree up, like they usually did before lunch the day of decorating the tree. Being the only men in the family, they felt the need to get the hard part done first, while the women laughed behind their backs.

"There they go, off to take an hour to put the tree up," Allie laughed to Marie.

"Wait for it." Marie stopped stirring and listened carefully, they heard the distant sound of the football game in the background. "And there's the annual classic playoff game."

The ladies laughed while they finished up the lunch. Maddy nibbled on a piece of the fresh bread while she kicked her legs from the high counter top.

"Is Bill going to eat too?" Maddy asked curiously.

"Oh honey, Bill doesn't eat hot soup," Marie answered with a smile.

"Bill would like this soup." Maddy nodded eagerly.

Allie laughed and picked up her daughter. "Maddy, Bill is made of snow. Snow is very cold. If Bill ate the hot soup, it would hurt him." They stood at the sliding glass door overlooking the big, snowy backyard. Bill the snowman stood in the middle. Allie set her daughter down and Maddy put her fingers on the glass. She stood for a moment, silently contemplating.

"What does Bill eat?" Maddy seemed highly confused. Allie knelt down beside Maddy and thought about her words carefully.

"Maddy, Bill eats snowflakes. Each time the snow falls from the sky, when you aren't looking, Bill sticks his tongue out really far and grabs the yummy snowflakes."

"Like this?" Maddy stuck her tongue out and danced around the floor.

"Just like that." Allie smiled, hugging her daughter tightly.

"Lunch is ready!" Marie announced, carrying the large pot of soup to the dining room table.

"Has anyone tried to call Annabelle today?" Marie asked as everyone sat down at the table set for six.

"Evan tried calling her this morning but her phone was off. She was working late last night so I assume-" Allie glanced at the clock, 12:35, "-she could still be sleeping."

"Ma, today is her first day off in six days," Evan pointed out, taking a seat at one end of the table

"Why aren't those Meyer's working that son of theirs as much as Annabelle?" Marie questioned, serving large helpings of her soup.

"That's what I asked." Evan shrugged. "I can't stand that kid."

"Relax," Allie whispered patting his hand.

"Well I'm going to try and call her." Marie walked back to the kitchen.

The conversation continued while Marie tried calling her daughter once, then twice, and a third time.

"Each time I call her, it goes straight to her voice mail."

"Her phone must be off," Allie assured her. "We will give her until two o'clock, if she doesn't answer, we will go and get her."

"Sounds fair, now let's eat." Mark quickly changed the subject, receiving a glare from his wife. She shook her head and took a seat next to her husband. The family of five chatted while they ate their food. Time raced by until Marie heard a strange noise.

"Do you hear that?" Marie questioned, everyone looked up at her. "It sounds like a drill or a saw, something vibrating."

"Oh," Allie said with a mouth full of bread, "that's probably my phone." She got up from the table and went to the kitchen. The noise continued, she listened carefully and smiled. "It's just my phone, Marie!"

"Oh, is it Annabelle?" Marie's voice was excited.

Allie dug her phone out of her purse and saw that it was the station calling, "No, it's work." Allie opened her phone. "Hello Chief."

"Allie, sorry to bother you, are you busy?"

"No sir, what do you need?" Allie asked, knowing she was going to have to leave.

"Well, the Meyers, again." Jeff's voice was annoyed. "They went to open their store at noon today and they found something you might want to know about." He paused.

"What is it, sir?" Allie was interested to see what the Meyer's could possibly want now.

"They found Annabelle's car in the parking lot." Jeff paused again. "All her windows are broken."

"What?" Allie's surprised tone carried into the dining room. Marie got up from her seat and walked into the kitchen. She stood curiously at the door.

"Allie, have you talked to Annabelle today?" Jeff's tone was low.

"No..." Allie's mind spun, thinking of all the possibilities.

"Richardson found a set of keys in the parking lot too."

Allie didn't respond. She looked up at Marie and quickly turned away from her. "I'll be right there." Allie shut her phone, shoving it into her pocket.

"What was that all about?" Marie questioned quietly. Allie was putting her coat on.

"That was Chief Michaels; he needs me to go check something out at the Meyer's Bookstore, sounds like a break in."

"Oh, be careful," Marie told her daughter-in-law.

They both walked into the dining room and Allie bent over to kiss her daughter. Evan looked up at his wife with a questioning glance.

"I'm sorry I have to leave," she told everyone. She kissed Evan on the forehead and said, "I'll be back soon. On my way home, I'll pick up Anna."

She left the house quickly and got into Evan's truck. She had a bag with her belt, gun holster and badge in the backseat. She reached for it as she pulled out of the driveway.

On the way to the bookstore, images ran through Allie's head. She worried about all the things that could have happened to her best friend, her sister-in-law, Annabelle. She didn't want to think the worst, but her career didn't offer the thoughts of a best case scenario. She got to the bookstore in record time, ten minutes. Jeff's cruiser was sitting, lights flashing, in the parking lot. Allie parked the truck, throwing on her holster and badge, jumping out of her truck.

"Where is the set of keys that Henry found?" was Allie's first question. Jeff handed her the set of keys found in the parking lot. Sure enough, Allie's fears were coming true. On the set of keys was a silver sun burst keychain that she had bought Anna on their last trip to Hawaii.

"Those are Annabelle's," Allie said as her thoughts raced through her mind. She handed the keys back to Jeff. She looked over at the small gray sedan. The windows were no longer smooth, and solid panes but little pieces of glass, scattered across the snow and covering the seats inside the car. Allie walked closer to the car where a new dent had made itself at home in the driver's door panel. Allie knelt down and ran her fingers across the dent. She took a step towards the car and felt something crack underneath her shoe. Allie picked up a piece of broken plastic. She moved more of the snow out of the way to find more broken pieces.

"Annabelle's cell phone," Allie thought aloud. Chief Michaels was standing behind her.

"Allie," Michaels spoke from behind her. She looked up as he handed her a piece of laminated paper. Allie quickly recognized the name tag. Allie turned it over to see **Annabelle** printed in bold letters.

Discouraged, Allie looked around the area again. That is when she saw the small spots of discolored snow. She got closer to the stained snow and realized it wasn't just dirty snow, but bloody snow.

"Allie," Michaels' began but before he could finish, Allie stood up and handed him the pieces of the phone and said, "I'm going to Annabelle's apartment. I'll call you as soon as I'm there."

Allie raced to Anna's apartment complex. She used her key to get into the building and ran up the stairs to her sister-in-law's apartment. Allie stopped at the door, B2, and knocked. No answer. Allie knocked harder, almost pounding; still no answer. She used her key and opened the door herself. She walked into the warm apartment, quickly searching the small area. Annabelle wasn't there. Allie stood in the middle of the apartment, hands on her head. Her breathing increased and the tears begged to fall.

"No…." she whispered. She ran her hands through her hair roughly. "Where are you Anna?"

She quickly thought of everything that could have happened to her best friend. *What if she was hurt? What if she was raped? What if she was kidnapped? What if-.* Allie's terrible thoughts were interrupted by her phone vibrating in her pocket. Tears forced their way into Allie's eyes. Everything was happening so quickly.

"Hello?" her voice cracked as she answered her phone, never looking to see who it was.

"Allie? Are you okay?" Evan's voice questioned. Allie's tears pushed to escape her eyes.

"Evan, honey, what is it?" Allie cleared her throat, forgetting the question he had asked.

"Billy Jean just called me. She was worried about Anna. Billy said Anna promised to call her when she got off work last night and she never called. Billy's been trying all morning to call her but Anna's phone is off. Is she with you? Could you tell her to call Billy?"

Allie broke down. "Evan, Annabelle's missing."

Sunday December 14th

"What do you mean Annabelle's missing?" Marie's voice was quiet and tight.

"Her phone, keys and car were left in the parking lot at Meyer's Bookstore last night. The windows in her car were shattered. She never came home last night according to her neighbors. There is no other place in town she could be." Allie's voice was flat; her eyes stared back into her mother-in-laws eyes with sorrow.

Mark sat silently, holding his wife's hand. He avoided all eye contact. Evan stood watching his wife tell his parents news he had already heard. His fists clenched the back of the couch his parents sat on. The Rockart's living room was eerily silent and the four adults sat in disbelief for a brief minute.

"I bet you it was that son of a bitch Meyer. I'll kill him."

"Now Evan, don't jump to conclu-"

"Don't give me that bullshit, Allie. You know about Friday night, don't play sheriff right now. Act like Anna's sister, like her best friend, you're thinking the same thing I am." Evan spat.

Allie stared back at Evan, fury burned out of her eyes, hot tears streaming down her cheeks.

"Friday? What happened Friday, Evan?" Marie's voice questioned.

Evan's face burned red, remembering the promise he made to his sister. It didn't matter now.

"Anna had Dolan over at her apartment. He was his usual self, not treating Anna any better than he used to. Good thing I showed up when I did."

"Evan James! Why didn't you tell me this?" Marie exploded. She started on a rant when Mark cut her off.

"Marie! This isn't the time for this." Mark's voice was hard. He looked at Allie. "Has anyone gone to question this kid?"

"As of last night, Dolan is missing."

Voices shouted across the living room, none audible over the volume of each person's rage.

"Everyone! STOP IT!" Allie screamed as loud as she could, instant silence filled the air with the exception of a faint voice in the corner of the room.

"Mommy?" Madison's voice cooed. She had been preoccupied in the family room watching a children's program.

"I'm sorry honey, come here." Allie picked up her frightened daughter. Maddy looked around at everyone's faces.

"Where's auntie?" Maddy questioned.

Allie looked to her husband for help. He looked to the ground then to his parents then he approached his daughter. He held out his arms for her. She gladly went to her father and Evan set her down on the couch next to his parents. He knelt down to her eye level.

While he did this, thoughts went through his mind. *She won't understand. She is too young. I don't want to scare her. I could tell her Anna is on vacation with Billy...That might make her mad... What would a three year old understand? Maybe she's playing a game...*

"Auntie Anna is playing hide and seek, Maddy." Evan chose his words carefully. Maddy squinted her eyes at Evan. "Anna is in a really good hiding spot and it's taking a long time for us to find her."

Maddy digested her father's words for a few minutes. The four adults waited patiently as the little girl contemplated these facts. She looked up at her dad, curled her lower lip towards her nose and crossed her arms.

"I'm mad at Auntie."

"Why are you mad at Auntie, honey?" Allie's voice was hurt.

"She promised," Maddy announced. "She promised she would play games with me."

Everyone sat in silence, unsure of what to tell the little girl. Instead, Madison hopped down off the couch and left the room to pout. Initially stunned by the little girl's words, the adults knew not to take her words personally. She was three, she didn't understand the circumstance.

Allie's phone rang and everyone nearly jumped out of their seats. They waited patiently as Allie listened to Chief Michaels. The phone call was one way, Allie ended it by saying, "I'll be right there."

"What did he say?" Evan's reaction beat out the rest.

"Dolan's home." Allie's two words set Evan on a race to the coat rack.

"Evan, this is work. You have to stay here," Allie tried to remind him. Evan stood in front of her, coat in hand.

"No, that's my sister. I can't just sit here and wait." Evan's breaths were fast and heavy; he was obviously holding back tears. Allie stood in front of him; she placed her hand on his chest.

"Evan, please," Allie whispered to him. He looked into his wife's eyes. "Please," she repeated. His tense stance went limp and he nodded, closing his eyes. Allie kissed him on the forehead, lingering longer than just a peck. Before Evan could open his eyes again, Allie was gone.

"I told you people, I don't know anything about where she is!" Dolan's voice carried through the Meyer's Bookstore.

"We're under the impression that you and Ms. Rockart haven't been on the best terms as of late." Chief Michaels remained calm as Allie stood behind him, clenching her fists.

"Yeah, you're right. I proposed to a prude bitch. My fault." Dolan's snarky comment made Allie lunge. Chief Michael held her back, reminding her to stay professional.

"He's got a motive, Jeff," she pleaded with him.

"He wasn't anywhere near Meyer Bookstore last night." Michaels' reminded Allie. Allie turned and hit the wall, leaving the bookstore. Dolan's voice rang in her head, "I should have known that family was crazy."

Allie flew back into the bookstore faster than anyone could react. She pushed Dolan up against the counter, holding him up by the collar of his coat.

"If I ever find out that you did something to my sister, so help me God, I will make sure you never open that pretty little mouth of yours again." Allie's voice was threatening to break, tears threatened to fall and her temper threatened her job. Dolan's eyes were stunned, filled with fear. Allie felt a strong hand on her shoulder and she sighed heavily.

"Get a hold of yourself, Rockart," Michael reminded her. After staring Dolan down for another few seconds, she jerked her hand from his coat and left the bookstore.

Chief Michael's followed her and met her at the side of Evan's truck. She rested her hands on the fender, taking a deep breath to regain her composure.

"Maybe you should go home. Be with your family for now. Let us handle this right now. We have no leads and no trace of her yet. You need to relax and be with your family, Allie," Michaels explained.

"How would you feel if your sister was missing Jeff?" Allie questioned.

"I would stay focused on finding her, not on things others say. Go home, Allie." Allie looked up at him and nodded.

Monday December 15th

"How are there no leads on her or who took her?" Evan's voice was annoyed, a loud whisper to not wake Madison upstairs. "Aren't there cameras on the store?"

"We've tried that. The lens was iced over. All we can make out are two vehicles, nothing else," Allie whispered, feeling a bit guilty for her husband's anger.

"Are you kidding me?" Evan growled.

"Evan! We're trying everything," Allie pleaded. Allie finally gave up arguing and sat on the couch. She put her face in her hands and let out a painful sigh. Forcing her fingers through her hair, Allie let tears fall down her face. She felt defeated and helpless. *Why couldn't they find any trace of her? Where was Annabelle? Was she still alive?*

"I'm sorry." Evan sat down, wrapping his arm around his wife's waist. He pulled her close and kissed the top of her head. "I'm sorry for yelling."

They sat exchanging silent looks of empathy and sorrow. Evan looked at the doorway, seemingly in a daze. After a few more minutes of silence, Evan took a sharp breath in.

"You know…" Evan began, stopping short of his thought.

"What?" Allie encouraged through her tears.

"I feel like she's going to walk through that door any minute and act like nothing's wrong. I don't feel like any of this is real. It can't be." Evan's words were drowned in his tears. "She's supposed to be graduating today…" Allie felt Evan's strong hold go limp and his body shook with tears.

Even after nearly six years of marriage, Allie had seen her husband cry only a handful of times. Once the day Madison was born and the rest were since his sister had gone missing.

"I'm so sorry, Evan. I wish I could do more." Allie held her vulnerable husband close to her chest. "I should have prevented this. I should be able to keep this town safe. I didn't do my job."

"Allison, stop talking like that." Evan's immediate response stopped his tears in their tracks. "No one could have possibly seen this coming. I don't know anyone who would want this to happen to Annabelle."

"Except Dolan..." Allie whispered.

"Don't get me started at that piece of work." Evan's rage bubbled in his throat.

Allie patted his hands. She kissed his cheek and wrapped her arms around his neck. He lifted his wife into his lap and nuzzled his face into her neck.

"We will find her, Evan. No matter what it takes, we will find Annabelle." Allie's words lingered in the air. The couple sat silently.

"Do you think Madison will continue to stay angry?" Evan's voice sounded regretful. "Should I have told her the truth?"

"How do you tell a three year old that their aunt was kidnapped? She wouldn't understand that either." Allie tried to convince her husband.

"Mommy?" Maddy's voice startled her parents. They turned to see Madison at the bottom of the stairs, Baby close behind her, tail wagging.

"What's wrong, honey? It's late, you should be in bed," Allie told her daughter tiredly looking at the clock. 12:40 am.

"Where is auntie?" Madison stood in the doorway in her pink pajamas. Her curly blond hair was tangled and disheveled. Allie stood up and opened her arms for her daughter. Maddy walked to her mother. Allie picked up her three year old and sat down on the couch.

"Madison, Auntie Anna is missing. She is lost." Allie's words were soft and flat.

Madison contemplated her mother's words for a minute then looked at her father.

"You said she was playing a hide a seek," Maddy pointed out to Evan. He nodded. "Why don't you just say you give up? Auntie will come out."

Allie's eye filled with tears and she hugged her daughter tightly. "It's not that easy honey." She composed herself quickly and Madison looked up at her.

"Auntie was taken, Madison." Evan tried to explain, "A bad person took auntie away from us when we were playing. They won't bring her back to us."

Madison cocked her head to the side thoughtfully. "That's not nice."

"No, it's very naughty. That's why everyone is so upset." Allie nodded.

"That person isn't going to get any Christmas presents," Maddy commented angrily.

Tuesday December 16th in Texas

"How could she be missing? That town isn't that big!" Billy screamed in frustration. Her Granny sat on the edge of the bed watching her only granddaughter suffer.

"Honey, anyone can go missin' anywhere, you know that."

"Not helping, Granny!" Billy shot back.

"Honey, you know I'm sorry. There's nothin' you can do here, screamin' into the heavens."

"I know. I just don't understand… why Anna? Where could she be? What if she's hurt?"

"Billy-Jean, you don't talk like that! Stop thinkin' all of these negative thoughts right now." Granny moved closer to Billy. She gently lifted her granddaughter's face into her hands. "Annabelle is a strong woman. She is going to be just fine. You can't worry yourself sick."

Tears streamed from the young woman's eyes. She nodded at her grandma and buried her face into the old lady's shoulder. Billy's granny wrapped her arms around her shaking frame and held her close.

"It's goin' to be alright, child. You will be there tomorrow. For all we know, Annabelle will be there waitin' for you at the airport."

Billy-Jean smiled at that thought and she dried her tears.

Wednesday December 17th

Annabelle was not waiting at the airport when Billy-Jean arrived that afternoon. The snow brushed across the ground as Billy approached the familiar car in the lot. Ronnie opened his arms to his tear stained fiancé. She buried her face into his neck.

"Come on, let's go home," Ronnie told Billy, kissing the top of her head.

The car ride was quiet. The music played softly in the background. Billy's left hand clung to Ronnie's right. She let tears fall silently as they drove through the small town of Fort Kent.

"I hate this place," Billy muttered.

"Hey, if it weren't for this place, you would have never met me or Annabelle," Ronnie reminded her.

"If it weren't for this place, Annabelle would still be here." Billy's words were cold.

"Billy-Jean, you have to understand that the town has nothing to do with that. Someone took Annabelle. We don't even know who it was. For all we know they could be Canadian!" Ronnie took defense of his town. He had lived in Fort Kent since birth.

Billy's eyes were puffy and red when they arrived at their apartment complex. Ronnie turned off the car and turned to his fiancé. He put his hands on either side of her face and looked into her green eyes.

"Annabelle is strong. I've known her since first grade, Billy. She beat me up in sixth grade because I made fun of her lunchbox." Ronnie smiled, Billy didn't return the gesture. "We will find her and everything will go back to normal. You have to be strong for your friend." Ronnie's words met Billy's ears. She let more tears fall from her eyes.

"You're right." Billy sniffed.

"Now, you're exhausted, it's late. Let's go to bed. We need to rest up for whatever tomorrow brings." They walked to their first story apartment and Ronnie set Billy's suit case on the couch. Billy set Felix's carrier down on the kitchen floor and let out the fluffy feline. He darted passed them and into the bedroom.

The couple made their way to the bedroom, hands still tangled together. They both climbed into bed, shoes and all. Ronnie wrapped his arms around Billy and kissed her softly.

"I feel like she's just going to call any minute now. She'll say that she lost her phone and everything will be okay," Billy whispered. They lay there quietly for a short while. Billy sighed heavily, obviously worrying.

"Sleep, sweetheart," he told her softly.

She fell asleep quickly, but not without worries swimming through her mind.

Friday December 19th

"What do you mean?" Evan yelled. Allie was holding back her husband from beating Dolan Meyer to the ground.

"What's your problem, Rockart? I don't know where your stupid sister is!" Dolan's words infuriated Evan more.

"You're pushing your limit, kid. I'm holding him back, so you don't want to piss off me too," Allie reminded Dolan.

"You two can get off my property now. I'm sick of getting shit for things I have NOTHING to do with." Dolan slammed his front door closed.

He turned to see his mother and father standing at the bottom of the stairs. They both stood with raised eyebrow, mouths slightly open.

"What?" Dolan's voice was angry.

"We didn't say anything, son," Matt commented.

"Don't call me son. I'm not your son." Dolan's words cut deep.

"How dare you?" Nancy's words were shaky. She closed the distance between her and her son. He stood, shoulders squared and chest out.

"No mother, how dare you? How dare you think that you could keep my own father away from me?" Dolan questioned, pushing his way past his mother and he stormed up the stairs.

"Don't walk away from me!" Nancy screamed, following Dolan up the stairs.

"Just leave me alone!"

Dolan slammed his bedroom door closed in Nancy's face. She quickly reopened the door to see her son packing his things. He shoved handfuls of clothing into an old duffel bag. It pained her to watch him in such a fury.

"What are you doing?" She questioned, tears begging to fall from her eyes. She blinked, letting a few loose.

"What I should have done a long time ago, leave this place." Dolan never looked up at his mother. He continued packing with a rapid, violent pace. Dolan felt just as hurt as Nancy did, both feeling betrayed.

Wednesday December 17th

"What do you mean you kidnapped her?" Dolan's voice was surprised.

Hector, Dolan's biological father stood before him in the parking lot of the gas station.

"Son, we had to take the closest thing to the cop. The Rockart girl is just like a sister to her. It's a fool proof plan. The cop will come searching for her sister and I will have my revenge."

"That's the dumbest plan I've ever heard. You have no idea what you are getting yourself into. Allie won't come alone to find Annabelle." Dolan finished filling his gas tank and replaced the nozzle onto the pump.

"How dare you doubt my plan? I know exactly what I'm doing." Hector got into the passenger's side of the car. "This is completely genius. Plus, I get to teach Janis how to properly fight."

"What?" Dolan's voice was curious to the meaning of his father's words. "What are you talking about old man?"

"Janis wouldn't hit a fly. I need her to be stronger for future travels and ... things." Hector's statement confused Dolan. He ignored his father's madness and continued with his questions.

"You're just going to kidnap her, right?"

"And teach her a lesson or two. She's not going to get away with making my son look foolish. Why would I let her get away with putting shame to our family? I will get back at her for you."

An evil switch went off in Dolan's head, revenge.

"When can I help?

"When can you move in?" Hector smiled at his son.

Dolan's mother broke through his thoughts.

"Where will you go?" Nancy's teary eyed questioned disgusted him.

"To live with my real father." Dolan looked straight into Nancy's eyes when he said these words. She let a small whimper leave her lips and she collapsed to Dolan's bed. She reached out for his sleeve, but he ripped it from her grasp.

"He's not a good man Dolan. He will lead you down the wrong path, son."

"At least he loves me." Dolan zipped his bag and threw it over his shoulder.

"Dolan..." Nancy whispered. Dolan twisted the knife of betrayal in her chest.

Dolan walked past her, never turning around, and left the room. Nancy sat for a minute, stunned by her son's words.

160

"Dolan," she called. She got up from his bed and followed his path out of the room and down the stairs. Dolan was standing in the door way, facing Matt.

"Get out of my way." Dolan growled.

"Not until you sit down and talk rationally to your mother and I," Matt said calmly.

"I don't need to talk to either of you. You have no say in what I do." Dolan jabbed.

"Dolan, how could you think that we don't love you?" Nancy asked.

"Why would you lie to me if you loved me? Why would you lead me to believe that this man is my father?"

"Because this man is more of a father than Hector Martin would have ever been to you!" Nancy yelled in defense of her husband.

"Hector Martin loves me. He is the reason I know the truth. He is the reason I have the chance to leave this hell hole. He is the reason I see the real you, mother." Dolan pushed past Matt and opened the door.

But before he could leave, Nancy slammed the door shut and stood in front of her only son. She stared him in the eyes and realizations set in.

"What is the real reason you are leaving, Dolan?" she questioned.

This caught Dolan off guard. He furrowed his eyebrows at his mother. "I just said, because you don't love me."

"You know where Annabelle is," Nancy accused.

"Oh great! You too?" Dolan spoke defensively.

"Dolan, look at me and tell me you have no idea where that girl is," Nancy demanded. Dolan's eyes focused on his mother's piercing glare.

"Dolan, you can't be a part of this. You can't do this. Don't become your father," Nancy begged.

"Get out of my way!" Dolan yelled. She lost her balance after Dolan's strong arm pushed her away. Nancy fell to the floor, shock written across her face.

Matt grabbed Dolan's jacket and pulled him back, causing him to stumble onto the stairs. Matt helped his wife up off the floor. Nancy walked straight to Dolan and slapped him across the face.

161

"If you leave this house, you are no longer a part of this family. If you leave this house you are no longer allowed on this property," Nancy threatened.

"Good." Dolan spit back. He got up and snatched his bag from the ground beside him.

"One more thing," Matt spoke from beside him.

"What now old man?" Dolan complained, turning to Matt.

"Answer the question," Matt said calmly.

"What question?"

"Do you know where Annabelle is?" Matt repeated.

"I told her, I told them and now I'll tell you. I have no idea *WHERE* that bitch is," Dolan screamed at his parents.

He wasn't lying. He didn't know *where* Annabelle was. He only knew who took her. Dolan knew that his biological father was a raging lunatic who had kidnapped Annabelle Rockart for revenge.

"Fine." Matt turned and left the room. Nancy stood, arms crossed, staring at her son. Dolan took one look at his mother and left the house for the last time. As he crossed the front porch, Nancy followed him outside. She watched him leave the property for the last time.

Dolan got into his car and drove away quickly. He looked into the rearview mirror to see his mother collapse on the front porch in tears. Dolan felt a pang of guilt hit his chest with a force greater than he expected. She was the reason he was alive. She was also the reason he never knew his real father. For that reason, Dolan could never forgive her.

He would join the Martin family where he would be wanted and loved. Dolan told himself he would not return to his mother. He would never come back to this house of lies he called home for his entire life. That was the reason he knew his life would never be the same.

Sunday December 21st

It had been an entire week since anyone had heard from Annabelle Rockart. For reasons unknown to her family, Annabelle had been taken against her will. The search for Annabelle had been at a standstill for days. Dolan Meyer was still a main suspect in the eyes of Annabelle's family. However, no evidence supported their instinct.

"Where could she be?" Marie whispered to Mark. They sat quietly in the living room of their home. Marie's head was tucked into

162

her husband's shoulder. His arms were wrapped protectively around his wife and he rocked her back and forth ever so slightly.

"I don't know honey. I don't know," Mark whispered in response.

"I want my baby girl back." Marie cried quietly.

"We'll get her back, Marie. I don't care what it takes. We'll get her back." He kissed the top of her head and hugged her tighter. "I promise."

The couple sat quietly for an hour or two sharing comforting words of encouragement that their daughter would return home safely. When Marie began to fall asleep and Mark had been resting his eyes for only a few minutes, the front door open and slammed shut.

"Mom? Dad?" Evan's voice called through the house.

Marie ran to the front of the house, hoping to see three adults standing in front of her. To her dismay, only Evan and Allie stood at the front door. They both appeared to have been crying; eye red and puffy.

"What is it? Why do you look upset?" Marie questioned.

"Where's Dad?" Evan asked avoiding Marie's eyes. His anger wasn't easily hidden from his mother. His tears of anguish were falling freely.

"Living room." Marie kept her eyes on her son.

"He needs to hear this too," Allie commented looking down at the floor. Feelings of guilt and worry filled Allie to the point of breaking. She held back her tears as they threatened to fall.

The three adults made their way to the living room. Allie and Evan sat down on the couch opposite of their parents. Marie sat with Mark and waited a minute until their son and daughter-in-law dropped whatever news they were holding.

"The station got a phone call today. Someone has her, someone is keeping Anna." Evan fumed to his parents. His words bubbled between tears and gasps of rage.

"What?" Marie gasped. She grabbed for her husband's hand and she felt tears in her eyes plead to fall.

"A man called the station today. He stated that he had Annabelle. He wants me," Allie commented quietly. She hated thinking that the reason for Annabelle's disappearance was caused by merely doing her job.

"What....you? I don't understand," Mark spoke finally. His tone was low and full of confusion.

"Even though the man did not relay his name to Chief Michaels on the phone, it is obvious who this man is." Allie took a deep breath and finally raised her tear stained eyes to meet those of her in-laws. "Hector Martin is a man I put in jail for domestic violence in 2003. Hector Martin is also the biological father of Dolan Meyer."

Marie and Mark stared at their daughter-in-law in complete silence. Marie was the first to speak after nearly five minutes.

"I understand where you would make the connection...but... I just don't understand why he would choose Annabelle."

"Hector Martin is a crazed lunatic who should have never been released from jail. His mind is not one of logical or rational thought," Allie explained.

"The Meyer boy... wasn't he cleared of suspicion?" Mark questioned.

"Yes, but Nancy Meyer has been worried about her son. I have been called there several times in the past week because Dolan has gone missing. He is associating with Martin more often. Nancy has noticed violent behavior in Dolan."

"Should you be telling us this? Isn't that personal?" Mark questioned, acting nervous.

"In this case, everything is personal," Evan commented with a low grumble.

"As far as I'm concerned, I am sharing information with you that you might already know from the gossip in this little town." Allie's voice was sarcastic but confident. She wasn't concerned with privacy anymore. She would do whatever it took to get Annabelle back.

"Do you have an address of this Martin character?" Mark asked.

"I went today. House looks abandoned. The neighbors say they left over two weeks ago," Allie explained sadly.

That night, Evan, Allie and Billy-Jean continued to search for answers. After searching Annabelle's apartment from wall to wall and floor to ceiling to find absolutely nothing out of place, Evan began to believe that Annabelle was never coming home. Allie tried her hardest to convince him that she would find his sister while she was tearing herself inside out with guilt.

"I should have seen this coming. I should have known a lunatic like Hector Martin would retaliate. I should have seen this." Allie cried to Billy-Jean in Billy's apartment late that night after going through Annabelle's things.

"Allie, stop it. You are only going to drive yourself insane by putting that much guilt and blame on yourself. No one could have seen this coming." Billy's words didn't touch Allie.

She continued to think to herself all the things she could have done to protect her loved ones. She thought of the precautions she should have taken when Martin was released from jail. Allie remembered Hector Martin's laugh when he saw his knife protruding from her chest. He was an evil man and she was positive he was the same man who took Annabelle.

Allie stood up from the couch and walked towards the window. It overlooked the hills of Maine. "She could be anywhere," Allie whispered.

Billy stood and pulled Allie into a hug. Allie didn't pull away. She embraced her friend tightly and let tears fall from her eyes. Billy returned the squeeze and pulled away, looking into Allie's tear stained face.

"Anna is a strong woman. She won't let just anyone get to her. She will be okay. We will find her. Stop blaming yourself, it's not going to bring her home any sooner if you sit and feel guilty," Billy pointed out. Allie nodded slightly and returned her gaze to the window.

"It's hard not to think that I might be the reason she's gone," Allie said. Billy gave her a sympathetic look. Billy was out of words of encouragement. Allie was beyond the point of support. She was too far into a state of shock and guilt that only Annabelle could bring her out of.

"Why the hell would you call the police station?" Dolan questioned, outraged.

"No one was even looking for her. Officer Rockart never even left home today!" Hector yelled back.

The father and son were sitting at the kitchen table of the tiny motel outside of downtown Fort Kent. The Martins had left their home over two weeks ago to prevent questioning from the police. Paying with cash to avoid a paper trail; the Martin family was now known as the Parker family in the motel's records. The trusting small town staff never asked the Parker's for an ID or reasoning for their lengthy stay.

"Well she is probably sucking her thumb and crying to her husband like the child she is," Janis commented from the living area. Hector shot her a glance to remain quiet.

"What phone did you use?" Dolan questioned.

"The payphone down the road." Hector smirked at his son. "Did you think I was dumb enough to use the hotel phone? Please, Dolan, give me more credit. I am much more experienced at this than you will ever know."

"The officer hasn't got any clue where to look for the girl. She isn't thinking to look in the hills. How are you planning on leading her there?" Dolan questioned. Hector glared at his son.

"How dare you question my plan? I am in no hurry to finish this. I'm having fun torturing the girl." Hector smiled devilishly.

"And she almost escaped yesterday! Explain that!" Dolan yelled, getting out of his chair beginning to pace the small kitchen.

"That was a minor mishap." Hector added, "She was punished and we fixed the hole in the wall." He crossed his arms over his chest tightly and watched his pacing son.

"Why are you getting all the fun? When do I get the chance to have a go at the bitch? Even your pathetic excuse for another son had a chance to teach her a lesson!" Dolan pointed out with a growl. Janis laughed from the other side of the room.

"Sit down, Dolan," Hector said calmly.

"No," he protested. "Give me a chance!"

"Sit down son," Hector repeated. Dolan stood his ground. Hector laughed, standing from his chair. He approached Dolan with a fist clenched. Hector stood two inches from his son's face. "Sit down," Hector threatened. Dolan sat down with a heavy sigh.

"The only reason Lucas got a chance was because we needed him to watch her over night. I wasn't going to risk her getting out. It's not my fault he surprised us all by teaching her a lesson." Hector smiled and patted Dolan on the back. "You'll get a chance, be patient. For now, stay here and let us do our job."

Hector left Dolan at the kitchen table and joined Janis on the couch. Dolan scoffed at his father and turned to the cabinet for a drink.

Lucas stood in the doorway to one of the two bedrooms of the motel. He was unnoticed by his unloving family. He eyed Dolan drinking straight from a liquor bottle; glowering at his half-brother. He quietly shut the door and sat on the dusty bed. Lucas took a deep breath and held in his anger. He had hated his family for almost his entire life. Now to add a brother into his dysfunctional family was the breaking point. Lucas needed to get out, he needed to help Annabelle.

Lucas had managed to almost get Annabelle out of the hole in the wall of the old cabin the woods. He had taken the truck each night, without his parents ever knowing differently. Ever since she tried to escape, they had been on high alert. The easiest option, the phone, was guarded by his mother. The keys to the truck, a slightly harder option, pushed deep into the pocket of his father's pants. Leaving the motel for long period of time would only cause them to question his whereabouts.

Annabelle, Annie. Lucas thought to himself. She was the person that made him feel needed. She needed him. Annabelle was the only person that had ever needed Lucas. It helped that she actually spoke to him like a human being instead of a pet like his parents did. She didn't deserve the torment from his family. She deserved much more than anything Lucas could offer her.

She only needs you because you are her way out. His thoughts jabbed him in the side. *You could never get a girl like Annabelle any other time.* Lucas shook his head. It wasn't about 'getting the girl'; it was about helping an innocent person escape a terrible fate.

But it was about getting the girl. Lucas felt closer to Annabelle than he had ever felt towards anyone. He wanted to know more about her life, her family, and her dreams. His heart pounded in anticipation. Lucas felt the need to protect this woman with his own life. He wanted to save her from his parents the way Mable had for him.

Lucas would make himself be the reason Annabelle Rockart will be found, *alive.*

- 17 - Christmas without Annabelle

It was Christmas Eve on the calendar, but no one in the Rockart family felt like celebrating. Annabelle was still missing and they had hit another dead end. The only lead they had was Allie's gut feeling.

"Mommy?" Maddy asked, pulling herself up onto the couch next to her mom.

"Hmm?" Allie looked up from her present wrapping. Maddy looked down at the gift in her hands then back up at her mom. The gift Madison was holding said "To: Annabelle," Allie's heart sunk. Madison thought for a minute.

"If I'm good, Santa will bring me what I want," Maddy said.

"Yes honey, if you are a good girl all year round, Santa will bring you what you asked for," Allie pointed out. Madison looked down at the gift again.

"I want Auntie." Maddy looked up at her mom with a tear in her eye. Allie's heart broke watching her daughter cry over her missing aunt. Allie pushed the gift she was wrapping to the side and pulled her three year old into her lap. Maddy held tightly onto the gift for Annabelle in her arms.

"Oh, Madison, everyone wants the same thing this year." Allie rocked her daughter, tears streaming down her own cheeks. She didn't know what else to say to Madison. She had run out of things to say.

Evan rounded the corner of the living room and saw his wife and daughter crying on the couch. Evan took his coat off and sat down next to them. Madison looked at her dad and held out her arms for him to hold her. Evan took his little girl in his lap and put his arm around his wife. They stayed that way for hours. All crying and comforting one another, this wouldn't be Christmas without Annabelle.

Thursday December 25th

Christmas Morning, the snow covered hills of Northern Maine had been greeted with a fresh layer of snow. The untouched hills held more secrets that any Fort Kent resident really knew, except the Martin family.

"My disappointment for you has been replaced with complete confidence." Hector's voice echoed through the motel room. Dolan sat in the chair, smiling back at his father.

"I knew that would happen when you gave me the chance to prove myself." Dolan said. Hector nodded in agreement. Janis sat quietly in the corner of the room.

Janis was filled with mixed feelings. Lucas had indeed betrayed their family. He picked the enemy over his own father and brother. But was Lucas wrong for going against their crime? Janis had begun to question the plan. She began to question her husband's sanity, even her own. When had she become ugly?

"Janis, you will need to stay home tomorrow. We will return with Lucas. I'm not sure what we are going to do with him yet. Maybe you could think of something while we're gone." Hector brought Janis from her thoughts.

"We aren't going to hurt him, are we?" Janis let the question slip her lips before she could think. Hector turned slowly in his chair to face his wife.

"Why would we let him get away with betrayal? His loyalties are no longer to this family. As far as I'm concerned, I have one son." Hector smiled at his wife and she nodded quietly.

Janis knew she was outnumbered and would never dare standing up to her husband. Hector's strength was too much for Janis to beat. She would surely lose in a fight with her husband.

Tomorrow would be a long day.

"Merry Christmas," Evan greeted his parents somberly. Using the word 'merry' just didn't seem right today. Annabelle's smile was burned into his eyes and he felt the ache in his chest each time he let his mind wonder.

"Hi, honey." Marie refused to return the greeting. As far as she was concerned, it was not Christmas and would not be until her daughter was returned to her.

Evan set his box of presents down on the floor near the Christmas tree. Madison followed him closely, still clinging to the present marked for Annabelle. She hadn't let it go in 24 hours, even during the night.

"Where's Allie?" Mark asked from the kitchen entrance.

"She went into the station for an hour or so. She'll be here later." Evan spoke distractedly. "She's going to pick up Ronnie and Billy on her way."

Marie nodded and sat down on the couch. Madison climbed up next to her grandma. Marie smiled and pulled the little girl into her lap.

"What do you have, Maddy?" Marie asked. Madison showed her the present marked for Annabelle. Marie felt tears burn her eyes and she squeezed her granddaughter tightly. She kissed the top of Madison's head and the little girl turned and faced Marie. Maddy set the present next to them on the couch and wrapped her arms around Marie. Marie wrapped her arms around the little girl and rocked her slightly. "I love you, Madison."

"I love you, Gama," Madison replied.

Evan left the room and sat down at the kitchen table with his father.

"How is Allie?" Mark asked concerned, knowing the guilt Allie felt.

"Not good." Evan started picking at his thumbs. "She won't stop blaming herself for this. Nothing I say changes her mind."

Mark took in his son's words and sat quietly, thinking of the right thing to say. Mark felt just as helpless as the rest of his family. Not knowing where his little girl was, was tearing him apart. He had been able to keep her safe for her entire life until now. Where had he gone wrong? What could he do to keep her safe now?

"I feel like I should have seen this coming." Evan broke Mark's thoughts.

"Don't you start, too," Mark begged. Evan shook his head, letting a few tears fall from his eyes. He had never let his father see him cry, even as a child.

Mark watched his son struggle with his emotions. He sighed heavily, feeling his own tears run down his cheeks. Evan felt his father's eyes on him and looked up.

"I just want to find her," Evan said.

Both men were vulnerable. Never in their relationship had they felt so close. Evan stood, embarrassed by his tears. He walked to the back door of the house, watching the neighbor's grandchildren playing in the snow. This reminded him of his childhood when he would play with Annabelle in the snow on Christmas Day. Tears streamed from his eyes. Would he ever get the chance to see his sister smile again? Would he ever see his sister again? Was she alive? The thought sent a chilling feeling through his spine.

A hand touched his shoulder. Evan turned around to see his dad standing behind him. Mark pulled his son into a hug. Evan let tears fall freely from his eyes. Mark patted his son's back and they let go of one another.

"We'll find her, Evan," Mark promised.

"Mark!" Marie called from the living room.

Evan and Mark rushed into the living room to see what caused Marie to yell. They saw a picture of Annabelle on the TV. The afternoon news was reporting on Annabelle's disappearance.

"Today is everything but a Merry Christmas for one Fort Kent family. The Rockart family is still mourning the disappearance of their daughter, Annabelle. Annabelle Rockart was reported missing on December 14th when her car was found, abandoned outside the Meyer Bookstore. The local police are continuing to search for the missing 22 year old. We interviewed Chief Michaels last night; Jenna James has the rest of the story, Jenna?"

The young reporter stood outside of the Meyer Bookstore. "Yes, Diane. Chief Michaels told us last night that this is only missing person's case that he has seen last this long in his 25 years of service as Chief of Police here in Fort Kent. He remains hopeful for Annabelle's safe return, but claims that the station has hit a dead end in the search. If you have any information, please call the local police station at 207-834-0124. Back to you, Diane."

Marie turned off the TV. They sat in silence for a few minutes, all with mixed emotions. Marie clung to a now sleeping Madison and rocked her gently. Marie was saddened by the news report.

"A dead end?" Evan repeated the words of the reporter. He shook his head and ran his hands through his hair.

Two hours passed and Allie showed up with Billy and Ronnie. They greeted the somber family with fake smiles and false wishes of happiness. Billy didn't bother with make up or dressy clothes. She sat down on the couch next to Marie and Madison climbed into her lap.

"Any news?" Ronnie asked Evan. Evan shook his head and took Ronnie's coat.

Mark nodded. "No."

"I'm still on call, so if I have to leave, please forgive me."

"That's all right dear," Marie told her daughter-in-law. She smiled at Allie who didn't return the gesture. Allie walked into the kitchen without a word.

"I'll go-" Evan started but his mother interrupted.

"Let me." Marie stood up and followed Allie into the kitchen.

Allie stood at the counter, cutting up a block of cheese for the cracker platter that sat in front of her. She had tears streaming down her face. Marie walked to stand next to Allie and touched her hand.

"Allie…" Marie started. Allie looked up at Marie with sad eyes. Marie took the knife from Allie's hand and pulled the woman into a strong hug. Allie cried out loud, sobbing softly into Marie's shoulder.

"I'm so sorry Marie."

"Stop that, stop that right now." Marie pulled Allie away from her shoulder and looked at her. "This is not your fault any more than it is mine or anyone else in this house. You did nothing wrong. Stop blaming yourself," Marie told Allie sternly.

Allie stared at her mother-in-law for a minute before she spoke. "I just want her home."

"Just like everyone else, dear." Marie smiled sadly. She pulled Allie into another hug.

"Now let's finish this platter so we can feed everyone." Marie smiled.

When they joined the group in the living room, the room was quiet. Maddy had left Billy's lap and had joined Ronnie on the floor to play with Fig. Allie smiled slightly when she saw Madison having fun. It was the first time she heard the little girl laugh in a days. Marie set the platter of appetizers on the coffee table and joined her husband on the couch. Mark kissed her cheek gently.

"Madison honey, would you like to open your gifts?" Marie asked, trying to make the best of the day. Maddy smiled at her grandma.

"Okay, take a seat right here," Evan told his daughter pointing to the floor in front of the love seat where he and Allie sat. Maddy petted Fig on the head before she crawled to the spot where Evan told her to sit. Billy joined Ronnie on the floor and kissed his cheek lightly.

Marie passed out presents to everyone and the room was filled with the sound of ripping paper and words of thanks. After Madison opened her last present from Billy and Ronnie, she frowned.

"What's wrong, Maddy? Don't you like your present?" Ronnie asked, worried they bought the wrong doll for the young girl. Maddy shook her head and set the doll down on the floor next to her. She

172

stood up and walked to the tree. The little girl climbed under the tree and searched for something.

"Madison, what are you doing?" Marie asked her granddaughter. Everyone's side conversations stopped as they watched the little girl fret over something.

"Did you get what you wanted?" Allie asked, trying to figure out what Madison was looking for.

"No," the little girl said plainly. Allie looked at Evan. They both understood what Madison was looking for.

"Did Santa forget to bring you something?" Billy questioned, oblivious to Madison's wishes.

"Yes." Maddy climbed out from under the tree. "Auntie."

The room when silent, each person held their breath. Madison looked at her parents with a pain struck face. She still didn't understand why Annabelle was gone.

"Was I a bad girl?" Maddy asked with tears threatening to fall from her eyes.

"No, Madison. Not at all, come here." Evan held out his arms for his daughter. Madison climbed in her father's lap. She wrapped her arms around his neck and he hugged her tightly.

"This is not your fault honey," Allie reminded the little girl. She brushed the blonde curls from her face and nodded at her mother.

"Auntie will be home soon," Marie promised. Her heart broke with the empty promise to the little girl. She *hoped* her daughter would be home soon. She *wanted* her daughter to be home soon. But just like everyone else in the room, she was clueless to where Annabelle was, when she would be found, and whether or not she was okay. The thought took Marie's breath away and she held her husband's hand tightly.

It just wasn't Christmas without Annabelle.

173

Later Christmas night, Allie was called back into work to cover the phones for Chief Michaels. She didn't care too much about leaving the family party. The family spent the day in an awkward silence. Laughter remained a rare occasion. Allie was happy to get away and give herself time to think.

Allie answered the phone, "Fort Kent Police, this is Officer Rockart." The automatic recording system clicked on and the hum of the ancient machine shook Allie's desk. She held onto her cup of coffee and listened to the woman on the other side of the line complain about her neighbor's music being too loud.

"Mrs. Anderson, it's Christmas," Allie reminded the old store keeper. She smiled slightly and shook her head at the old woman.

"I want something done," Mrs. Anderson threatened.

"I'll tell you what Mrs. Anderson," Allie began, bargaining with the woman. "If the music is not turned down by," Allie glanced up at the clock, 11:40pm, "midnight, give us a call back and we will send a car out to check out the scene."

"Fine, expect my call in twenty minutes." Mrs. Anderson hung up.

Allie shook her head and set the phone on the receiver. Allie knew the people of Fort Kent too well. Twenty minutes passed, thirty minutes… Allie never received another call from Mrs. Anderson that night.

Friday December 26th

Allie found herself straightening the station to keep her mind off Annabelle. After two hours of deep cleaning, the station bathrooms sparkled. Allie sat at her desk, satisfied with the station's appearance. Chief Michael's would be pleased with her later that morning.

Around 4:00am, Allie tapped her pencil on the edge of the desk while she looked for the word 'marvelous' in her word search. The phone rang and Allie set her pencil down on the desk. It was unusual for the phone to ring between the hours of 1:00am and 5:00am.

"Fort Kent Police. This is Sheriff Rockart," Allie recited. There was a breath on the other side of the line. Allie sat forward in her seat when the hum of the recorder began. She turned the volume of her phone up.

"May I help you?" Allie asked, after a moment of silence.

"I know where she is," the woman's voice whispered. Allie's heart dropped into her stomach.

"Who is this? Where who is? Annabelle?" Allie jumped to conclusions. She held her breath, waiting for an answer.

"Yes…. The hills east of Fort Kent." The woman spoke softly and nervously.

"Who is this?" Allie repeated. The line went dead.

Allie quickly dialed Chief Michaels. It was a little after four in the morning and Allie knew the Chief would be awake by now, getting ready to work.

"Michaels," Jeff answered the phone quickly.

"Jeff, its Allie," she began, her heart in her throat. "I got another anonymous phone call. This time it was from a woman. She said Annabelle was in the hills east of Fort Kent."

"Is that the only information she gave you?"

"Yes, sir."

"What's the number?" Michaels questioned.

"Same pay phone as last time, just outside of town on Market Street," Allie said. Michaels sighed on the other end of the line. Allie swallowed hard.

"I'll be in as soon as I can." Michaels hung up his phone.

Allie sat at her desk with a map of the hills in northern Maine. She shook her head and sighed. It would take weeks to cover the entire area.

"Where are you Anna?" Allie whispered to herself.

"Janis!" Dolan called from the door of the motel. He dragged his half brother into the apartment by his arms.

Janis stood at the edge of the room, fearful of her son's condition, prepared never to show it. Her plan however, *had* to work.

"Get a rope from the bedroom," Hector called, slamming the door closed behind him. He locked the door and closed the curtains. "I don't think anyone is following."

"What should we do with him?" Dolan kicked Lucas to his back. Lucas was unconscious.

"Teach him a lesson in betrayal, son." Hector smiled. Dolan nodded.

Janis handed her husband a bundle of rope and stood silently in the corner, her arms crossed tightly over her chest and her face blank.

"Get up!" Hector yelled at the unconscious man. Hector knelt down and tied his arms behind his back. He pulled Lucas up by the knotted rope and pushed him against the wall. Lucas moaned slightly with the sudden jolt to reality.

Lucas tried to open his eyes. His right eye remained closed, completely swollen shut from the bashes his family provided him.

"Well, it looks like you survived the ride home. Would you like to guess your time of death or do you like surprises?" Hector smirked. He drove his knee into Lucas's stomach. Lucas buckled to the floor. His gasps for air were heard loud and clear across the room. Janis cringed away. She held her breath, thinking of a way to get Hector to lock Lucas in the bedroom.

"Do you have anything to say for yourself?" Dolan questioned his younger brother.

Lucas took in a deep breath. He looked up at his family and growled, "Go to hell."

"Well son, that's no way to talk to your family. Especially after we gave you what you wanted." Hector smiled. "We let your bitch go."

Janis stood quietly, taking in this new information. "You did what?" she finally spoke, Dolan stopped to stare at his father.

Hector turned to his wife. "Excuse me?"

"You let the girl go?" Janis questioned, keeping her voice angry.

"You put her back in the shack, you locked the door," Dolan pointed out.

"Yes, but she was of no use anymore." Hector's tone was annoyed. "I locked the lock to the door, not to the building."

"No use? Did the officer come to the woods? Did you have your revenge? Are they both dead?" Janis questioned, sounding annoyed herself.

Hector stared at them as if he had seen a ghost; Janis threw her hands in the air. "What was the point of all this then?"

Janis shook her head and walked towards the three men. She lifted the youngest man to his feet by the knotted ropes. Lucas groaned loudly in pain. Janis's heart broke silently. She glared at Hector and Dolan.

"You two will have no fun with him until you figure out how to get to the officer now." Janis felt a wave of relief. She felt like she made her point and saved her son from death. She pushed him forward into the bedroom, making sure he landed on the bed.

Before she closed the door, she turned back to Lucas and said, "Note on the dresser."

Lucas didn't have time to react before she slammed the door loudly and locked it from the outside.

Feelings of exhaustion took over his body; Lucas remained still on the bed for several minutes. He felt a sharp pain in his chest with each breath. It was either the loss of the one person he would truly give his life for or the fact that his ribs were caved in.

After a struggle with the blade left on the dresser, Lucas freed his arms from the tight ropes. He found the note his mother spoke of and read it:

> The window is unlocked; we are on the first story. It's not a long jump. Please get yourself out. This is the only way for you to get out alive.
>
> I'm sorry.

The note was short. No, I love you. No, I'll see you later. No ounce of love was put into this note; only guilt. Lucas stuffed the note into his pocket. Without his family knowing, Lucas had used this window to escape each night, while his family was sleeping, to go to Annie before he ever knew her, before he loved her.

He didn't have time to over think the note. He walked to the window, opening the dirty glass pane. The cold air hit his injured face gently. Without another thought, he jumped from the window.

The short jump caused him to gasp loudly. He landed on his feet. Lucas held his side tightly, catching his breath. He began the three mile walk to the Fort Kent Police station.

"Go home, Allie," Michaels begged his co-worker.

"There has to be some way we can get more people to help us search these hills, Jeff," Allie pleaded. Jeff looked back at Allie with sympathetic eyes. She shook her head and turned around to stare at the area map on the wall. She felt tears creep into her eyes. A hand touched her shoulder.

Allie had been at the station all day trying to get him to budge. The phone call yesterday made Allie that much more eager to drive out to the hills to search for Annabelle. It was now 7:30 at night.

"Go home, please. Get some rest and we will start at day light when this storm lets up. You know these hills at night just as much as I do. There's no way," Jeff reminded her. Allie sighed. She knew he was right. The hills were impossible and much too dangerous to travel at night.

"Call me if you get any more calls," Allie reminded him, sliding on her coat.

She turned to leave when Michaels said, "Please Allie, get some sleep."

Allie left the building silently. Snow fell heavily around her. She zipped her coat as she walked toward her car. As she unlocked the driver's door she heard a noise from the side of the building. She stopped in her tracks and waited to hear it again. It sounded like an animal in the trash can until she heard someone cough.

Immediately on her defense, Allie put her hand on her gun, grabbing for her flashlight with the other hand. She walked slowly to the edge of the building waiting for the person make a move. After a moment of silence, she took her gun from her holster and took a deep breath before stepping around the corner.

"Who's there?" Allie called out. The light shined around the tiny alley.

"Allie…" This man's voice was soft and unthreatening. She moved around the dumpster to find a young man leaning up against the brick building. His face was badly swollen and bleeding. His expression was exhausted, completely drained of energy. He was familiar.

"Do I know you?" Allie questioned.

"Lucas Martin," he said cautiously.

She knew exactly who he was when he said his last name. She recognized his face. Allie watched him carefully as he struggled to contain his tears. He quickly wiped his face, wincing at his swollen injury.

"Who did this to you?" Allie questioned.

"My father…" Lucas began.

178

"Say no more." Allie stopped him. "I am going to take you to a hospital."

"No…" He tried to straighten up his posture. "I know where she is. I have to take you to where she is. You'll never find her."

"What?" Allie stopped in her tracks. Her heart skipped. "Annabelle?"

"I have to take you to her. You'll never find her," Lucas repeated.

"You are in no condition to travel anywhere but a hospital," Allie spoke sternly. With no response, Allie stepped closer. His eyes were closed as he stood leaned against the wall.

"Lucas?" Allie questioned. She shook his shoulder. His eyes opened and he looked back up at Allie. She felt her heart break for him. "Let's take you inside."

"No." Lucas stood his ground. "You can't let anyone know about this, I have to take you to her. My father will kill her if you send the whole town after her. If we go now, he would never know." Lucas rested his head back against the wall, closing his eyes.

"Lucas, you can barely stand. I have to get you to a hospital," Allie repeated.

"NO!" Lucas practically yelled. Allie stepped back. She watched as Lucas broke down. He slid to the ground, his hands covering his face. Lucas cried, his body trembling.

"Lucas, please-" Allie began.

"Please, Allie. We have to get to her before he does. You don't understand. My father is insane. He wants to kill you." Lucas looked up at Allie with tears rolling down his cheeks. "He took Annabelle to get to you. He wants you."

Allie stood, stunned at the facts that poured for Lucas's mouth. Her heart dropped into her stomach. She looked down at Lucas and took a deep breath in.

"Where is she?" Allie whispered.

"Glass Hill area, to the east of the town," Lucas answered with a strange tone, swallowing hard. Allie nodded, remembering the phone call from the morning.

"We can't go tonight. There's no way to get through those hills at night," Allie said, feeling her heart sink deeper into her chest. Leaving Annabelle alone for another night felt like leaving her daughter alone in a cage of wild dogs.

"I've done it before. I know where to go." Lucas stood up. His legs shook as he leaned against the building.

"Lucas, you can't go through the woods like this," Allie pointed out. What was she going to do? She couldn't take him home to Evan. She had to go home, Evan would be expecting her. She couldn't leave Lucas here. A sudden idea pierced Allie's mind. "If I promise you we will leave before the sun rises, will you agree to letting me take you somewhere for the night?"

Lucas focused on Allie's face. His heart told him no, but his body begged for him to say yes. He looked down, thinking about Allie's offer.

"Lucas, please. You know where she is and I have the resources to get to her. I can't believe I'm even considering hiding you, but I will to keep her alive," Allie added.

"I'll do it. We will have to leave before 5 am. Hector and Janis usually go to the hills around 8. We can't waste time," Lucas whispered.

Everything inside of these two strangers told them they were doing something wrong; neither cared. They knew it was the only way to find Annabelle and get her home safely. Without letting the other know, their hearts ached as they thought about leaving Annabelle out there alone for another night. Lucas felt his stomach twist into knots at the thought. Allie felt her head spin with the amount of information she had to process. She would have to lie; lie to her family, her co-workers, to herself.

Allie broke the silence. "Come on." She looked at Lucas with a strange sense of maternal instinct. She didn't know the entire story. She didn't understand why Lucas was here. She didn't know what tonight would bring. Nothing mattered if it meant bringing Annabelle home.

"Where are we going?" Lucas questioned.

The hair on the back of Allie's neck stood up. If she led Lucas to her car parked in the front of the station, Chief Michaels would see him. She turned around and looked down the alley.

"I'll pull my car around the back of the building. Can you meet me there?" Allie watched as he struggled to balance himself. Lucas nodded and turned away from her.

Watching him hold onto the building and stumble towards the opposite side of the alley, Allie worried what tomorrow would be like.

She returned to her car, starting the engine quickly. Avoiding attention, Allie pulled away from the station in her normal direction. She took a quick right and circled around the station. Her headlights pointed Lucas out in the snowy darkness. He stood with his head back, leaning against the building. She parked the running car near the alley. Allie unlocked the door, Lucas opened the passenger door. Holding his side, he cautiously sat down in the seat. He buckled his seat belt and sighed heavily, his body happy to be sitting.

Once he was in the car, Allie picked her phone up and dialed the only number she could think of. The phone rang twice before Allie heard the other line picked up.

"Billy-Jean, I need a huge favor."

"If he won't go to the hospital, why can't we make him go?" Billy questioned Allie in a harsh whisper. "If everything he just told us is true, Anna wouldn't want him going back after her. I don't know how I feel about either of you going through the hills without someone who knows the area."

"Billy-Jean, you heard what he said. If either of his parents find out we're going out there, they are going to kill her. I can't take the chance of anyone finding out. I can't risk her life anymore than it already is. It's the only way." Allie's voice was low and miserable. "He knows the area; I can't do it without him."

Billy sighed in defeat. There was no getting around the situation. The snow fell heavily around them. They were standing on Billy's balcony, avoiding the ears of Ronnie and Lucas. The night had been long and full of information. Lucas had showered and let Allie clean his injuries. Having dealt with broken ribs himself, Ronnie suggested ice and pain medicines. Lucas was now resting on their couch, trying to sleep.

Billy-Jean looked at Allie's concentrated expression.

"Are you going to tell Evan?" Billy asked already assuming the answer would be no.

"I can't. He'll over react. You know Evan, it's his little sister and he's protective of her." Allie exchanged looks with Billy. They both nodded in agreement.

"I won't tell anyone." Billy paused. "Unless you aren't home or haven't called by noon tomorrow. We've lost Annabelle, we can't lose you too."

Allie felt tears fall from her eyes. She turned to Billy and hugged her tightly. "Thank you so much. Call me if you need me. I'll be here around 4:30 tomorrow morning."

The two women returned to the warmth of the apartment. Without bothering Lucas, Allie slipped through the front door after saying goodbye to Ronnie. She ran down the stairs and to her car. Once her car door was closed, Allie broke down. The weight of the world rested on her shoulders. The truth was out; tomorrow would be the day Annabelle would be found.

In the mind of Evan Rockart, he kissed his wife goodbye and watched her drive away to a normal day of work. But Allie was hiding something from him. She had received vital information last night straight from the source; today she would find Annabelle.

Billy greeted Allie at the door of the apartment building. Her face was pale, worried and anxious. Allie hugged Billy tightly and promised her they would be okay. Walking up the stairs to Billy-Jean's apartment, Allie's heart pounded with anticipation for the day.

Allie followed Billy inside the apartment where Lucas sat quietly at the dining room table. Sitting on the table next to him was a winter coat Ronnie was letting him borrow. Allie noticed his face was significantly smaller than yesterday, the swelling had subsided. He looked up at Allie when she walked into the room. His eyes were red and tired. She sighed heavily and nodded. "Everything inside of me is telling me otherwise, let's get going before I change my mind."

Lucas thanked Billy and Ronnie and turned to leave. Before he left Billy-Jean pulled him into a hug. The sudden hug from a person he barely knew stunned Lucas. Billy pulled out of the hug and kept her hands on his shoulders.

"I trust you to bring both of them home," Billy asserted.

He nodded and followed Allie out of the apartment. Allie opened the door to Evan's truck and started the truck. Lucas climbed in, wincing as he twisted his body. Allie kept her mouth closed as her conscience screamed in her head for her to go straight to the hospital. She took a deep breath and pulled out of the parking lot, heading for the hills.

The night had left Fort Kent, Maine covered in a fresh foot of snow. She knew if the family knew as much as she did, they would have wanted to come with her. The condition of the hills was no place for large groups of people to wander in the winter. The twists and turns of the woods; cliffs and steep slopes nearly invisible under the fresh blanket of snow; taking a group of people would only raise the risk of someone being separated from the group.

As they approached the area, Lucas became more alert. He directed Allie through the unmarked paths of the woods. He did know the area very well. Allie was amazed how he predicted each turn and swerve as they went deeper into the forest.

"Park here, we'll have to walk the rest of the way. It's not too far," Lucas promised, opening his door as the truck came to a stop. The adrenaline surged through Lucas. He wasn't going to let anything keep him from Annie, he was too close.

Allie stuffed the keys into her pocket and grabbed her bag of supplies. She had packed blankets, water and a first aid kit. Sliding her arms through the straps of the back pack, Allie closed her door.

Lucas met Allie at the front of the truck and pointed towards the woods ahead. "Annie was locked in a building that is straight through these trees. I don't know if she's still there or if they actually let her go."

With a hesitant nod, Allie followed Lucas through the thick tree line. Allie's thoughts went wild. What if I find her body? If she is still alive, what condition will she be in? What if she isn't in the cabin? Will she be alone? Will Hector Martin be there, waiting for the perfect time to pounce? The pictures flashed through her mind and she felt tears freeze to her cheeks.

The hike was rough. The snow covered trees made it hard to see far ahead of where they walked. Allie couldn't help but feel lost. She was in a foreign area, off the beaten path and with a stranger. *Was Annabelle feeling the same?*

"It's around here," Lucas spoke to Allie. His breaths quicken as he felt a wave of optimism.

Allie nodded quickly and slowed her pace, watching her footsteps carefully. As she followed Lucas, she reached the bottom of the small slope in the front of the structure. They watched the doorway of the building as it swung open, swaying in the breeze. Approaching the doorway carefully and quietly, Lucas looked down at the handle of the door, which clanged loudly.

Allie looked down to see the large metal lock that hung loosely on the door handle. She felt her rage boil inside her chest. She took a deep breath and tried to calm herself down.

Once she stood inside the structure, her hope was ripped from her chest. An empty room stood in front of her. The air was musty and stale. The floor was dirty, and wet in spots from the leaking ceiling. A sink sat in the corner of the room, a wooden chair broken into pieces on the center and a metal framed bed sat across from the sink. She walked closer to the sink, checking for any signs or clues of Annabelle's presence.

Allie reached for her flashlight and looked into the sink. She brought the hand that hovered over her gun to her mouth and took a sharp breath in. She reached for the piece of cloth that lay at the bottom of the sink. She shined the light at it to get a closer look; blood. The sight made her stomach twist. She dropped the cloth back to the bottom and saw small spots of blood, splattered on the floor. The edge of the sink was covered in dried bits of blood as well.

"Allie?" Lucas's voice startled her. She pulled her gun out and pointing at the door. Lucas put his hands up in defense. Allie's breaths were sharp. She realized her overreaction and apologized.

"She's not here. We've got to keep looking," Lucas said, feeling the lump in his throat grow. Where was she? How far had she gotten? Lucas felt the weight of the world resting on his shoulders.

Allie felt like she was in a dream; floating behind Lucas like she had seen Annabelle's ghost. She had been standing in the very building that Annabelle had been kept in, like an animal. She shook the thoughts from her head and focused her attention on the surrounding area.

"Allie." Lucas pointed at the ground. Footprints littered the ground leading in all different directions. Allie's heart thumped loudly in her chest.

"The path is just through this tree line," Lucas pointed out, moving forward. A set of the footprints did lead towards the path.

Allie and Lucas navigated the thick tree line. The hardened snow made it difficult to avoid stumbling now and again. Allie kept her eyes on Lucas, afraid his adrenaline would wear off too soon. What would she do if he got any worse? How could she handle taking care of him and finding Annabelle? Her conscience poked her brain again. She shook it off and continued to follow Lucas.

"Careful, there is an old perimeter fence buried in the snow." Lucas stepped forward, on to the path. Allie copied him only to lose her balance. Lucas reached his arms to catch her but Allie fell, face first, on the path. Landing with a grunt, Allie lifted herself up on her hands. Shaking her head slightly, her eyes landed on a person in the middle of the path.

"Are you okay?" Lucas bent down to help Allie up. Her focus remained straight ahead. Lucas's eyes followed her line of sight to see the same person about two yards in front of them.

Allie helped herself up, her eyes frozen to the person wandering down the path in their direction.

"Annabelle," Allie and Lucas whispered almost simultaneously. With each step, Annabelle was closer to them. But as they gained speed, Annabelle fell to her knees.

"Help me," Annabelle whispered. Allie's heart broke as she watched Annabelle fall to the snow. Her body remained motionless and Allie's thoughts went wild.

Lucas reached Annabelle first. On his knees, he lifted Annabelle's head onto his lap. He cupped his hands around her face and felt tears fall from his eyes.

"Annie? Open your eyes, Annie," he whispered through his tears. Lucas couldn't help but notice the state of Annabelle's clothing. Her pants and shirt were destroyed beyond the damage they had yesterday. Maybe when she fell? Lucas didn't want to even think about the possibilities.

Allie collapsed next to her sister-in-law's seemingly lifeless body. Taking what felt like hours to look over Annabelle's emaciated body Allie noticed the terrible condition her sister-in-law, her best friend, was in. Annabelle's face was bruised and sunken in; dark circles under her eyes. Her lips were cracked and bleeding; chapped from the cold weather. Her arms and legs were bruised and boney from her sudden, forced weight loss. Allie's eyes finally fell upon a wooden object protruding from her side.

Taking a deep breath, Allie reached out for Annabelle's hand. Allie felt a heavy rock sitting in her stomach. Rage, nausea, heartache, uncertainty; emotions pierced Allie's heart.

Annabelle's eyes opened suddenly. She pushed them away, her eyes frightened. Lucas put his hands on either side of her face.

"Annie, look at me. It's okay. No one is going to hurt you." Lucas spoke sternly. Annabelle's face was terrified.

"I d-didn't want him to h-hurt me. I d-didn't f-fight back." Annabelle's words were choked with her tears. "I just let h-him do it again."

Lucas looked down at her, confused.

"Let who do what again?" Allie questioned anyone who would answer. She looked up at Lucas, then down at Annabelle.

Lucas focused on Annabelle's humiliated expression. The same expression she had after Dolan had sexually assaulted her. A painful light went off in Lucas's mind.

"Who?" Allie questioned.

"Annie? Where did he go?" Lucas was suddenly paranoid about the surrounding area and who was lurking in the woods.

"He just left me, left me…" Annabelle's voice faded away. Her eyes closed again, not responding. Her body went limp in his arms.

"Annie?" Lucas called, turning her face towards him. Tears streamed down his cheeks. Lucas looked down at Annabelle with a pained look on his face. His body shook with fear. Allie stiffened, taking a deep breath in. She needed to be the strong person in this situation. She wiped her tears.

"We have to get her to the hospital. She needs to go to the hospital." Allie shuddered. She watched as Lucas took his coat off and wrapped it around Annabelle. Leaning forward, he tucked her head into his chest and slid his arm under her legs to pick her up. Allie put her hand on his arm.

"Let me carry her. You don't have the strength. You're going to hurt yourself more if you try and carry her all the way to the truck." Allie felt her tears break her voice. Lucas looked up at her; his eyes were overcome with pain as he nodded. Allie gently tucked her arms under Annabelle's neck and knees. The wood that protruded from Annabelle's side sent a wave of nausea through Allie's mind. Taking a deep breath through her nose, she pushed through it and stood up. As the trees past, paying no attention to her surroundings, Allie focused on keeping her footing on the uneven, snowy ground. Lucas led Allie back through the woods to the truck without any delay.

"The keys are in my pocket," Allie told Lucas. Lucas grabbed the end of the keychain that stuck out of Allie's pocket. He unlocked the truck and looked at Allie. She was thinking the same thing. "Get in the back seat; I'll lay her across your lap."

Lucas didn't waste any time, he swung the door open and pushed himself to the other side. Allie gently lifted Annabelle into the back seat. As Lucas held his arms out to cradle Annie's head, he felt his ribs ache violently. Taking her head in his lap, he winced with a grunt.

"Are you okay?" Allie asked concerned. He lied with a nod. Allie handed him a blanket to keep Annabelle as warm as possible.

After getting Lucas and Annabelle situated in the back seat, Allie got into the driver's seat and turned the truck around. Using her instinct and memory, Allie navigated through the woods, back to the main road. Allie reached for her cell phone and dialed Billy-Jean. As the phone rang, she looked at the clock and saw 8:43am.

"Hello?" Billy's voice was alarmed.

"Billy, we found her. We are taking her to the hospital. Please call Evan. He'll know how to tell his parents." Allie spoke just as fast as her heart pounded.

"Is she okay, Allie?" Billy questioned, hoping for the best. Allie didn't answer. "Allie? Is she okay?" Billy's voice broke.

"I don't know," Allie answered softly. Tears streamed down both women's faces. Allie caught her breath and said, "Please call Evan."

-

"Okay," Billy cried and hung up the phone. Ronnie stood behind her, waiting for her to tell him something.

"Well?" he finally asked. Billy's face was pale and stunned.

"They are taking her to the hospital." Her voice was quiet. She shook her head and took a deep breath. "I have to call Evan."

-

Lucas watched as Annabelle's eyes flickered. He waited for Annabelle to look at him, but instead, Annabelle's eyes closed again. Lucas rubbed his thumb across her checks, avoiding her wounds. He held her hand with his other hand.

"Annabelle?" Lucas begged. Annabelle suddenly began to breathe heavily. Her face was twisted in pain and Lucas tried to get her to look at him. Annabelle gasped for air.

"Please, don't do this to me Annie."

I opened my eyes slowly, afraid to see what waited for me on the other side of my thin eye lids. The bright light shined into my sensitive eyes. I blinked twice before I gave up. My eyes remained closed while I tried to remember what happened. *That's when I felt the pain.*

Death... Was I dead? *You can't be alive...* I felt exhausted, completely drained of all energy, hope and thoughts. *That's when I felt the pain.*

I felt a person's hand in mine. I tried to move my fingers in this person's hand. I tried to open my eyes to look and see this person's face. Nothing worked. I felt helpless and trapped in my own body.

You know you're dead, there's no way you could have survived. Survived? Why did I need to survive? Did something so torturous happen that I needed survival? *You don't remember?* No, what was I missing? *That's when I felt the familiar pain.*

Familiar pain ripped through my body as I was jolted to life. Air hit my lungs, cold and brisk. The burn of the hot blood in my veins rushed over my body. The mixture of oxygen and blood ran its course through my limbs, filling them with warm circulation. I gripped the surface underneath me with a great pressure that I never knew my body was capable of.

"Annabelle?" The familiar voice cried out, hopeful.

I couldn't speak. The blood had not reached my voice. I could not find my voice. *There's not enough blood to go around.* I've lost blood, but how? *Remember... That's when I felt the pain.*

"Please, don't do this to me Annie," the voice begged through obvious tears. It was familiar to hear this person's voice. It was familiar to feel their touch on my hand. Who, who is this familiar person? *That's when I felt the pain.*

I moved my hand to my right side, feeling for the source. *Remember...* I felt the object protruding from my body. The sticky, warm area around the protrusion reminded me of my loss of blood. I tightly squeezed my eyes shut and opened my mouth, gasping for help.

The blood pounded through my chest. I felt the warmth run up my neck and into my face. I opened my mouth again and let out a scream of torture. My voice filled my head and my ears with a high pitched shrill.

"Annie, please open your eyes and look at me," the voice begged again.

I wanted so desperately to open my eyes and recognize the person who begged for my presence. I forced myself to open my eye lids. I struggled with the simple task while a brilliant light attacked my eyes. I didn't dare blink this time; too afraid to never open my eyes again.

"Annabelle?" The familiar voice choked. I moved my eyes slowly to try and focus on the face that hovered above me. I gripped their hand as tight as I could. I felt another hand brush my cheek and saw the figure move closer to my face.

Lucas. *It's a figment of your imagination.* His face came into focus. I felt tears burn into my eyes. I held his hand tightly to my chest. I watched as he cried above me. He didn't say anything for a long time. It didn't bother me. I was just happy to see his face. *He's not real.* I didn't care. It comforted me to see him.

"Annie, I'm so sorry," Lucas whispered. I looked at him strangely, furrowing my eyebrows at him. My voice was lost.

I was lying in the back seat of a truck. Lucas, the only person I could see, was not driving. A blanket was wrapped around my body, the warmth sent shivers up my spine. Lucas tucked the edges closer to my chin, rubbing his hand up and down my arms.

I looked back at him, hoping it wasn't a dream. He watched me with a pained look on his face. Something was wrong, he wasn't okay. *Annabelle, you need to focus on yourself.*

That's when I felt the pain. I gritted my teeth and let out a strange noise of anguish. I felt my breaths quicken and my heart pound. Lucas looked at me helplessly and ran his hand over my face. Another voice entered my mind.

"Hold on Annabelle, we are only ten minutes away," Allie's voice called from the front of the truck. More tears forced their way out of my eyes. Lucas looked at me, lost for words.

He reached for something and brought a bottle of water to my lips. He put his hand underneath my head and lifted to help me drink. The water ran down my dry throat with a vengeance. After one swallow, I closed my mouth, refusing the water. *That's when I felt the pain.*

"Please drink Annie. You need water," Lucas begged again. I closed my eyes and shook my head slowly. I pointed at my throat. He sighed and set the bottle down.

I tucked my face into his chest, taking another shallow breath in. I clung to his shirt and prayed this was real. *It's not real, Annabelle. That's when I felt the pain.*

"Rest, Annie. You're okay now," Lucas whispered.

I wanted to believe him. I wanted to believe that this was the end of my suffering. I cried out, feeling the pain of uncertainty.

"I'm not going anywhere," Lucas promised. I closed my eyes again. Exhaustion took over my body.

After what felt like seconds, his hand left mine and my eyes shot open. I searched for him in the pool of strangers that surrounded me. *That's when I felt the pain.*

I let out a scream when one of the people lifted my right side. I squirmed from their grasp. I couldn't speak. I couldn't find my voice.

"I'm right here, Annie," Lucas whispered, holding my hand. "We are at the hospital. They won't hurt you."

They lifted me onto their stretcher, which I now assumed is where they were trying to move me to before. I rested my head on the stretcher as I looked up at the building. A bright red sign read EMERGENCY above the entry. I closed my eyes slightly.

A new voice entered my mind. "Is this Annabelle?" I opened my eyes to see a tall blonde woman standing above me. Allie was talking to her as they pushed me into the hospital. "I've heard about her story."

"We just found her in the woods." Allie's voice was quiet.

"Annabelle? Can you hear me?" the blond asked. My voice continued to hide. I nodded up at her. "My name is Michelle, I'm a nurse. Can you speak, honey?" she questioned. Tears streamed down my cheeks as I shook my head no, that's when I felt the pain.

A panicked feeling ran through my body as Lucas and Allie left my line of sight.

"It's okay, they're right behind us." Michelle smiled. I relaxed, closing my eyes again. My ears continued to listen to the area that surrounded me. Was I still dreaming?

"Lucas?" I heard Allie's voice from behind us. "Lucas? What's wrong?" My eyes opened as the stretcher stopped.

"Lucas?" I heard Michelle's voice this time. "He passed out. Has he been ill?"

My heart pounded in my chest, I needed my voice. I panicked when I realized I was strapped down.

"His ribs, he injured his ribs," Allie answered Michelle.

"Macie, get him a wheelchair," Michelle called.

"Lucas?" I cried. My voice was silent. I tried again, pushing my voice out of my body, "Lucas?"

"Relax Annabelle." Allie came to my side. I looked up at her and shook my head. She watched me struggle with my emotions.

"What happened?" I assumed that was Macie's voice. I looked up at Allie with wide eyes.

"It's okay Anna; he's going to be fine. Relax." Allie ran her hand down my arm.

Allie watched my expression. I felt the blood drain from my face. My breaths quickened and I felt my heart break in two. I knew I needed to relax, but I couldn't control myself. Panic developed and I began to cry.

"Annabelle, calm down honey," Michelle told me, returning to my side. I shook my head.

"Anna, hey, slow down. It's okay. You're okay." Allie's hand found my face and I looked back at her face. She smiled. "Calm down."

My breaths were rapid and my heart pounded. I knew I was hyperventilating. I couldn't catch my breath and control my nerves. He is my light…

"Anna…." Allie's voice faded out. I looked up at the ceiling as the edges of my vision blurred. Devastation settled into my chest.

"Anna, please calm down," Allie's voice reminded me. I felt my breaths slipping away from me. The darkness consumed me. *That's when you felt the pain.*

I felt pressure on my forehead when someone pulled open my right eye lid and shined a light at me. I flinched away from their touch and my body felt heavy. I tried to move my arms but they didn't respond to my brain.

"Annabelle?" a man's voice beckoned. I squeezed my eye shut tightly. *Hector is back...* I desperately gasped for air, using all my energy to cry out. "Annabelle?" the voice was loud and close. *Hector is close by...* I flinched again at the sound of my name.

"Dr. Morris, stop it. It's your voice," a gentle woman's voice scolded. "Anna, I'm Macie, you're in the emergency room."

I opened my eyes slowly to see a young woman standing above me. Her gloved hand rested on my shoulder and her face was bright. She smiled at me.

"What..." I whispered but my voice broke and pain rushed through my body. I screamed in torture. It felt like my side was being crushed by a boulder.

"Stop," the man's booming voice, who I now knew to be Dr. Morris, ordered. "She needs to be taken to surgery. Don't try and cut it any shorter. Let surgery handle that."

"Her pulse is dropping to 52, 50... Her oxygen level is 83." Another woman's voice spoke from beside me. CT, hypothermia, TBI, hematomas, MRI, pneumonia, bilateral fractures; meaningless words and letters filled my head.

A sudden movement caused me to flinch again. The nurse, who identified herself as Macie, pushed an oxygen tube in my nose and a cold, crispy air blew through my nostrils. A feeling of relief surrounded the pressure in my chest. The pain in my chest, however, remained.

I let out another moan, this time I reached out for the person closest to my hand. Raged breaths, followed by cries of pain filled the room. I cried softly.

"You're in good hands, Annabelle. Try to relax," Macie reminded me.

Relax? How was I supposed to relax when I felt my insides twist painfully and my head pound loudly? I closed my eyes tightly. I let another whimper leave my lips.

"Annabelle?" a voice filled the room that stopped my heart.

I cried, reaching out with my left hand. A warm, strong hand enveloped mine. I opened my eyes to see my brother standing beside me. His eyes were sad, red and he looked as though he'd been crying. Tears immediately filled my eyes, blurring my vision. I cried out loud.

"I'm right here." Evan was standing above me, tears resting on his eye lids. He held onto my hand tightly.

The pain surged through my body again, causing my muscles to twitch and tense. Evan stood by, watching helplessly. The nurses and doctors ran around the room, adding things to my IV and poking my arms with needles. I tried to cry out again but I choked on my words. Bile worked its way up my throat and into my mouth. I began to choke and gasp.

"She's vomiting," called one of the nurses that surrounded me. Immediately, my body was being pushed to the left, causing the vomit to leave my mouth. I cried out as I vomited in to a bucket, feeling completely feeble and humiliated.

They turned me to my back and Evan's face was different. He was pale and clammy. His hands were sweaty and cold.

"Are you all right, sir?" Macie asked Evan. Her hand rested on Evan's shoulder and she patted him on the back. "You need to go have a seat in the hallway. Deep breaths through your nose," Macie explained, pushing him out the door of the trauma room.

He was gone. My eyes begged to Macie. She smiled and touched my arm gently.

"Anna?" a voice called from the other side of room. I looked to my right and saw Allie approach the bed. Her demeanor was just as bad as Evan's; pale, crying and sweaty.

She smiled and leaned over to kiss my forehead. "Your parents are on their way, Anna." I tried to ask a question, when someone touched the right side of my rib cage. I screamed, almost directly into Allie's face.

"What are you doing?" Allie snapped at the nameless nurse. She went pale at the tone of Allie's voice. Allie rested her hand on the bed near my head. She looked nervous to be in the same room as me, afraid to break my fragile body.

I felt tears burn my frozen cheeks as I began to realize the possibility of seeing my family again. I took a breath, looking up at Allie. I opened my mouth to speak, crying out loud.

194

"What is it, Anna? Tell me." One of Allie's hand closed around mine and her other found the side of my face.

Braving all the pain it would take, feeling my thoughts all jump at once to be heard. One begging fear ran to the front of my head and pushed everything else aside. I opened my mouth and through my tears, I cried, "I don't want to die."

Allie's face turned to panic. Her eyes began to well up with tears and she put both hands on either side of my face. Through her tears she sternly said, "Don't even think about that. You are strong, Annabelle. You can get through this."

I heard her words, but her eyes said something different. She spoke confidence, but her eyes read worry. I let tears continue to fall from my eyes and she leaned down to kiss my forehead.

"Surgery is ready for us. We have to go, now." Dr. Morris immediately left the room.

It was a sudden chaos that surrounded my bed. Allie was pushed aside and I never got to ask my question. I never got to ask her about Lucas. I reached into the air where she had been standing.

The stretcher moved faster than my eyes could follow. Dizziness caused me to shut my eyes and I gave up searching for Allie.

The journey to surgery was short and quiet. I kept my eyes closed, waiting for someone to tell me what was going on. The hallways were bright on the other side of my eye lids. I heard the doors open and we moved over a small threshold.

"Annabelle, we are on the elevator." Macie's voice warned. *Duh, lady.*

"Mm hmm…" I moaned too exhausted to form words.

We arrived in the operating room and were greeted by a team of people. I kept my eyes closed and listened to the words and conversations around me.

Nothing made sense. The words they spoke, the statements they made. Everything was starting to blur. I knew the IV fluid and whatever medicines they were giving me began to run their course on my body.

"Annabelle, we are going to be putting you under a general anesthetic. In a few hours, we will bring you back out of the surgery. After the anesthesia wears off, Dr. Morris will be there to greet you. Do you have any more questions?" the woman asked, her mouth covered with a mask.

I was exhausted; too exhausted to open my eyes, let alone ask a question. The darkness filled my thoughts.

"What is his name?" a female asked urgently.

"Lucas Martin," another female voice answered.

Darkness surrounded his mind as if it was trying to keep him from the reality of the situation. Lucas remained still. His body throbbed in a dull pain. His chest began to rise and fall in a hurried pace.

"Lucas, can you hear me? My name is Michelle, I'm a nurse. You are in the emergency room," the first female explained.

Lucas continued to lay motionless, his eyes closed. Michelle continued to talk to him as if he answered her. Lucas felt his heart ache painfully for the woman he desperately wanted to be with. He couldn't hear her breathing, her heart beating or feel the warmth of her body next to his. She was fading away from the world without him.

"I have to go." His words were sudden, muffled by the oxygen mask.

Michelle looked down the young man, startled by his voice. "You have to stay here, sir. You need to stay still. You are dehydrated and-" Michelle began before Lucas cut into her statement.

"Where is she?" he questioned louder, opening his eyes for the first time.

"Who?" Michelle questioned.

"Annie, where is she?"

"The women you came in with are in the trauma room. Don't worry about that right now, you need to relax," Michelle reminded him.

Exhausted, Lucas closed his eyes again feeling anxious not being by her side. Tears streamed from his eyes; guilt and pain surfaced. His physical pain suddenly worsened as he yelled through the oxygen mask. Darkness surrounded his mind.

Waking up with a heavy chest, Lucas opened his eyes to find himself in a different surrounding. The room was dark and quiet. The beeping of a monitor close by kept his mind occupied momentarily. The sound of someone entering the room startled him, his breath catching in his throat.

"Oh, you're awake," a smiling woman commented as she turned a dim light on. He suddenly realized he was no longer in the emergency room; he was in a hospital room instead. He tried to sit up, shifting his body as pain struck violently. He growled in frustration.

"Just relax, nothing to get worked up over. You are going to need all the rest you can get," the nurse explained, checking the monitor next to his head. He squinted at her nametag; reading Gretchen, RN.

Gretchen smiled at him in silence. Suddenly, tears fell from his eyes as he thought of Annabelle. Lucas took another breath, feeling the pressure in his chest.

"You are going to be sore for a couple days. Broken ribs are not an easy healer," Gretchen commented looking down at him.

Lucas finally spoke quietly. "I need to find Annabelle." She smiled.

"I know you feel that way right now, but I'm sure you will see her soon."

"You don't understand what I'm saying. She is in this hospital, dying." Lucas shut his eyes tightly and added, "because of me." He clenched his teeth together tightly.

Gretchen looked at him sympathetically. Lucas explained the situation briefly. Gretchen's smile faded into a sunken, faded look of disappointment.

"I need to make sure she is okay." Lucas whined, tears streaming slowly down his cheeks.

"You are lucky to be alive." She spoke loudly.

"I need to find out where she is."

"You can find this girl when you are strong enough to stand on your own. Until then, stay in bed and call me when you need me." Gretchen said, quickly pausing to look at the distressed look on her patient's face, "Lucas, will it make you happy if I checked to see where Annabelle was in the hospital?"

"Please." He coughed loudly. "I need to know if she's okay."

"Rest." Gretchen turned to leave the room. "I'll be back to check on you," she called as she closed the door. Within two minutes, Gretchen appeared at the foot of his bed.

"There is a woman here to see you."

"Where is she?" Marie Rockart greeted her son with a panicked expression on her face. Mark stood close behind his wife, waiting for an answer.

"They took her to surgery," Evan told his parents with a somber tone. They both took in a sharp breath in. Without another word, they sat down next to Allie and Billy. Billy had her right hand tightly wrapped around Allie's left. Allie's face was blank, tear stained and pale.

"How was she?" Marie asked to anyone who would answer.

"She is…" Evan began quietly, "in bad shape."

Marie held her breath. She didn't want to hear the rest. Marie looked at her daughter-in-law. She felt her heart break with the sight of Allie's face. Marie set her purse down in her chair and knelt down in front of Allie.

"Allie?" Marie spoke softly to Allie. Allie continued her blank stare, never hearing her mother-in-law. "Allison, look at me." Marie took her hand and placed it on Allie's cheek.

Marie's warm hand caused Allie's eyes to well up with tears. Allie looked into Marie's eyes and immediately began to cry.

"I'm so sorry, Marie." Allie cried.

"Allie, stop apologizing to me!" Marie scolded with tears now falling from her own eyes. "I don't blame you for this. How could I? You have nothing to do with this." Marie hugged Allie tightly. "I should be thanking you."

Marie pulled away from Allie and looked into her eyes. "You brought my little girl home." Marie smiled with tears streaming down her cheeks. "Thank you, Allie."

Evan sat down next to his father.

"How bad?" Mark questioned in a low tone.

"Dad, I've never seen Annabelle's face so drained of life. She might have lost twenty pounds. Her face is covered in marks and bruises…." Evan's voice turned into rage.

"Relax," Mark reminded his son. "Be calm for Anna right now. We'll deal with the man another day. Right now, stay focused on your sister."

Mark told his son to stay calm while his emotions raged inside of his head. He was furious with whoever did this to his little girl. He would find this person and make them beg for death. Mark had to control himself right now, for his entire family.

"I need to go for a walk," Allie announced, walking out of the small waiting area. Once she was far enough away from her family, Allie found a service desk. The round desk sat in the middle of a large lobby area. High vaulted ceilings created an echo with each step Allie took.

"How can I help you?" the young woman at the desk asked with an annoyed smile.

"I was wondering if you could help me find a patient." Allie spoke softly, afraid to cause too much noise in the big open room.

"Sure, what is the patient's name?" the woman began to type something into her computer.

"Lucas Martin," Allie answered, still whispering. After Annabelle had gone to a trauma room, Allie had lost track of Lucas.

Allie waited as the employee typed the name into her computer. She tapped her finger in the mouse once or twice before she asked, "What is his date of birth?"

Allie's heart dropped. "Actually, I'm not sure."

"Okay, we asked to make sure we have the right patient." The woman rolled her eyes and grabbed a visitor pass from the drawer. She quickly scribbled a number and handed Allie the sticker. "Hold on to that, the nurse should ask for it. If you use these elevators behind me and take them to the second floor, follow the hallway to the right and it's the last room on the left. Room 213."

Allie tried to take in the information she had just been given as fast as possible. Instead of asking her to repeat the directions, Allie decided to figure it out on her own.

"Thank you," Allie told the clerk as she walked past the desk.

Allie pushed the up arrow and waited for the elevator to pick her up. She shoved her hands into the pockets of her jacket and shivered nervously. What would she say to him?

The elevator opened and three women, all dressed in dark green scrubs exited the small closed space. Allie walked onto the elevator quickly, holding the door for a woman with a stroller.

"What floor?" Allie questioned the mother.

"Three, please," she answered, never looking up from her phone.

Allie pressed two and three and waited for the elevator to move. The ride was silent and quick. Allie was relieved of the awkward silence when the doors opened on the second floor.

She looked up at the sign and remembered to follow the hallway to the right. Allie walked down the white walled hallway as she heard sounds of beeping monitors and the shuffling of papers at the nurse's desk.

Allie reached a dead end and tried to remember which direction she was supposed to go.

"Can I help you find something, officer?" a woman asked as she walked by. Allie had forgotten she had her uniform on.

"Room 213." Allie smiled. The nurse pointed to the right.

"It's going to be the last room on the left." The nurse continued on her way in the opposite direction.

"Thank you," Allie called after her.

Allie walked down the hallway, trying to figure out what to say to this complete stranger. She approached the room labeled 213. The door was cracked open and Allie could hear the nurse talking.

"You are lucky to be alive." She spoke loudly.

"I need to find out where she is." A low, male's voice spoke. He sounded exhausted, his voice was rough.

"You can find this girl when you are strong enough to stand on your own. Until then, stay in bed and call me when you need me." She spoke as if she was his mother. There was a pause. "Lucas, will it make you happy if I checked to see where Annabelle was in the hospital?"

"Please." He coughed loudly. "I need to know if she's okay."

"Rest." The nurse's voice was closer to the door. "I'll be back to check on you."

The door opened and Allie was startled when a woman dressed in dark green scrubs with wild blond, curly hair exited the room.

"Can I help you, ma'am?" she questioned with a wide, white smile.

"I... umm... is this Lucas Martin's room?" Allie stumbled with her thoughts.

"Yes, it is. How do you know Mr. Martin?" the nurse questioned curiously.

"I am... I am Annabelle's sister-in-law." Allie spoke softly. She felt like the nurse would understand who Annabelle was by the conversation she just overheard. "Could I speak to him?"

The nurse eyed Allie for a moment. She slipped back into the room and left Allie standing in the hallway. The door closed tightly

201

behind the nurse, leaving Allie in silence. Allie stood nervously in the hallway, waiting for the woman to return. A few minutes passed before the wild-haired nurse returned.

"Go on in." She smiled, holding the door open for Allie.

Allie walked into the dark hospital room with a nervous stomach. She wasn't sure what to say to the young man.

"Hello." She sat down near the head of his bed.

"Is she okay?" Lucas questioned, skipping straight to the point. Allie looked at him, his face was hopeful.

"She's in surgery. We don't know anything," Allie explained. Lucas's face went from hopeful to dead in a second. He turned his head away from her, looking out the window.

"What did they say about you?" Allie wondered about his condition.

"Dehydration, pneumonia, cracked ribs," Lucas listed off his diagnosis. Allie watched him struggle with tears that threatened to fall.

"You are the reason she is alive," Allie pointed out.

"I should have given my life to save her from what she went through. I'm no hero." Lucas took a breath. "Annabelle shouldn't be in surgery right now, fighting for her life, I should be."

Allie sat quietly, listening to Lucas doubt himself. She wasn't sure what to say to him. Allie could only imagine what Annabelle had been through. She pushed the thought away. Lucas looked up at Allie.

"I love Annabelle. I would give anything to see her. I would give my life to make and keep her safe. It sounds crazy and completely impossible, but it's the truth."

Allie watched as this man she barely knew poured his heart out to her. She had spent the day searching the woods with this young man and she definitely understood he had feelings for Annabelle.

"Why?" Allie inquired, curiosity getting the best of her.

"I love her because she treats me like a human being. Annabelle is the only person who has ever spoken to me like I have feelings. She listens to me and she trusts me." Lucas struggled with his breaths again. After catching his breath he added, "Something pulls me to her, something inside of me feels right when I'm with her. She makes me feel needed, wanted and loved."

Allie watched as Lucas's eyes lit up when he talked about his feelings for Annabelle. Allie felt like she just stepped into a fairytale. How could they possibly be in love after two weeks?

Realizing she barely knew Lucas, a question popped into her mind. "Lucas, do you have anyone I can call?"

Allie felt compelled to do something for this *child* sitting in front of her. He was so young, so vulnerable, and so alone. He had found the only thing that kept him sane, Annabelle. Lucas shook his head no. Allie swallowed hard; she needed to do something for this seemingly orphaned child.

"Lucas, I have an offer for you." Allie smiled, thinking of the best way to protect this young man and keep him close to Annabelle.

- 23- Annabelle: Waking Up

I felt like I was floating. It was like the feeling you get as a child after you've spun around really fast and fall to the ground. I was lying flat on my back in a bed. I couldn't open my eyes. My eyelids felt like cement curtains over my eyes.

My head was spinning. I couldn't remember where I was. What happened? *What day was it?* Where was my family? My heart pounded with fear.

I tried to move my body, nothing responded. I couldn't feel my arms or legs. I squeezed my eyes tightly, searching my brain for answers. What happened? I felt a tear slip out of my eyes.

I took a deep breath in and felt the cold air of the oxygen tube in my nose and the sore, dry feeling in my throat. I needed a drink of water. I wasn't sure if anyone was near me, I couldn't hear anything. *Open your eyes, Annabelle.*

I struggled with the thought of opening my eyes. I squinted slightly, slowly opening my eyes. The bright florescent lights reached my eyes quickly. I blinked several times to adjust to the light.

The white ceiling was a welcoming sight. The thought of electricity and a solid structure warmed me. I looked around the room, never moving my neck. The room was small and enclosed by two glass sliding doors. The room had three chairs lining the walls. Coats hung loosely around the back of each chair. *No one is here...*

I could see people outside of my glass doors. I thought about a way to get their attention. Call button, *you're in a hospital room.* I looked at the railing of the bed to see a little red button. I wiggled my left fingers slightly, noticing a pain in the middle of my palm. I slowly reached out for the button with my left index finger. I pressed the button and waited.

Three people standing outside my room all turned in my direction. One man and two women rushed in.

"Annabelle?" the male's voice was deep and he was dressed in khakis and a long white jacket. The name on the jacket said, *Dr. James Morris, MD.*

"Honey, do you know where you are?" the blond nurse questioned.

"Do you know what year it is?" Dr. Morris continued to question.

"Good Lord, give the girl a break." The second nurse, a red headed, stocky woman, reached for a glass of water with a straw floating in it. She brought the straw to my lips and I took a drink. The ice cold water hugged each crevice of my mouth. As I swallowed, the pain quickly disappeared. She pulled the glass away and set it back down in the table.

"Annabelle, you've suffered a traumatic brain injury. I spoke to you four days ago before you were taken to surgery. We originally thought you suffered a concussion. However, after a CT scan, your brain showed signs of swelling in the frontal lobe. We placed you in a medically induced coma for the past four days," Dr. Morris explained. "Your last CT scan was taken about six hours ago. The swelling has significantly subsided. After we discovered this, we took you off the ventilator. That was about five hours ago." The doctor took breath. "Unfortunately that is just the tip of the iceberg, with your list of injuries and the serve hypothermia, it's truly a miracle you're awake."

This information hit me like a tidal wave. I had been asleep for four days. *What did you miss?* Where is my family? My heart ached at the thought of my family and the panic they must be in. But could I have suffered such an injury… *injuries…* and not remember what happened? My memory was blank. Why am I in the hospital? *What happened?*

"Your family should be back soon. They stepped out to call family members that you were taken off the ventilator," the red headed nurse explained.

I closed my eyes in exhaustion. My right arm was in a sling, wrapped tightly to my body. I moved my right hand to feel the bandages that were wrapped around my side. My chest ached with each breath. I moved my left hand to feel my left cheek, another bandage rested on my cheek bone.

"Would you like me to explain what we did?" Dr. Morris questioned.

I opened my eyes to look at him. The red headed nurse remained in the room, the blonde nurse had left.

"Well your left cheek bone was fractured; we did a small reconstructive surgery to rebuild the bone. It will heal and you'll look like new, minimal scarring. Your right shoulder was dislocated which is why it is in a sling. That will be sore for a week or so but you'll be able to use it in a few days.

"We removed three inches of a wooden post from your right side. The angle that you fell onto the post missed your vital organs and we were able to sew you back up; good as new. You did dislocate your right hip which is why you're in a brace. You have five broken ribs; three on the right, two on the left that punctured your lung, which was also repaired in surgery."

I stared at the doctor with wide eyes. *What else did you expect, Annabelle, a few cuts and bruises?* I wasn't sure what I was expecting him to say, but that wasn't it. I blinked several times, adjusting my mind slowly to the fact that I had fallen. *Are you sure?* He just said I fell... right?

"I know this is a lot to take in, but we will take everything one day at a time. Recovery, rehabilitation, and therapy are things that cannot be rushed," Dr Morris explained. "You'll spend a day or two in ICU, once you're strong enough, you'll be moved to a regular hospital room in our rehabilitation wing." Dr. Morris continued to read his charts, muttering things out loud.

I tuned him out, tears burned my eyes. I couldn't go home. *Not for a while...* I wanted to go home. I needed my family, my bed, my home. I let my tears escape. My eyes begged to close, exhaustion and pain still weighed heavy on my chest.

"Dr. Morris, this is too much for her," the red headed nurse whispered. Dr. Morris stopped and looked up at my tear stained face.

"I'm sorry, Annabelle. This must be a lot of information for you." He placed his clip board down at the end of the counter. He approached my bed. "Are you in any pain right now?"

His questioned lingered in my head for a moment before I answered, "My head..." The two short words were all I could manage. I closed my eyes again.

"Your family is here, Annabelle." The blonde nurse had returned to the doorway.

My heart leaped into my throat when my mother, father and brother walked into my tiny room. Tears streaming down my mother's face caused my eyes to water. She approached my bed with her arms out.

"My Annabelle," she cried. She put her face into my neck, crying into my left shoulder. She kissed my forehead gently and stood next to my bed, holding my hand. She smiled, tears still streaming down her face.

I felt another hand gently touch my right cheek. I turned my head to the right slowly. My dad's face was at my level, smiling widely.

"We are so glad you're home, Anna." My dad let a single tear slide down his cheek. *Home...* This wasn't home. I had to ignore the specifics and focus on my family.

Evan walked around to my left side and kissed my hand. "Good to see you awake, sis."

I felt a slight pain in my right hip, I closed my eyes tightly. The pain was numb and annoying, like a cramp. I took a deep breath.

"Are you okay, Annabelle?" my mom's panicked voice questioned.

I gritted my teeth, feeling the pain worsen.

"This will help that." Dr. Morris spoke up finally. He stepped past my mother and brother and did something that was out of my range of sight. *Pain medicine...*

The numbness set in quickly, the floating sensation occupied my body again. I looked up at my family again, knowing I would lose consciousness soon enough. I gave them a gentle smile as I closed my eyes.

"Sleep, Annabelle. We will be here when you wake up," my mom whispered into my forehead. I fell into a numb slumber.

I felt a warm hand tangled with my left hand. I opened my eyes slowly to see Billy-Jean standing next to my bed. Her face wasn't looking down at me but across the room. I heard a voice, that's when I realized that Evan and Allie were also in the room. I noticed that Billy wasn't smiling. I closed my eyes again to listen.

"They released him today." Allie spoke first. *Who?*

"That soon?" Billy's voice questioned.

"What did you expect?" Allie asked.

"Thought they would keep him for more than four days," Billy sighed.

"I picked him up at noon." *Pick him up? Who?*

"It's nice of you guys to let him stay with you for a while," Billy added.

"It's the least we could do," Allie commented.

"Are you going to let him see her tomorrow?" Billy asked.
Who's him? Who's her?

"I don't see what it could hurt." Evan added, "The doctor told him to rest for a few days, but I know we won't be able to keep him away for much longer."

The room was silent. I waited silently to see if their conversation would continue. *Eavesdropping is not normal for you...* I ignored the voice in my head.

"Do you think she'll talk to him?" Billy's voice was whispered.

"What?" Evan questioned.

"Do you think he can get her to talk? She hasn't said anything to us," Billy whispered, her voice cracking with tears. A sudden pain struck my body. I felt tears beg to fall behind my eyelids.

"Would you want to talk after what she's been through?" Allie questioned.

What I had been through? Why is everyone acting like I had died and come back to life? The room fell painfully silent. I knew I couldn't hold my tears much longer. I let out a small whimper, shifting slightly in my bed.

"Anna?" Billy's voice called. "Annabelle, can you hear me?"

I felt my tears fall, my breaths left my mouth with rapid speed. A pain deep in my chest made me gasp loudly. The burning in my lungs continued as I cried out loud.

"Annabelle? What's wrong?" Evan questioned. I felt his hand on my right cheek. "Look at me."

I opened my eyes to see a blurry figure standing above me. I couldn't tell which direction was up, the room spun. I quickly closed my eyes again a let out another whimper.

"I'll get her nurse." Allie ran from the room.

"Anna, look at us. What's wrong?" Billy questioned me.

I shook my head, eyes still closed. *Find your voice.* "Lungs," is all I could manage.

"Lungs? Are you having trouble breathing?" Evan asked. I nodded, opening my eyes slightly. The room held still this time but I gasped for air. I could feel the oxygen tube in my nose, but I continued to gasp.

"What's wrong?" The red headed nurse rushed into the small room. Billy let go of my hand and moved out of the way.

"She can't breathe." Evan's voice was panicked.

"Lungs," is again all I could say.

She checked the wires and tubes that left my bed and went to the monitors behind my line of sight.

"Ah ha," she said from behind me, "Your oxygen tube came unplugged."

She must have plugged it back in as she said that. The cold air hit my nose and I took a deep breath in. The relief that came over my chest was incredible. It was as if someone flipped a switch to my oxygen supply.

"Is that better?" the stubby red head asked with a wide smile. I nodded at her. "Good, now that we are settled, I'm Renee. I'll be your nurse. Is there anything I get for you?"

I settled down slightly, feeling the pain in my chest subside tremendously. I shook my head no and she patted my arm gently.

"I'm just a button push away," she added and left the room.

I sighed and looked at Billy. She smiled at me and replaced her hand in mine. She was my best friend. I smiled the best I could back at her. She touched my cheek slightly and kissed my hand.

"I'm so glad you're home." She smiled with tear glazed eyes. There was that word again. *Home...* This wasn't home.

I looked up at Evan and Allie. Evan smiled sweetly at me when my eyes caught the board behind him. *January, 1st*... That's not right. I'm graduating on December 15th, that's in a couple days. Panic shook my body as I felt the hair on my arms stand up.

I opened my mouth slightly. Everyone's attention was on me as they anticipated my words.

"What-" my words horrified me. My voice sounded like another person; low, raspy and broken. I cleared my throat slightly. "What happened to me?"

I saw Allie's reaction first. I will never forget the terrified look on her face as she turned to her husband. Billy-Jean looked down at me, her eyes full of tears.

The room remained silent as Evan and Allie exchanged looks. After another minute and a quick whisper from Allie into Evan's ear, Evan stood up and nodded towards the door to Billy. Billy hesitantly stood up from the side of the bed and kissed my forehead gently. I watched as my best friend and brother left the room, closing the glass door quietly behind them.

Allie approached my bed, sitting in the same spot that Billy-Jean had just been sitting in. I looked up at Allie. Her face looked sunken in and dark circles surrounded her red eyes. Her warm hand held mine firmly. She looked from our hands to my eyes and opened her mouth.

"Anna, do you remember anything that happened? Think really hard."

I closed my eyes and tried to remember the last things that happened to me. I opened my mouth and spoke what came to mind. "I had to work until close. I was locking up the door to the store. There was a truck parked near my car..."

I opened my eyes to look at Allie. She smiled and nodded. Her silence signaled me to keep trying to remember.

"There was a guy." I looked down at my hands. I traced the bandages around my palms silently. The movement felt familiar. I looked back up at Allie.

"Lucas?" Allie questioned.

Lucas... The name was burned into my head. I felt my heart break without knowing why. I couldn't put my feeling into words. I felt sad at the thought of this name.

"Lucas?" I asked. I looked down again, closing my eyes. The dark corners of my memory began to brighten. "Yes, Lucas. He was there. It was his truck. He was acting strange, like someone was watching him."

Without knowing why, these thoughts brought up a question that went unanswered earlier today.

"Allie?" I whispered. "Who are you letting stay with you? Who were you talking about earlier?" My question felt childish. I completely changed the subject and asked the first thing that came to my mind.

"Someone who I owe a huge favor." Allie smiled. "His name is Lucas."

"Is Lucas-" I whispered, stopping myself. I didn't understand the question or why it came to mind. "Is he okay?"

Allie watched me carefully. She smiled. "He's okay."

Sudden warmth ran through my body and I felt a shiver crawl up my spine. *He's okay.* I wanted to understand the sudden relief that filled my body. I couldn't help but feel like I had missed a chapter in the story.

"Allie, what happened to me?" I felt tears fall from my eyes.

Allie began to tell me what happened. She filled in the empty, dark corners of my memory. Nothing made sense. From Hector Martin to the fact that I was in love with a man I barely knew.

I couldn't comprehend the truth. I felt panic hit me as I thought about my graduation.

"I missed graduation," I whispered.

"The college knows what happened. They are mailing you your degree. Don't worry, Anna. Everything had been taken care of."

I closed my eyes, pushing the rest of my tears out of my eye lids. I lifted my left hand to wipe my face dry. I looked down to my right hand and saw stitches. It began to sink in, the amount of injuries that I had.

"We are all so glad to have you home." Allie smiled at me.

That word again....

"This isn't home," I said to her softly. Allie's smile disappeared.

"You're right. But compared to where you were–this is home," Allie reminded me. I took her comment to heart. I felt like something was missing.

Light... I looked around the room to find no windows or sunlight. I felt a bit trapped in this tiny hospital room. It was overwhelming to be thrown from one extreme to another. According to Allie, I had gone from danger to comfort in a matter of a day. I had spent days in an unconscious state, giving myself no time to adjust. The room I was currently in offered me no source of *light.*

"This just doesn't make any sense," I whispered.

"I know you're confused right now Anna, but why don't you rest? Try to take a nap," Allie suggested, sliding off the bed. "Evan and I will be down the hall in the family waiting area. You need to rest."

I nodded to Allie, feeling my eyes beg to close.

"I missed you, Anna." Allie hugged me tightly. I smiled at her and watched her leave the room.

Me too, I thought, thinking about the double meaning to that statement. *Have you found yourself yet, Annabelle?* Not yet, I've only just woken up.

As I fell asleep, images filled my head. The images were graphic, detailed and painful to even remember, I wasn't seeing these images for the first time. The first time I had seen these events, I had lived them. Tortured, humiliated, broken by people, one of which I thought I loved.

As I fell in a painful slumber, the images turned into dreams. They came to life, replaying over and over in my head. Like a movie set on repeat, I relived the hell that I had forgotten. I found security in a man's arms that I never knew I could love. I found pain in the loss of his existence. New questions began to appear in my mind.

As I opened my eyes, new tears slid down my cheeks. Had it all been a dream? Were the dreams delusions? Was I as broken and tormented as I had seen?

Like I was struck by lightning, the memories shot into my body. It was a painful realization of the difference between truth and delusion. I remembered the people who tortured me and the man who saved my life. The man I love.

I never thought it could happen to me.

"Annabelle?" The voice was quiet, whispered. I looked around the room, unsure of who called my name.

Allie appeared in the doorway, Evan close behind her. She smiled sympathetically at me as if she read my mind.

"Why me?" I whispered to her from my tear soaked face. Her smiled turned into a grimace as she closed the space between us. Her arms wrapped around my small, malnourished body. Evan sat on the opposite side of the bed and held my hand gently.

"I don't know why, Anna," Allie whispered into my ear, "But what I do know is that you are safe now. You are never going to go through that pain again. You have people who love you here to protect you, to keep you safe."

"We won't let anything hurt you," Evan added.

I rested my head on Allie's shoulder, letting my tears subside. A sudden question came to mind as my heart ached for a certain person's touch. I sat back and looked at them quietly.

"When can I see him?" I asked, adding, "When can I see Lucas?"

Allie smiled. "Tomorrow."

Friday January, 2nd

I leaned against Billy as she brushed my wet hair. Billy was sitting behind me on the bed, slightly holding my body up. I was weak, unable to sit or stand by myself. The brace on my right hip limited my movement. My right arm rested gently on my side, without the sling and I rested my head on Billy's shoulder tiredly.

Billy rested her chin gently on my forehead, wrapping her arms gently around me. It felt good to be embraced so lovingly. She had just washed my hair for me. It had been the first time in almost three weeks. Allie had helped Billy give me a shower earlier that day. Being unable to move or wash by myself, it was embarrassing to be so helpless. *Would you rather a complete stranger give you a shower?*

Billy and Allie had been at the hospital with me since 8:30 that morning. Around nine o'clock this morning I was moved from ICU and into a regular hospital room. It was now noon. Allie sat across the room in a chair reading the newspaper in her uniform. She had to work in an hour and she wanted to stay as long as possible.

I glanced at the clock. Billy noticed my nervous glance and she smiled. She finished the long braid down my back and helped me lie down in the bed.

"No worries, Ann. He'll be here," Billy reminded me.

Allie looked up at us while she folded her newspaper. She shook her head with a smile.

"Are you tired?" Allie asked. I nodded.

"Rest for a little while, we'll wake you up when he gets here," Billy suggested.

I nodded, closing my eyes again. I was exhausted. I couldn't go for more than a couple hours without taking a nap. Dr. Morris said I should expect this for a couple weeks until I was myself again.

"We'll be back in a little bit. Let the nurse know if you need us, we'll be down the hall in the family room," Billy whispered, closing the door behind her. The family room was on the opposite side of floor from mine. I was put farthest away from the nurse's station for no particular reason.

Glancing around the room, I really looked at where I would be staying. It was painted a pale green. It was a warm color. To my left was a large armchair. It was a pale cream color to match the curtain that covered the floor to ceiling window in the corner to my left. A long, striped couch sat in front of the large window. Straight ahead was another door that led to my own bathroom; a perk that my nurse,

Renee, claimed to have begged for. To the right of the bathroom was the door to the hallway, a door through which I wouldn't leave for a very long time. Directly to my right was another armchair, behind it was a counter lined with cabinets and a sink.

For being a hospital room, it was quite comfortable. Renee explained that unlike the ICU, I could have whatever I wanted to have. Any personal items, pictures, or even food that I wished to have, I could. However, freedom and home were the only two things I truly desired.

I sighed and moved the blanket up to my chin, closing my eyes tightly. I wouldn't admit it, but being alone bothered me. I needed to get used to being by myself at night again.

I began to drift to sleep, feeling the darkness creep into my vision.

After what felt like a few minutes of sleep, I heard the door to my room open. *He's here.* My nerves went wild. Why was I so nervous to see the man I love? *Because you barely know him…* No, I know a lot about him. *Like what?* He is sweet, caring and sacrificing. *Is that enough?*

I pushed my thoughts aside when I heard someone approach my bed on the right. I turned my head to greet whoever entered my room. In the dark shadows of the room, I saw the outline of a man standing next to my bed. I squinted to focus on his face.

"Lucas?" I questioned. No answer. "Evan?" I tried to guess. The male form moved closer, revealing his face. "Dolan…."

Before I had a chance to react, his hands closed around my neck. I gasped for air. I couldn't believe this was happening to me again. *It's a dream…* I put my hands on his wrists, trying to resist his grip. It didn't feel like a dream. I panicked and began to punch his shoulders as I struggled to breathe. *It's a dream…*

I tried to push him away. I had no strength to even faze him. *You need someone else's help.* The red button caught my sight. Letting go of his wrist with my left hand, I struggled to reach for the button. I gasped for air as he pushed harder. I didn't have much time. It was on my finger tips and I grabbed the small device, pushing the button as hard as I could.

"Can I help you?" the nurse's voice rang from the speaker on the wall. I gasped loudly. *Was it loud enough?* "Annabelle?"

I closed my eyes, losing hope. I couldn't believe this was happening. I felt my body twitch as I gasped for air. *Not again…* I had just gotten my memory, my family back. I could only pray someone would come to save me. I would never see the end of this torture.

"Annabelle?" The voice was closer than the speaker on the wall.

A sudden relief came over my exhausted body. I didn't open my eyes as the air filled my lungs. I coughed, gasping the air in sharply. I cried out loud, taking a deep breath.

"Annabelle, open your eyes," the voice begged me. Warm hands touched my cheeks gently. I opened my eyes to look into a pair of familiar blue eyes. I could never forget those eyes. It didn't take me any longer to wrap my left arm around his neck.

"Lucas," I cried inaudibly, holding him close. This couldn't be a dream.

"It's okay, I'm here." He wrapped his arms around my waist, putting his hand on the back of my head. I cried softly into his shoulder, unable to find my voice. My breaths continued to slow their rapid pace as I filled my injured lungs with air.

"Is she okay?" Billy's voice was clearly out of breath. I opened my eyes to look around the room. Lucas was sitting at the edge of my bed, Billy-Jean stood in the doorway.

Lucas looked down at me, searching for an answer. I felt my throat constrict as I looked into his eyes. He took my breath away. I nodded once. I rested my head on his shoulder. It felt right to be in his arms.

Lucas held me tightly. I looked up at him while he talked to Billy. Tuning out their conversation I looked at his face. The sight of his features made my pain go away. His gentle eyes, his forgiving, loving smile, everything about his face made me feel right.

"I'll be right back," Lucas whispered to me, kissing my forehead. I couldn't speak. I put my hand to my throat, feeling the burn of Dolan's hands. Billy sat on the edge of my bed.

"Anna," Billy-Jean lifted my chin to look at her. Her cheek was bleeding. *What happened to her face?*

I touched the side of her face gently.

She shook her head. "No worries, and he looks worse."

"I'll kill her!" I flinched at Dolan's angry voice that shouted from the hall. Billy brought my head into her chest.

215

"He's talking about me. Ignore him, Allie's got him handcuffed," Billy assured me.

"Get off me you stupid woman!" his voice yelled.

"If you don't shut your mouth, I'll shut it for you! There are patients in this hospital!" a woman's voice yelled back.

"You could never make me! I'd like to see you try!" Dolan laughed. His laugh was quickly silenced and the hallway was peaceful.

"How's that?" the woman's voice called, obviously she shut him up.

"You really shouldn't have done that," I heard Allie's voice laugh sarcastically.

"I have too many patients for him to disturb, it had to be done." The woman's voice entered the room. I recognized Renee as soon as her red hair came into view.

"I'm going to step in the hall for a minute to let Renee do her job," Billy told me slipping out of the room. I never had time to object, *probably going to give Dolan a piece of her mind.*

"Did he hurt you?" Renee asked, standing near the monitor to my left. I opened my mouth to speak but she took in a sharp breath, her eyes rested on my neck. I could only imagine what my neck looked like.

"Don't say anything." She shook her head in disgust. She continued to mumble things under her breath and she checked my vitals. "I should have gave him an extra kick in the face, bastard," was the only bit I heard her say. I closed my eyes as she continued her job.

My heart begged to see Lucas again. I needed him with me. I cleared my throat. I needed to find my voice. I thought about my words and looked up at her.

"What's wrong?" she questioned.

"Lucas," I whispered. I wasn't even sure if she heard me. She understood.

"I'll be right back." Renee smiled, patting my left arm lightly.

The room stayed silent as Renee went to get Lucas. I felt my hands shake nervously, anxiously waiting for Lucas to return. I touched my neck gently, wondering what I looked like now. I smoothed my hair slightly, tucking the fallen pieces behind my right ear. I took another deep breath, trying to readjust my position in the bed.

I tried to adjust myself. My right shoulder still ached, preventing me from lifting my body. I tried to turn to my left side, taking my weight off my hip, but I couldn't move my own body. I felt frustrated tears filled my eyes. *Sick of tears...*

"Would you like help?" His voice filled my ears with music. I turned my head to look up at him. The tears fell and I nodded yes.

Lucas approached the bed and slid his right arm behind my back and his left underneath my knees. I put my left arm around his neck and shoulders and he gently lifted my body. When he set me down, I didn't let go of his neck. He looked down at me and took the hint. Lucas sat down on the left side of my bed. I moved my hand to his chest and leaned into his shoulder.

"I missed you," I whispered into his shirt, taking in his scent. I felt him kiss my head.

"I missed you," he returned. He smiled and looked down at me. "You smell amazing."

I smiled at his joke, feeling the laughter escape my mouth. I quickly stopped, feeling the pain in my cheek. I put my hand on my face and looked away from Lucas.

"I'm sorry," he apologized; I shook my head at him.

"It's not your fault." I looked up at him. His blue eyes gleamed back at mine. "I needed to smile." A few tears fell from my eyes, the reasons blurred together. Lucas wiped my cheeks.

"He can't hurt you anymore," Lucas promised.

"He always finds a way." I sulked.

"Don't say that," Lucas scolded softly. I looked down at our hands.

"Don't ever leave me, okay?" I choked on my words, feeling tears fall. Lucas looked at me helplessly.

"Why did you think I would leave?" he questioned, almost sounding offended.

I shook my head, not sure what made me say that. I looked at him with sad eyes. *Will you ever be happy again?* Would I ever be normal again?

"Annie, stop worrying about me leaving. I will never leave you," he promised. His face was true, his eyes were wet with tears and I felt close to him. *I'm warming up to him...*

He moved, sitting with his back against the bed, putting his right arm around my shoulders. I leaned into his shoulder, feeling right at home. *That word...*

"Do you need anything?" Lucas questioned.

"No." I smiled to myself, I held him tighter. "I have everything I need."

<u>Saturday January 3rd</u>

3:25am

The nurse had just left the room after giving Annabelle a dose of pain medicine and checking her vital signs. After the Dolan event, Lucas refused to leave the hospital last night. It played back in his mind.

Billy-Jean and Allie met up with Lucas and Evan as they approached the family area at the end of Annabelle's hallway. Allie hugged her husband tightly and explained that Annabelle was resting.

Lucas smiled nervously at Billy and felt his heart pound in his chest. The excitement of seeing Annabelle again filled his body with a tingling sensation. He longed to hold her in his arms.

A sudden ring from the nurse's station startled Lucas from his thoughts.

"Can I help you?" the clerk asked. A loud rustling sound could be heard. "What's the patient's name in 12?" the clerk asked.

"Annabelle," another nurse responded.

"Annabelle?" the clerk asked over the intercom. No response.

Lucas's thoughts matched Billy's. They both began running down the hallway, Allie and Evan on their heels.

"Annabelle?"Billy reached the door before Lucas did and shouted.

Lucas entered the room as Billy-Jean pulled Dolan off the bed. Dolan reached back and punched Billy in the face, sending her to the floor.

Rage took over his body; Lucas grabbed the back of Dolan's clothes and pushed him up against the wall.

"What's-" Allie's voice stopped at the sight of Dolan Meyer. She took him from Lucas's grip and shoved him out into the hallway.

Coughing, gasping and crying could be heard from the other side of the room. Lucas turned around to see Annabelle curled up in her bed, her eyes closed.

Lucas approached the bed cautiously, afraid to startle her. With his hands, he gently touched her cheeks. "Annabelle, open your eyes," he begged.

He shook the picture from his mind. It was too close for him to handle, regardless if Dolan was in jail or not. He made a promise to keep her safe; he would not break it.

"Madison, time to wake up." Evan smiled as he walked into his little girl's pink bedroom. The curly, blonde four year old sat up in her bed.

"Daddy." Madison stretched. "Do I get to see Auntie today?"

"Yes, you do." Evan smiled. Madison had only talked to Annabelle on the phone.

Madison had a cold after Annabelle woke up from a coma. The doctors suggested keeping Madison home until she was better to prevent Annabelle from getting the virus on top of the pneumonia and her injuries.

"Daddy!" Maddy jumped up in her bed. "Today is my birthday!"

Evan laughed at her enthusiasm. He waited for her to remember on her own. He picked her up off the bed and set her down. "Even the birthday girl can't jump on her bed."

"Why?" Maddy questioned.

"You don't want to fall off and hurt yourself, do you?" Evan pointed out.

A look of astonishment and worry struck Madison's face. "Oh no."

Evan shook his head and patted her on the head. "Good girl. Now, what does the birthday girl want to wear on her special day?"

Madison took her father's hand and pulled him to the closet. He stood to the side and watched as his little girl ran around the closet, chatting up a storm about what colors Auntie would like best. Evan smiled; nodding to her each time she would turn to show him a shirt. Evan secretly held in his nerves. What would Madison think when she saw Annabelle? *How do you explain to a four year old that their aunt can't get out of bed to play?* What kind of questions would Madison ask Annabelle?

"Stop worrying," Allie's voice whispered into his ear. Evan smiled when his wife wrapped her arms around his shoulders. It's like she could hear his thoughts. She kissed his cheek and walked past him.

"Mommy!" Madison squealed showing her a pink dress.

"Madison, it's cold outside. Auntie wouldn't want you to be cold." Allie knew exactly what to say to their daughter. Evan watched his wife and daughter with a hollow smile on his face. *What could today bring?*

At the hospital, Marie sat at the edge of Annabelle's bed. She was brushing her daughter's hair after helping her shower. Annabelle's progress was slow but she could now sit up straight on her own. Marie's back was to Mark, who sat silently in the corner of the room.

Mark and Marie had arrived early that morning to find Lucas sleeping in the chair near Annabelle's head. His hand was tangled in their daughter's hand. Marie pushed her concerns out of her mind when she saw the look in Annabelle's eyes. Annabelle watched Lucas sleep like he was her child. She had a different light to her face when Lucas was in the room. Marie felt uneasy about this connection they held.

"Mark, how does she look?" Marie smiled, standing up from the bed. Annabelle smiled at her father.

"Beautiful, as usual," Mark gushed. Annabelle shook her head at her father and took a deep breath.

"Are you okay?" Marie asked her daughter. With every breath Annabelle took, Marie asked that same question.

"Nervous," Annabelle spoke quietly. Today she was feeling anxious. She hadn't seen Madison in over three weeks.

"Don't be worried," Marie encouraged. Annabelle tried to listen to her mother talk but she felt uneasy. She had felt nauseous and light headed today. Trying to keep the symptoms to herself to prevent worry, Annabelle closed her eyes while her mom continued to speak.

"Marie, let her get some rest before they get here," Mark pointed out. Marie stopped speaking and patted her daughter's arm.

Annabelle silently struggled through her nausea and dizzy spell. She drifted to sleep.

"Now Madison, Auntie is sick and she can't be jumped on," Allie explained in the elevator ride to the third floor.

"Okay, Mommy." Madison clung to the present that she had been holding onto since Christmas. The tag read To: Annabelle. It was a gift that Madison had picked out for her aunt the day after Annabelle went missing. Madison had begged Allie to buy it for Annabelle for days before Allie broke down and bought it. Madison insisted her aunt would *need* it.

As the small family made their way down the long, quiet hallway, they were met by Lucas. He was leaving the family room, a cup of coffee in his hand.

"Mr. Lucas." Madison smiled happily to him as they approached him. Lucas smiled at the three people that had taken him in.

Lucas felt welcomed by Evan and Allie. They hadn't doubted him from day one like Marie and Mark. Madison made his day each time she smiled. He understood Annabelle's love for the little girl.

"Miss Maddy," Lucas responded to the little girl. She hugged his legs with her free arm. He patted her gently on her head.

Evan greeted Lucas with a hand shake. "My parents are here, aren't they?" Evan knew Lucas felt uncomfortable when his parents were around. When Evan told Marie and Mark that he and Allie would be letting Lucas live with them, they nearly died.

Lucas wasn't sure how to talk to Annabelle's parents. He avoided the situation as much as possible. When he woke up this morning, Mark was sitting silently reading the newspaper in Annabelle's room. Mark briefly spoke to say that Marie was helping Annabelle shower. Lucas excused himself and hadn't been back since.

"They've been here for about an hour," Lucas answered as they walked towards Annabelle's room.

Madison stopped at the door and looked up at her parents. She took a deep breath and sighed heavily.

"Wait here," she proclaimed. Allie raised her eyebrows at the little girl and looked at her husband. He shrugged in surrender.

"I don't see what it could hurt," Evan pointed out. Allie shook her head and waved her daughter to go ahead.

Madison took another breath as her mom gave her the okay to go in. She held the gift in her tiny arms. She walked into the quiet room with light footsteps. She saw her grandparents sitting on the couch in the corner of the room. Allie stood in the doorway and signaled her parents to remain quiet. They watched their granddaughter approach the hospital bed. She used the chair that sat near Annabelle's head to get on the side of the bed. She sat down softly, barely making a sound. Madison set the gift in her lap and thought about how to wake up her aunt.

Annabelle was secretly peaking through her eye lids at her niece. She suppressed her laughter as the little girl struggled with her thoughts.

Madison scrunched her nose and giggled when Annabelle tickled her side unexpectedly.

"Auntie, you're supposed to be sleeping," Madison scolded with a tiny giggle.

"How could I sleep when my favorite little woman is here?" Annabelle pointed out.

Allie, Evan and Lucas took the laughter as a sign to come into the room. Lucas stayed behind Allie and Evan as they entered. He stayed close to the door when Evan approached Annabelle's bed.

"I'm glad the mean person brought you back to us," Maddy told Annabelle. The four year old looked up at Annabelle with her green eyes sparkling with tears. Annabelle pulled the little girl close to her chest. Madison wrapped her arms gently around Annabelle's neck.

"I missed you so much," Annabelle whispered into the little girl's hair.

Madison sat up again and said, "I have something for you." Annabelle pushed the button on the side of the railing to reposition the bed to sit up and Madison handed her gift to Annabelle.

"It's your birthday, Maddy. Why are you giving me a gift?" Annabelle smiled, taking the gift.

"You didn't get any Christmas presents," Madison pointed out. "Open it, I picked it out."

Annabelle smiled at the little girl's enthusiasm. She ripped open the Christmas paper slowly as everyone watched silently. As she opened the present, Annabelle's head spun. She needed to lie down. She took a deep breath and continued as if she was fine. *Keep it together, Annabelle.*

Annabelle looked down at the object she subconsciously unwrapped. It was soft to the touch and colorful. It looked like a ball of fabric until Allie grabbed either end and unfolded it. It was a blanket. *Not just any blanket...* It had a picture of the entire Rockart family. It was a picture from last Christmas when Madison was only two years old. Annabelle's eyes watered as she looked at the frozen faces of her family staring back at her.

Annabelle smiled through a wave of nausea. She took in a breath slowly, letting it subside. Lucas noticed Annabelle's deep, concentrated breathing as the room filled with multiple conversations. Annabelle tried to listen, desperately trying to ignore the dizziness that caused her vision to blur.

"She picked it out the day we told her you were missing." Allie smiled slightly, remembering the day vividly. "She wanted to keep you warm and close to your family."

Annabelle looked at her niece with tears in her eyes. "Thank you so much Maddy." Annabelle wrapped her arms around the little girl tightly. Madison smiled and returned the hug. "I love you," Annabelle whispered to her niece.

"Me too Auntie." Maddy pulled away from the hug and continued talking to Annabelle. Annabelle felt her stomach flip painfully. She closed her eyes, still listening to her niece. Annabelle could feel her hands shake. Taking another deep breath, she sat the little girl up with a smile.

"Now it's time to celebrate your birthday, Maddy." Annabelle let Madison turn around and sit next to her in the bed. Allie grabbed a wrapped object from behind her husband. It was a tiny box wrapped in bright pink paper. There was only one thing Annabelle could think to give to her niece on her fourth birthday. Madison looked up at her aunt with a big smile.

"Go ahead, open it," Annabelle told Madison. The little girl ripped into the paper with an excited giggle. Annabelle closed her eyes quickly to take another breath. Lucas watched Annabelle carefully. He knew something wasn't right. Quietly, without anyone noticing, he slid behind Evan and stood near the head of Annabelle's bed.

Madison ripped the pink paper away to see a small silver box. She handed the pink paper to her mother and set the box in her lap. She slowly took the lid off the box and dumped its contents in her lap. Madison picked up the delicate silver chain in her hand and gasped at her aunt.

"It's just like yours!" Maddy pointed at the silver heart charm that dangled from the chain.

"It is mine," Annabelle corrected her. "I'm giving it to you"

Madison smiled widely and hugged her aunt. "Can I put it on?" Annabelle nodded at her. Once again, nausea caught up with Annabelle, taking her breath away, she sighed heavily and let her head rest on her pillow. Madison turned to her mom to put on her necklace.

"Are you okay?" Lucas whispered to Annabelle.

Annabelle looked up at him and smiled. "Yes, I just need to go to restroom." Annabelle felt nausea twist her stomach.

"I'll help you," Allie volunteered. She quickly fastened the necklace around her daughter's neck and lifted the girl up off the bed and set her on the floor.

"Why don't you and I go to the cafeteria and get some cupcakes for everyone?" Mark suggested to his granddaughter. Madison took his hand and smiled.

"We'll be right back auntie!" Maddy smiled as she pulled Mark out the door.

Lucas helped Allie get Annabelle to her feet. With the brace, movement was quite limited. Even the slow movement caused Annabelle's head to spin; she leaned back on Lucas, tiredly closing her eyes.

"What's wrong, Anna?" Allie asked her sister-in-law. Annabelle took another deep breath.

"Light headed." Annabelle took a breath through her nose, blowing it out her mouth slowly.

"Do you feel like you're going to get sick?" Marie asked in a concerned tone.

"I'm not sure." Annabelle opened her eyes.

Annabelle felt the blood pulse through her veins with the next step. A strange sensation came over her body, feeling as though she was going to faint. Her grip on Allie tightened and Lucas held onto her waist. Spots formed in Annabelle's eyes and she felt her knees shake.

"I feel like I'm going to pass out," Annabelle whispered, closing her eyes. Lucas took the initiative to pick her up off the ground. He placed Annabelle back into bed. Allie grabbed a basin from the bathroom.

"What are you doing?" Marie scolded Lucas.

"Ma, relax," Evan said quickly to his mother. Shocked, Marie closed her mouth tightly.

Annabelle put her hand to her mouth, feeling her throat tighten. Allie pulled Annabelle's hair back, holding it away from her face. Allie rubbed Annabelle's back softly as she vomited. Lucas felt crowded around the bed. He took a deep breath as he passed Evan who stood at the end of the bed. Evan patted his back as he walked by and said, "Relax," to his mother before she said anything. Marie tightened her mouth again and pushed passed Evan to the head of the bed.

"Your mother hates me." Lucas spoke softly, feeling out of place.

"Give her time. She doesn't understand yet," Evan encouraged. Lucas sat down on one of the chairs and ran his hands through his hair.

"It's okay, Anna," Marie told her daughter, kissing her head. Annabelle rested her head on Allie's shoulder. Annabelle's throat was on fire.

"What do you need?" Allie questioned, trying to help.

"Water." Annabelle's voice was hoarse.

Marie filled a glass with water from the pitcher. She held the cup to Annabelle's face and Annabelle took the glass in her shaking hand. The water was cold and felt soothing as she swallowed.

Renee entered the room and saw the people gathered around the bed. "Did I miss something?"

"She's not feeling well," Allie answered, running a cool cloth across Anna's forehead.

"Do you have any pain anywhere?" Renee questioned.

Annabelle nodded. "My head, throat, and now my stomach."

"I'll see if I can get you something for your nausea. You're in a lot of pain that your body is not used to, that will cause nausea. I'm sure you'll be just fine."

"She said she felt like passing out. What do you think caused that?" Marie pointed out. Renee looked at Annabelle.

"Light headedness could be a number of things; her body being under stress, possibly a minor virus, blood sugar." Renee explained. She pulled a device from the ledge behind Annabelle's head. She quickly checked Annabelle's sugar. "It's just a little low. When is the last time you ate something?"

"Breakfast," Annabelle whispered with her head rested on a pillow.

"How about a snack?" Renee asked. Annabelle nodded, eye closed.

"Should we get the doctor?" Marie asked.

"I'll let you rest. I'm going to page Dr. Morris and I'll be back in a little while." Renee smiled and patted Annabelle's arm.

"Auntie! Cakes!" Maddy announced pulling her grandpa behind her. Mark smiled at the enthusiastic little girl.

226

Annabelle smiled at Maddy. The little girl happily got into the bed next to Annabelle. Maddy was holding a DVD that Annabelle recognized as Madison's favorite movie.

"Let me guess, Princess and the Field Mice?" Annabelle asked her niece. Madison smiled with a frosting face.

"Can we watch it?" Maddy questioned.

"Of course." Annabelle smiled; Allie took the DVD from her daughter.

Allie turned and put the DVD in and Madison snuggled up with her aunt. Not wanting to watch the DVD for the millionth time, Evan, Allie, Marie and Mark excused themselves from the room for lunch.

Anna looked up at Lucas who stood quietly in the corner. She smiled at his look of concern. He walked to the side of her bed, kissed her cheek and whispered, "I love you."

"I love you too, Lucas." Annabelle returned his kiss.

Madison was excited about the movie for the first ten minutes. Slowly her enthusiasm faded into a heavily sleeping four-year-old. Annabelle was exhausted. She soon let her own eyes close. Annabelle drifted into a deep sleep of her own.

Lucas saw that both Annabelle and Madison had fallen asleep. Feeling his stomach rumble, he stood from his chair and left the dark room. Once in the hallway, he saw Allie and Marie returning to the room. Allie smiled and greeted him like a friend, while Marie glared. Allie stopped to talk when Marie pushed past Lucas into the room.

"Don't mind her, she'll come around," Allie reminded him. Lucas shook his head and sighed.

"I'd love for that day to hurry up and get here."

"Where are you headed?" Allie asked.

"I was going to get a cup of coffee." Lucas improvised, not really sure what he was going to eat without any money.

"Are you hungry?" Allie questioned, she put her hand in her pocket and pulled out a five dollar bill.

"You don't have to do that." Lucas couldn't take her money.

"Please, I know you're hungry. Just take it," Allie insisted, putting the money into his hand. "Pretend it's for babysitting Maddy while we were gone." Allie smiled and patted his arm, walking into Annabelle's room.

"But." Lucas stood for a moment, when he turned, Allie had closed the door. He sighed and walked towards the family room where the vending machines were located. When he turned the corner, he nearly ran into Mark Rockart.

"I'm sorry, excuse me." Lucas felt his face flush and his hands shake. He stood to the side and let Mark pass. Mark didn't say anything to Lucas and walked by, leaving the small waiting area. Lucas exhaled loudly, walked to the corner and stood in front of the machines.

Mark walked from the room and stopped in his tracks when he heard Lucas sigh. Mark felt unlike himself, not giving Lucas a fair chance. Mark was usually a welcoming person, like he raised his children to be. He wasn't setting any kind of example for his granddaughter.

Mark spun on his heel and reentered the room. Lucas was knelt down at the vending machine retrieving something out of the bottom. When Lucas stood up and turned around, he took a sharp breath in, startled by Mark's presence.

"I have to apologize to you." Mark spoke calmly and in a gentle tone.

"You really don't have anything to apologize to me for," Lucas insisted. Mark watched as the young man shifted nervously. His nerves hurt Mark.

"Sit down, let's talk." Mark gestured to the chair behind them. Lucas hesitantly took a seat and Mark sat next to him.

"Lucas, son, I have been completely unlike myself this past week. I am normally very kind hearted, welcoming and happy to meet anyone. For some reason, I haven't been able to give you that same respect. For that I am sorry." Mark spoke genuinely.

"Mr. Rockart, you honestly don't have to apologize. I understand your concern for Annabelle. To have such a wonderful, innocent woman like Annabelle ripped from your family, I would never want to imagine the feeling. Now, to have a stranger tell you that he loves her-"

"Wait, love?" Mark stopped Lucas.

"Yes, sir, I love Annie. I have never been more certain of anything in my life. I would do anything for her. She has given me trust and I do not intend on ever losing it." Lucas felt confident speaking these words, even if they were to Annabelle's father.

Mark sat and watched Lucas speak these words of trust and love about his little girl. *She's not little anymore.* Mark had to remind himself that Annabelle was a woman now. She wasn't a child anymore. Mark smiled at Lucas and shook his hand.

"She deserves a new chance at love. She needs someone to take care of her," Mark pointed out.

"I plan to be that person, sir." Lucas spoke assertively.

"I like confidence in a young man." Mark stood from his chair. "I'm glad we had this discussion."

"Thank you, sir." Lucas also stood up from his seat.

"Please, call me Mark," Mark insisted, patting Lucas on the back. "You know, Annabelle doesn't even let me or her mother call her Annie anymore. Consider yourself lucky."

The two men left the room, smiling and no longer uncomfortable together. Evan watched as his father and Lucas approached him, together.

"What did I miss?" he asked with his mouth full of food.

"I've come to my senses," Mark admitted and turned to Lucas again. "Give Marie time. I'll talk to her. She'll need a bit more convincing. She's very protective of her children."

As the three men walked into Annabelle's room together, smiling, the women looked at them with confused faces. Annabelle looked at the three most important men in her life. They all winked and smiled at her. She smiled tiredly and shook her head. *One step in the right direction...*

<u>Sunday, January 4th</u>

It was a feeling that couldn't be described with words, waking up, in a hospital bed, exhausted and anxious.

I looked around the room to find Lucas sleeping in the chair next to my bed. His head was resting on the mattress near my hand, our fingers tangled together. I took my other hand and ran it through his hair. He lifted his head and looked up at me. He smiled up at me and kissed my hand.

"Good morning." He spoke quietly. "How are you?"

I smiled at him, unable to contain my tears. *Now, why are you crying?*

Lucas sat on the edge of my bed; he pulled me into his arms. I rested my head on his chest, crying softly. We sat in silence; no words to express our feelings, his hands rubbed my back gently.

I needed him more than I had ever needed anyone. Lucas was my rock, my soul mate, my light. *Slow down, Annabelle.* I didn't want to slow down. How could one person have such an impact on me? *You let him.*

I thought about the feelings that ran through my head as Lucas held me. One thing I had never thought of suddenly dawned on me. *What now?* Where does our relationship go now? *What will happen when you are ready to go home?* Will I be able to live alone? *Who will take care of you?* Will Lucas stay with me? *Will he get a place of his own?* What about his parents? *His parents…*

I pulled away from Lucas so suddenly that he looked hurt. I held his hand and tried to think of what to say without sounding rude or impatient.

"Have they found your parents?" It was easier to say than I had imagined.

Lucas, a bit surprised by my sudden need to know, looked at me for a moment. I studied his face. Before he could say anything, I understood. I looked down at our hands.

"You don't have to worry about them," Lucas reassured me, "They abandoned everything they own in that hotel room. If they come within a ten mile radius of this town, everyone will be here to protect you." He lifted my chin to look into his eyes. "I will never let them hurt you again."

I watched his face change from worry to a smile of assurance. His eyes were passionate and his words were confident. Silence filled the room. It was an easy silence, one that shouldn't be interrupted. However, another question swam through my head.

"What happens now, Lucas?" I broke the silence with a whisper, almost fearful.

"What do you mean?" His voice was small, bemused.

"What will happen when I go home? Will I be able to live alone?" My voice trailed off a bit, I looked up at him. "What will happen to us?"

"Annie, are you worried about us?" Lucas paused. "Do you think I'm going to just disappear?"

I avoided his eyes. *Everyone always does...* My confidence level was nonexistent. I was hitting my low point. I hadn't felt this insecure of myself since my first date in junior high, but even back then I held more confidence than I did today. *This isn't like you.* I know. Was I overreacting? Was this really the end of my pain? Would something else ruin my chance of a new beginning? *Why are you questioning your relationship with the man you love?*

"Annabelle?" Lucas brought me from my thoughts. I looked up at him. *No tears,* no tears.

"I don't want you to disappear. I need you here with me. I need your strength to keep me grounded. Lucas, you mean everything to me," I confessed. *Should this be a surprise?*

"Annie, if I can ask one favor of you? Please, stop worrying about me leaving you. I am not going to leave you. I promise." He kissed my cheeks, my forehead and then my lips and whispered, "I can't live without you."

My heart jumped in my chest. I felt my fears melting away, *for the moment.* I knew he was speaking to me from his heart when I felt his tears on my cheeks as he kissed me. I pulled away, wiping his tears.

"Why are you crying?" I smiled sweetly. He laughed and shrugged. I smiled and pulled him close. There was a knock at the door.

"Come in," I invited.

My mom and dad walked around the corner with smiling faces. I smiled back and I felt Lucas stiffen next to me. His grip on my hand went rigid and I squeezed his hand gently. He looked at me and I smiled at him. His nerves were obvious. Usually the mornings when Lucas stayed with me, my mother always suggests that he take a walk or get a cup of coffee when she arrives. This morning she got straight to the conversation.

"Good morning, honey." My dad greeted, kissing my forehead. He sat down on the chair in the corner of the room. My mom walked to the side of the bed opposite of Lucas. She kissed my cheek and tucked my hair behind my ear.

"Good morning Annabelle, how are you feeling today?" Her face was gentle. "How did you sleep?" my mother asked, waiting patiently for my answers. I opened my mouth to answer her question but I couldn't get over her sudden change of attitude. She continued the conversation. "Your father and I can't stay long. We have to go to your Aunt Fiona's for her 60th Birthday." I looked up at her with my mouth open slightly. She smiled and patted my hand.

"I have to apologize to you," my mom said hesitantly, "to both of you. I haven't been fair to either of you since you've been here."

I looked at Lucas. His face was pale and you could see the worry in his eyes. I squeezed his hand again.

"I judged Lucas before I had a chance to even get to know him, Annabelle. It's not fair for us to treat him with disrespect. We have to be on the same page if we want any chance to help you on your road to recovery."

The room went silent, awkwardly silent. I didn't know what to say or do. My mom rarely admitted she was wrong. Lucas was a complete stranger to my parents and they were finally going to give him the chance he deserved.

"Thank you, Mom," I spoke quietly, unsure. She shook her head.

"Don't thank me. It's not a favor. I should have been like this from the beginning." She looked up at Lucas. "I should have given you a chance from the beginning."

Lucas finally closed his mouth. Shock still written across his face, he nodded to her. I chuckled in the awkward moment. My dad sat quietly in the corner, grinning at me. I knew he was the reason behind my mother's change of heart. He knew how to talk to her. I had always been a Daddy's Girl. He winked at me. I smiled back at him.

I took a deep breath in and sighed heavily. It was a sigh of relief. With one thing off my mind, I could focus on the next step to my new beginning.

Bringing me from my thoughts, Billy-Jean, Evan, and Allie walked into the room with their hands full of coffee, muffins and a bag of things I needed from my apartment. I smiled at Allie when she threw a cranberry-lemon muffin at me. It was my favorite. I set it down on the tray of untouched breakfast. I was too nauseous to eat anything.

"Are you still feeling nauseas?" my mom asked, feeling my forehead for fever.

I nodded, taking another breath. "Dr. Morris should be in today to see me."

My family sat around the room and we talked. No topic in particular, just talking. It felt nice to have conversations that didn't revolve around me or my *experience*. I hated calling it an experience. When I thought of new experiences, I thought excitement and it was everything but exciting.

After an hour, Dr. Morris showed up and joined the conversation about Madison's snowman, Bill.

"My daughter would most definitely get along with your niece, Annabelle." Dr. Morris laughed. "Well, back to the reason I'm here today. I talked to Renee yesterday about your concerns. Nausea, like fever, is the body's way of telling you it's fighting something. It could be as minor as a cold virus or as major as brain injury. I am going to order a brain scan to make sure everything is still looking good. I don't have any reason to believe we'll find anything abnormal, but to be on the safe side considering your head trauma."

My cheeks flushed with a nervous panic. Dr. Morris patted my shoulder. "Don't worry, Annabelle. You're in great hands."

Dr. Morris left the room and soon after, two women came in to take me to get the test done. My parents kissed my cheeks and my mother begged my father to stay and forget the birthday party.

"Ma, please go, for me. I want you two to enjoy your day. I will be fine; I have four other people to take care of me today." I smiled, my mom held my face in her hands.

"I love you, Annabelle. I will be back tomorrow morning, bright and early." She leaned forward and kissed me.

"I love you too, Ma."

It was now about three hours after my parents had left. I returned from the brain scan about two hours ago. Nothing abnormal showed up in the scan. Dr. Morris told me to keep an eye on when I felt nauseous or dizzy and let him know. For now, he was convinced my body was dealing with the stress of my injuries.

Billy was sitting next to me in bed with a bridal magazine open in her lap. Evan, Allie and Lucas were playing a riveting game of Go Fish in the corner.

Barely paying any attention to the magazine in her lap, Billy talked to me about her ideas.

"I don't really enjoy the idea of having an outdoor wedding around here. It's either snowing or raining around here. When it is sunny, a rain cloud could be lurking around the bend. We'll have to find a hall. Granny suggested having the wedding at her house in Texas. I like the idea but I couldn't imagine asking everyone to fly down there. It's expensive."

"Billy! That's a great idea! You know how much your Granny misses your family. It would give everyone a chance to get out of the cold too. I wouldn't mind flying down there. Plus, you love Texas, where better to have your wedding?" I pointed out as she took in my words. She frowned.

There was a knock on the door and Allie got up to answer it. "Don't look at my cards!"

"Maybe we could fly Texas's weather here. Ronnie hates flying." Billy shook her head.

Allie turned around and closed the door behind her.

"Who is it?" I asked laughing at Billy's comment.

"It's an investigator; he is here to talk to you." Allie had a strange look on her face. "If you aren't ready for this, I can tell him to go away."

My face went from laughter to panic. I hadn't thought about having to tell my side of the story, let alone to a complete stranger. I thought about the details they would want.

Memories flooded my senses; the cold breeze that hindered my body each night and day. The smell of the odor of my own bodily fluids and rotting wood that surrounded me as I lay helplessly dying. Starring up at the rotting ceiling, watching the sun rise and fall through the cracks in the walls. My ears tingled with the sound of jingling keys to warn me of the danger that lurked behind the walls.

"Annabelle?" Billy-Jean brought me from my memories. Tears lingered in my eyes as I looked at her.

"I'll tell him to come back another time," Allie told me, turning to door. *They'll come back and you'll have to tell your story eventually.*

"No," I stopped her. "It's okay. I'm going to have to eventually."

"Are you sure you're okay?" Lucas questioned.

I nodded at him and smiled.

"Do you want us to leave?" Evan asked.

I shook my head. "No, I don't have anything to hide."

Allie let the man in while Billy-Jean stood up and gathered the wedding planning explosion that covered the bed in papers. She shoved the stack into her bag and switched seats with Lucas. Lucas sat down next to me on the bed.

"Are you sure?" he whispered to me.

"I am," I assured him.

I panicked inside thinking about reliving my two weeks of hell. I shook my head, reminding myself to stay calm and not to cry. I looked up to see a man in dark jeans and a gray sweater standing near the door of the room. He looked to be in his 30's, short cut, dark hair, gentle features. *Not intimidating at all...*

"Hello Ms. Rockart, I'm Brian Stanley and I am an investigator with the state. If you're up to it, I would like to ask some questions." He put his hand out. I shook it and he took a seat in a chair to my right. He smiled and asked, "Who do we have with us?"

"This is my brother Evan, my sister-in-law Allie, my best friend Billy-Jean and..." It suddenly dawned on me that I didn't have a title for Lucas. "This is Lucas." Lucas looked at me with a strange look when I paused before his name. I tried to ignore it.

"Well it's nice to meet you all." Brian smiled. He seemed genuine. He looked down at the tablet of paper he was holding. "I want to be as gentle about this as possible. I am sure the last thing you would want to do right now is relive your experience."

I nodded in agreement. I took a deep breath and prepared myself for the next question.

"Let's start by asking who abducted you?"

"Janis Martin."

"Janis Martin, married to Hector Martin?" Brian questioned. I nodded. "Was anyone else involved in the actual abduction? Was anyone else there to witness?"

I closed my mouth, *Lucas.* I couldn't bring myself to speak his name. He wasn't guilty of anything but saving my life.

Lucas squeezed my hand and I looked up at him. He nodded. I shook my head no at him. He tilted his head at me, defeated. I sighed heavily, thinking the subject would disappear.

"I was there." Lucas broke into my thoughts. I looked down at my hands, nervous.

Evan looked at us, struck with a bolt of shock. Allie and Billy-Jean sat quietly, knowing the whole story.

"He didn't do anything wrong. He tried to stop her," I pointed out.

"I should have done more," Lucas sulked.

"Lucas," I whispered. He looked at me, sadness in his eyes. "She had a gun." I told Lucas like he was hearing it for the first time.

"Janis Martin is my mother; I shouldn't have let her do the things she did to you." Lucas was angry with himself.

"You are Lucas Martin? Son of Hector and Janis Martin," Brian questioned, Lucas nodded.

"Lucas, you didn't have a choice. You are not the reason for this. Please, stop blaming yourself," I begged. "Lucas, look at me." He avoided my eyes. I felt tears beg to escape. I held my breath and pushed them away. "Next question." I looked at Brian.

The conversation continued. We went through the entire first days. I explained Hector's reasoning for taking me. Allie's face began to pale with each lesson I explained. I continued on to talk about Janis feeding me poisoned mashed potatoes. Billy-Jean hid her face in her blanket with each detail. Evan and Lucas remained stone faced, both boiling with anger. Lucas hadn't heard all the details of my first seven days in captivity.

Feeling everyone's eyes on me as I explained my '*experience*', I felt embarrassed, overwhelmed. I closed my eyes, holding back tears; I continued the story starting at the night Lucas stayed with me. I described how he took care of me, cleaning my injuries and feeding me food and clean water. I watched Lucas's face as I explained the impact his presence had on me.

236

"The reason I had a chance to escape was because he had been trying to loosen the boards on the building. Lucas risked his own life there, treating me the opposite of what his parents taught him. I owe him my sanity and my life."

Lucas continued to look at the floor. I furrowed my eyebrows at him and looked back to Brian. I resumed my story. Dolan Meyer now entered the story line. I explained his first visit, reliving the molestation with a blank face. I carried on about Hector realizing that Lucas was no longer on their side.

"They tortured him as if he wasn't their son; as if they had never met," I remembered. I reached for Lucas's hand. "I felt like it was my fault that they hurt him." His eyes finally glanced up at me for a brief second. His cheeks were red with anger.

I remembered the pain and humiliation I felt as I told the story of my sexual assault. I saw the look on Evan's face as I explained the details; rage. Allie hid her face, obviously in tears. I let tears fall from my own eyes as I remembered the feeling I felt when they took Lucas away from me. Billy-Jean had tears streaming down her face. Evan and Lucas continued to stare off into oblivion.

Brian watched me with a curious but gentle look on his face. I looked into his eyes when I said, "They left me, alone, for dead."

"Dolan Meyer raped you?" Brian confirmed. A sinking feeling hit me. *Twice.*

"Twice," I whispered. Lucas stiffened his body. Allie and Billy held their breath in disgust. Evan just about jumped out of his seat. My heart fell onto the floor, humiliated, ashamed and broken. I didn't do anything to stop him.

Brian nodded, adding something else to his notes. The room went silent.

"Lucas came to the police station on December 26th. He is the person who took me to where Annabelle was," Allie added to the story.

The conversation happened around me as I felt the tears fall from my eyes. Brian continued to ask Allie and Lucas questions from their perspective. I looked at Billy's face as she stared back at me. Her eyes were swollen and her cheeks were red. I felt like I had caused her pain by telling her my story. I looked away from her, unable to watch her face.

My eyes found Evan. His face was angry. His knuckles were white, his fists clenched together in his lap. I couldn't look at him either. I returned my sight to my hands. I let go of Lucas's hand and put mine together in my lap. I shivered slightly, letting a nervous wave of guilt run through my body. I closed my eyes, taking a deep breath in.

"Annabelle?" Brian's voice asked. I looked up at him. Everyone in the room was looking at me. *He asked you a question...*

"I'm sorry, I didn't hear you," I said calmly.

"Are you okay, Anna?" Billy questioned.

I nodded, feeling tears fall from my eyes. *Liar...* My nod turned into a tremble. I felt a strong wave of tears burst from my eyes. I cried out loud, feeling Lucas pull me into his arms.

"I didn't mean to push." Brian's voice was concerned. I shook my head at him.

"No, you didn't," I told him.

"I am going to get going. I'll leave my card for you if you have anything to add or any questions."

Brian said his goodbyes and Evan walked him out of the room. Allie followed quietly. Lucas let me go when I caught my breath.

"I'm sorry." I spoke softly.

"Don't apologize, Anna." Billy spoke with a look of admiration on her face.

Lucas got up from the bed and Billy sat down next to me. As Billy hugged me, I watched Lucas walk to the window. He was distant, not himself. Billy let go of the hug and watched my face as I looked at Lucas.

"I'll be right outside. Talk to him," Billy whispered, wiping my cheeks with her thumbs. She smiled and left the room.

It was quiet after Billy closed the door. Lucas continued to look out the window, avoiding me.

"Luke," I spoke softly, feeling tears fall, "Please Lucas, look at me."

I watched his fists clench, then he turned around. His face was red and his eyes were swollen with tears streaming down his cheeks. I felt my chest pound with guilt. I held my breath, holding my tears back.

"Talk to me," I pleaded. He processed his thoughts.

238

"Why did you pause when you said my name?" His words came slowly. *He heard the hesitation.*

"I'm sorry. I was going to say boyfriend but-"

"Do you not think of me as your boyfriend?" he shot at me. *Ouch...*

"Of course I do, Lucas. But saying it felt odd to me."

"Odd? Are you ashamed of me?" His words cut into my chest like a knife.

"Never, how could you think that?" I cried.

"Then what is it Annabelle? What is wrong?" Lucas had never talked to me like this. *You hurt his feelings...*

"Lucas, I love you. I owe you my life. Using the term boyfriend doesn't feel justified." I paused. I had his attention. "The word boyfriend feels much too immature for our connection. I want to call you my soul mate, my hero, my savior. Boyfriend is an elementary word."

His features softened. Relief filled my chest.

"Using words like soul mate, hero and savior wouldn't make sense to anyone other than us. Telling a detective that you were any of those things would have sounded strange considering our situation." I watched his barrier fall.

"Luke, come here." I cried. He walked towards me and climbed into bed. He sat down beside me, wrapping his arms around me. He kissed my nose, running his hands through my hair.

"From now on, please use boyfriend. I would much rather know the things I do now than believe you don't love me. I won't be offended in any way." Lucas smiled.

I smiled and hugged him tightly. *Boyfriend....* An inferior word compared to the man that sat beside me. *It will have to do,* for now.

.

Wednesday January, 14th

A week and a half after Madison's birthday and Annabelle's brain scan, her nausea had mostly subsided. Yesterday, Dr. Morris explained that her improvements were beyond their expectations. He briefly mentioned the idea of sending her home within the next week. Without letting anyone know, Annabelle panicked inside. How could she live in her own home like this?

Last night, Lucas reluctantly left with Allie to get a good night's sleep in a real bed, possibly even shower. Annabelle told everyone she would be fine alone, lying through her teeth. Annabelle had been out of harm's way for almost three weeks but she hadn't gotten used to spending the night alone.

Annabelle readjusted the pillow underneath her head. Comfort was a rare occasion in the hospital bed. She gave up and pushed the button to move her bed into the sitting position. She reached for the remote that sat on the nightstand to her left. Her finger barely grazed the side of the remote. She grunted slightly, stretching her arm to the limit to reach for the remote. Moving slightly to her left, she tried again. This time, she managed to push the remote off the nightstand.

"Damn it," she growled. Her eyes landed on the red button that said call on the railing of her bed. "No, I can't call them for every little thing, especially if they want to send me home."

Annabelle leaned forward, uncovering her legs. She told herself that she didn't need any help getting up. Even though each time she had been out of bed in the last week, someone was there to catch her if she slipped.

"I don't need help," Annabelle told herself as she dangled her feet off the bed. Her right hip remained braced, still limiting movement. Annabelle put her left foot down on the ground. She got a good grip on the railing of the bed with her left arm and stood up. Once her left leg was straight underneath her, she stepped down on her right leg. Normally, this caused her minimal pain with the influence of pain medicines. Tonight, however, she forgot that she declined the need for pain medicine. As she stepped down, pain shot up her leg and Annabelle yelled out in agony. She felt her knees shake and beg to fall. Luckily, her grip on the bed remained tight and she fell back onto the bed.

"Annabelle?" A young, blonde haired nurse entered the room. Her name was Donna, Annabelle's night nurse. She saw Annabelle hanging onto the bed. Donna helped Anna back onto the bed. "What happened?"

"I was trying to get the TV remote." Annabelle felt her face burn with embarrassment. "It fell behind the night stand."

"Why didn't you call for me?" Donna asked, retrieving the plastic object from the floor. She set it on the side of Annabelle's bed. Donna watched her patient struggle with tears. She pulled up a chair and sat down. "What's wrong, Anna?"

Annabelle felt her tears find their familiar path down her cheeks. She quickly wiped them away and looked up at Donna. "I can't do anything for myself."

"No one expects you to this soon. There are certain things you can't expect to do this soon." Donna reminded her.

"This soon? It's been almost three weeks since I've been here. How long is it supposed to take? Plus, Dr. Morris talked about sending me home. How am I ever going to live a normal life? I don't want to be a burden to my friends and family." Tears streamed from her eyes, as she breathed in and out with ragged breaths. "I feel terrible, my hip won't stop aching. I look terrible; my face is bruised and scarred. I cry all the time. I'm a blubbering, whining, pathetic mess."

"Annabelle, settle down." Donna held Annabelle's hands. "You look great. You've been through a terrifying ordeal. You are going to be just fine. Your family loves you and you know that. You'll never be a burden to them. Dr. Morris isn't talking about sending you home tomorrow. He means in the next week. Please, relax. Try and get some sleep. And if you need anything, please push the button. It's what I'm here for." Donna winked and got up from the bed and handed Annabelle a box of tissues.

Annabelle nodded and wiped her face with the tissue. Donna smiled and left the room.

Laying her head back on the pillow, Annabelle closed her eyes. Comfort lulled her to sleep that night, far from panic free.

Thursday January, 15th .

Annabelle was sleeping soundly when Lucas arrived the next morning. Allie dropped him at the hospital before she went to work.

241

He closed the door quietly behind him and tip toed to the side of her bed. Not wanting to wake her up, he sat in his usual chair on her left. He watched her sleep peacefully.

Lucas felt closer to this woman than he felt to anyone in his life, even to his grandma. He wanted Annabelle to know the impact she'd had on his life. She made him realize his worth. He felt needed around Annabelle. Lucas was sure he wanted to spend his life with Annabelle. He also knew that marriage was not the solution to their problems. His parents had not been found yet.

Lucas shook his head and pushed the thought from his mind. He leaned back in the chair and relaxed. His eyes closed slightly, sending him into a light slumber.

Annabelle's dreams threw her into a terrible nightmare. She was stranded in a dark room, unable to walk on her own. She screamed for help, pawing at the floor with her hands. Crying loudly, Annabelle struggled to get to the door in the corner of the dark room. A single spot light followed her desperate attempt to escape. With each inch she moved, the door moved farther.

Finally, another person's voice called from behind her.

"Annabelle," the familiar voice called.

Annabelle turned around to see herself standing, without limitations or injuries. The unharmed Annabelle smiled and knelt down beside herself. She tucked the hair behind her mirror image's ear and snickered.

"I hope you have a plan. No one will be here to save you this time." The unharmed Annabelle stood up and disappeared. As the figure disappeared, the room lit up, revealing Annabelle's apartment. Her possessions surrounded her. But when she reached for the couch to help herself up, it moved away. She turned to the coffee table and watched as it slid away from her.

Confused, Annabelle pounded the floor, defeated.

"No one will help you this time." Her voice rang through the small apartment.

Annabelle jerked awake with a sharp breath. She painfully, caught her breath, feeling her heart pound in her chest. She looked to her left and saw Lucas sleeping in the chair next to the bed. The sight caused Annabelle to smile. She stretched slightly, feeling her muscles tense.

"Lucas," she whispered. His eyes flickered. "Lucas, how long have you been here?"

Annabelle watched as he opened his eyes slowly and looked at her. Lucas smiled when he met her eyes. He sat up and stretched his arms over his head.

"I've been here for-" He looked at the clock on the other side of the room, 12:20pm "-Wow, for two hours."

"You should have woken me up." Annabelle pouted. Lucas laughed and sat on the edge of her bed.

"Why would I wake you up when you were clearly sleeping so peacefully?" Lucas hugged Annabelle tightly and kissed her forehead.

"I wouldn't have called that peaceful," Annabelle whispered, remembering her dream.

"Why? What's wrong?" Lucas questioned. She shook her head, "Come on, you can tell me. Did you have a nightmare?"

"More like foreshadowing," Annabelle grumbled.

"What's wrong?" Lucas repeated.

"Dr. Morris is thinking about sending me home in the next week."

"That's great news." Lucas smiled happily.

"No, it's not!" Annabelle argued, "How am I supposed to take care of myself?"

"Annie, that's what I'm here for." Lucas looked at her with a look of concern. Annabelle looked at Lucas with a defeated face. He smiled and shook his head. He put his hand on her chin and leaned forward to kiss her. Annabelle's lips met his with sweet, soft warmth. Lucas's heart pounded with his love for her.

Lucas cuddled with Annabelle for a few minutes until there was a knock on the door. Lucas got up to answer it when Ronnie and Billy-Jean walked in. Lucas sat back down on the edge of Annabelle's bed when he saw the door open.

"Morning, how are you today?" Billy hugged her best friend. Annabelle put her head back on her pillow and smiled.

"Just fine, more tired than I have been," Annabelle commented. Billy gave her a strange look and then turned to Lucas.

"Want some coffee? Ronnie and I were going to stop at the coffee shop on the way up here but they were closed for lunch." Billy turned to Annabelle. "So we decided to come up here first and see if ya'll wanted anything. They are going to open back up in ten minutes at one o'clock."

"You can stay here with Annie and I'll walk down there with Ronnie if you'd like," Lucas suggested.

"Sure, I could use some girl talk," Billy agreed, sitting down on the end of Annabelle's bed. The guys left and Billy lay down on her back. She moaned slightly.

"If only men knew the pain of menstrual cramps," Billy joked. Anna laughed at her friend's dramatic face. "I can't wait until the end of this week is over. I swear if it's not cramps then it's…."

Annabelle tuned Billy Jean out while something suddenly came to mind. She calculated in her head and panic struck. She calculated again, again and again.

"Anna? Hello?" Billy waved her hand in front of her friend's face. Annabelle looked up at Billy Jean with a dazed look. "What's wrong, Anna?"

Friday January 16th

Dr. Morris walked into the room. Lucas stood next to Annabelle's bed, Billy-Jean sat in the corner of the room.

"Do you have the results?" Annabelle asked with a strained voice.

"Yes," Dr. Morris sighed, "you're pregnant."

Annabelle felt like her chest caved in. She couldn't say anything. Annabelle was pregnant. Not only was she pregnant, but it was Dolan Meyer's baby; a result of rape. Her thoughts were distraught and her eyes showed it. Thoughts flooded through her mind but one thought jumped to the front of the line.

"But I've been on birth control for months. How is this possible?" Annabelle gaped at the doctor.

"The pill is only effective if taken regularly. With the timeline of the events that occurred, the two weeks you were without your birth control attributed to a higher chance of pregnancy."

Annabelle stared at Dr. Morris as if he grew a second head.

"We are lucky we found out this soon. Most women don't know until they're almost two months pregnant. Unfortunate circumstances, of course." Dr. Morris was obviously uncomfortable.

244

He was struggling with telling this young woman that she was pregnant after being raped. "Calculating from the date of the first," he paused, "You are three weeks pregnant."

The room was silent. How would Annabelle tell her parents? How would she raise a child? Could she really take any more bad news? Annabelle felt Lucas pull her close to his chest. Billy said goodbye to Dr. Morris and joined the couple on the bed.

"What am I going to do?" Annabelle begged with tears streaming down her face.

"It's okay, Annie. It will be okay," Lucas promised, rocking her back and forth.

Saturday January 17th

I put my hands on my face. Lucas rubbed my back soothingly. He pulled my hands off my face and held them tightly. I looked up at him.

"Tell them," he whispered encouragingly.

I had to tell my family the news Dr. Morris broke to me yesterday. Telling my family about my pregnancy wasn't the only news I would be breaking today. My parents did not know that I had been raped. I hadn't been able to find the right way to tell them. *How do you find a right way to tell someone that?*

"Tell us what?" Allie looked at Lucas, then to me, "Annabelle?"

"What's going on, Annabelle?" my mom questioned, her tone dropped to a lower octave.

"Dr. Morris told me that I," I took a breath, "that I am pregnant."

Each person around the room, except Lucas and I, took a sharp breath in. I felt the temperature of the room rise ten degrees in an uncomfortable embarrassment. I felt my cheeks burn and my throat went dry. Lucas squeezed my hand to remind me that he was still there.

My mother's face was shocked. Her mouth hung open and her eyes were wide. She took a breath to speak when my father put his hand on her arm. "Let her talk, Marie."

I took a few breaths in, shuddering slightly. I would have to relive the night of humiliation and torture. I wiped my tears and spoke softly. *Too soft...*

"I was raped," I whispered. My mother recoiled as though I had slapped her in the face. "Dolan Meyer raped me."

The room was silent. I looked at my family's scared faces. My mother's hand covered her mother, her face struck with pain. She stepped closer to bedside.

"The entire two weeks I was kept in that abandoned cabin I pleaded with death to take my life. I begged for the end. The pain, the smell, and the horrible cold; I wanted it to just go away. I wanted to die. Each day was a new day for them to torture me; a new day to find a new way to humiliate and violate me and my confidence."

Renee and Dr. Morris had entered the room in the middle of the conversation.

I watched as my mother glared at Lucas. Taking in a heavy breath, my mother's eyes returned to me. I shook my head.

"What are you thinking?" I asked her. Knowing my mother, she was creating an elaborate story in her head.

"Where was he during this? Why didn't he stop him?" My mother spat.

"How dare you blame him for this? You couldn't even imagine the hell I've been through. I was close to giving up when Lucas was told to watch me but instead he took care of me. He was the only person there for me when I wanted nothing more than to die. He was there for me, risking his own life. He is the reason I made it out alive. I love him and I owe him everything."

My chest pounded and my breaths were heavy with anticipation. Lucas kissed the top of my head. I held him closely, watching my family's faces. Allie had tears streaming down her face. Evan and my father both had looks of protective disgust and anger; neither looked me in the eye.

My mother sat silently in the chair to the side of my bed. Her face was blank, on the verge of tears. Her cheeks were red with no doubt, embarrassment and irritation. She stood from her chair and approached me. Her face was like stone. When she reached for my face, the stone wall crumbled and she broke down into tears. She pulled me close to her chest. Her arms wrapped around my body warmed me.

"I'm so sorry, Annabelle." She cried heavily. "Please, don't hate me. I'm so sorry."

"Ma, I don't hate you. I love you." I cried back to her. We held each other, crying and whispering things to each other.

Dr. Morris broke the silence by explaining that I wasn't out of the woods yet. He continued to say this was going to be a difficult pregnancy for me.

"With the weakened condition her body is already in, any amount of stress could be harmful to both her and the baby."

"Dr. Morris, when can Annabelle come home?" my mom asked, still holding my hand tightly. My heart pounded with the thought of going home. *It's what you've wanted...* I wasn't ready to be alone.

"Soon, with a few more days of therapy, we can determine a day to send her home. For now, Annabelle will continue with Clara and Heather from the therapy to gain strength and independence," Dr. Morris explained.

I cringed at the thought of Clara and Heather's visits. They were like a pair of annoying sisters, sitting on either side of me on a long family road trip. Constantly poking me, hovering around me saying, "I'm not touching you," or using my own hand to slap me across the face and repeat, "Stop hitting yourself; stop hitting yourself."

I loathed therapy or as Clara would say in her abnormally high voice, "OT." Clara and I were about the same age. Her intent to help me was genuine, but her ways of helping me were cruel and unusual punishment. Heather, the other therapist, was not as hyper as Clara was; however, her overly optimistic outlook on life was possibly as annoying as Clara's energy.

The combination of the two women could be lethal to anyone allergic to happy. Luckily or unfortunately for me, I was not allergic to happy and had to deal with these women on a daily basis. Lucas had to remind me every day to tolerate them for my own good. I trusted his sanity more than my own. It was our deal for him to endure them with me or I would have been arrested by now.

My mom brought me from my thoughts of therapy when I heard her say, "Annabelle won't have to worry about a thing. Her father and I will take great care of her."

My mother had the idea that I was moving home with them. *Sadly mistaken Marie...*

Lucas looked at me with eye brows raised. I shook my head at him. Dr. Morris promised another visit later and said goodbye. Once Dr. Morris left, I felt the need to explain our plans to my mother.

"Ma, when you say you and Daddy will take good care of me, what do you mean?" The subject was delicate; I needed to treat it like a crystal bowl.

"I meant when you move home after you've been discharged, Daddy and I will be able to take care of you." She smiled at me sweetly. My heart broke at her hopefulness. *Be careful of how you say this...*

"Ma, we never discussed this." I felt like I was playing in a mine field.

"I didn't think it had to be discussed. Who else could take care of you? You didn't expect us to let you live alone, did you?" Mom's confusion only made this conversation harder.

"I like my apartment and," I paused before I jumped into the line of fire. "Lucas is moving in with me. He is going to take care of me." *Bull in a china shop.*

My mom looked at me, not stunned, but hurt. She liked Lucas but I knew she couldn't stand the thought of anyone but herself taking care of me.

"I see," was the only thing my mom could say. She smiled and patted my hand. I watched as she fought her inner thoughts.

"Ma," I began. She shook her head and smiled. "Please, don't make a big deal out of this," I begged.

That was the last thing I needed, more stress. I couldn't help but feel guilty when I looked at my mom. She was fighting tears. It's like I was moving out again. She cried like a baby when I begged her to let me move out into my own place.

"I won't, Annabelle. I promise." My mom kissed my forehead and walked across the room. She sat down next to my father on the couch in the corner.

Between the stresses of the day, my body begging for sleep and the fact that Clara and Heather would be arriving at any moment, I felt horrible. I sighed heavily. Lucas looked at me with a knowing smirk. He was thinking the same thing I was.

My parents said their goodbye and headed home. Allie and Evan decided to stay and experience Clara and Heather.

"Are you sure you want to do that?" Lucas questioned with a nervous laugh.

"I don't believe that these women are *that* bad," Allie commented. I laughed out loud.

"Well, you're in for a rude awakening."

"We'll see," Evan added. I shook my head at them.

A loud high pitched giggle rang through the hallways of the hospital. It was followed by loud chatter, similar to a crowd waiting for the latest pop star to arrive at a concert. I cringed slightly, knowing exactly the cause of the horrid sound.

"Here they come," I warned. Allie gave me a crazy look that made me giggle girlishly. I couldn't help but feel anxious about the activities that would be occurring within the next hour. Nerves shook my hands and sweat soaked my palms.

"Hello!" Clara burst into the room with her pink duffel bag in hand. Heather followed, with her matching turquoise bag, smiling brightly. I felt the urge to hurl at the sight of them. Lucas patted my hand softly, reminding me to be nice.

"I'm Clara, you are?" Clara introduced herself to Evan and Allie. Allie gave me a look of 'are you serious?' and I laughed at her. Evan shook Clara's hand and introduced himself. Allie did the same.

"I'm Heather." Heather waved at the couple. I snickered at their faces.

After all introductions were complete, Clara turned to me. "You, my dear, are going to walk down the hallway today."

I stared at her with fire in my eyes. "Ha ha, funny." *Sarcasm... not your best quality...*

"No joking, darling. It is time for you to get up on your feet." Clara set her bag down and dug through it. She happily pulled out a pair of rainbow slippers. "These are a present for you. They have good, hard souls that will be PERFECT for these slippery hospital floors." Clara managed to add a happy squeal at the end of her sentence.

"I've been on my feet." I added, "I don't like it." I gave her a look of revulsion. Disgust covered my fear with no sugar coating. Raw feelings begged to spill from my mouth. I wanted to tell this chipper woman what I really thought of her Rainbow Bright socks.

"Come on Annie, it will be fun," Lucas nudged. I moved my look of disgust from Clara to Lucas.

"I tried to stand up on my own three nights ago. I nearly fell on my face. You really expect me to go parading down the hallway? Especially in those." My voice reached a higher volume.

"Annabelle, can I tell you something?" Heather chimed in. I looked at her with a dull look in my eyes.

"Why not?" I answered.

"You doubt yourself." Heather spoke simply. Giving her a strange look, I listened to her speak. "You have to believe that you can walk down the hallway. It's not going to be easy. It probably won't be pain free. But the steps you take in that hallway are the steps to a new beginning. You have to start somewhere. If you don't walk down that hallway-"

"I have a choice?" I cut her off mid statement. Lucas nudged me. I sighed, "Sorry."

"If you don't walk down that hallway, you are telling yourself you are not ready to move on from your struggles. You are not ready to let go of your pain and suffering. If you don't walk down that hallway, you're letting them win." Heather, along with everyone else in the room, watched me in silence.

Not that I will ever admit it to them, but Heather was right. I needed to take steps towards recovery. I had to believe I could do this. Believing in myself would help me believe in a normal life again.

"Do it for your unborn child," Clara added with a smile. I instantly felt nauseated with the thought of the growing baby inside of me. Lucas shook his head at Clara and she wiped the smile from her face.

"Do it for yourself, Annabelle," Heather corrected.

I nodded. *Time to move on…*

Lucas sat in the guest room of Allie and Evan's home. His bags were packed and ready to move into Annabelle's apartment later today. Annabelle wasn't aware that she would be leaving the hospital tonight. He was excited to watch her reaction and ready to move in with her.

Baby rested her head on Lucas's knee. Lucas smiled and patted the golden retriever's head.

"Are you ready to go?" Evan asked from the hallway. Lucas nodded and grabbed the duffel bag from the end of the bed. "Are you really ready for this?" Evan questioned Lucas.

"Nervous," Lucas admitted, "but ready. I love your sister."

Evan smiled and patted Lucas lightly on the back. The two men walked downstairs where Madison and Allie waited in the kitchen. Maddy laughed when Lucas stuck his tongue out at the little girl.

"Annabelle should be doing physical therapy until four this afternoon. I'll get off work around five. If everyone gets there before me, just go ahead as planned. You know how things just happen," Allie explained to her husband. Evan nodded as he ate a piece of toast.

"I get to see Gamma and Gampa today, Mr. Lucas," Madison explained happily from her booster seat.

"Do you? That sounds fun. Are you going to play with Fig?" Lucas smiled.

Madison moved her head up and down excitedly. "Gampa said we can play outside today."

Lucas laughed at her excitement and rubbed her hair. She giggled and continued eating her scrambled eggs.

"Lucas, I'll take you to your parent's house today to get the rest of your things. I have a few boxes in the truck to get all your clothes," Evan explained.

Lucas nodded with his mouth full of cereal. He wasn't interested in visiting his house. They had lived there for about six years. No meaning lay in the rooms of the house. Only terrible memories and tragic events happened within the walls.

"Are you okay?" Allie asked Lucas.

"Nervous." Lucas smiled at her.

Allie returned the gesture and watched her daughter eat her eggs. Allie couldn't help but have maternal instincts and feelings

252

towards Lucas. She knew the struggle he's had since his father was put in jail. She remembered back to the first night he stayed in their house while Annabelle was still in the ICU.

New Years Eve, 2008

"The bathroom is across the hall. There are fresh towels in the cabinet under the sink." Allie spoke as she set the small bag of his belongings on the dresser. Lucas nodded, never looking at her.

Allie watched Lucas look around the room, quietly taking in his surroundings. He looked at the pile of clothes that sat at the end of the bed.

"Oh, those are some of Evan's old clothes. You can wear them if you'd like," Allie pointed out. Lucas nodded again. She watched as he sat down cautiously on the bed, holding his injured ribs. "How are you feeling?"

Lucas took in a deep breath slowly. "To be honest, I don't know how I feel. I am so grateful to you and Evan for taking me in. My body aches from head to toe. I get to sleep safely in a warm bed." Lucas finally looked up at Allie. "My feelings are quite mixed."

Allie leaned against the door frame and said, "That's understandable. You need a good night's sleep in something other than a hospital bed or the ground." Allie smiled.

Lucas looked down at his hands. Allie watched as he fought tears. She approached the bed and sat next to the young man. He looked up at her, eyes red with tears.

"I'm so sorry for letting this happen to her. She never deserved this." Lucas cried to Allie.

"Look at me." Allie gently turned his face towards her. "Do not blame yourself for this. What your parents did has nothing to do with you. You saved her life, Lucas. You got her through this."

"I should have stopped Janis from taking her." Lucas sniffed. "I was a coward."

"Stop it. You didn't have a choice," Allie told him sternly. Lucas wiped his tears.

Allie stood up and gave Lucas a hug. "You probably don't believe me, but I'm glad you're here. I'm so happy to have the chance to give you the same kindness you gave Annabelle. It's your turn to receive generosity."

"Thank you, Allie." Lucas returned the hug. "For everything."

Allie was brought from her thoughts when she heard Madison laugh loudly. Allie looked up to see Lucas tickling her daughter. Allie smiled and watched her four year old bond with her new friend.

"Mr. Lucas, why do you have to leave?" Madison asked.

"Well, Miss Maddy, your auntie is leaving the hospital today and when she gets home, someone has to be there for her," Lucas explained.

"Mommy and Daddy take care of me when I get sick. Isn't that what Gamma and Gampa do?" Madison pointed out.

"Of course they do, but auntie doesn't live with them. She doesn't want them to have to leave their house, so she asked me to stay with her." Lucas watched the little girl process the information.

Madison chewed on the corner of the piece of toast as she thought about what Lucas had just told her. She smiled and said, "I love auntie." She paused and swallowed her bite. "Do you love auntie?"

"Yes I do," Lucas answered. Madison smiled bigger.

"Daddy loves Mommy too," she pointed out. Lucas looked up at Allie and Evan. They returned his smile and joined in on Madison's laughter.

When they were done eating, Allie and Lucas cleaned up the kitchen while Evan took Madison to get dressed and ready to go to his parents' house for the day. Once everyone was ready to go, Allie and Madison loaded into Allie's car and Evan and Lucas loaded into Evan's truck.

"I'll see you at the hospital later tonight. I love you," Allie called out of her window as she pulled out of the garage. Evan blew his wife a kiss and they headed off to 3rd Avenue.

The roads were surprisingly clear of snow. The sun had been out for the past two days melting the snow on the roadways and sidewalks. The trip from Pleasant Road to 3rd Avenue was short and traffic free. Lucas pointed to Evan which house it was and he pulled into the snow covered drive.

Lucas sighed heavily. His heart pounded as he remembered leaving the house in a hurry.

Sunday December 14th 2008

"We have to leave." Hector burst into the house in frenzy. Lucas watched his father scramble around their small living room from the stairs.

"Why?" Janis questioned. Hector stopped to stare at his wife.

"Staying here would be stupid. If the cop even begins to suspect I had anything to do with this, she'll be at our door in a second."

"So lie, I don't feel like living in some hotel." Janis lounged on the couch, flipping through the channels.

"We all know that you can't lie if your life depended on it and I don't want to take the chance of getting caught."

"Lying is one of my best qualities! Why do you always insist on controlling my life?" Janis yelled turning the TV off.

"If it weren't for me, you would still be living on the streets! Don't question me and get a bag packed!" Hector yelled at his wife.

Lucas sat quietly on the stairs, keeping to himself. When he heard Janis stomping in his direction, he quickly moved out of the way. As his mother came up the stairs, she glanced at him.

"Are you packed?" she questioned. He shook his head no. She sighed and pulled him up the stairs with her.

"Let go of me." Lucas snapped at her. She slapped him across the face.

"How dare you speak to me like that?" Janis growled. Lucas pulled his arm from her grasp. "Get in your room and pack a bag of clothes."

"It'd be easier if we just let her go," Lucas mumbled turning to his room he added, "She didn't do anything wrong."

Hector flew up the stairs and cornered Lucas in the doorway of his bedroom. "Do you have an issue with my plan?"

"She didn't do anything wrong!" Lucas yelled at his father. Hector pulled Lucas closer to him by the collar of his shirt. Inches away from his face, Hector glared at Lucas.

"If you ever try to disobey me or betray me," Hector spat. "I will kill you. Do you understand?"

Hector gave his son a deadly glare and released his shirt. Pushing Lucas into his room, Hector added, "Pack a bag. You have ten minutes."

Lucas sat on his bed, taking in his father's words. He hated his father with a passion that no person could understand. His father stuck to his word. If he said he would kill Lucas, he would surely kill him.

Lucas grabbed a back pack and shoved handfuls of clothes in it; not caring what he did or didn't have. That's when a shiny object

255

from the other side of the room caught his eye; a brand new hammer that Lucas had bought to fix the broken dresser in the corner of his room. Lucas grabbed the hammer and shoved it in the bottom of the bag.

"Lucas!" Hector yelled up the stairs.

Lucas zipped the bag closed and threw it over his back. Lucas didn't know it yet, but that would be the best decision he could have ever made.

"Ready?" Evan asked turning off the truck. Lucas nodded and opened his door.

Evan grabbed the boxes from the back seat. The two men walked through the deep snow to the front door. Finally on the front step, Lucas pushed the door open. It was unlocked, which didn't surprise Lucas at all. They walked into the dark, cold house and Evan flipped the light switch. Nothing...

"No power," Evan commented. Lucas was focused on something else when he approached the stairs.

Lucas reached out for the piece of paper that was taped to the railing of the stairs. He pulled it off and recognized his father's handwriting.

I KNOW YOU'RE WITH THEM. MY GUESS IS YOU'LL BE COMING HOME SOONER OR LATER. DON'T WORRY I'M NOT GOING TO BE HERE TO MEET YOU. JUST REMEMBER, I KEEP MY WORD SON.

A PROMISE IS A PROMISE.

Lucas reread the note. Evan stood behind him and read it as well. Lucas felt his body shake. He knew his father would find him. He couldn't put Annabelle in danger. How was he going to keep her safe by living with her?

"We have to show this to Allie." Evan brought Lucas from his thoughts. Lucas nodded and folded the note, shoving it into his pants pocket.

Lucas looked up the stairs and sighed heavily. He climbed up the stairs slowly, in no hurry to gather what little clothes he owned. When he reached the top of the stairs, he walked into his small excuse for a room. Evan followed quietly behind him.

The room had one window which was covered by a heavy blanket. Without power, the room was like a dungeon. Lucas climbed through the mess and pulled the blanket off the window. Dust flew into the air and the room became a cloudy mess.

Lucas discarded the blanket and looked around the room. It was packed full with only a twin sized bed and a broken dresser. The tiny 7 x 8 room was like a small walk in closet. The walls were gray, barren of any decoration or color. The plaster on the ceiling bowed and cracked from obvious water damage.

The twin sized box spring and mattress that sat frameless on the floor. There was a broken dresser that leaned against the wall in the corner. Its drawers were laid out on the bed. As Evan looked around the room, he noticed a milk crate that sat next to the mattresses. It held a single wooden picture frame that had an elderly woman hugging a teenage Lucas.

Evan stood in the door as Lucas packed the boxes with clothes from the drawers on the bed. Lucas quickly filled the first box and Evan noticed that the four drawers were now empty.

Evan watched as Lucas noticed the same picture frame on the milk crate. Lucas reached for the frame and set it on the top of the clothes in the box. Without Evan noticing, Lucas grabbed the small velvet box that sat behind the frame and shoved it in his pocket.

"That's everything." Lucas spoke uncomfortably. Evan looked at the younger man that stood in front of him. Lucas looked embarrassed and ashamed of his belongings. Evan felt his heart break for Lucas. How could anyone treat their own child like this? Living like an animal with no love or care; it's amazing that Lucas is alive.

"Let's go drop that note off with Allie and head over to your new home." Evan turned and walked down the stairs. Lucas stood is his room for a minute, looking around. He felt nothing. No attachment to anything left in the room or even to the room itself. Lucas picked up the box and walked out of his past and towards his future.

After taking the note to the station, Evan and Lucas were on their way to Annabelle's apartment. Lucas tried to remember directions to and from places. He would be Annabelle's connection to the outside world. They arrived at Annabelle's apartment complex.

Lucas got the box of his clothes out of the back seat. Evan grabbed his book bag and they headed to the door. Lucas remembered the first time he met Annabelle as he walked up the stairs to the second level. The memory of why he was in her apartment building flooded into his mind.

Saturday December 13th

"Just go in there and find out where she lives." Janis growled at her son.

"How am I going to find out where she lives? Knock on every door?" Lucas questioned from the back seat with a sneer.

"Shut up! Both of you." Hector concentrated on the door of the small apartment complex. He watched as a mailman propped the door open with a rock. The mailman returned to his truck and shuffled through boxes.

"Now is your chance to get in. You're going to start on the second floor and knock on each door. Act like you are selling something, I don't care what," Hector demanded.

"What if someone-"Lucas began to ask.

"I don't care, just go!" Hector yelled and Lucas got out of the car.

Evan unlocked the door to apartment B2. Flipping the light switch, Lucas looked around the living room. The walls were a tan color filled with artwork and pictures of Annabelle's friends and family. The couch was red, covered in brown pillows and a multi colored throw draped across the back. Across from the couch was a small, dark wooden entertainment center that held a good sized TV. Lucas smiled as he noticed how tidy Annabelle's home was. She had explained to him how compulsive she could be about cleaning.

To his right was the kitchen. It was a good size kitchen with a four person table; the color matched the dark wood of the entertainment center. The kitchen was another example of Annabelle's obsession with cleanliness. Each appliance was squared off the counter. The towels were folded neatly across the handle of the oven. Not a speck of dirt, dust of clutter to be found.

Through the living room was a short hallway. At the end, there were three doors; to the left, straight ahead, and to the right.

"You can fill the dresser in the guest bedroom. All except for the top drawer are empty." Evan pointed at the room to the right. "The bathroom is through the door between the two bedrooms. I need to go downstairs and talk to the landlord about a key for the elevator."

Lucas walked into the room that Evan called the extra bedroom. The room was a warm color of green. The full size bed was in the far corner of the room. A white dresser sat to the right of the bed. Lucas set the box down on the bed and looked around the room. To the left of the door was a desk, neatly organized with school books and a laptop computer. Above the desk was a CD case filled with all sorts of music. Lucas took a moment to look at her taste of music; Lily Allen, Paramore, Rascal Flatts, Van Halen, Elvis Presley, and Alanis Morissette were some of the names that popped out at Lucas. He smiled at the wide range of music. He turned to the dresser that he was supposed to use.

He quickly folded his clothes and filled two of the three empty drawers. Curiosity struck Lucas as he remembered Evan saying all the drawers but the top were empty. Lucas slid open the top drawer to find it filled with pictures. It was the closest thing to chaos that Lucas had found in the apartment. He dug through the pictures to see Annabelle as a child, teenager and holding Madison as an infant. He found high school dance, graduation and school pictures. Lucas smiled as he found a picture of Annabelle smiling widely; her teeth covered in braces. Her eyes were bright and her face was excited. Lucas set this on the top of pile and closed the drawer.

He picked up the picture frame from the box and wiped off the dust. He looked down at his Grandma Mable and smiled. He propped the frame up on the dresser and walked out of the room.

Setting the box down by the door of the guest room, he peeked into Annabelle's bedroom. It was slightly bigger than the guest room and painted a bright yellow color. The bed was covered in a luscious comforter and tons of pillows. The colors ranged from yellow to orange to red. Above the bed was a piece of artwork that caught Lucas's eye.

He reached for the light switch and moved closer to the painting. It was of a sunset. It wasn't a typical sunset on a beach picture, but instead a sunset from a hillside. Snow covered the hills and trees that outlined an opening in the tree line. Yellows, oranges, and reds reflected off the untouched snow. It seemed to be the inspiration for the color pallet of the room.

"Annabelle painted it." Evan spoke from behind Lucas. Lucas jumped slightly at the sudden sound of his voice. "Sorry, didn't mean to scare you," Evan joked.

"It's okay," Lucas laughed. He focused on the painting again.

"She painted it about three years ago. She took a trip with Billy Jean to Canada. I'm not even sure where in Canada. She painted it from a picture she took outside of their resort." Evan smiled looking proudly at the painting.

"It's amazing," Lucas commented. Both men stood staring at the painting, admiring.

Evan dropped Lucas off at the hospital entrance.

"I'll be back later. My parents will probably get here before me," Evan informed Lucas.

"Okay, I'll see later." Lucas closed the truck door.

As he walked through the lobby of the hospital, he saw some familiar faces of the staff. He smiled and waved at those who noticed him. He pushed the button for the elevator and waited for its arrival.

On the ride up, Lucas thought about the note his father left. Hector would find Lucas. He knew living with Annabelle was going to be putting her life in danger. However, not living with Annabelle wasn't an option. He would protect her with his life.

Shoving his hands in his pockets, he felt the small green velvet box. Lucas pulled the ring box out and opened it. Adorned with a single diamond mounted in the center, a small silver ring shined back at him. Lucas sighed heavily and put the box back in his pocket as the doors opened.

He walked down the long hallway to Annabelle's room. Donna smiled at him as he walked past the nurse's station. Lucas entered Annabelle's room to find a note on the closed bathroom door.

Lucas,

I needed a shower. I'll be out in a little bit. Don't worry, I'm fine. Make yourself comfortable.

I love you,

-Annie. 4:35pm.

Lucas smiled and looked up at the clock; 4:45. He knew that she would be in there for at least another ten minutes. He sat down on the edge of couch and thought about his grandmother's ring. Was it really the answer? Would she think he was rushing things? Lucas shook his head. He knew they were head over heels for each other. Is it enough? Of course… right?

Lucas continued to fight with his thoughts when he looked up at the clock. It was five o'clock. Annabelle wasn't out of the bathroom yet. He got up and paced in front of the door. He tried to tell himself that she was fine. If he went into the bathroom, she would think he didn't trust her. She told him not to worry. Five more minutes, he thought to himself. If she isn't out in five more minutes then he would knock on the door.

Just as he moved to listen to the door, it opened. He quickly moved away and acted as though he was looking at something on the wall. He looked at Annabelle and saw a smile appear on her face.

"I love you," Annabelle whispered.

- 30- Annabelle: Healing

Earlier that day…

After four days of intense therapy, I was exhausted. I sat on the seat in the tub, dangling my feet in the warm water as it drained. I was finally able to bathe myself. Unfortunately, it was like I was five again, taking a bath. I wrapped the towel around my body and lifted my legs out of the tub. I sighed heavily looking at the forming scar on my right hip. The incision was about eight inches long. It ran from the front of my body around to my lower back. It was almost healed, luckily, showing no signs of infection.

My wounds were healing and my strength was returning. I had regained half of the twenty pounds I had lost. Feeling happier with each day, my emotions began to stabilize and I could go through the day without crying. I knew I would be sent home sooner rather than later. Preparing for that day was harder than walking down the hallway anymore.

Once I was dry and clothed, including my rainbow slippers, I stood up, holding onto the bars around the shower. A dark blue walker stood a couple feet away from me. It was another gift from Clara; donated by the hospital. I reached out for the metal frame and leaned against it. I felt old with a walker, but it was also a freeing experience to be able to do it on my own.

I stood in front of the sink, glancing at my reflection in the mirror. My left eye was healing, the bruising was turning yellow. The scar underneath my eye was small, fading with time. I looked into my own eyes, seeing a dim light gleam at me. I smiled and turned to leave. I opened the bathroom door to see Lucas leaned up against the door frame. I smiled as he jumped away from the door, acting as though he wasn't waiting for me to call him.

"I love you." I smiled at him. He blushed and kissed my cheek. I moved to the chair, near the end of the hospital bed. Lucas propped a pillow behind my back and I sat down slowly. Once settled into the chair, Lucas moved the walker out of the way.

"Annie, there is something I wanted to ask you," Lucas said, returning to stand in front of me. He shoved his hands into the pockets of his jeans. He stood tall in front of me, his face was nervous. As I opened my mouth to reply, there was a knock at the door.

"Come in," I called.

Dr. Morris walked in, smiling. He shook Lucas's hand and said, "Good news, Annabelle." I looked up at him with wide eyes. *Here it comes...* "You can go home."

Excitement quickly fizzled when I thought about the obstacles that lay ahead. Dr. Morris noticed my anxiety and quickly said, "Don't worry. You're ready for this."

"Ready for what?" My mom's voice rang from the doorway. I looked to see my parents walk into the room.

"I get to go home," I said softly.

"That's great news!" Mom exclaimed. Her excitement filled the room. I couldn't help but smile. "When?" she asked Dr. Morris.

"Tonight, as soon as you'd like to leave. I'll have Donna get the papers ready," Dr. Morris told me with a grin on his face. He continued to talk to my mother as I sat, staring forward. I felt a hand on my shoulder and looked up to see my dad.

"Annabelle." He smiled at me. "You are just like your mother. You are ready for this. Lucas is going to be there to take care of you. Your mother and I are just a call away. Stop worrying." I looked down at my hands.

"I know, but I'm scared. I've been here for almost a month. It's a safety net," I explained.

"You'll find a new safety net, I promise." My dad nodded to Lucas, who was involved in a conversation with my overly excited mother and Dr. Morris. I smiled. My dad kissed my forehead and gave me a hug.

"Thanks Daddy." I spoke softly.

He walked over to the conversation while I thought silently in my chair. I looked around the room. It was filled with flowers, new and old. Cards, hand-made and bought, plastered the walls and table tops. A bundle of balloons, half deflated, floated in front of the window. The couch was covered in bags and gifts from friends and family. My eyes found the chair that sat near the head of the bed. It was the same chair that Lucas refused to leave every night he spent here with me. I thought of the first night I stayed in this room, Lucas's hand never leaving mine.

A lost tear found its way down my cheek. Not another tear followed its lead as it traveled down my chin and to my collar bone. A pensive, melancholy smile formed across my face and I thought of the good memories that happened here. Finally walking by myself, playing with Madison on the bed, watching Lucas sleep each morning, the good and bad seemed to equal each other. Leaving would be a bitter sweet departure.

Donna entered the room with a clip board of papers. I subconsciously signed the dotted lines. Once I finished signing and Dr. Morris had explained the details of home care to my parents and Lucas, there was another knock at the door. I snapped out of my day dream when Renee said hello. She was my primary day nurse and I didn't expect to see her tonight.

"What are you doing here?" I asked. She smiled and put the walker in front of me.

"We are going to take a walk." Renee held her hand out to help me stand. She led me outside of the room and we walked together down the long hallway.

"Annabelle," Renee started, "I've been at the hospital for ten years and I have never been as inspired as I have been by you. Your courage and determination are incredible. What you went through could have broken most people twice as old as you, but you made it through. You accomplished so much in the past 26 days. You are special young woman."

I stopped walking and looked at Renee. Tears formed in her eyes as she looked back at me. I felt humbled by her words.

"Thank you." I hugged her tightly with one arm, still holding onto the walker. I pulled away and added, "Thank you for helping me get this far. I couldn't possibly have gotten here without your care, compassion and protection." I smiled.

She pulled me into another hug, "Come back to visit."

"I will," I promised.

"Let's go back to your room. You've got some packing to do." Renee wiped her face.

We made our way back to my room, chatting causally as we walked. The door was closed. Renee walked in front of me to open it. As the door opened, applause filled my ears. I walked into the room that was now filled with people: nurses that had been a part of my care, Clara and Heather, other hospital workers I had met, friends, and my family.

Warmth filled my body when I saw the faces of all the people who got me through the past month. I knew I was going to be well taken care of even after I left. It was the first time I felt confident in leaving the safety net of the hospital.

As I walked through the crowd, I was hugged, kissed, poked and pinched. I couldn't stop smiling as everyone said wonderful things to me: "I'm so proud of you," "This is the beginning of a new life," "You look so good," and "You got through the hardest part."

I had been on my feet for a good twenty minutes, much longer than I had been used to. My knees grew weak under the weight of my body. I looked at my mom. She knowingly pushed a chair behind me and I sat down.

"Annabelle," Dr. Morris spoke. The room went silent. "Everyone here has come together to do something for you. I, personally, am so very proud of your progress and accomplishments this far. We all know the struggle that you've been through and the journey that still lies ahead. With that said, we have started a fund to help pay off your medical bills. After the word got out around this small town, I'm happy to tell you that your medical bills are paid off."

As the words left his mouth, my jaw tightened. I felt tears fill my eyes as my mother wrapped her arms around me. Words could not describe the feeling that spilled from my body. I cried heavily, overwhelmed with gratitude.

The room got quiet and I knew it was my turn to speak. I took a deep breath and thought carefully about my words.

"Thank you, thank you all so much." I paused, tears still streaming down my cheeks. "Words cannot describe the gratitude and love I feel for each and every one of you. This is more than I could ever ask for. More than I could ever imagine. You are truly the reason I pushed so hard through this past month and half." I paused again, thinking back to the two weeks of hell. "You are the reason I pushed through the pain and the humiliation. You all kept me alive." My eyes fell on Lucas as I finished the statement. His face was red with tears. Evan stood next to him, tears streaming down his cheeks.

"Auntie!" Madison yelled from behind her father. Madison ran up to me and hugged me. I kissed the little girl's head. I pulled her onto my lap letting her sit on my left leg. The room quickly emptied, leaving my family and me alone in the room. Madison sat in my lap, chatting away about her day at day care. Her broken sentences and missing words took my mind off the battle that lay ahead.

"Where's Allie?" I asked Evan. He glanced at the clock.

"She should be here anytime."

As if she had heard us talking about her, Allie walked into the room.

"Speak of the devil." Evan greeted his wife with a kiss. Allie tried to smile, but her composure was shaken and nervous. Maddy jumped down from my lap and ran to her mother. Allie picked up the four year old and kissed her cheek.

"What's wrong, honey?" my mom asked.

Allie looked at my mother, then at me. She placed Madison on the couch and said, "We found Janis Martin today."

Her words were plain, and to the point. I felt a piece of the world fall off my shoulders with her news. *That's great news.* I watched Allie for a moment. Her disposition said there was something more to the story. I thought about her words, *'We found Janis Martin today.'* Why didn't she say caught? *What about Hector?* Why isn't she more excited? *What about Hector?*

"What aren't you telling us?" I spoke in a low tone. Allie looked into my eyes with fear.

"She's dead." Allie spoke in a blank tone. She wasn't hurt by the news, rather worried. Her words began to sink in as she continued. "She was found in a motel five miles outside of town. We got a call from the motel saying there was a disturbance. When we arrived at the motel, she was found; shot in the chest."

I closed my eyes as the picture of Janis, dead, filled my head. I shook my head. *It was Hector.* Hector killed his wife. Fear pained my chest, feeling like a boulder had been set on it. I looked up at Lucas. His expression was blank. He didn't look back at me, nor did he say anything.

"Did you find Hector?" Evan questioned. Allie shook her head at her husband. Evan clenched his fists. "He did it." He nodded. "He killed her."

"Nothing has been proven," Allie reminded him.

"Who else? We live in Fort Kent, Maine, Allie, who else?" Evan questioned.

He turned towards the window and stood silently.

Lucas's expression went from blank to pain within a few seconds. I wished I knew what he was thinking. I reached for his hand. He looked down at me and I realized he was holding back tears. I

266

pulled him closer. He knelt down in front of me and I wrapped my arms around his neck.

"It's okay, Lucas. We'll be okay," I whispered. He rested his head on my shoulder, nuzzling my neck. Deep down, I hoped Lucas loved his mother. I felt the need to protect him. No one deserves to be murdered. Criminals don't even deserve to be killed; it's the easy way out.

The room turned silent. I continued holding Lucas as my parents stood in the corner with Allie and Evan. Madison sat tiredly on the couch while her parents chatted with my parents. Lucas pulled out of the hug and looked at me. His tears rested on his lower eye lids. Leaning forward to kiss me, Lucas let a single tear slide down his cheek. I quickly wiped the tear with my thumb.

"I love you," he whispered into my lips.

"I love you." I kissed his lips again. Our eyes met and I added, "We'll be okay."

"Annabelle, you're free to leave whenever you're ready." Donna spoke from the doorway. I looked up at her and smiled.

I suddenly realized how ready I was to go home. I was ready to sleep in my own bed, eat my own food and be on my own schedule. As thoughts flooded into my head, I thought of Lucas. I was ready for him to live with me, in my own home. I was ready to start our new journey together. I knew it was time for me to move forward and let go of my fears.

"Are you ready?" my mom asked cautiously, bringing me out of my thoughts.

I nodded at her with a smile. "Yes, very ready."

Donna pushed a wheelchair into the room and I shook my head at her.

"I'll walk." I smiled. She nodded and smiled knowingly back at me. "But we can use that for all the stuff we have to carry."

My mind was clear for the first time in weeks. Happiness was beginning to find its way back into my life. I felt the need to be confident; not only for myself, but for my family. I didn't feel the need to look to them for every decision I made. I was healing; mentally, emotionally and physically.

PART THREE

I walked towards the elevator with my family behind me, Lucas and Donna on either side of me. I held onto the handles with all my strength. With each step I took, my limits lessened and my movement was smoother. My left leg took one step forward and then I had to pivot my right leg forward. Clara told me it would get easier to bend my hip with practice. For now, it was best to avoid bending the joint at all.

Evan walked ahead of us to pull the car around to the front. He was taking me and Lucas home on his way. Everyone agreed to go home tonight and let us get settled into our new life.

I smiled to myself thinking about living with the man that walked along side of me. We had *lived* together, but never in a voluntary atmosphere. I admitted to myself that I was excited to live with him. My mother gave me a small but adamant reminder earlier this morning that the guest bedroom in my apartment was ready for Lucas. *She's right. Don't rush anything…*

No, I didn't want to rush anything. I wasn't going to tell Lucas where to live or sleep. If he wants to sleep in the guest bedroom, I was okay with that. But if he wanted to climb into bed with me I definitely wouldn't say no. Nothing sexual was on my mind. I wasn't ready for that kind of a relationship. *Especially with what's on the way…* Pregnancy thoughts stayed in the back of my thoughts. I pushed them away again, focusing on right now.

"The elevator door will be a tricky maneuver. The walker wheels could easily get stuck in the ridges." My mom's voice brought me from my thoughts.

"Actually, since wheel chairs and walkers are used so often in hospitals, she'll barely even notice the difference," Donna explained. "Your apartment building will be another story. Getting on and off the elevator at home will need your full and careful attention until you're used to it."

I nodded at Donna as the elevator doors closed behind us. I leaned up against the wall as we descended. Donna smiled at me and whispered, "Plus, this walker isn't going to be a permanent attachment. You'll be up and down the stairs before you know it."

I smiled back feeling the elevator move. Nerves bubbled in my chest, my knees shook anxiously and I felt my palms sweat. *Relax, you're going home.* Easier said than done...

I closed my eyes slightly, taking a deep breath. I felt Lucas wrap his arm around my waist. I looked up at him and smiled. He kissed my forehead and whispered, "Relax."

Comfort was a light way of putting his touch into words. My body begged to be held by Lucas. He was safety for me. He knew my thoughts before I thought them. He knew my actions before I made them. Only knowing him for a month felt like knowing him my entire life. *You have plenty of time to learn more...* I owed him my life.

The elevator finished its slow decent and the doors opened. Evan stood on the other side, waiting for us. Everyone exited the elevator leaving Lucas and I. Donna stood holding the doors open. I pushed the walker in front of me, gliding without restraint through the threshold of the elevator. The lobby echoed with the movements of the people scattered around the large area.

Walking through the wide open lobby reminded me that I was leaving the safety of the hospital. I tightened my grip on the walker. We walked silently to the door. Lucas stayed close to me, like we were glued at the hip.

I stepped outside into the fresh, cold air for the first time in weeks. Apprehensive to say the least, the cold air brushed my cheeks and tickled my nose. A once welcome and once feared feeling took hold of my body; winter air.

Memories of both love and loathing for the cold weather danced in my brain. Happy to see the sunset in the distance and sad to leave the safety of the hospital, I took another step into the world.

With Lucas close at my side and Evan ahead of me, waiting by the open car door, I moved closer.

"Careful of the ice," Mom chimed in my ear. I smiled, gliding over the smooth patch of ice.

Lucas held my arm close to his body and he assisted me to the edge of the side walk. Donna took the walker from in front of me.

"Pivot on your left leg and sit down on the seat, facing me," Donna explained, holding onto my waist. She helped me turn around and back into the car. Once I felt the seat underneath me, I sighed. "Now lift your legs into the car."

Holding onto my right leg, I shifted my legs into the car. With a deep breath, I hid the pain that radiated through my hips. I smiled at Donna, giving her a thumbs-up. She leaned into the truck and hugged me tightly.

"Come back and visit," Donna whispered.

"I will," I promised.

She pulled away from the hug and looked into my eyes. "If there is anything that you ever need, don't hesitate to call me."

"I will." I smiled. She touched my cheek, stood up and closed the door.

The running truck roared as the heat poured from the vents. I put my hands in front of the vents, rubbing them together. After the short time outside, my hands burned from the cold.

My parents, Allie and Madison said goodbye. Lucas got in the back seat of the truck and Evan got into the driver's seat.

"All set?" Evan smiled at me. I nodded, feeling a nervous shiver climb up my spine.

As we drove away from the hospital, a light snow fell from the sky. The setting sun was interrupted by cloud cover. I smiled and I watched the flakes dance across the pavement. It was a familiar site. My town covered in snow, snowflakes falling from the sky and the sun setting in the background. I was home.

As we turned down Main Street, the local Rite Aid's sign caught my eye. It read, "We are all behind you, Annabelle." I looked at Evan as he tried to hide his smile. Without a word, I watched as we passed each little business, store and restaurants, all their signs reading words of encouragement and wishes of good luck. Tears filled my eyes happily. Quickly, the Meyer Bookstore appeared on my left. The dim lights indicated the store was closed. The sign in the front read, "Never give up, Annabelle."

Emotions flooded into my chest as we passed the store. The memories of that night haunted my dreams and thoughts. Seeing it again brought back the pain, the fear and the helpless feelings.

Lucas gently squeezed my shoulder from the back seat. I instantly felt calm, reminded of what I have now because of that day.

We turned down the street to my apartment complex. I felt my nerves bubble inside of my chest. I knew this was the beginning of a new life for me. I was stepping into my new life.

We pulled up to the door. "I don't have a car any-"

271

Evan cut my statement off and added, "Don't worry about that right now." My brother smiled at me and jumped out of his door.

Evan walked around to my door. Lucas got out of the truck and opened my door. Evan grabbed a handful of the bags in the back seat and headed for the apartment building. Lucas placed the walker in front of me. I hung my feet over the seat, just barely reaching the ground.

"Take your time," Lucas reminded me. I looked at him and the corners of my mouth began to curl. He was holding onto the walker tightly, watching my every movement as though I was taking my first steps. He noticed my stare. "What?"

"Nothing," I lied, putting my hands on his shoulders. I pulled him close, hugging his neck tightly.

"What?" He laughed. I shook my head in his shoulder.

"Nothing," I repeated. I pulled away from him, placing my grip on the walker. My left foot touched the ground first, gently baring my weight. Lucas held onto me as I stepped down with my left. I took a deep breath in of relief.

"Are you okay?" he questioned. I smiled and looked up at him. *This guy is attentive.*

"Yes." I moved forward and he closed the truck door behind me. He grabbed the duffel bag from the back seat and closed the last door.

Once we were inside the building, I remembered meeting Lucas. I looked at the stairs as we passed them. I smiled inwardly as I replayed falling into Lucas's arms rushing down the stairs to work. We passed the stairs and the two down stairs apartments. As we passed A2, Jolene, my neighbor, was leaving her apartment.

"Anna." She was startled to see me. She excitedly put her hands out to hug me. I flinched slightly, waiting for her fierce hug. "Oh, I'm sorry." She quickly put her arms down at her side.

"No, it's all right." I let go of the walker with my left arm and held it out to hug her. She approached me slowly and gently wrapped her arms around me. While I hugged my friend, Lucas kept his body close behind me, preventing me from losing balance or falling.

Jolene held me for a minute and then said, "I'm so glad to see you. I'm so glad you're okay." She pulled out of the hug but kept her hands on my shoulder. "If you need anything, please, don't hesitate to call me. Even if it's for a hug, I'll be there." Jolene smiled at me.

"Thanks Jo." I smiled back at her. She was dressed for work, her name tag pinned to her chest. I suddenly worried if I still had a job. *Not the time to think about that.*

"I've got to run." Jolene said. "It was good seeing you." She quickly rushed past us and left the building. Lucas stood behind me, waiting for me to continue forward to the elevator ahead.

When I didn't continue, Lucas leaned forward around my shoulder. He asked, "Are you okay?"

I took a breath, said, "Yeah, sorry," and took another step forward.

"Don't apologize. If you need to stop, we aren't in a hurry," Lucas reminded me.

"No, it's okay. I'm fine." *Liar, stop worrying.*

Lucas stayed close behind, unsure of my answer. We finally reached the utility elevator and waited for Evan to return. We weren't standing there for less than 10 seconds when the doors opened.

"Going up?" he joked. I smiled at my older brother. I was exhausted; *too much worrying,* or excitement. Evan stepped forward and helped me push the walker over the uneven threshold of the old elevator.

The elevator was small, only big enough for two. Lucas opted to walk up the stairs. Evan closed the door to the elevator and pushed the only button on the elevator. As we made our way up, Evan asked me a question.

"Is he the one?" Evan's voice wasn't completely serious. I could hear at hint of joking in his tone. I looked up at him and furrowed my eyebrows.

"What do you mean?" I asked.

"Is Lucas the guy?" Evan smiled. As he paused to let me answer, the elevator beeped. "We're here." He opened the door and Lucas was standing on the other side. As Evan walked forward, I looked down at my hands gripping the walker. *You're over analyzing.*

Again, Evan helped push the walker over the threshold and straight ahead was the open door to my apartment. The smell of vanilla and sandalwood soaked the air around me. *You're home.*

I stopped at the door and Evan shook Lucas's hand. My older brother then turned to me and smiled. "Time for me to go and let you get settled in. Allie went through your kitchen and got rid of all the expired food. Mom went shopping for you last night and you should be fine for the next couple weeks." Evan rolled his eyes. I shook my head at my mother's preparedness. Evan wrapped his arms around me and gave me a bear hug.

"Thank you, Evan," I whispered. I returned the hug and kissed his cheek.

"Don't hesitate to call," Evan reminded me, "either of you." He looked at Lucas. Lucas nodded. *We have an entire list of people to call, for any imaginable reason.*

"Night, sis." Evan patted my back softly. "See you tomorrow."

Lucas waited for me to pass him into the apartment and then locked the door behind him.

"It smells the way I left it." I smiled at the air freshener that sat on the counter; sandalwood and vanilla. I stepped forward, looking around my home. It was warm, bright and welcoming.

Everything was the way I left it. Each item I owned felt insignificant to the man that now shared the place I called home. I turned to glance into the kitchen. A bouquet of my favorite flowers, orange and red Gerber daisies, sat in the center of the table. I moved forward and pulled the chair out. I sat down and leaned forward, smelling the bouquet. Picking up the envelope, sliding the card out, I looked down at a beautiful picture of a sunset. I opened the card to read:

Annie,

Together, we will get through this.

I love you,

- Lucas.

I smiled at the bold handwriting that I had never seen before. Placing the card in front of the flowers, I noticed that Lucas had not followed me into the kitchen. I stood up slowly from the chair and held onto my walker. I walked into the living room to see Lucas standing at the door, his hands in his pockets.

"What's wrong?" I questioned, smiling curiously at him.

"This is different," he admitted. I stood in front of him.

Lucas was right. We had never lived together on a voluntary basis. We had been forced together by his parents, never meant to fall in love.

I leaned forward, just the metal of the walker between us. I kissed his lips softly, feeling the corners of his mouth curl upwards. I smiled back as he wrapped his arms around me.

"It will take time." I added, "I promise it will get easier."

Lucas finally walked into the apartment, trailing behind me. He picked up my bags and took them into my room. I went into the bathroom to get ready for bed. It felt good to be home, especially to have Lucas home with me.

I walked into my bedroom after changing into a tank top and sweat pants to see Lucas unpacking my bags. He turned to look at me and smiled. Lucas had turned the blankets down on my bed and helped me into bed.

"Go to sleep." Lucas smiled, kissing my forehead. I rested my head on the pillows. Lucas walked across the room and continued unpacking my bag.

"You don't have to do that." I yawned.

"You are tired," Lucas pointed out. I shook my head and closed my eye tiredly. As I reopened my eyes, I heard his gentle laugh.

"No, I want to stay up," I insisted, opening my eyes wider only to feel them protest. "I want to stay up and talk with you."

"We have plenty of time to talk. Sleep, Annie," Lucas insisted approaching my bed with an empty suitcase.

"It goes in the closet of the other room." I yawned again. Lucas nodded and left the room. I closed my eyes again, shifting my body. Before I had time to get comfortable, I was asleep.

- 32- Annabelle's Smile

"It goes in the closet of the other room." Annabelle yawned tiredly. Lucas smiled at his exhausted girlfriend. He walked across the hallway and placed the suitcase on the top shelf of the closet.

Crossing the hallway again, Lucas entered Annabelle's room to find her sleeping soundly. A smile crept across his face as he noticed the strange position her body was in. Without hesitation, Lucas shifted Annabelle's body into a visibly comfortable position and covered her with the blankets. Touching her forehead with his lips, he noticed Annabelle's unconscious smile. Lucas turned out the light and closed the door partially.

Having just gotten home before Annabelle fell asleep, sleeping arrangements had not been discussed. Marie had made it very clear to both Lucas and Annabelle that the guest bedroom was perfectly suitable for Lucas to stay in. While he could assume Annabelle wouldn't mind him sleeping in the same bed with her, he didn't feel comfortable doing that without discussing it first. Knowing how easily she was startled, waking up next to someone she hadn't fallen asleep next to didn't seem like a good way to start their living together.

In the bathroom, Lucas ran a hand full of cold water across his face. He sighed heavily and returned to *his* room. Closing the door halfway, Lucas slipped out of his jeans, hanging them over the computer chair. He slipped off his t-shirt and threw it into the corner.

As he stood in front of a full length mirror, Lucas couldn't help but look at himself. The bruising on his ribs had diminished and the scars on his face were faded. Running his fingers through his hair, Lucas shrugged off the reflection.

Sitting on the edge of the bed, Lucas felt the expectation weigh heavily on his shoulders. Today was the first day of a very rough journey for both Lucas and Annabelle. He was stepping into a new world, a new life style of being needed and counted on. Growing up, no one counted on him for anything; no one expected anything out of him. Now, Annabelle counted on him for everything. She needed him to do the things she won't be able to do herself.

Inhaling, Lucas felt confidence fill his chest. He could only take on this responsibility with complete confidence in himself. He could only accomplish his expectations if he knew she was worth the struggle. A smile appeared on his lips; Annabelle was worth a lot more than a struggle. She was worth anything and everything he could fathom.

Clicking the light off, Lucas crossed his arms behind his head and reclined back in the bed. Staring up at the ceiling, Lucas pictured Annabelle smiling up at him from his arms. Within minutes, Lucas fell into a light slumber.

Thursday, January 22nd

An abrupt noise woke Lucas from his hollow shut-eye. Rubbing his eyes tiredly, he glanced at the clock; 2:34am. The apartment was silent. He stretched his senses, waiting for another noise to catch his ear. He heard Annabelle mumble from across the hallway. Knowing how often Annabelle talked in her sleep, he waited for the silence to return. Instead the mumbling grew louder and quickly turned into a cry for him.

Without delay, Lucas was on his feet and in Annabelle's room before the second hand had time to click. He switched on the lamp on the night stand and sat at the edge of Annabelle's bed.

"Annie?" He spoke softly, gently touching her jaw with his hand.

She squirmed underneath him, letting out another cry for help. Lucas put both of his hands on her face. She finally opened her eyes, letting her tears flow freely.

"I'm right here," he promised.

Eyes terrified, Annabelle sat up and wrapped her arms around his neck. She tucked her face into his neck and whispered, "I couldn't find you."

Annabelle felt like a lost child who couldn't find her way home. Panic and abandonment overwhelmed her sense of right and wrong. Waking up from a nightmare alone was like being back in hell to Annabelle.

"I'm here now. Don't worry, I won't go anywhere," Lucas promised. Inside, he beat himself up for leaving her alone, knowing how many nightmares she had.

Running his fingers through her hair, Lucas rocked her gently, calming her nerves. Annabelle suddenly became conscious of his lack of clothing as she rested her hand on his bare chest. Noticing, for the first time, the muscles in his chest, Annabelle became self aware of her own body. It had never crossed her mind to look at Lucas in a physical sense. Unexpectedly responsive of their close proximity to one another, Annabelle's nerves formed goose bumps along her arms and neck. She shivered slightly.

Noticing, Lucas pulled her closer and wrapped the blanket around them, thinking she was cold. He kissed her forehead and rested his cheek on her head.

As Annabelle's nerves got the best of her, her body involuntarily shuddered in response. Her mild went wild feeling the heat of his breath on her neck. Feeling overwhelmed, Annabelle blushed.

"Lucas," she whispered, feeling ashamed. He looked down at her crimson cheeks. "Umm…" An anxious smirk appeared on her face as she sat up in bed.

"What's wrong?" Lucas sat up, watching her curiously.

"You're making me nervous," she whispered, an awkward giggle escaping her lips.

"What?" he questioned. He didn't understand what he was doing differently.

Annabelle looked at his face, then at his bare chest then back up at his face again. As if someone flipped a switch in his mind, Lucas realized what Annabelle meant. He jumped out of the bed and ran into the other room. Before Annabelle had time to think, Lucas was back wearing sweat pants and a t-shirt.

"I'm sorry, I didn't even think about-" Lucas began as he sat down on the edge of the bed.

"Don't worry about it. Forget it." Annabelle moved closer to Lucas, pulling him into bed with her. She kissed him softly and rested her head on the pillows. Her eyes looked at the neon numbers to her right. "It's 3 am. We should probably go to sleep." Annabelle yawned quietly.

Lucas kissed her forehead and rested his head on the pillow. He looked up at the ceiling as the room fell silent. He thought about making the woman lying next to him nervous. He smiled wistfully, the confidence growing inside his chest. It felt good to know Annabelle was physically attracted to him.

With that thought, Annabelle shifted in bed and placed her head on his chest. His arm wrapped around her and brushed her bare arms. A shiver ran up his spine, sending a wave of fervor through his thoughts. With a quick inhale, Lucas felt the hair on his neck stand up

278

and his heart pounded with anticipation. Annabelle rested her hand on his chest and snuggled closer to him. Feeling the heat of her body on his, Lucas felt his nerves scream.

Lucas stopped his thoughts abruptly in their tracks. Mentally scolding himself, he pushed the inappropriate notions from his mind. Their relationship was just getting the chance to mature, sex wasn't what he wanted.

With a sigh, Lucas yawned and rested his chin on Annabelle's head. Keeping his thoughts clean, Lucas fell asleep with nothing more than Annabelle's smile on his mind.

Lucas woke up feeling refreshed; his mind clear. Without waking up Annabelle, he looked at the clock on the nightstand; 10:20 am. Annabelle's family would be here in less than two hours.

Not wanting to wake Annabelle up yet, Lucas remained still. He looked up at the ceiling remembering his thoughts from last night. He remembered the promise he'd made to his Grandmother before she passed.

November 13th, 2003

"How are you doing today, Luke?" Mable sat with her grandson on the couch of the nursing home living room.

"All right, I guess," Lucas lied.

Mable smiled and patted his knee. "You were never good at lying, Luke."

He smiled at his grandmother and said, "Mable, it's terrible at home. Hector wrote a letter to Janis. She got it in the mail yesterday. After she read it, she left it sitting out on the kitchen counter."

"You didn't read your mother's mail, did you?" Mable smiled knowingly.

"I was just curious." Lucas shrugged. "He never mentioned anything about me, not even to see if I was okay."

"Lucas, you know your father. He doesn't care about anyone but himself." Mable sighed. "You are more of a man than your father will ever be."

She reached for his hand and held it tightly. She patted the back of his hand. "Oh that reminds me." She reached for something on the table beside her. "Happy 16th Birthday, Lucas."

Mable set a small white box on his lap. *"I've wanted to give this to you for a while. It means a lot to me and I wanted to make sure it would be passed down to you."*

Lucas opened the white box to find a green, velvet box inside. Dumping the velvet box into his hand, Lucas found a ring inside. It was a silver wedding ring with a single diamond mounted in the center.

"Mable, I'm only 16. What about Janis?"

"If I would have given this ring to your mother when she married Hector, they would have pawned it for money long before you were even born." Mable sneered. Lucas looked down at the glistening diamond ring. *"Luke, before you know it, there will be a girl that you fall so in love with that you won't know which direction is up. When that day comes that you want to spend the rest of your life with a special lady, you'll be prepared."*

Closing the small ring box, Lucas hugged his grandmother. *"Thanks, Mable."*

"Anything for you, Luke." She kissed his cheek. *"Promise you'll take good care of that and give it to a sweet girl who will take good care of you."*

"I promise, Mable."

Thinking of his grandmother brought tears to his eyes. Lucas let a few slide down his cheeks as he thought of her words. The ring had been the only reminder of the promise he made to Mable. Until now, five years later, the ring held an untouchable destiny. Now, with a sweet girl in his arms, the ring held a purpose.

Annabelle was the girl Lucas wanted to spend the rest of his existence with. No person could ever match the feelings he felt for her. Marriage, unfortunately, felt like a rushed decision right now. Lucas knew it wouldn't solve the problems that lay ahead.

Was he ready for that commitment? With the weight of the world on his shoulders by accepting the responsibility of Annabelle's care, did Lucas really want to add the commitment and obligation of marriage?

Visibly frowning, Lucas threw the negative thoughts from his mind. Annabelle wasn't a burden in his life. He wasn't obligated to be here. He felt privileged that Annabelle would put her life in his hands. He was blessed to be trusted by anyone after the hell his parents created.

Shifting slightly, Lucas looked down at the woman who depended on him with her life. How could he let himself think of her as anything other than a gift? She was the reason he was no longer in the care of his parents. She was the reason he pushed himself to take a risk. Annabelle was the reason he was alive.

Bringing him from his thoughts, Annabelle's face twisted in pain. The hand that rested on his chest, clenched into a fist. Her finger nails dug into her palms and she let out a tiny sob.

Sliding his arm out from underneath her pillow, Lucas sat up and slipped his hands into hers. "Annie, wake up."

She continued to sob quietly, suffering in her nightmare.

"Annabelle." Lucas brushed her cheek with his thumb. With the touch of his thumb, she opened her eyes and looked up at him. Tears fell from her eyes as she opened her mouth to speak.

"My hip..."She sobbed.

"I'll be right back." Lucas got out of bed and went to the bathroom. He returned with her pain medicine and a glass of water.

Annabelle sat up in bed, wiping her tears. She felt her hip ache and throb. With a shaking hand, she took the pills. The small pills felt like boulders as she continued to drink the water. Coughing slightly, she handed the glass to Lucas. He set it on the nightstand and waited for Annabelle to say something.

"I'm still tired." Annabelle grumbled as she sat against the headboard and rested her head on Lucas's shoulder. Her eyes fell on the neon numbers of the clock and she sighed. "It's 10:50. My family is going to be here in an hour." She yawned again.

"Do you want to take a shower?" Lucas suggested. Annabelle shook her head.

"Do you want me to make you breakfast?" Lucas offered. Again, Annabelle shook her head. She crossed her arms over her chest and frowned. Lucas could see it wasn't going to be any easy morning.

"You're acting like a child," Lucas pointed out with a smirk on his face.

"I hate feeling like a child." She agreed with him. "I can't do anything for myself."

"Annabelle..."

"Don't. Just go take a shower."

Instead of leaving her alone, Lucas leaned forward to kiss her neck playfully. Continuing to frown, Annabelle suppressed her smile.

Lucas wasn't satisfied and kissed her lips tenderly, tangling his hand in her hair. Annabelle's senses came to life with his touch. Her frown instantly melted into a smile and she giggled against his lips.

"You're doing it again," Annabelle reminded him of last night.

"I just wanted to see you smile," he joked and gave her one last peck on the cheek before he left the room. "I'll be out in a few."

Lucas closed the bathroom door and started the water of the shower. Taking a moment to catch his breath, his body trembled with infatuation at the thought of Annabelle's smile.

- 33- Annabelle: Depression to Happiness

I heard the bathroom door close and I rested my head back on the pillows. I never imagined living with Lucas outside of hell. While I was in the hospital, thoughts of our relationship seemed to stop while time continued. Looking forward was overwhelming.

Now, lying in my own bed, living with my boyfriend, it seemed surreal. *Will you ever get used to this?* I knew I could get used to living again, but how soon?

I shook the thoughts from my head. I didn't feel like having a heart to heart with myself. I brushed my hair back and sat up. Gently readjusting my legs to hang off the side of the bed, I waited for my body to respond. Knowing the pain would soon numb with the medicine, I reached for the metal walker that stood near the bed. I sighed heavily at the elderly contraption. *It's better than a wheelchair.* Was it?

Again, pushing the negative thoughts from my head, I stood up with the walker. Feeling the blood rush back into my feet, I took a few steps forward and closed the door. I needed to get dressed. I stood in front of the dresser for a minute. *What are you waiting for?*

With a frustrated growl, I pulled open the drawers and picked out something comfortable to wear. Throwing a sweater and pair of decent sweat pants on the bed, I felt my anger get the best of me.

Why did this happen to me? When can I be myself again? *Will I ever be myself again?* I have never hated anyone in my life as much as I do right now. I'm glad Dolan is in jail. Janis never did anything to prevent her murder, serves her right! *Annabelle!* I don't care! I didn't deserve this! *You waited this long to get* this *angry?*

I felt my breaths quicken and my chest rise and fall with rage. My blood boiled as I thought of the people who ruined my life. The potential I had, before my untimely kidnapping, was gone. I was a different person. I couldn't feel happy. *You're just having a bad morning, relax.*

I clenched my fists, feeling angry tears burn my eyes. I thought of Hector's face as he coached his wife in her boxing match against me. I remembered his sadistic laugh each time he entered my prison. Anger surged through my veins as I remembered Dolan's disgusting touch as he took my innocence.

I looked up at the mirror that reflected my face and I couldn't help but exhale noisily. Even though I looked better, in my eyes I still looked fragile and unpleasant. *Glad to see that you've decided to wake up with a positive attitude…*

Looking down at my hands, I watched them shake. *What's wrong with you?* Feeling dizzy with emotion, I slammed the drawer closed. The motion knocked the mirror off the dresser and it crashed to the hard wood floor.

Feeling even more stupid, I lowered myself to the floor. Completely disregarding the precautions I was told to take because of my hip, I sat on the floor. Bending forward, I began to pick up the pieces of broken glass.

"Annie?" Lucas questioned as the bedroom door opened. He walked into the room and was completely clothed, his hair barely wet. "I heard something fall. Are you okay?"

My body shook involuntarily. Lucas approached me and let out a strange sigh as he reached for my hands. He knelt down in front of me. I avoided his eyes, feeling ridiculous.

"You're bleeding." His voice was flat. I looked down and flexed my hand. Blood ran from a cut in the palm of it. Sudden nausea overwhelmed me; I felt the need to lie back down.

"I'm sorry," I whispered as Lucas stood up.

"Why are you sorry?"

"I didn't mean to break the mirror," I answered sadly.

"Stay here for a minute; let me get something to clean up your hand." Lucas left the room. I sat silently on the floor, my mind drained of negative thoughts.

What is wrong with you, Annabelle? I felt depression scratch at the inside of my brain. No, I refuse to let myself down that path. I will not let myself become depressed. I am alive. I have a family that loves me. I have a wonderful boyfriend who takes care of me. I have been through hell and I survived to tell my story. Blessed with an amazing support system, there wasn't any room for depression.

Lucas reentered the room with a wet cloth and bandages. He gently cleaned my hand, bringing me back to the first day we spent together. I remembered his kind looks and his gentle touch in my fragile state. He took care of me then and continues to take care of me now.

"Talk to me," he begged, sitting next to me as he finished bandaging my hand.

I looked down at my hands, remembering the angry thoughts that brought me to this depressing state.

"I'm so angry." I paused and took another breath. "I am so angry with the people who put me here; the people who did this to me. I have never felt this angry before." I felt my hands shake again.

Without a word, Lucas gently ran his hand down my cheek. His other hand sat on my knee, holding my fingers cautiously. I looked into his eyes, feeling my anger fade. He could control my emotions with a touch of his hand.

"You have every right to be angry," Lucas said. He looked down at my hands. "But you need to talk about it before you let it get to you."

I leaned against him, feeling his arms wrap around my body. I felt foolish for letting my anger get the best of me. Lucas kissed my head softly.

"Don't ever apologize for your feelings," Lucas reminded me. We sat silently for a few minutes on the floor while we both pondered the situation. I felt my head spin with emotions.

"Let me help you up," Lucas suggested as he stood up.

I nodded silently to him, rubbing my right leg. My hip ached after being pushed too far. Lucas bent down and lifted me to my feet. He helped me to the bed.

"I have to get dressed," I said as I looked at the clock. "My family is going to be here any-" The door buzzed. "-minute." I sighed heavily.

"Relax, I'll get the door while you get dressed. Once you're dressed and out in the living room, I'll come and clean this up. Okay?" Lucas suggested. I nodded and he left the room, closing the door behind him.

I could hear Allie's voice. Thankfully it was Allie and Evan and not my parents. My mother would have come barging into my room if I didn't answer the door. I knew I had a few minutes, so I didn't rush.

As I finished getting dressed, a knock on the door made me jump.

"Annie?" Lucas called.

Relieved to hear it was Lucas, I called, "Come in."

He walked into the room and smiled. "Allie, Evan and Madison are here. Your parents and Billy should be here any minute."

I couldn't help but smile at his nervous expression. In return, he smiled back.

"That's a wonderful sight." He leaned forward and kissed me. I returned the kiss, thanking him for his help. Lucas helped me to my feet and I left him alone in the room to clean up the mirror.

Madison jumped off the couch happily as I walked around the corner.

"Madison!" Evan's voice boomed from the kitchen. Madison froze mid step as she looked up at her father. "What did we talk about?"

"I am not allowed to run at Auntie's," Madison replied. Evan gave her a knowing look as she stepped towards me slowly. I couldn't help but laugh at the little girl's enthusiasm. Madison stopped in front of the walker and looked up at me.

"We brought your presents, Auntie." She pointed at the little tree in the corner.

Before, the tree had a few gifts scattered underneath. Now, boxes and bags had made themselves at home underneath the tiny shrub. Overwhelmed, the tree had begun to tilt to the right. I smiled and patted Maddy on the head.

"Would you like to sit down with me?" I asked. She nodded her head eagerly with a huge smile plastered on her face. We walked to the couch and I slowly sat down at one end. Madison waited until I was situated before she jumped on the couch. She sat right next to me, snuggling her face under my arm. Hugging her tightly to my side, I smiled at Evan.

"Good morning, sunshine," he joked. I knew I was a mess. Careless, I stuck my tongue out at him.

"Morning, Allie!" I called to Allie in the kitchen. She popped her head out and smiled.

"Morning, Anna. How are you feeling?"

"I've been worse." I shrugged.

"I hope you're hungry," Allie warned, disappearing back into the kitchen.

I shook my head as I heard a knock at the door. Evan opened the door for Billy and Ronnie and soon after, my parents arrived. Once everyone was there, Lucas joined the party, kissing my forehead

286

before he went to help in the kitchen. My apartment was filled with conversations, laughter and the sounds of family and friends having a good time. I quickly remembered why depression wasn't an option for me.

With my niece tucked under my arm, I listened to my family happily. It was good to be home where I belonged. Maddy pulled a book out and pointed to the pictures. She told me the story, without any clue what the words on the pages actually said. It was amazing to see her creativity blossom. I thought back to the first time I held her; her blue eyes barely open, her little pink nose and her tiny hands.

A jolt of reality hit me. I would soon have a baby of my own. Overwhelmed with the thoughts of motherhood, I felt my face drain of color and my hands sweat. I held back the nervous tears and focused on Maddy's story.

"The frog jumped over the big rock." She pointed at the boulder on the page and looked up at me. I forced a smile and she giggled happily.

Panic begged to take over. I took a deep breath and pushed the thoughts from my head. Within seconds, they stomped through my brain. I would be a mother in less than nine months. I was four weeks along, much too early to tell what my future would hold. A sickening feeling sat in my stomach thinking about the reason behind the pregnancy.

"When the frog met the piggy, the piggy said 'Hello frog, will you help me find my family?'" Madison explained.

Listening to Madison read her book to me caused my body to shake with a frightening anticipation. A terrifying future rested on my shoulders, one I had not prepared myself for. *You have nine months to prepare.* I was pregnant. The statement sent a shiver up my spine.

"Lunch is ready," Allie called from the kitchen.

Emotions running high, I let Madison get up and run into the kitchen before I got up. Closing my eyes slightly, I took a deep breath. I had to calm my nerves down before I stood up.

"Annie?" Lucas approached me. I looked up at him with a half-hearted smile. "What's wrong?"

"Thinking too much," Billy-Jean commented from behind Lucas. I smiled at my best friend. "She does this."

"I'm fine," I lied, reaching for my walker. Billy's hand touched mine as she sat down next to me.

287

"No you're not." Billy said and I looked up at Lucas.

"I'm fine," I promised him.

"Annabelle." Billy's voice rang in my ear. I looked at her sternly.

"I'm fine, Billy-Jean." I gave her a dirty look. She took the hint and got up from the couch. Lucas replaced her and held my hand.

"Would you tell me if something was wrong?"

"No." I smiled sarcastically. He looked at me with a knowing look. "I promise you, I will talk to you about this later. As soon as the last person is out the door, we can talk." I kissed his cheek and softly whispered, "I love you."

"I love you too," he promised.

While everyone was finishing their dessert, Allie and my mom collected dishes and took them into the kitchen. Madison was excitedly waiting by the tree to hand out gifts. I had a strange feeling that most of the gifts under the tree were either from me or to me. That's how my family worked.

"Is everyone finished?" Mom asked. There was a unanimous yes that mumbled through the group of people in my living room. Then Madison jumped up and down and picked up a gift from under the tree. It was a small box, wrapped in blue metallic paper. She skipped to my spot on the couch and handed me the first gift.

As she walked away from me, she continued around the room until each person had a gift, including Lucas. Once everyone had their gifts, the room was filled with sounds of ripping paper and a low mumble of conversation.

I opened my blue gift from Allie and Evan to see a new cell phone, paired with shiny new necklace. I set the cell phone aside and opened the necklace. It was a silver chain, with two charms. One was a tiny letter A with a diamond in the middle, the other was a sun burst, filled with orange and red rhinestones. I smiled at Evan and Allie and asked Billy to help me put it on.

"Thank you," I called across the room. They both nodded back at me.

I watched as my family opened gifts unable to hold back a smile. It felt amazing to be in the presence of the people that meant the most to me. As I looked around the room, Madison placed another box in my lap. I smiled down at the little girl before she said, "Hurry up, you have the most."

I couldn't help but laugh. She was growing up to be such the little diva. Her attitude was hilarious and she brightened my darkest days. The impending hysteria of having my own child scared me. I shivered and ripped into the gift.

After opening my gifts, I ended up with a large amount of gifts from my family. I had a feeling most of the gifts were bought after Christmas. Billy and Ronnie bought a set of lamps for my living room. They claimed my living room was too dark for them. Evan and Allie added a new set of throw pillows for my living room.

My parents are the people who I believe bought more gifts after Christmas. To begin with, I received a box set of the classic TV shows and movies. My favorite, "I Love Lucy" came with a set of six coasters. My mother was determined to pass down her obsession with coasters. Also, they got me another winter coat; fluffy, thick and dark orange. It was way too expensive. I couldn't help but give them a knowing look when I opened the box. Finally, my parents handed me my last gift; the tiny box with a solitary bow on top.

I eyed my mother curiously and she smiled back at me. "Open it."

"This is your graduation present," my dad added.

I opened the little box to see a car key. I instantly felt my eyes water. I looked up at my parents and shook my head.

"I can't take this…" I whispered.

My dad shook his head. "Don't worry. It was our plan for a while. It's not a problem. Take it."

I looked down at the key and smiled, tears falling from my eyes. I looked up and added, "Well, do I get to see it?"

The smile that came across my father's face was one I had only seen a few times in my life. Once when I graduated high school, once at my brother's wedding and once when Madison was born. My father was a very happy person, but this smile was something special; child-like.

Lucas helped me with my shoes and I slipped on my new coat. As a group, my family went outside into the bitter cold to look at my new car.

"It's a used car. We bought it from Hopewell Auto Sales in New Canada. I think the color will be your favorite part." Mom giggled as we stepped outside of the building.

A rust-colored Pontiac Vibe sat in the spot where my car was normally parked. I smiled at her and nodded happily.

"It's so cute." I laughed, pushing my walker forward. My excitement was short lived as I felt my feet slip on the invisible patch of ice under the snow. As my feet lost traction with ground, I gripped onto the walker tightly. As I began to fall backwards, I felt a pair of hands cradle my shoulders. I looked up to see Lucas catch me.

This all happened in a matter of seconds. My mom rushed to my side as Lucas helped me stand back up.

"Are you all right, Annabelle?" she questioned frantically.

"Yeah, Ma, it was just the ice," I answered in a frustrated tone.

"Let's go back inside before you slip again." My mom ushered us back to the door. Lucas kept a close distance behind me until I was back inside.

I looked up at my dad and smiled. I reached out to hug him and whispered, "Thank you."

He smiled and kissed my cheek. "Anything for you."

As my family went up the stairs, Lucas and I took the elevator. As the doors closed, I leaned against the wall of the tiny area. Lucas turned around to look at me.

"Thank you." I smiled at him and held my hands out for a hug. He slipped his arms around my waist and pulled me into a warm hug. I tucked my face into his neck and took a deep breath. He kissed my cheek gently and I returned the kiss on his neck. He pulled away, putting his hand on the side of my face. He leaned forward, pressing his lips against mine. I felt the elevator slow down, signaling the doors would open at the second floor. I giggled and whispered, "We should stop; the doors are going to open."

Lucas smiled and pecked my nose quickly as the door opened. As he turned around, my mom was on the other side of the open elevator waiting for us.

"This elevator is very slow," she pointed out and added, "You should tell your landlord."

I rolled my eyes and we entered the apartment again. Madison was sitting with a present in her lap. She smiled up at me and I realized it was the gift I had bought her. I nodded at her and she ripped through the silver paper before I had a chance to sit down.

"Auntie!" She squealed as she picked up the box happily. It was a dress up station. Complete with a pink vanity, costumes, jewelry and shoes, it was perfect for Madison's diva attitude. "Can I play now?"

"Wait until we get home to open it, Maddy. We'll be leaving in a little while," Allie promised her daughter. I nodded at Allie, thanking her. I couldn't imagine playing with a high strung four-year-old right now. My body was begging to lie down. I glanced up at the clock above the TV, 6:54pm.

Lucas sat down next to me and Madison set a box in his lap. Before he had a chance to look at me in protest, Madison set another box next to him. I smiled at him and chuckled softly.

I nudged him to open them. He shook his head and opened the gift from my parents. Inside was a pair of winter boots. I smiled remembering the condition of his current boots. He thanked my parents and grabbed the second gift from Billy-Jean and Ronnie. He ripped through the paper to find two smaller boxes inside. The first box held a gift card to the local mall. The other box was a set of keys.

Lucas looked up at Billy curiously.

"You have the same set of keys as Annabelle: a key for our apartment, Allie and Evan's house and the Mr. and Mrs. Rockart's house. If you're going to be a part of this family, might as well give you all the same respect," Billy joked. The car key on the key chain was identical to mine.

"One more, Mr. Lucas." Madison handed Lucas another box.

This last present was from Evan and Allie. I looked down at the box and then up at Allie and widened my eyes. She smiled with a giggle as Lucas opened it. My suspicions were correct. Inside was a cell phone, identical to mine. Also in the box were two phone covers; green and orange.

"To tell them apart, Lucas can pick which color he wants," Evan pointed out smiling. He knew I would want the orange, but he wanted to torture me a little longer. Lucas laughed and picked up the orange, handing me the green. Without complaining, out loud, I took the green like a team-player. Lucas laughed and quickly switched the covers, giving me the orange.

"Thank you," I whispered with a sigh. He laughed and patted my knee.

"Thank you. I really didn't expect any of this." Lucas spoke to my family and friends.

"Like I said; if you're going to be a part of this family, might as well give you the same respect." Billy smiled.

A warm feeling came over my body as everyone continued the conversation. *Fever?* No, happiness; I was elated. My family welcomed Lucas into our family like they had known him forever. *Isn't that what you did?* I thought back to the time it took for me to accept Lucas into my life. It took a couple hours for me to understand the sincerity of Lucas's intent. It took me days to fall in love with his compassionate heart and soul. It took weeks for me to want to spend forever with him. Happiness filled my body. Peace relaxed my mind. Love entered my heart. I was home.

The clock chimed eight o'clock. As her family began to say their goodbyes, Annabelle yawned silently from the couch. Lucas smiled watching her try to keep her eyes open. Evan and Allie had left first, after Madison had begun to fall asleep in Annabelle's lap.

Billy-Jean leaned down to hug Annabelle, giving her friend a kiss on the cheek. Annabelle smiled tiredly and gave Ronnie a hug.

"Call us if you need anything," Billy reminded Lucas as she gave him a strong hug.

"Thanks for everything, Billy," he said.

She smiled and said goodbye to Annabelle's parents.

After Ronnie and Billy left, Marie sat down next to Annabelle. Putting her arm around her daughter, Marie whispered, "I love you."

"I love you too, Ma," Annabelle replied, adding another yawn to the end.

Marie laughed. "Lucas will be right back. Are you sure you don't want me to stay up here while they carry the stuff to the car?"

"Ma, go home. I'm just going to sit here and wait," Annabelle promised her mother.

Mark smiled and kissed his daughter goodnight. Marie gave Annabelle a final kiss goodbye and left the apartment.

Annabelle lifted her legs up onto the couch next to her. She pulled the brand new blanket up around her shoulders and rested her head back on the arm of the couch. After desperately trying to keep her eyes open, Annabelle finally let herself fall asleep.

Lucas put the last item into the trunk of Marie and Mark's car and closed the hatch. Marie turned to give Lucas a hug. Lucas felt her tighten the embrace and he could feel the emotion pour from Marie's eyes. She pulled away from him and said, "Lucas, you take care of her. She deserves it."

"That is my plan, Mrs. Rockart," Lucas promised with a smirk. Marie returned the smile and got into the car.

"Thanks again, for everything." Mark shook Lucas's hand.

"No, thank you. I wouldn't be able to do this alone," Lucas insisted. Mark smiled and patted Lucas on the back.

"Good night," Mark said as he got into the car. As he closed the car door, Lucas walked to the steps of the apartment building and waved as they drove away. Opening the building door, he shivered slightly and closed the door tightly behind him.

As Lucas walked up the stairs, he thought of the ring box that sat in the bottom of his dresser drawer. His heart pounded in his throat as he thought of proposing to Annabelle. Tonight would be perfect, but too soon. Lucas knew the thought marriage would frighten Annabelle. She had enough to deal with right now. He remembered the promise Annabelle made to him earlier to him as soon as the last person left.

Opening the door to the apartment, silence hit Lucas's ears. He locked the door and turned off the hallway light. Slipping his shoes off at the door, he turned the kitchen light off as well. As he entered the living room, he saw the reason for the silence.

Annabelle was sleeping soundly on the couch. Her sandy hair was brushed down, around her shoulders. Her chest moved up and down, steadily. He watched as her face relaxed and a brief smile crossed her lips; causing him to smile. Lucas approached his peacefully sleeping girlfriend.

With a gentle, slow movement, Lucas lifted her off the couch. She readjusted her head onto his shoulder and continued sleeping. Deciding to leave the walker, Lucas left the living room and walked into Annabelle's bedroom.

With his elbow, Lucas flipped the switch on the wall to turn the light on. Setting her down gingerly, Lucas removed her slippers. Figuring her sweat pants and sweater were suitable for bed, Lucas didn't bother waking her up to change. He turned to leave when Annabelle's hand found his.

"Don't go," she whispered, her eyes remained closed. "Sleep with me."

"Are you sure?" She opened her eyes slightly to look at Lucas.

"I love you." She smiled.

Lucas felt his heart pound as she whispered the words. It sent shivers through his body. He leaned down to kiss her lips before he said, "Let me change out of my jeans, and clean up the living room. I'll be right back."

Annabelle nodded, closing her eyes again. Lucas left the room and returned to the living room. He began by arranging the new pillows and blanket on the couch. He picked up the few wrapping paper scraps that littered the ground.

Setting the new items neatly in a pile under the tree, Lucas noticed a package that was tucked behind it. Bending down on his knees, he reached for the small package. It was unmarked. Unsure of what to do with it, Lucas set it on the coffee table. Hopefully Annabelle knew who it was for. It could wait for the morning.

After he threw away the scraps of paper, he turned the lights off and went to the guest room. Quickly changing into a pair of pajama bottoms, Lucas slipped his sweat shirt off; he replaced it with a plain t-shirt.

Taking another breath, Lucas walked back into Annabelle's bedroom. Looking at the pile of clothes on the floor, Lucas knew she had taken off her sweater and sweat pants. She blushed tiredly and pulled the blanket up to her chin.

"My walker is still in the other room. Could you hand me a t-shirt?" Annabelle smiled, her cheeks burning red.

Lucas laughed slightly and headed to her dresser.

"Third drawer, there should be a light purple t-shirt on the left side," Annabelle directed. Lucas found exactly what she was looking for. It was an oversized t-shirt that read, **TROUBLE.** Again, Lucas laughed and handed Annabelle the t-shirt.

"Shut up," Annabelle warned as Lucas turned around. Annabelle slipped the shirt over her head. "Okay, I'm done."

Lucas turned back around, the smile wide across his face. Annabelle glared playfully at him.

"Shut up," she repeated.

"I didn't say anything," Lucas said with a chuckle. He flicked the light switch off sending the room into the darkness. The faint moonlight bled into the room from the curtains. Annabelle looked up at Lucas as he got into bed next to her. She smiled, remembering the moonlight on his face the first night he stayed with her.

"I love you, Mr. Lucas." Annabelle smiled.

"I love you too, Miss. Annie." Lucas kissed the end of her nose.

Annabelle snuggled closer to his chest, tucking her arms between their bodies. Lucas wrapped his arms protectively around her small frame. As they settled into a comfortable position, Lucas yawned quietly. He let his thoughts wander as he began to fall asleep.

"Lucas," Annabelle whispered.

"Hmm?"

"I promised I would tell you what I was thinking about when everyone left," Annabelle whispered tiredly.

"It's okay, you're tired. We can wait for morning."

"I promised."

Lucas smiled to himself hearing the tone of her voice emphasize it.

"Okay, if you want to talk now, we'll talk now." Lucas opened his eyes to look down at her. "What were you thinking about earlier?"

"I'm scared," she whispered, avoiding his moonlit eyes.

"About what?" Lucas questioned, taken by surprise.

"I'm not ready to have a baby."

Lucas wasn't sure exactly what to say to her. He, himself, was worried about the idea of being a potential father figure. He was afraid of becoming his father. He had never experienced a decent father until he met the Rockart family.

Suddenly, a thought popped into his mind. Annabelle had a beautiful family. She had a beautiful niece that she helped take care of from birth. If Annabelle was worried about being a mother, he didn't have a chance.

"Lucas?" she questioned quietly, bringing Lucas from his thoughts.

"I'm sorry." Lucas looked down at her. Her eyes begged for his response. Lucas took a breath and thought of his words carefully. "Annie, I'm scared too."

Annabelle's face turned away from him, obviously not expecting that response. Lucas tilted her chin back up to look at him. "But being with you, I know we can get through this, together."

Annabelle's eyes welled up as Lucas smiled down at her. She felt her heart leap, faithfully, into Lucas's hands. She trusted this man with her heart, and now with her future.

Lucas watched as his words brought emotions out of Annabelle. He knew his words meant something to her. His heart pounded in his chest. Silently, he reminded himself tonight wasn't the night. Waiting to ask Annabelle to marry him, he could gain more of her trust.

Feeling her breath on his neck, Lucas pulled her closer. Inhaling her scent, Lucas kissed the top of her head. Annabelle pulled her arms close to her chest as she felt herself fall into a deep sleep.

Lucas rubbed her shoulders gently, watching her eyes close slowly. Smiling to himself, he let his eyes close and waited for sleep to take over his thoughts.

Friday January, 23rd
4:40am

Feeling her chest pound, Annabelle opened her eyes quickly. Her hands searched for Lucas in the dark room. Shivers ran down her spine as she realized the bed was empty. A sudden panic overwhelmed her body as she rolled to the side of the bed.

"Lucas?" she called, reaching for the lamp switch. Her voice sounded pained, worried.

"What's wrong?" Lucas rushed to the bedroom as he heard Annabelle's worried cry.

"Where did you go?" Tears burned her eyes.

"I was in the living room. I couldn't sleep. I didn't want to wake you up." Lucas sat down on the side of the bed. "I'm sorry." He wrapped his arms around her gently, feeling her heart pound.

Annabelle tucked her head into his neck and pushed her tears away. She took a deep breath and said, "Don't be sorry. I had a nightmare. I woke up and you were gone; I panicked."

"Do you want to talk about it?"

Annabelle shook her head and yawned slightly.

"Go back to sleep, I won't leave," he promised.

Annabelle rearranged herself and Lucas lay down next to her, pulling the blanket over them. Closing her eyes tightly, the nightmare replayed in her head.

The scene flashed to her kitchen where Dolan had first presented her with the ring box. A flash of panic rushed through her as she answered, "yes."

Another quick change of scenery, a dark gloomy night in Fort Kent, Annabelle was standing outside the bookstore. Dolan stood a few feet away, unaware of her presence. She overheard him say, "She would never expect this. It's perfect. Tomorrow night, I promise." Annabelle watched as Dolan shook Hector Martin's hand. Hector proceeded to his truck and Dolan returned to the store.

The picture changed again, sending Annabelle to center stage. She watched herself as Dolan Meyer picked her up for a night out. She was dressed in a black dress, her hair pulled back into a tight pony tail. Dolan's expression was evil, unmasked and eerie.

Annabelle felt herself being punched, stabbed and stomped on. Her eyes opened to see Dolan Meyer standing above her, blood on his hands. Her body was numb; the sensation of pain was numb to the feeling of sudden terror. She tried to move, but her body would not respond.

"Is she dead?" an angry growl broke into her thoughts.

"No, not yet," Dolan answered.

"Go wash up, we can get you back home before anyone knows your gone."

"Annie?" Lucas questioned. Annabelle opened her eyes, feeling Lucas's touch. "Are you all right?"

She opened her mouth to answer when she felt her tear stained cheeks. She had been crying.

"What's wrong?" Lucas asked, wiping her cheeks.

"The nightmare," Annabelle whispered, remembering the dream. Taking another breath, Annabelle explained the dream, briefly, to Lucas.

"Annie," he whispered, wrapping his arms around her. "It was a dream. They will never hurt you again. I promise you."

Unable to express her feelings in words, Annabelle nodded and closed her eyes. She fell asleep, dreaming of nothing at all.

Lucas finished making the bed as Annabelle took a shower. His mind was scattered, thinking about last night, the ring and Annabelle. Lucas felt himself panic inside as he reminded himself Hector was still on the run.

Lucas sighed, shaking off the thought. He walked across the hall, stopping to listen to the bathroom door. Without letting Annabelle know, Lucas had noticed she would hum while she showered. It was his secret security system to make sure Annabelle was okay. Hearing the soft humming through the running water, Lucas smiled and continued into the guest room.

The room was more of a holding room for his things instead of his room. It was the second morning waking up in his new home and he still felt as though everything would change in an instant. Someone new could come along and take Annabelle from him again. It shook Lucas to think about all the possibilities.

"Stop it," Lucas mumbled to himself.

Without another negative thought, Lucas slipped on a pair of jeans and a long sleeved shirt. Tossing his dirty clothes in the box in the corner, Lucas turned to the mirror. His hair was barely wet from his earlier shower. Rubbing his palm along his cheek, he realized how badly he needed to shave. Sighing slightly, Lucas heard the shower turn off.

Smiling to himself, he left the guest room and went to the kitchen. It was still early enough for breakfast and he knew Annabelle would be hungry. Looking through the pantry, he found what he was looking for.

Before the bathroom door opened, the pancakes were nearly done. Annabelle felt her head pound and her stomach turn over angrily. Pushing the walker forward, the smell of pancakes filled her nose. The scent was welcoming. Smiling, she continued into the kitchen.

Lucas plated the last pancake as Annabelle entered the kitchen. Setting the pan on the stove, he pulled out the chair for Annabelle.

"Thank you." Annabelle smiled, sitting down gingerly. She winced slightly, feeling her hip ache.

"Is it your hip?" Lucas questioned knowingly. Annabelle nodded. Lucas stood up and grabbed a bottle from the counter. He handed her two pills and returned the bottle to the counter. Sitting down across from her, he watched as she took the pills. He smiled as she made a strange face.

"Disgusting," she mumbled, taking another drink of her juice.

Both laughing, the breakfast remained quiet and peaceful. It was a welcome change for Annabelle. She felt good, at least better than she had felt. *Can't ask for more than that...*

Looking up at Lucas from her glass, Annabelle felt her heart flutter and the hair on her neck stood up. A shiver ran through her body, feeling the connection with the man across the table.

Lucas felt her eyes on him. Smiling inwardly, he continued to eat his pancakes, acting oblivious to her stares. With another bite, Lucas stole a glance at Annabelle. Her eyes darted to the ceiling, a smirk danced across her face. Lucas couldn't help but smile back.

"You know, if you want to stare at me, you don't have to hide it," Lucas announced, looking down at his food.

Annabelle's cheeks burned red. She laughed and looked up at him. "I'm terrible at being sneaky."

Lucas nodded in agreement. With smiles on their faces, breakfast continued in a euphoric silence.

Later that day, Annabelle was returning her multiple e-mails while Lucas relaxed on the couch. Glancing at the time, 3:45pm, Annabelle clicked send. Closing her laptop, she noticed a new picture frame sitting on the dresser. Pulling her walker closer, she stood up. She realized that the picture was of a young Lucas, hugging an elderly woman. The frame was engraved. Picking it up, she ran her thumb along the bottom to read the message: *"Mable, I owe you for everything wonderful I have. I thank you for every terrible thing I don't have. I love you for the person you've helped me become. Love, Luke."*

Setting the frame down, Annabelle smiled heavy-heartedly at the picture. Lucas spoke about his grandmother one of the first nights they spent together. She was his safe haven. Annabelle felt her heart pound with grief, remembering the tears in his eyes. Taking a deep breath, she turned around and went to the living room.

"All done?" Lucas yawned.

"Can I lay with you?" Annabelle asked quietly.

"Are you okay?" He sat up slightly. She nodded silently. He moved towards the arm of the couch, resting his head on a pillow. Annabelle positioned herself on her side, between the back of the couch and his legs, her head on his chest.

"Are you comfortable?" he questioned. She looked at him and smiled. Glancing at the clock, it was only 4:20pm.

"I don't want to fall asleep yet," she warned. Lucas nodded and smiled to himself.

He put his arms around her, running his fingers through her hair. She rested her head on his chest, closer to his shoulder, listening to his heart beat. The feeling of his fingers in her hair and steady beat of his heart began to put her to sleep.

Lifting her head, she smiled at Lucas's closed eyes. Taking the opportunity, Annabelle leaned forward and kissed his neck gently. Leaving a trail of kisses, she continued to his lips.

Lucas moved his hand to the back of Annabelle's head. Kissing her lips softly, he gently pulled her closer. Without hesitation, Lucas moved his lips to her cheeks, kissing them freely. He moved to her jaw line, one kiss after the other, down her neck and to her collar bone.

Feeling her body respond to his touch, Annabelle inhaled. With an impulse of enchantment, Annabelle kissed his neck. Her shirt revealed bare skin as Lucas moved his hand to the small of her back. He moved his hand delicately across her back. The teasing touch caused Annabelle to tremble pleasantly.

Feeling the heat of her skin underneath his finger tips, Lucas continued to kiss her eagerly. The heat intensified as Annabelle pushed her body forward. With a giggle, Annabelle felt Lucas kiss her collar bone. Lucas smiled as she brought his face back to hers. Parting their lips, the kiss deepened. With their bodies electrified, they continued to deepen the kiss.

Annabelle put her hand on his chest, propping herself up. She gasped, breathing heavily.

"Sorry," Lucas mumbled, also out of breath.

"Don't apologize. I needed to breathe." She smirked at him.

Lucas returned the smirk with a wide eyed smile. Annabelle leaned forward, planting another kiss on his lips. This time, Annabelle felt the passion pierce her like a blade. The delight of the moment deepened and Lucas pulled her closer.

Feeling his heart pound, he moved his hand to her neck, caressing the side of her face. Annabelle kissed the side of his face and whispered into his ear, "Take your shirt off."

Lucas obeyed and removed his shirt. Annabelle put her hands on his chest, feeling the muscles under his warm skin. Leaning down, she kissed his chest softly. Moving towards his neck, leaving kisses across his collar bone, Annabelle felt her body beg for more. *Slow down, Annabelle.* Her conscience poked. She pushed it away.

Lucas pulled her closer, bringing her lips to his. Moving his hands up the back of her shirt, he ran his fingers down her spine. Annabelle shivered at his touch. *Too much, Annabelle.* Annabelle pushed the thought away, feeling her body react to Lucas's body. She deepened the kiss in spite of the voice in her head. Moving her hands down his chest, Lucas felt Annabelle tug at his belt.

"Annie," Lucas whispered as he felt her body shiver. "Slow down."

Annabelle heard the words, but couldn't help herself. Kissing his neck feverishly, Annabelle continued. *You're going to regret this.* Annabelle felt the pang of guilt in her chest.

Lucas put his hand on her hand. Her breaths were raged and rapid.

"Annie, it's okay. Relax," Lucas promised her. "Let's stop before we do anything we will regret."

Annabelle felt tears settle into her eyes. Lucas noticed and put his hands on either side of her face. "No, don't cry. I'm not upset."

He wrapped his arms around her, bringing her face into his chest. He felt her tears fall silently onto his bare chest.

"Don't cry," Lucas begged her.

"I'm sorry," Annabelle whispered. Lucas pulled her away from his chest, looking into her eyes.

"I'm not." He smiled, kissing her lips softly. Annabelle felt her heart pound. She pulled away from him and rested her head on his chest. He placed his hands on her head. "It's okay."

Annabelle wasn't upset with Lucas. She was upset with herself. She couldn't figure out why she let herself get that involved and let herself go that far. *Told you to slow down...*

Lucas lifted her up, moving her to a sitting position. She wiped her face and straightened her shirt. Lucas wiped another tear as it fell and kissed her forehead.

Annabelle rested her head on his shoulder. Lucas wrapped his arms around her tightly. Kissing the top of her forehead, he whispered, "I love you."

"I love you," Annabelle answered.

The more time they spent together, the closer their hearts became.

Friday, January 30th, 2009

"Could you be any more obvious?" Evan blurted out during an intense game of poker.

"Shut up!" Allie pushed him lightly. I laughed quietly from the couch. Lucas ran his fingers through my hair silently.

I yawned quietly, letting my eyes close slightly. I was exhausted from the day's events.

Lucas and I had woken up early to go to therapy. After two hours of physical therapy, my appointment with Dr. Morris, an hour at the grocery store, taking the groceries home, Evan picked us up for dinner at his house.

Madison burned the rest of my energy by convincing me to play house with her in her room after dinner. Hours later, the current poker tournament began. I began falling asleep in Lucas's lap while Ronnie and Allie finished the last game. I drifted to sleep only to see what nightmare my unconsciousness would bring.

"If only you knew the real reason we brought you here." Hector's voice rang in my head.

"If only you understood the danger you face." Dolan stood behind his father with an evil grin plastered on his face.

"If only you felt the pain I feel." Another figure lurked into view. I could not make out their face but they shook my shoulders violently.

Pain exploded from my head. I screamed out, only to hear silence. I was suddenly alone in a room without windows or doors. The walls were white, splattered with red. The smell of rotting wood and mold filled my nose. Nausea overwhelmed my head, blurring my vision. I clutched my stomach, feeling myself writhe in pain.

A hand touched my shoulder. "Annabelle," a voice whispered.

Startled awake, I sat up quickly. My head jerked upwards, colliding with something. I instantly brought my hand to my head, feeling the pain of the collision.

"Are you okay?" Allie nearly yelled. I turned to look at her, embarrassed by my sudden outburst. Expecting her to be looking at me, her eyes were focused behind me. I turned around to see who she was talking to.

"I'm fine," Lucas answered, holding his face with both of his hands. I could see the blood running from his nose into his hands. A wave of panic devastated my body, guilt weighing heavy in my stomach.

"Come on, let's go into the kitchen." Allie helped Lucas up from his seat, his hands still covering his face. He looked down at me, his eyes sad. I felt my eyes burn with tears.

"I'm sorry," I whispered as he left the room.

The room went silent. I sat up, bringing my left knee into my chest. I tucked my chin into my chest and let tears fall. Cowering down like a child, I sat silently crying.

"Annabelle." Billy sat down next to me. "It was an accident."

"You didn't mean to do it, Lucas knows that," Ronnie added.

I felt my chest pound with guilt. I looked up at Billy. She smiled sympathetically at me.

"I don't even know what scared me." I spoke quietly.

"Lucas tried to wake you up," Evan answered. "It was getting late and everyone was getting ready to leave."

I looked down and played with a loose string on the edge of my shirt in silence. *Don't worry, he'll be fine.* A few minutes passed and Billy continued to tell me that it was an accident.

After another five minutes, Lucas entered the room holding a cloth over his nose. With no visible blood, he sat down next to me. I looked up at him, tears sitting on the edge of my eye lids.

"Don't worry." Lucas smiled. "Just a bloody nose."

"I'm sorry," I whispered.

"It's okay." Lucas put his arm around my shoulders and kissed my cheek. "Nothing to worry about."

He pulled me closer. I tucked my head carefully under his chin. I felt his arm tighten around me. I couldn't help but feel guilty. *Don't...* It's hard not to.

Pushing the thoughts away, I yawned again. Lucas looked down at me, pulling the cloth away. His nose was red, but no longer bleeding.

"Ready to go?" he asked. I nodded my eyes heavy.

"I'll grab your shoes," Allie announced.

I glanced up at the clock; 11:32pm. *This is the latest you've stayed up for a long time.*

Allie set our shoes in front of us and I slipped my boots on. Carefully bending my legs, I pulled them up. Things were getting easier the more I worked with Clara and Heather. Regrettably, I actually began to enjoy therapy.

"I'll take them home," Evan said slipping on his coat. "I'll be back in a few."

Evan kissed Allie good-bye as Lucas and I said good-bye to Billy and Ronnie.

"Tell Madison good night for me." I yawned to Allie. With a laugh, she agreed and gave me a hug.

"Walk or carry?" Lucas offered. I smiled up at him. This was a question I had experienced several times in the past week. Any time I was tired or in pain, Lucas would offer to carry me. Most of the time I turned him down, however, tonight seemed like a good night to change things up.

"Carry?" I answered with a question.

"Why the question? I wouldn't offer if I didn't want to," Lucas pointed out with a whisper. I smiled shyly at him. He shook his head with a smirk and lifted me effortlessly off the couch.

I heard giggles and jokes from Ronnie. I stuck my tongue out at him. He returned the favor and I couldn't help but giggle.

Saying goodbye, Lucas carried me to Evan's truck. Evan set my walker in the back seat next to Lucas and we headed to our apartment.

Saturday, January 31st, 2009

After Evan left, Lucas and I sat quietly on the couch watching the midnight news. The news for the area was normally quite boring. However, since I made news in December, the news had become a part of the daily routine. Hector Martin was still out there. Janis Martin had been murdered and Dolan was in jail, awaiting trial.

I sighed as the weather report ended. Lucas turned the TV off and pulled me closer. I looked up at him and he smiled tiredly at me. I couldn't help but return the gesture, leaning up to kiss his lips softly.

"Ready for bed?" Lucas questioned. I nodded, feeling my eyes beg to close. Without any hurry to get up, we continued to cuddle on the couch under a blanket. I rested my head on his chest, wrapping my arms around him. He kissed my forehead and pulled the blanket closer to my face.

I began to fall asleep, feeling my body relax. Taking another deep breath, I hugged Lucas tighter. As both of us began to fall asleep, a hard pounding noise came from the hallway of the building.

Startling me, I sat up to listen for it again. Lucas stood up and walked towards the door. Another pounding sound rang through the halls. This time, however, a blood curdling scream was added to the end.

My heart pounded, almost into my throat. Lucas turned the lights out in the apartment. I watched as his figure vanished into the darkness of the apartment.

"Do you have your phone?" Lucas whispered.

Nodding into the darkness, I answered with a whisper, "Yes."

"Get it ready, I'm going to look into the hallway-"

"No! Just stay here," I begged in a loud whisper. Another loud noise came from the hallway. *Gunshot...*

"Annie, listen to me. Please, stay here. Call Allie," Lucas whispered. I felt his hand touch my face gently. His lips followed and pressed against my forehead.

"Lucas," I whispered into the air.

I saw the light of the hallway form a thin line across the floor as Lucas peaked out the door. Soon after, the room filled with light, bleeding from the hallway as Lucas stepped out into the hallway.

My heart pounded in my chest. I felt my head swarm with different thoughts and ideas. Comprehending the situation, I couldn't think straight. *He had found us.* Hector was going to kill us.

With a sharp gasp, I remembered Lucas's request for me to call Allie. I fumbled for my phone and opened it. The sudden light from the screen temporarily blinded me. I squinted and held my breath as I dialed the number.

As I listened to the ringing line, the clock on the TV glowed 12:35 am. I felt my breath catch in my throat as another loud bang came from the hallway. It wasn't the same noise as the first commotion.

"Hello?" Evan's scratchy voice answered.

"Evan," I whispered, afraid to draw attention.

"Annabelle?" Evan was suddenly wide awake. I felt my eyes well up with tears.

"Evan, he found us."

"Who, Anna? Who found you?" Evan questioned.

"Hector, he's here, in the apartment building. We need help, Evan." My tears fell silently.

Another noise from the hallway caused my body to jerk. I held my breath as I watched a shadow approach the doorway. The light shinning underneath the door disappeared.

As the door opened and the room filled with the same bleeding beam of light, I dropped to the floor in front of the couch. Feeling my hip protest, I bit my lip to keep my whimper quiet. Crawling forward, I slid behind the couch. Turning my face away from the light, I held my breath.

"Who the hell are you? What are you doing in here?" Grady's voice growled from the hallway. As gunfire echoed through the building, I began to tremble.

"You stupid bastard! You nearly shot me! I'm calling the police." Grady's old voice was followed quickly by his door slamming.

"Annabelle," the whisper stopped my heart.

"Lucas..." I choked quietly.

Before either of us could speak again, a deafening hammering came from the door. It continued until I could hear Hector growl under his breath.

Sudden hands around my shoulders caused me to cry out loud. Lucas put his hand gently over my mouth.

"It's me," he whispered softly into my ear. Careful of my hip, Lucas lifted me off the ground. Before he could take one step another thunderous noise came from the hallway. I quickly realized that Hector had fired his gun at the apartment door.

Lucas darted into the kitchen. Quickly looking for a hiding place, he moved to the corner of the room. The rest of the kitchen was covered in a glow from the moon light. The corner however, was dark and shadowy.

Another shot rattled the dishes in the cabinets and shook my body. I clung to Lucas's shirt as the front door of the apartment burst open.

"Shit," Lucas whispered. He wrapped his arms around me protectively and we held as still as possible.

"Here, kitty, kitty, kitty." The voice brought bile into my throat. A disgusted chill climbed up my spine. The hairs on my arms stood at attention, sending my body into an involuntary tremble.

"I know you're in here." Hector's presence, voice and scent filled the air. The smell of whiskey brought tears to my eyes as the door closed with a slam.

Feeling my body shake, I began to beg myself to hold still. My hip throbbed in pain from the cramped position. I felt my tears drip down my chin and roll down my chest.

"Come out and play." Hector continued to move in our direction. His footsteps approached like a roaring train.

Lucas was on his feet before I had time to react. I watched as Lucas threw himself at his father. The sounds of wrestling continued as the two men slammed into the living room wall, then to the floor. Stretching my legs forward, I crawled to the side, out of the corner. I could hear Lucas yell out as the loud thud of skin forcefully contacting skin. I couldn't look up, fearful of what I would witness.

A piercing bang was followed unexpectedly by an eerie silence.

Before I had time to think, a hand grabbed my hair. I let out a pained scream as Hector pulled me to my feet.

"There you are princess." Hector's sadistic smile sent a thundering panic through my body. I felt my head spin as he whipped my body around, sending me head first into the floor. Darkness surrounded me.

Lucas closed the door quietly behind him. The sounds that came from the lower level were disheartening. A soft, terrified, female voice, sobbed, begged and gasped for help. Lucas felt his heart leap into his throat as he recognized Jolene's voice. Lucas dropped to his knees silently. He watched through the railing as a man pounded loudly on the lower level doors. The man turned around and Lucas instantly felt the urge to vomit. Hector Martin had found them.

Knowing he needed to keep Annabelle safe, Lucas kept quiet. Feeling the guilt sink in as he listened to the sobs of their young neighbor.

Without making any progress on the lower level, Hector pulled the gun from his pocket and aimed it towards the sobbing female. The gunfire echoed through the corridor. Panic shook Lucas's body.

Moving away from the stairway, Lucas looked down through the railing. His stomach twisted at the sight of Jolene lying motionless on the ground in front of her open apartment door. Looking away, Lucas held his breath, holding in his nausea. He heard Hector reach the steps.

Sudden thundering footsteps came from the apartment next to theirs. The door swung open and Grady, their neighbor, came bursting through. His eyes darted around the hallway and fell upon the figure that moved swiftly up the stairs.

As Grady left his apartment, Lucas took the brief opportunity to dart across the hall to their apartment door. With Grady in Hector's line of sight, Lucas slipped into his apartment, locking the door behind him.

The darkness consumed his sight. Feeling in front of him, he walked forward. Wanting to let Annabelle know it was him, Lucas opened his mouth to call her name.

"Who the hell are you? What are you doing in here?" Grady's voice growled from the hallway, cutting Lucas off.

"You stupid bastard! You nearly shot me! I'm calling the police," Grady's old voice was followed quickly by his footsteps as he ran back into his apartment, slamming the door behind him.

Lucas needed to find Annabelle.

"Annabelle?" he whispered loudly.

"Lucas." Her voice was from across the room. Pain pierced his chest as he could hear the panic in her voice.

As Lucas opened his mouth to ask her where she was, an annoying pounding ensued on the apartment door. Feeling around, Lucas guided himself to the couch. Listening carefully, he reached forward, knowing Annabelle couldn't be far. He was right.

His hands met her shoulders gently. Feeling her body jump, he quickly placed his hand over her mouth as she cried out in fear.

"It's me," Lucas whispered into her ear. He gently lifted her off the ground, knowing he needed to hide her.

As he stepped forward, earsplitting sounds shook the floor. Realizing the door had been shot, Lucas rushed into the kitchen.

As they huddled in the kitchen, Lucas held Annie close. His mind raced, wanting nothing more than to keep her safe. He felt her heart pound against his chest. Hearing his father's voice sickened him. He listened as Hector Martin walked through the apartment.

The foot steps into the kitchen were the breaking point for Lucas. Leaping to his feet, Lucas threw himself at his father. Catching Hector off guard, the two men stumbled backward into the living room.

Lucas swung his arm around and connected with Hector's cheek. His adrenaline running high, Hector recovered quickly and pointed the gun at Lucas. The gun fired and sent Lucas falling back onto the floor. His head connected with the end table, sending him into the darkness.

Hector turned to the kitchen and he giggled with happiness. He would finally finish the plan and kill the Rockart girl. His wife was gone. Both of his sons disgraced him and he was determined to find solace in finishing the plan that he began.

He slowly walked forward, waiting and listening for the girl. Hector could make out a shadow with in the shadows of the corner of the kitchen. Without warning, Hector jumped on his prey. Bringing the girl up by her hair, Hector threw her to the floor.

As the car sped down the street, Allie felt her heart pound. Why hadn't they left a parked cruiser in front of the apartment building? Why hadn't they thought to keep Annabelle under surveillance? She kicked herself for all the ways she could have prevented this from happening.

She finished slipping her arms through her vest, Chief Michaels pulled into the parking lot. The outside of the building looked normal. Just driving past the building, nothing would look suspicious. Allie knew something terrible could happen at any point in time. She pulled the gun from its holster and swung her door open. With her partner behind her, Allie approached the door of the complex. Using her personal key, she let herself in. As she opened the door, the siren of an ambulance filled the air.

Nausea hit Allie in full force as she saw Jolene lying in a pool of her own blood. She heard a slam from upstairs as Michael's called for the paramedics. Allie's mind was racing. She knew that Annabelle and Lucas were upstairs. What she didn't know, terrified her.

Opening his eyes Lucas heard Annabelle's cry echoing through the building. Sending waves of fear through Lucas's chest, he felt his body shake. Feeling a pressure in his chest, Lucas quickly realized he had been shot. Blood streamed from the wound on his right shoulder. He remembered falling into the table as Hector fired his gun.

He couldn't focus. Waves of pain, guilt, nausea and anger flushed through his system. One thing pushed itself forward in his mind.

"Annabelle," he whispered. He quickly searched the area for either Annabelle or Hector.

The apartment was still dark. Lucas strained his ears and listened for sounds of life. Crying quickly filled his ears. He turned over with a groan, pressing down on his bleeding wound with his hand. The blood continued to flow. As he looked towards the doorway, Lucas could see Hector standing over Annabelle.

Hector was laughing, pointing the gun down at Lucas's helpless girlfriend. Her face was covered with blood, her hair sticking to her cheeks.

"Please, don't." Her whimpered voice echoed through the quiet apartment.

Lucas moved forward, wincing as he got to his knees. Hector was oblivious to his son's movement as Lucas used the wall to stand up. Feeling the blood drain from his head, Lucas closed his eyes briefly, letting the dizziness subside.

Hector laughed and flinched towards Annabelle causing her to cry louder.

Lucas squared his shoulders and stepped into the kitchen. "Hey."

Hector grabbed a handful of Annabelle's shirt, pulling her to her feet. Annabelle cried out in pain as she attempted to balance herself on her unstable legs. Lucas watched as Hector wrapped his arm around Annabelle's neck and backed into the hallway of the building.

As they moved farther away from the apartment door, Lucas felt his knees weaken. Taking a few steps forward, something caught Hector's attention. Lucas watched as Hector pointed his gun towards the stair well, out of Lucas's line of sight.

As he walked forward, Lucas thought of ways to disarm his estranged father and save his girlfriend from whatever fate threatened to take her from him. Lucas made a final step to the door frame. The groan of the floor board sent a wave of panic and regret over Lucas.

Hector spun around, dropping Annabelle from his grip, his gun pointed at Lucas. As he pulled the trigger, Annabelle screamed, "No!"

As Allie met the stairs, her fears were met with Annabelle in the hands of Hector Martin, his gun pointed at her head. As she climbed to the first landing silently, his attention was still focused on something in the apartment.

Allie took another step up when the stairs betrayed her. The squeak of the stair made Hector's head snap in her direction like he knew exactly who was there. A smile crept over his sadistic face as Allie took another step forward. Her gun pointed forward as Hector's gun pointed at Annabelle.

Allie looked at Annabelle struggle with his grip and her balance. Her hair covered her eyes, stuck to her forehead, glued on by a bleeding laceration. Annabelle panicked with a tiny cry as Hector spun around.

Allie's heart broke as Annabelle struggled to stay on her feet, the barrel of Hector's gun sharply pushing into the side of her skull. Allie took another step towards the landing. Hector laughed maliciously.

"So nice of you to show up," Hector growled in Allie's direction.

Allie held herself and her partner back as Hector stepped backwards. She watched as he laughed again, pushing the gun harder into Annabelle's head. Annabelle cried out, stumbling slightly.

"Hold still, Anna," Allie encouraged. Annabelle nodded, her sight still blocked by her hair. Allie lifted her gun, pointing it past Annabelle's head. Hector smiled and shook his head at Allie.

"Not that simple," Hector mused.

The floor suddenly groaned near the entrance of Annabelle's apartment as Lucas stepped into view. Hector spun around in such frenzy, Annabelle twisted uncomfortably, screaming out in pain. As her eyes followed the barrel of Hector's gun and saw that it lead straight to Lucas, she screamed, "No!" As she fell to the ground, her head collided with the floor sending her into unconsciousness.

Allie's mind raced as the next few seconds passed by. Before she knew it, Michaels fired his gun. Instead of silence following her partner's gunfire, an echoing gunfire rang through the building. Reacting, Allie ducked forward, a bullet missing her head.

Hearing the multiple shots fired, Annabelle began to open her eyes. The sounds echoed through her head. Annabelle was unprepared for the pain that settled into her skull. Letting out a cry, Annabelle closed her eyes again. She moved her hands to her face, clenching her hands to her temples.

As she gripped the sides of her face, Annabelle opened her eyes to see Hector lying on the floor in front of her. Panic struck Annabelle as she watched his face curl up at her aggressively. His hand reached for his fallen gun. Annabelle watched as he pointed his gun toward her.

Stunned, Annabelle was paralyzed with fear. Unable to react, she watched as he clenched his fist, ready to pull the trigger. Flashing through her mind within the couple seconds she waited, Annabelle saw her life. She thought of all the things she had done in her life and what she hadn't be able to experience yet. Closing her eyes, Annabelle heard him pull the trigger. As if time stood still, Annabelle waited for death.

Death never came. Annabelle opened her eyes, Allie stood over Hector, her gun still pointed at his head. The sight of blood caused Annabelle to clamp her hand over her mouth. Nausea followed as she felt tears stream down her face. Taking a deep breath, Annabelle rolled away from Hector's lifeless body. Crawling forward, Annabelle dragged herself, moving towards the entrance of the apartment.

Blindly moving forward, nausea hit her like a wall when her hands reached a damp, sticky substance on the floor of the hallway. As she looked up to see what she was in, panic struck her as the crimson substance covered her hands. Utter fear and pain shook Annabelle to the core as her eyes fell on Lucas's unconscious form, leaned up against the wall.

"Lucas," her voice trembled. His eyes remained still. "Lucas?" Her voice was choked, crying out for him to answer. She took her blood stained hands and touched the side of his face. As if she pushed a button, Lucas's eyes opened at the touch of her finger tips. A sigh of relief escaped her lips as she rested her head on his left shoulder.

Meanwhile, Allie remained frozen above the man she had just killed. Her hand shook as she looked down at the blood streaming from his head. Her eyes welled up with tears as she felt a hand take the gun from her hand. Michaels took her shoulders and guided her to a chair. He knew exactly the feeling she felt. She had never had to fire her gun, let alone shoot a person. Allie trembled slightly, regaining her composure. She was quickly reminded of the original situation when a paramedic rushed into view.

Allie's eyes searched the room to find Annabelle. She was curled up against the wall, her head leaning against Lucas. Her eyes were closed as a paramedic knelt down in front of her.

"Miss? Can you hear me? Have you been shot?" the younger gentleman asked. Annabelle slowly opened her eyes to look at him. She couldn't process the question.

Had she been shot? The pain in her head had taken all of her attention when she regained consciousness. Annabelle looked down at her own body, feeling panicked. Her hands traveled down her arms, finding a sore spot around her right forearm. The pain in her head pounded, reminding her of her fall, Annabelle ran her hand across her cheek. Looking down at her hand, blood stained the skin.

"Annabelle?" the voice was pained, begging. Annabelle looked up at Lucas, who sat next to her. Her eyes continued to stare as she saw the blood stain on his shirt. Her body froze, her mind stopped. She felt the pain of the shock settle into her chest. Choking on her tears, the lump in her throat threatened her breathing.

Letting a gasp escape her lips, Annabelle struggled to turn and face him. The young male paramedic, trying to examine her, put his hands gently on her shoulders.

"It's okay, Annabelle. Just hold still." Lucas comforted her.

Adrenaline drained from his body, Lucas could only lift his arm to hold Annabelle's hand. The sudden loss of energy brought pain to the front of his mind. Feeling the blood streaming from his body, Lucas held his breath slightly. Another paramedic appeared in front of him. His focus was elsewhere.

Lucas looked over to Annabelle as she looked back at him, her face stained with blood and tears. Guilt weighed heavily on his chest as he moved his eyes away from her face. As his eyes wandered, they soon fell on the lifeless form on the floor. One of the officers was covering the form with a sheet.

Pain, anger, rage, guilt, agony, the need for revenge; all the emotions hit Lucas at once with the force of hurricane winds. His father was dead. His suffering was over. His life could begin again. Lucas wanted nothing more than to jump up and down in delight that he could live without fear.

Instead, revenge and rage took hold of his body and pushed him forward. Standing from the floor, he pushed the paramedic away, ignoring Annabelle's beg to stay sitting. Lucas stood over his father's body and stared down at it.

"Sir, please sit down," one of the police officers demanded. Lucas tuned everything out and lifted his leg. With every bit of energy he had left, Lucas slammed his foot into the back of Hector's head.

More than one person sprang forward, pulling Lucas away from the body. Allie took Lucas, sobbing and mumbling, to the chair she had just been sitting in. Kneeling down in front of him, Allie pulled him into her arms.

"He can't hurt you anymore," she promised him.

Annabelle sat silently, feeling her mind process the scene she had just witnessed. Lucas had every reason to hate his father. She had never seen him so angry. Her heart pounded, wanting to be with him, to comfort him.

She looked up at Allie comforting her boyfriend. Jealousy filled her. Not because she was mad at Allie for comforting him, but because she physically couldn't get up to be with him.

Annabelle opened her mouth to speak as the paramedic cleaned the blood off her face. He waited for her to say something. "Please, help him."

After her whisper registered, the paramedic smiled and said something to Annabelle. Not listening, Annabelle nodded absently. Her eyes were focused across the hall on Lucas. She couldn't hear anything the paramedic said to Lucas but she watched his reaction. Sadness was an easy emotion to detect in Lucas's features.

Annabelle watched as a group of people appeared at the top of the stairs. One of the men began to take pictures. Another man began to question Chief Michaels. Annabelle was suddenly swarmed by people, all asking her questions. She felt her head spin. Pushing a paramedic away, Annabelle looked across the hall to see another group of people enter.

Overwhelmed, Annabelle let her eyes close and let her mind stop. *Just close your eyes, forget it all.* She let the darkness consume her once again.

- 37- Annabelle: Despair to Euphoria

I opened my eyes slowly, hoping it was all a dream. My eyes burned with tears as I looked around the area. Allie was bent over me, holding me down.

"Anna, listen to me!" she yelled at me. Struggling against her arms, I tried to get up. "Please, you have to calm down!" She wasn't yelling, but begging.

I took in another sharp, hard breath. I felt the pain in my chest stab deeper as I realized I was no longer in the hallway. Lying on my couch, my head was cushioned with a pillow and I was covered in a blanket.

Allie continued to watch me, waiting for something to be said. We were alone in the apartment. The silence was unbearable. I choked on another breath as I watched the tears fall from Allie's eyes.

Had the worst happened? Was Lucas dead? Was he still here with us? Did Allie kill Hector? Was it all a dream? Had it all be a terrible nightmare?

These questions all begged to escape my lips. One beat the rest and spewed from my mouth faster than I had time to process my tone.

"Where is he?" I shouted, not realizing the volume of my voice.

Startled, Allie regained her composure and said, "Lucas is okay, Annabelle. The bullet didn't go through his shoulder, it grazed across his skin. He will be home later. Evan is with him."

I remained still, silently thinking. Overwhelming tears continued to fall from my eyes. I couldn't remember how to breathe until Allie placed her hand on my the side of my face. Her green eyes pierced through my mind.

"Annabelle, there's something else I have to tell you." Her tone was low, filled with sadness.

I didn't know if I was ready for any more bad news. I looked into her eyes and waited for the something else she was to tell me.

"Jolene is dead," Allie whispered quietly. She continued to pierce my brain with her green daggers waiting for my reaction.

The news was terrible. Thoughts of quiet hallways, lonely trips to the diner and never seeing my friend again stormed into my brain.

It was my fault. I was the reason Jolene was no longer alive. Hector came looking for me. Hector was here to kill me, not her. She never did anything to him. He just killed her as if she was just a fly on the wall. *It's not your fault.*

"Annabelle, look at me." Allie's face was in front of mine; her eyes piercing mine. I shook my head at her, staring back into her eyes.

"No." I closed my eyes. Allie leaned forward, wrapping her arms around my body.

"It's okay. It's going to be okay," Allie whispered, holding me tightly.

I couldn't even concentrate. I began to feel the guilt, pain and anger from the night's events. The neon glow of the time shined at me. 3 am...

"Allie, when... where..." I couldn't form the questions that swarmed my mind. Tears continued to stream down my cheeks. She sat on the edge of the couch, pushing my hair away from my face.

I remained silent for a few minutes until I began to feel the physical pain from the night. My head pounded from the blows to the face. I had a new cut that ran across my right cheek, not deep enough for stitches. Then I realized that my hip was throbbing as if my heart had fallen into the joint. The brace clung to my leg, strained from the swelling that I had caused by twisting and moving too quickly.

Squeezing my eyes closed tightly, I growled in frustration. Allie's hand fell into mine. I looked up at her in desperation.

"Why does this keep happening?" I cried quietly.

"It's over. Hector is dead," Allie promised in a low tone. I watched her face stare blankly across the room. I remembered the look on her face after she shot and killed Hector Martin. The empty stare that filled her eyes was eerie. The lack of emotion was what she was taught at the Police Academy. She was told to protect. She had never shot anyone before. The first time she needed to fire her gun, she killed.

"You saved my life." The statement left my lips before I had even considered the statement. It was nothing but the truth. Allie had saved my life, again. She was the reason I was still able to open my eyes and breathe another breath.

Allie looked up at me, her eyes glazed over with guilty tears. It was my turn to convince her of her heroism. It was my turn to comfort her. I placed my free hand on the side of her face. She blinked, letting tears fall down her cheeks.

"You saved my life, Allie." I cried to her.

The room filled with silence. I was afraid to speak, unable to form logical sentences. I was afraid to speak, unsure of what would come out. Exhaustion had begun to set in. I felt my eyes beg to close.

As I looked across the room, a small package on the coffee table caught my eye. I quickly recognized the neatly wrapped package. Without saying a word or making a sound, I sat up on the couch. Allie watched me quietly. I reached forward, ignoring the protests my hip screamed. I picked up the small box and opened it.

It was my gift to Lucas. I didn't have much time to come up with an idea. It was an improvised idea that I had thought up in the hospital room. With limited time and money, it was the best idea I could come up with.

Friday, January 2nd

I was leaning against the back of the chair after Billy and Allie helped me take a shower for the first time in weeks. My feelings were completely jumbled and my heart throbbed heavily with the thought of seeing Lucas.

Suppressing a yawn, I closed my eyes for less than a second before I heard Renee's voice enter the room.

"We received a bag of the clothes and belongings that you had with you when you arrived in the emergency room." Renee set the bag of items in front of me.

I leaned forward and looked down at the soiled, bloodied and torn clothes. Having no attachment, I pushed the bag away.

"Just throw it away," I whispered, leaning back in the chair. Billy took the bag from me and turned to toss it in the trash. As the bag swung forward, a tiny metal sound echoed across the floor. Bending down, Billy Jean picked up a slender metal chain with a charm attached to the end. I gasped slightly, remembering shoving the delicate chain into my pocket outside of my hell.

"What is it? Billy asked curiously.

"Lucas's necklace, from his grandmother." I spoke quietly, tears forming in my eyes as I pictured Hector ripping it from his son's neck, spitting the words, "No one loves you, no one ever will."

I shook my head, feeling tears well up in my eyes. I held the small package in my hands tightly. I looked up at Allie as I gathered everything I had in me to say, "When will he be home?"

"A few hours, maybe tonight?" Allie's voice fluctuated unsurely. I watched her face look down at the small envelope and then back up at my face. "I promised him to keep you home. You need to rest," Allie pointed out weakly.

I closed my eyes slowly, feeling tears fall down my cheeks. *Don't argue, she's right.*

Sighing, I nodded quietly. I leaned forward, setting the package down on the coffee table. The clock in glowed 4 am and I yawned in exhaustion.

"Why don't you take a hot shower and go to bed? You've had a long night," Allie suggested.

Allie was right, I had a long night. My body begged to lie down in my bed. Each joint ached as if I had run a marathon straight up a hill. I yawned again, watching Allie move my walker in front of me.

With Allie's help and close supervision, I prepared to shower. With just a towel wrapped around my body, I looked at Allie with a strange grin.

"I've got it from here," I promised.

"Oh, right. Sorry." Allie blushed. "Yell if you need me."

The hot water ran down my body, washing away the day's events. My mind wandered to the feelings that my mind had begged to forget. Feelings of pain, suffering and loss filled my body as the water ran down my pain soaked body. Weakness took over as I felt my knees shake. I felt around for the edge of the tub and sat down slowly.

A mixture of tears and water dripped down my cheeks. The salty lines disappeared as I ran my hands across my face. I thought about Jolene, her innocent life stolen because of a man that was trying to find me. I couldn't help but feel guilty. Her laughter and screams both haunted my mind, both equally painful.

I took a deep breath, turning the water off. I needed to sleep. I felt my head spin with the overwhelming feeling of remorse. With a shaking hand I reached for the robe that hung on the side of the sink. Wrapping the robe around my shoulders, tying it closed, I closed my eyes, resting my head on the wall.

"Allie," I spoke, barely even louder than a whisper. My voice cracked, tears falling from my eyes. With a deep breath, I opened my mouth to speak again.

"Allie," I called again, slightly louder. I listened to hear her footsteps approach the door. The door opened slowly and Allie poked her head in. She smiled understandingly at me.

With the walker under my hands, Allie close behind me, I walked into my bedroom. I sat down on the edge of my bed, groaning with the bending of my hip. Allie was prepared and handed me a handful of pills. She held a glass of water in front of me as well. I took the pain medicine and took a couple drinks of the water.

After slipping on an oversized t-shirt, I pulled the blankets up over my shoulders. Allie sat down on the side of the bed and brushed her hand over my hair. I could feel her maternal instinct as she hesitated to leave me alone.

"I'll be in the living room. If you need me, call me." Allie leaned over me and kissed my forehead gently. "Good night Anna, try and sleep."

"Good night Allie," I whispered, closing my eyes involuntarily.

Before I could take another breath, I drifted into a deep, dreamless sleep.

I opened my eyes slowly, feeling warmth behind my body. With a tired yawn, I turned over in my bed to see a pair of blue eyes that could melt any girl's heart. Instead of saying anything, I moved forward and planted a deep kiss on his lips. Feeling him push back, I felt my heart pound.

My mind was suddenly cleared of all worries, fears and feelings of guilt. I felt his hands touch the back of my head as he pulled me closer. Pulling my lips away from his, I burrowed my face into his chest. He wrapped his arms around my body and I took in his scent.

"It's over, Annie. You are safe now," Lucas whispered, kissing my hair firmly.

"I love you, Lucas," I whispered.

"I love you, Annabelle," he echoed.

With his arms wrapped tightly around me, we fell asleep.

<u>Sunday, February 1ˢᵗ</u>

The morning crawled into the afternoon slowly. As the afternoon came to a close, the sun would soon begin to fall behind the horizon and cast an orange glow through the bedroom. I adjusted my head slightly, continuing to run my hands through Lucas's soft hair. I could feel his breath on my arm as he slept peacefully.

As I looked up at the ceiling, my thoughts took me to a place I had pushed into the far corner of my mind. Before I had a chance to change my thoughts, emotions came flooding into my mind. As if propelled by a force unknown, I felt my body shake with anticipation of the coming months and events in my life.

One major point stuck out in my mind as if it were begging for my attention. The thought poked and squirmed its way into view. I didn't want to face the truth that needed so desperately to be dealt with.

In less than nine months, I would be a mother. There is a baby growing inside of me. I waited quietly knowing I would begin to cry at any moment. I would cry because of the fear of being a mother. I would cry because I didn't want to have Dolan Meyer's child. I would cry because of the terrible events that caused me involuntarily become a mother. I would cry because I didn't know how I was going to love something that came from such a horrible, violent and traumatic event.

I waited, but the tears never came. My tear ducts remained dormant as I stared up at the ceiling. 'I am going to be a mother,' I thought to myself. I didn't shutter. I didn't cry, blink or even sweat. I wasn't scared.

The epiphany settled into my mind and I thought about the future. I looked down at the man that was asleep on my chest. I felt my heart pound with the happiness he brought me. I ran my hand through his hair and touched his cheek gently with my thumb. His eyes fluttered slightly and opened slowly. Lucas looked up at me with a tired look across his face. A sleepy smile lightened his face.

"Hi," he whispered softly. He readjusted, slipping his arm around my waist. I moved closer to him, holding him tightly.

I heard him wince as I hugged tighter. Pulling my arms away quickly, I apologized.

"No, it's okay." Lucas smiled.

I looked at him as he moved his hand to his shoulder and closed his eyes slightly. I moved my hand to his shoulder gently. As he

322

watched my hand, I slowly moved the collar of his shirt to the side. It exposed the bandage of the gunshot wound. I rubbed my hand gently over the side of his shoulder, tracing the outline of the bandage. The movement reminded me of when he traced the bandages on my hands.

I leaned forward quietly and kissed the side of his neck. I felt him shiver with the gentle touch. I smiled and sat up in front on him.

"I have something for you." I finally broke the silence.

Lucas looked at him curiously. I reached behind me, keeping my eyes on him.

"It must have gotten lost in the shuffle of presents when my parents were here," I continued to explain as I handed him the small envelope. "It's nothing big. I actually didn't even buy it."

Lucas opened the wrapping paper on the envelope as I continued to babble on about the gift. Finally, he dumped its contents into his hand. Once the metal touched his skin, Lucas froze.

I watched his hand relax as he looked down the delicate chain in his hand. With a soft and tearful look, Lucas stared at me.

"I found it when I left the…" I didn't feel the need to bring up the abandoned building. "They gave it to me in a bag of my belongings from the emergency room. I thought you would want it back."

Lucas continued to stare at me. I began to feel nervous, like I had made the wrong decision to give him the necklace back.

"Luke?" I whispered softly, almost silently.

His eyes moved from my eyes down to the necklace. The room continued in silence, his eyes focused on the metal chain in his hands. He shifted the necklace from his right hand to his left, rubbing the charm between his fingers gently.

"Luke, say something," I begged.

Lucas looked back up at me, tears now streaming down his face. Guilt struck me like a train, my breath escaped my lips. Instant tears fell from my eyes as I watched him cry softly.

Before I had time to apologize for whatever I did wrong, he wrapped himself around my body tightly. I felt his body shake with tears. As I held him close to me, I felt Lucas reach his limit. I felt Lucas break down in my arms.

I held him tightly for the next few minutes as he clung to me as I had clung to him so many times before. It was my turn to be strong for him. He needed me just as much, if not more than I needed him.

His family was gone. Not that his family had ever meant anything to him before, but he was completely disconnected from them now. Lucas had only me and my family to be his support system. I had never been more willing to give up everything to help someone. I wanted to be his family.

After a few minutes passed, Lucas stopped crying. His eyes were closed, but I could tell he wasn't sleeping. I ran my hands across his back, soothing him in silence. I kissed the side of his face gently. Lucas returned the kiss on my lips. I felt a few more tears fall on my cheeks.

"What's wrong?" I whispered against his cheek.

"Overwhelmed," Lucas whispered. "Everything has happened so quickly, I haven't had the time to adjust to any of the changes. Three months ago my life was miserable. I was living at house with two parents who wanted nothing to do with me. I suddenly gained a brother that I never wanted. I was thrust into the role of a kidnapper's son and was expected to become a monster. After I met you, got to know you, my life changed right before my eyes. I began to see the things in life that meant something to me." Lucas looked down at his hands. "When I thought I lost you, I didn't want to live. When we were both given a second chance, I vowed to myself to never let anything happen to you again. After Janis was killed, I thought we could start to move on. I never expected for Hector to show up here. I never expected for you to hurt again." Lucas let another tear fall.

"Luke," I whispered. He shook his head.

"No, don't tell me it wasn't my fault. It was my fault. It will always be my fault when you are hurting. I am here to protect you. I am here to take care of you. I didn't do that."

I watched him silently struggle with his thoughts and feelings.

"Annabelle, when you gave this back to me-" Lucas held up the necklace. "-I remembered a promise I made to Mable. I remember a vow I made to her before she passed away."

Lucas was suddenly on his feet. I watched as he left the room and left me in the silence. My thoughts tried desperately to catch up to the events that unfolded before me. I sat up at the edge of the bed, waiting for Lucas to come back.

Lucas reentered the room and knelt down before me. I looked down at him curiously.

"I promised that I would take care of whoever I gave this to. Annie, you are the only person I have ever felt anything for. You are the only person I have ever truly loved with every bit of my heart and soul. You make me feel needed, wanted, loved and cared for. You make me feel like a man. I love you so much." Lucas had more tears sitting on the edge of his eye lids. My eyes began to water, tears beginning to descend down my cheeks. *He's kidding, right?*

I looked down at his hands as his opened a tiny green box. The diamond ring inside shined brightly in the setting sun. *He's not kidding...*

"Luke," his name left my lips in a breathless statement. I looked into his eyes, searching for the joke. I wanted to laugh, cry, scream and jump for joy.

"Will you spend the rest of your life with me, Annie?"

I felt my chest cave in with the overwhelming sensations of hope, love, and anticipation. I gasped slightly as Lucas slipped the ring over my left ring finger. I couldn't speak. I couldn't put my chaotic thoughts to words. I nodded my head as tears streamed down my cheeks. Lucas leaned forward and tucked his face into my shoulder. *This is crazy.*

I pulled his head forward and placed my lips on his. The kiss was soft and assuring. I pulled him back into bed bedside me. I couldn't feel my body as I floated into a peaceful slumber. The thoughts that filled my mind were both confusing and suffocating. We would be starting over, starting a new life, starting forever. I had never felt a more euphoric feeling.

- 38- Annabelle: Baby Steps

Monday, February 2nd

With his arms wrapped around me, I looked down at the ring that wrapped around my finger. I smiled quietly, turning my hand to see the light of the rising sun gleam through the diamond.

The slight shift of the bed reminded me of the reason I had woken up in the first place. A dull ache throbbed down my leg from my hip to my toes. I took a deep breath in and slowly moved Lucas's arms to the side, sitting up on the edge of the bed. I knew it would be hard to wake him up. The past two days had been exhausting for both of us.

I reached for my walker and stood up. Carefully, I opened the bedroom door and stepped into the hallway. The light from the new day began to fill the apartment and bring happiness to the dark feeling that hung over the building.

After taking a dose of pain medicine, I decided against going back to the bedroom. I didn't want to take the chance of waking Lucas up. He needed sleep more than anyone.

I sat down on the couch. The neon numbers read 6:43am. The TV remote sat on the coffee table in front of me. I looked down at it. I knew that if I turned on the TV this early in the morning, the news would be on. If the news was on, there would be breaking news. If there would be breaking news, it would be about me.

Don't you want to know what they are saying about you, Annabelle? Maybe, but am I prepared to hear it? *What could they possibly say?* Everything, they could say everything. *You are strong enough to hear it, Annabelle.*

Going with what my head told me, I reached for the remote and turned the TV on. Sure enough, the local news station was interviewing Chief Michaels.

"Hector Martin is dead. He was shot and killed by a Fort Kent officer at the Hill Bridge Apartments early in the morning on Sunday, February 1st," Chief Michael's confirmed.

"Chief, what was the motive behind Martin's brutal outbursts and calculated moves?" The reporter plunged into the subject before Michael's had time to finish the first answer.

"It's not clear what his motives were to attack an innocent girl like Annabelle Rockart. Martin was insane. He didn't know right from wrong."

"Is it true that Ms. Rockart is romantically involved with Lucas Martin, the son of Hector Martin?" another reporter interrupted.

"That is not my business to disclose. I will not be answering any more questions, thank you," Chief Michaels answered. The camera view then showed the police station swarmed with reporters. I clicked the remote to another station.

The national news broadcast was showing a picture of Hector Martin. It was a mug shot from a few years back. The report continued as the reporter explained my situation from an outsider's perspective. When he finished reading off his cards, he turned to his co anchor and said, "This case seems to be one of the worst stories of kidnapping that

I have heard in my time as a reporter. Ms. Rockart survived through this terrible ordeal and still refuses to tell her story."

"Do you blame her? Would you want to relive the horrifying two weeks she spent locked up and left for dead? As far as I'm concerned, Annabelle Rockart is a hero. She is a role model for girls all over the world. Her strength and courage to get through this on her own is inspiring and heartbreaking. She should be given privacy until she is ready to talk." The female anchor smiled at the camera and I felt as though she was smiling at me.

With another click of the remote, I turned the TV off.

Looking around the room, I took a deep breath. *What now?*

I couldn't bring myself to wake up Lucas. He was exhausted and needed his sleep. I felt my heart pound as my eyes caught the ring on my finger. *What will your family say? Is it too soon? Do they really like him?*

I shook the thoughts from my mind and decided to make myself breakfast.

Reaching for my walker, I stood up from the couch, ignoring the dull ache of my hip. I had gotten used to the everyday pains from my injuries. My right hip, shoulder and sides ached consistently throughout the day. I was slowly learning to forget the pain, but my physical scars reminded me of it each time I looked in the mirror.

I walked to the kitchen, flipping the light switch on. After gathering the milk, bowl and spoon for cereal, I sat down at the table gently. I pushed my walker away and poured myself a bowl of fruit and granola cereal.

As I continued taking small bites of my cereal, I stared at my walker. Thinking back to my most recent therapy session, I thought about what Clara and Heather mentioned to me.

"Annabelle, you know what you're capable of." Clara laughed.

"I know. I'm afraid of the pain," I admitted shifting my weight on the therapy mat. Heather was positioned behind me as Clara evaluated my progress.

"Your range of motion in your hip as improved tremendously. You really don't need the walker all day, mostly for longer distances. As long as you have the brace for support, the walker is unnecessary," Heather pointed out.

Thinking about the suggestion of not using the walker terrified me. Pain terrified me. I couldn't imagine feeling pain without feeling nauseous. *How much more harm could it do to take one step?* I cringed. *Just try, Annabelle.*

After finishing my bowl of cereal, I continued to sit and stare at the walker that sat two feet in front of me. With the voice in my head taunting me, I took a deep breath.

"What's one step going to hurt?" I whispered to myself.

I pushed the chair out from the table, placing my hands firmly on the chair underneath me. I took a deep breath in, anticipating the pain that would surely strike my body in a matter of seconds. Taking another breath, I lifted myself up, shifting my weight to my left leg. As I balanced on my left leg, my right leg hovered hesitantly over the floor. I looked down at my feet, the floor seemed so far way. I touched the cold kitchen floor with the toes on my right foot. With a gentle movement, I placed my foot firmly on the floor beneath me.

Shifting my weight from one leg to the other seemed so simple. It really was a simple task, a movement you learn when you first begin to stand as a child. I felt my body shake as I braced for pain. I shifted from my left to my right. I felt the brace around my hip tighten as I my muscle adjusted to the unfamiliar stance. The silence of the apartment was quickly filled with the sound of my heart pounding through my chest.

I was standing, on my own, without anyone or anything helping me. *Baby steps, Annabelle.* My lips curled upwards as I stood motionless in the middle of my kitchen. The joy of this improvement encouraged me. *Take a baby step, Annabelle.*

My adrenaline was running high. My courage was leaping and bounding forward. I knew that taking a step forward would only encourage my happiness. I thought about my family, my friends and Lucas. I needed to take this step for them. I needed to be happy for them. *Do it for yourself, Annabelle.*

With a smile playing across my lips, I did just that. I took a step forward with my right leg. Subconsciously bracing my body for pain, I stepped down. With a small gasp, I felt my foot meet the floor. It was cool, smooth to the touch. I waited for the pain to strike. I looked down at my feet as my left leg found its place next to my right. Still no pain followed. I took another step closer to my walker. I let out a tiny squeak of nerves as I continued forward. I heard a soft shuffle in the bedroom. Knowing Lucas was waking up, I made a quick decision.

Passing my walker, I continued to walk on my own into the living room. Wanting desperately to show Lucas, I giggled happily. I stood silently as the bedroom door opened. Lucas caught sight of me immediately. His eyes widened in a sudden panic.

I smiled at him, nodding. I took a step towards him. I watched as his hands flinched as I stepped closer to him.

Lucas opened his mouth to say something; instead he let out a small burst of air. He smiled and walked closer to me. Closing the distance between us, he wrapped his arms around my waist. I smiled as he leaned down to kiss me.

"I love you," Lucas whispered into my lips.

I opened my eyes, placing my hands on either side of his face. This was the first time we have ever stood together, nothing separating the distance between our bodies, including the thin metal of a walker. He opened his eyes at the touch of my hands. Our eyes met, sending a wave of passion through my body.

"I love you more than I could ever express." I spoke softly. With a smile on his lips, he placed a soft kiss on the end of my nose. Knowing I didn't want to push myself too far, I suggested we sit down on the couch.

"How long have you been awake?" Lucas asked. I looked up at the clock that read 9:45am.

"A while." I smiled knowing I'd been up for three hours.

"Why didn't you wake me up?" He yawned. I laughed.

"Because I know you're exhausted. Are you hungry?" I asked.

"No, I'm okay."

"How is your shoulder?"

"Sore, but I'll be fine." Lucas shook his head. "Don't worry about me."

"I can't do that," I admitted. Lucas laughed leaning his head back on the couch. I looked at him quietly and he closed his eyes. "Are you still tired?"

"A little." Lucas yawned. I smiled and kissed his cheek gently. I pushed off from the couch and stood up slowly. I felt Lucas move behind me.

"No, stay right where you are. I will be right back," I promised him. His eyes watched me hesitantly. "Don't worry about me."

"I can't do that," he admitted, mocking my earlier statement. I smiled at him and shook my head.

With my hands on the furniture around me, I walked into the hallway. The walls guided me into the bathroom and I grabbed the small white bottle of pills prescribed to Lucas for pain. I brought the bottle out into the living room and handed Lucas a glass of water.

"It's my turn to take care of you."

The day continued as Lucas and I lounged around the apartment. Evan had called around the middle of the day to see if we needed anything. I knew he was worried about me but I assured him we were fine. We just needed time to relax.

Lucas suggested watching some of the DVDs that I had gotten for Christmas, something to pass the time. Almost as soon as the first season of I Love Lucy began, Lucas had fallen back to sleep.

A surplus of thoughts ran through my head. From Jolene's death to the thought of what color dresses my bridal party would wear. I smiled at the ring each time it caught my sight. I reminded myself a marriage right now would be too much to handle. I knew the engagement would take time to sink into my family's heads. It still hadn't sunk into my head just yet. I didn't have to tell them just yet… right?

It felt right. I needed Lucas. He needed me. *Do you want him?* More than I have ever wanted anything or anyone. *Don't you think you're rushing?* What's the hurry? We have all time in the world to get married. It doesn't have to be soon. In time, it will happen.

As I continued the conversation in my head, I felt my phone vibrate on the couch beside me. Careful not to disturb Lucas, I stood up from the couch using the walls to move into the kitchen. I looked down at the phone to see Allie's name.

"Hello?" I answered softly.

"Did I wake you?" Allie questioned.

"No, Lucas is sleeping. I didn't want to wake him," I explained.

"Shoot."

"What?" I laughed softly.

"I am sitting outside your building. I was going to pick you two up for dinner. Marie is making dinner and insisted I picked you up."

I looked up at the clock, 6:13pm. Lucas had to be hungry by now.

"Well Lucas hasn't eaten anything today and I haven't had anything since early this morning." I paused to look across the room at Lucas. He stirred slightly, yawning loudly. "You can come up, we will be joining you."

Lucas looked at me from across the room as I hung up with Allie. I smiled at his sleepy look. He yawned and rubbed his hair lazily.

"Who was that?" he asked softly, resting his head on the back of the couch.

"Allie, she's picking us up for dinner." I leaned against the counter. My hip was aching slightly.

"When will she be here?" Lucas questioned. There was a tap on the door. I smiled.

"Now." I laughed slightly. Waiting another second, I pushed myself off the wall. With a slow pace, I walked to the door and opened it to see Allie raising her arm to knock again.

"Sorry." I smiled. I waited for Allie notice my lack of walker. She looked from my feet to my face, up and down. She smiled and opened her arms to me. With a step forward, I was in her arms and she hugged me tightly.

"I'm so proud of you." She spoke quietly to me.

Allie walked into the apartment behind me and Lucas stood up from the couch tiredly.

"You weren't kidding about him being exhausted," Allie commented. I laughed as Lucas stumbled tiredly into the second bedroom to change.

Within the next few minutes, we were ready to go. After a short ride in the elevator, we were on the way to my parent's house. Sitting in the front seat, I looked down at my hand and remembered the shiny ring that lived on my finger. I panicked slightly, unsure how to explain the engagement to my family.

I curled my fingers into a fist and put my hand in the pocket. Sliding the ring off into the pocket, I thought to myself, baby steps...

After we finished dinner, Mom and Allie cleaned up the dishes while Lucas and I kept Madison busy. Madison pulled on Fig's ears as the cat crawled across Lucas's lap.

"Fig is a kitty. Baby is a doggy." She laughed. I smiled at her. Her random declaration of common knowledge was absolutely adorable.

Lucas held my hand as I leaned back against his shoulder. I felt his fingers touch my hand and continue to search the surface of my fingers.

I looked up at him quizzically. I realized he was searching my left hand for the ring. I pulled the ring from my pocket and reassured him. He didn't seem to agree with the secret. His face dropped and he zoned out for a while.

Fantastic, *you upset him*. With good reason, *is there a good reason to hide your engagement? You love him, right?* Of course, but my family would instantly jump on the idea and tear it down. *How do you know that? They love him.* They like him. I'm not convinced they love him. *Yet...*

Lucas remained quiet as Madison continued to play with Fig. I excused myself and stood up from the couch. Neither paid any attention to my absence. I walked into the kitchen slowly, gaining more independence with each step.

Allie smiled as I joined them in the kitchen. I gave her a little smile but I couldn't hide my unease. Luckily, their focus was on the dishes and not completely on my expression. I walked past them to the family room.

My dad passed me as I stepped down into the room. He kissed the top of my head as I passed by. Evan was perched on the edge of the couch watching the football game. His eyes landed on me as I sat down next to him.

"Hey Anna." He smiled, and quickly did a double take. His face fell at the sight of my freshly watering eyes. "What's up sis?"

"Evan, can I trust you?" I whispered.

"Of course you can." Evan turned the TV down.

Tell him.

"I need to tell you something," I began, his face tightened. "It's not bad news. It's more or less, sudden news."

Evan watched me contemplate my next words. I looked up at him. I pulled the ring from my pocket and began to spill my secrets like someone had flipped a switch.

"I said yes. I knew everyone would be upset because of how little I've known him. But I love him more than anything in the world. I have found the one person I can trust my life with and I want to spend the rest of my life with him. But I know mom will object. And I don't want to upset anyone, anymore. Now, Lucas is upset because I'm not wearing the ring. I don't want him to be upset," I babbled in one breath. Evan smiled and chuckled at my panic. Taking in a deep breath, I sighed heavily.

"Sooner or later you need to learn to ignore what mom wants and doesn't want. It isn't her life, Anna. Your decisions are yours," Evan encouraged. He took the ring from my hand and examined it. "Put it where it belongs." He smiled.

Smiling pensively, I slipped the ring onto my finger, looking down at its simplicity. I looked up at my brother. "How did you tell Mom and Dad?"

"Straight forward. Don't hesitate; show your confidence in the relationship. If you are committed to being with him for the rest of your life, don't show hesitation or uncertainty. It's a big step, but you are not a baby. You can handle it. Look how far you've come." Evan smiled.

Baby steps... are for babies.

Lucas sulked silently on the couch. Thoughts of regret passed through. He felt an overwhelming sense that he had rushed the idea of marriage into Annabelle's mind. Was she second guessing the proposal? How could he think she was ready? He mentally scolded himself for putting her in that position.

"Mr. Lucas," Madison started. He looked down at her where she sat next to a now sleeping Fig.

"Miss. Maddy," Lucas echoed with a small smile.

"Auntie loves you." She smiled sweetly. As if she sensed the tension between Annabelle and Lucas, Madison stood up from the ground and sat down on the couch.

Unsure of what to say in response, Lucas continued to watch her. She smiled and patted his hand.

"If she did something naughty, she is sorry. Auntie makes mistakes like Maddy does. Mommy tells me that when I am naughty, if I am sorry, she will forgive me. If Auntie says she is sorry, you should forgive her. It's what Mommy does."

Lucas looked down at the little girl in amazement. She was full of little wisdoms as if she was a wise old woman. Lucas smiled genuinely down at Madison and pulled her into a tight hug.

After telling her family, her mother embraced the idea as if she was already anticipating the announcement. Taking Annabelle completely off guard, Annabelle was overwhelmed with feelings.

Hearing the happy commotion in the kitchen, Lucas looked down at Madison who had the same curiosity written across her face. She smiled and held out her hand for him to follow her.

Entering the kitchen, Madison leading the way, he heard the happiness swell. Rounding the corner, Marie had Annabelle in her grasp. Her arms were wrapped tightly around her shoulders, saying how happy she was. Annabelle was facing the opposite side of the room, Lucas could not see her expression.

Madison let go of his hand and she ran to her grandma. Lucas looked around the room. Evan was smiling, leaning up against the door frame that led into the other room. Allie stood near Evan, smiling with her arms wrapped around her husband.

Lucas ended his look around the room at Mark. His eyes were fixed on his wife and daughter. Lucas noticed the tears that threatened to fall from his eyes. Feeling a sudden panic, his eyes flicked back to Annabelle. Lucas realized that she had put the ring on again.

Marie was the first to acknowledge his presence in the room. She let go of her daughter and closed the distance between them. She put her hands on his shoulders and looked into his eyes for a second.

"You-" She smiled. "-have made my daughter happy again. I have not known you very long but I can see the kind of person you are. You are what she deserves, a real man. A man that will take care of her and love her." Marie pulled Lucas into her arms.

The sudden turn of events sunk into his mind. His eyes met a pair of tear stained blue eyes. A smile filled the rest of her face, genuine and beautiful. His heart pounded with happy anticipation that Annabelle's family was so welcoming of his proposal.

Marie let go of Lucas's shoulders and he closed the distance between himself and Annabelle and wrapped his arms gently around her waist. Annabelle tucked her face into his neck, taking a deep, relieved breath in. Things could only get better.

Later that night, Lucas cuddled close to Annabelle on the couch of their apartment. She tucked her face into his chest, yawning slightly. Glancing up at the clock, Lucas noticed it was 11:45pm.

"We should probably go to bed." His words were a whisper in the near silent apartment.

"I'm comfortable," Annabelle whined.

With all the movement that her hip had endured throughout the day, the aching had just begun to subside after a dose of pain medicine. Lucas twisted his fingers through her hair softly. She closed her eyes slightly, ignoring the fact that they should be going to bed.

"Annie…" Lucas whispered softly. She hummed in response.

Lucas shifted their bodies as he sat up on the couch. Annabelle reluctantly sat up next to him, her eyes barely opening. He smiled, watching her body wave back and forth, exhaustedly trying to stay awake. Leaning forward, he kissed her cheek softly. Her eyes opened with a smile and she looked at him.

"Come on," Lucas said standing up with his hands out for her.

With a heavy sigh, Annabelle slid her hands into his and stood up slowly. The pain, a now dull ache, was nothing compared to the nausea that overwhelmed her body. Letting out a nauseated gasp, Annabelle leaned forward onto his shoulders.

"What's wrong?" Lucas questioned quickly grabbing her shoulders, cradling her head.

Annabelle took a deep breath through her nose, exhaling audibly from her mouth. The nausea subsided slightly and she stood up.

"I think I just stood up too quickly." Anna spoke delicately.

"Do you need to sit down again?" Lucas suggested.

"No." Annabelle took another breath. "Let's just go to bed."

Lucas looked at her again, she smiled silently and nodded. He nodded in return and they turned around and headed towards the bedroom. Annabelle took a few steps and as the nausea subsided momentarily.

As she stepped into the hallway, the nausea struck again. She leaned against the wall, closing her eyes tightly. Lucas turned to see her shut her eyes.

"Annabelle?" Lucas questioned. He stepped towards her and touched her face with the palm of his hand.

Sweat beaded down her forehead as her body shook weakly. Heat radiated from her body as she opened her eyes to look at Lucas. He watched her eyes fall as she took another breath in. He hesitantly hovered around her, unsure of what she would do.

"Bathroom," Annabelle finally spoke breathlessly. Lucas stepped aside, looping one arm around her waist as she took a step forward. A few steps later, Lucas helped Annabelle to the floor as she leaned her head back on the edge of the tub.

Sweat dripped from her brow as she continued to take deep breaths. Lucas knelt down beside her, however unsure of what she wanted him to do for her. He watched her blink her eyes a few times before he took his hand and touched the side of her face.

"Annie," Lucas whispered lightly to her. She opened her eyes to look him in the eye.

Leaning forward, Annabelle felt her stomach turn violently. With her hand over her mouth, she fought the urge to vomit. The feeling in her abdomen increased as she silently lost the battle with her nausea.

Surrendering to the knot in her throat, Annabelle leaned over the toilet. Lucas slipped his hands through her hair, holding it out of the way. With a gentle touch on her back, Lucas patiently waited for her to finish.

Wiping her mouth, Annabelle sat back against the tub, shaking slightly. Lucas closed the seat of the toilet and moved to sit on it. Running his hands through her hair, she leaned her head forward onto his knees.

"Better?" Lucas questioned. Annabelle nodded silently. They sat in silence for a minute or two before Annabelle shifted, ready to get up.

"Gross," Annabelle commented, reaching forward to the sink to stand up. Lucas helped her to her feet. Reaching for her toothbrush, Lucas kissed the back of her head and stepped out of the bathroom to give her privacy.

Walking into the second bedroom, Lucas changed out of his clothes and into something comfortable for bed. His eyes lingered at the bandage across his shoulder. The pain was dull and barely noticeable. He remembered the sounds of her screams and the feeling of pure hatred towards his father. Letting out a heavy sigh, Lucas reminded himself it was in the past.

Friday, February 6th

The week flew by. Nearly every day and night, Annabelle experienced pregnancy related sickness. Feeling helpless, Lucas could only stand nearby as she would get violently sick in the bathroom.

Today, began differently for Annabelle. Instead of waking up around 6am to rush to the bathroom, she opened her eyes to a knock on the front door. She scrunched her nose and looked at the neon numbers; 8:30 am. With a grunt, she turned over to Lucas, ignoring the knock.

Another knock caused her to sigh out loud. Lucas was startled by the second knock, sitting up in bed.

"Just ignore it." Annabelle moaned, curling into herself under the blanket.

Lucas shook his head, rubbing the sleep from his eyes. With a noisy yawn, he flipped the covers off and stumbled through the apartment to the front door. Looking through the peep hole, he recognized the postal service worker.

Unlocking the door, he greeted the man politely. The postman apologized for the early delivery but mentioned it would not fit in the mailbox. Lucas signed the paper and took the small package from him, thanking him kindly.

Retracing his steps through the apartment to the bedroom, he read the front of the package.

"Annabelle Dawn Rockart." Lucas yawned presenting the package to a tired Annabelle. "Package for you."

With a grumble, Annabelle sat up to take the object from Lucas. She slipped her finger through the side and pulled out an emerald green folder. The white writing on the front read *The University of Maine at Fort Kent.*

Anna smiled excitedly and opened the folder to see her diploma staring back at her. She smiled, running her hand over her name on the certificate. Tears formed in her eyes as Lucas read over her shoulder; *Bachelor's Degree in Elementary Education.*

"It's real. I'm actually done with school," Annabelle whispered. Lucas smiled at her silent celebration. He leaned forward and placed a kiss on her shoulder.

After a few minutes of happy silence, Annabelle set the degree on her night stand. She turned to Lucas and hugged him tightly. He pulled her into his arms and relaxed back into the pillows. Annabelle snuggled her head into his neck and took a deep breath in.

"I'm proud of you." Lucas smiled into her hair.

"Thank you." Annabelle turned her head to look up at him.

Maybe it was the way the rising sun shined through the curtains or the way his face lit up when she looked at him, but Annabelle could have sworn Luke's face was glowing. She smiled happily, running her hand across his chest.

Lucas leaned down to kiss her forehead and she sighed blissfully. She turned her head and placed her lips gently on his. In the moment their lips touched, the world stood still and Annabelle felt every piece of her life fall into its place.

Later that day, Annabelle had a scheduled appointment with Dr. Stevenson her new obstetrician referred by Dr. Morris. Annabelle sat nervously with Lucas in the waiting room of the brightly colored office. Another woman sat across the room from them, reading a magazine with her free hand resting on her protruding abdomen. A quiet smile rested on this woman's lips as she flipped through the parenting magazine.

Annabelle watched her as she sat in complete happiness. An envious feeling came over her as she saw the ring that rested on the woman's left hand. A gentle squeeze of Lucas's hand reminded Annabelle of the ring that rested on her finger. Smiling inwardly, she didn't feel so alone or envious of the stranger across the room. She had support. She would be ok.

"Are you okay?" Lucas whispered.

Annabelle nodded quietly and smiled at him. He returned the smile and patted her leg softly.

"Annabelle?" The receptionist called from her desk. Annabelle looked up at the sound of her name.

"Dr. Stevenson is ready for you. You can go through that door and to the right," the receptionist directed her.

With Lucas close behind, Annabelle walked into the small exam room. Before they had a chance to turn around, a nurse entered the room and greeted them happily.

"Hello, I'm Bridgett. I'm Dr. Stevenson's nurse and I'll be helping her out today. Annabelle, if you could change into the gown and have a seat in on the exam table, I will be right back with Dr. Stevenson."

Annabelle nodded at the nurse and the nurse left the room. Lucas excused himself as well to let Annabelle change in private. After a minute or so, Annabelle opened the door and let Lucas back in. She sat down on the table. The rustle of the paper underneath her was the only sound in the room. Lucas sat in the chair next to her nervously. They exchanged anxious glances, neither knowing what to expect.

Within a few minutes, Dr. Stevenson entered and introduced herself. She explained what they would be doing today and that she would make the pregnancy as easy as she could.

"Now, this is your fiancé?" Dr. Stevenson questioned, nodding towards Lucas.

"Yes." Annabelle smiled and looked at Lucas as his cheeks burned a bright shade of red.

"The father?" She smiled. Annabelle's faced dropped. Lucas held her hand tightly.

Anna took a deep breath and quietly explained the situation to her new doctor.

"Has anyone discussed your options?" Dr. Stevenson asked.

"Options are not necessary." Annabelle told her doctor firmly. She watched as the doctor understood immediately the sensitivity level that needed to be maintained throughout.

Changing the subject, the doctor explained that this would be an early ultrasound to make sure of the pregnancy and to make sure everything looked normal considering the circumstances.

"I don't know what Dr. Morris has told you about what you should expect today, but I assure you I will explain every step as we go." Dr. Stevenson smiled sweetly. She explained that this would be a very early ultrasound that the baby would not look like a baby yet.

As Annabelle listened to the doctor, she kept reminding herself that she would be ok. But accepting the idea of a normal pregnancy seemed impossible. This was the farthest thing from normal.

The rest of the appointment flew by before Annabelle had a chance to comprehend the information that was thrown at her. Dr. Stevenson mentioned that slight abnormalities were seen on the ultrasound. However, because of the early stages of the pregnancy these could work themselves out within a week or so.

"I will have you schedule another appointment in about 4 weeks. I want to keep a close eye on you and your baby because of these slightly abnormalities. Nothing to worry about yet, just yet; judging by the dates you have given me and the circumstances of your situation I'm estimating you are around 6 weeks pregnant. I won't know your true due date until the next ultrasound." Dr. Stevenson continued to explain the things that Annabelle should be cautious of and what she should look for; if any complications should occur, call the office immediately.

Walking Annabelle and Lucas out to the lobby, Dr. Stevenson handed them her card and a number to call in case of emergency.

"Do you have any questions?" she asked politely.

Annabelle felt overwhelmed as no questions formed in her chaotic brain. She looked at Lucas and he too looked overwhelmed.

"I understand if you are a bit anxious or overwhelmed, please call me if any questions come to mind." The doctor smiled again, shaking their hands firmly.

After checking out, Lucas held Annabelle's hand on their way to the car. The silence was peaceful as they pondered the appointment. The car ride home remained silent as they continued to digest the information gained today. As they arrived at their apartment complex, Annabelle's phone rang.

"Hello?" Annabelle spoke quietly.

"Annabelle, how did your appointment go?" Her mother's voice rang.

Annabelle explained what she could remember and what she had processed to her mother. She spiked worry in her mother when she mentioned the abnormalities.

"Did the doctor seem concerned? What kind of abnormalities?" Marie questioned.

"She didn't seem worried yet. She said it could just be too early to see clearly." Annabelle sighed.

Her mother continued to ramble on about her cousin's pregnancy and the high risk that ran in the family. Annabelle sighed and looked at Lucas begging for mother to stop talking.

"When is your next appointment? I would like to go with you to see how this doctor is treating you," Marie explained to her daughter.

"It's in a month." Annabelle added, "I'm sure you have better things to do, Ma."

"Nonsense, you are more important than anything else going on. I will make sure I am available." Marie insisted.

Lucas smiled and laughed inwardly at Annabelle as she rolled her eyes.

"Well, Ma, Lucas and I just pulled into the apartment," Annabelle said having actually been in the parking lot for nearly 10 minutes while they talked on the phone.

"Okay, honey. I will talk to you later." Marie replied detecting the irritation in her daughter's voice.

"Okay, Ma. I love you."

"Love you too, sweetheart." Marie hung up the phone.

"That was fun." Lucas smirked.

"Oh yes, a picnic." Annabelle smiled sarcastically. "I have accepted the fact that my mother will always be overprotective, overdramatic and overwhelming."

"I like her." Lucas added. Annabelle rolled her eyes and shook her head.

Inside, Annabelle was having difficulty accepting what the day had offered her. Inwardly she panicked about the risks that this pregnancy was already threatening. If accepting the pregnancy wasn't hard enough, let's make it harder to deal with. Annabelle took a deep breath and pushed the thoughts aside.

Lying in bed, Lucas tucked closely behind me. I felt like the world couldn't be any more complete. I closed my eyes, smile on my face and fell into a deep slumber.

Dreams passed peacefully through my head; keeping my body and mind at ease. Subconsciously I rolled to my back, keeping my hand clasped around Lucas's arm.

I was 26 weeks pregnant, almost 7 months. I had been discharged from therapy about two months ago. I was nearly good as new. The nightmares still existed and I have had a few bad nights; but few and far in between. All physical scars nearly gone, emotional scars healing; we were moving forward with life.

We had just found out that we were expecting a girl. We had been unable to determine the sex of the baby the first few ultrasounds after the 5th month mark; due to the positioning of the baby. Finally about 2 weeks ago, we were able to see that we would be having a girl.

The look on Luke's face when we found out was priceless. He was overjoyed with the idea of having a little girl. We have decided to name her May Bell, after his grandmother.

Without warning, a sharp pain seared through my stomach. Letting go of Luke's arm, I clutched my growing stomach. I continued to lie on my back, my eyes closed; waiting for the pain to subside. Instead of waking Lucas up, I took a deep breath and sat up; pulling myself to the edge of the bed.

Blood rushed to my head as dizziness consumed me. I teetered at the edge of the bed, closing my eyes and clenched my fists. With a breath out, I pushed myself to my feet. I fought the urge to pass out and used the furniture to walk myself out of the room. I made it to hallway before I let out a small whimper of panic. I stood in the hallway, my hands pressed on either side of my abdomen. Leaning forward I took another deep breath; in and out.

The pain eased, giving me a chance to catch my breath. Walking into the kitchen, I grabbed a glass from the cabinet. Using the counter to lean on, I turned the faucet on. Running my fingers under the cold water, I shiver ran through me. I was reminded of the nights I spent in the freezing cold; scared and alone.

Pushing the thought quickly from my mind, I smiled at the thought of the many nights since that I have spent in the arms of my rescuer and fiancé. We both struggled with the thoughts of raising a child conceived by force, out of hate and cruelty.

I filled the glass with water and took a few sips; testing my nausea. The water didn't seem to affect my nausea and took another drink. Standing at the counter, I waited for the pain to return; hoping it would not. After a few minutes, it seemed safe to return to bed. I refilled the glass with water to take it back to the bedroom. I glanced at the clock in the early glow of the morning, 6:45 am.

As I turned and took a step forward, the pain returned with a quick and cruel jut to the stomach. I involuntarily let go of the glass, letting it fall to its quick demise. I clutched my stomach, bending forward in pain. I let out a ragged breath followed by quick gasps and whimpers. I kept my feet firmly planted; knowing the amount of shattered glass that now surrounded my bare feet.

"Luke," I spoke as if he were sitting across the room; unable to speak any louder. I felt tears burn my eyes for the first time in months. Taking a deep breath in, I tried again. "Lucas!"

The sound echoed through the silent apartment. I could hear the frame of the bed squeak in response. Seconds later I could hear, Lucas stumbled from the bedroom. The light from the hallway flashed on and I closed my eyes quickly. Sweat beaded down my forehead; I took another breath in.

"What?" He questioned; his voice sounded panicked. I looked up him as he approached, disheveled, in the doorway to the kitchen.

"Wait," I breathed. I pointed towards the floor. "I broke a glass. Don't step on the glass."

Lucas reached for the kitchen light switched. I squinted into the light as I tried to stand up straight. I put my hand on the edge of the counter top and took a deep breath in.

"What's wrong, Annie?" Lucas asked, watching me carefully.

"Lots of pain," I breathed out, quickly taking another sharp breath in. I fought the urge to pass out. I hadn't experienced pain like this in months. Sweat beaded off my forehead, onto the back of my hand, as I rested my head on the counter.

"Do you want me to call Dr. Stevenson?" Lucas suggested. I turned my face to him and watched as he silently panicked.

"No, I just need to sit down." I insisted.

Lucas took the broom from the hallway closet and quick moved the glass out of the way; pushing it aside for cleaning up at a later time. Closing the distance between us, he put his hand gently on my lower back.

"Do you need me to carry you?" Lucas offered as I turned around. I shook my head, grabbing his hand with mine. With another deep breath in, we walked into the living room.

Once we were sitting on the couch, I let silent tears slide down my cheeks. Lucas sat quietly, looking unsure of what to do. I, myself, was lost for words or what actions to take next. I took another deep breath in only to feel a sensation of warmth spread through my body. It continued for a moment and the pain worsened.

I thought about the possibilities that could be happening to my body. Were these normal pregnancy pains? Was I going to wake up in a few hours, good as new? Should I ignore them? What if I am losing the baby? What if I'm unable to have children? What if the injuries from the few months before permanently damaged my body?

I shook my head, pushing the negative thoughts from my mind. I looked at Lucas. He watched me, waiting for me to speak.

"What do you want me to do?" He questioned with worried eyes. I continued to be at a loss for words. My hands rubbed side to side along my growing belly as I tried to soothe myself. The pain continued to rear its nasty head, keeping me from any comfortable feelings.

I took another deep breath. What was I supposed to do? If I call Dr. Stevenson and this all turns out to be nothing, my mother would be right.

I thought back to a conversation we had about two weeks ago.

"Annabelle, you are worrying too much."

"Ma, I was just saying that I have some back pain." I defended myself. *I stood in the kitchen of my childhood home, my hands rubbing my own lower back.*

"Yes, you did. But I know my daughter and you are worried." *Marie stepped closer to me and put her hand on my cheek.* *"You have a baby growing inside of you. Aches and pains will happen. I promise, everything will be okay; but you have to stop worrying. It's not good for the baby."*

"I'm not worried about the aches and pains." I muttered. *I looked at my mother to see her shake her head silently.*

"Whatever you say, Annabelle," she smiled.

I worried every day since I found out I was pregnant. I had worried about keeping myself healthy. I kept it to myself, making sure Lucas was settled into this new life, keeping him happy. I worried my family would leave, unsupportive of my choices. I worried if I would be a good mother to this child; afraid to ruin another life.

I kept my mind tied around the fact that Dolan was still alive, haunting my dreams; day and night. I never felt 100% safe in my own skin after weeks of torture. Never knowing what was waiting for me at the end of the road, around the corner or in the car parked next to me. I lived this worry in a silent world; inside my head. Another consequence of worrying; I didn't want anyone to know I was suffering.

You need to get over your pride…

I didn't want to acknowledge the voice in my head. Not wanting to swallow my pride, was a trait I had inherited from my mother.

"Annie?" Lucas put his hand on mine. I looked up at him. My eyes felt heavy, I was unable to decide what I should do.

Let someone else decide for you…

"Okay." I whispered.

"Okay?" Lucas echoed. I realized I had responded to my thoughts.

"Call Dr. Stevenson, I'll get dressed." I spoke calmly.

As if he read my mind, Lucas kissed my cheek and stood up from the couch. I took his out stretched hands and pulled myself up. Lucas pulled me into a hug.

I tried to give him a smile, but the pain in my stomach continued. I took a few steps toward the bathroom when I felt a warm sensation. Something made me look down at my legs. In the partial darkness of the day break and a lamp on the end table, I could see that something was wrong. I reached forward, to the light switch inside the bathroom.

As light struck my eyes, it took a minute to adjust. My light pink pajama bottoms were discolored with red. I took a sharp breath in, creating a gasping noise that caught Luke's attention. As I turned, shaking with panic, Lucas bought me a chair to sit on.

"Forget getting dressed, I'm calling Dr. Stevenson and we're leaving." Lucas took charge.

I watched him walk to the kitchen counter and pick up his phone. I sat silently, listening to one side of the conversation with Dr. Stevenson.

From my position on the chair, my eyes caught the newly painted purple walls of the second bedroom. The world around me seemed to continue as I stared across the room. I faded into a place in my mind that I had not visited in several months; the part of my brain that held doubt, pain, suffering, and uncertainty. I had tittered on the edge, never letting myself fall into its darkness. I had been trapped somewhere between happiness and worry for the past months. But something about this moment sent me falling into a deep, dark, abyss.

"Annabelle." I heard his voice, stern and calm.

Lucas was in front of me, his face level with mine. His hand touched my cheek gently, bringing my eyes to his. I let another tear slip down my cheek. His thumb caught it and wiped it away.

"We have to go." Lucas explained. "Dr. Stevenson is going to meet us at the hospital."

I looked down at my lap. My hands sat in their familiar place, on either side of my pregnant stomach. I was frozen. I couldn't move. Lucas waited, close by, for me to stand.

"Annie." Lucas called my name.

"I can't-" I looked up at him. Tears continued to fill my eyes.

"What?" Lucas watched me with a gentle expression on his face.

"I can't leave the house… not like this." I looked down at my stained pants.

Lucas took another look at me and walked out of the room. I shut my eyes tightly, shaking my head from side to side. With one hand firmly around my stomach, my other hand pushed off the seat of the chair and I stood from the chair. Before I could turn to walk into the bedroom, Lucas returned. I looked down at his hands and saw my black robe. For a second I wanted to protest to put on new clothes, but the pain in my stomach reminded me of the importance of the situation. I nodded and let Lucas help me into my robe.

Before I knew exactly what happened, we were downstairs, leaving the building and heading to the car. The cool summer morning sat heavy on the windshield. The dew easily wiped away with one push of the wiper blades. Lucas sat down a towel in the front passenger seat at my request. He helped me sit gently into the front seat.

The drive to the hospital was silent. Lucas took my hand in his and held it the entire way. Thoughts of complete failure pushed into my mind. I held onto my belly with my right hand, internally apologizing to my unborn daughter. My mind raced and tears began to stray from my eyes. I hadn't cried in weeks and not shedding a tear for anything negative in months. Staring down at my hand, I ran my palm across my out stretched stomach. After coming to terms with this pregnancy and this new path my life was taking, I couldn't imagine my future without my daughter, our daughter.

I felt Luke's hand graze my cheek with his thumb. I looked into his eyes. He looked back and said something I didn't register. I looked forward to see the red glow of the Emergency Room sign. A man dressed in blue came to open my door for me.

"Do you need a wheelchair?" He questioned.

"Yes, please hurry. She is pregnant and bleeding." Lucas spoke across the car to the man.

I looked at Lucas again and gave him a worried look. Words could not form into comprehendible sentences. Lucas took his hand and placed it on my face.

"I am going to park the car. I will be in with you in just a minute."

I nodded silently to him as the man in blue returned with a wheelchair. I turned my feet to step out of the car and another pain shot through my abdomen. I took a sharp breath in and gained my composure. The man in blue offered his hand to help me into the wheelchair. I took his hand and pulled myself up. Grabbing on to the arms of the wheelchair, I took another deep breath and pushed myself to stand up. Not giving my brain a moment to process, I continued my momentum into the wheelchair.

I watched as Lucas pulled away from the curb and felt the world move around me. I put my face into my hands and closed my eyes. I knew the man in blue was asking me questions, but I couldn't form any words to answer his questions. I wiped my silent tears away and opened my eyes we entered the building. The man in blue asked another question as my eyes adjusted to the florescent lights of the emergency room waiting area.

"How far along are you, ma'am?" His question registered.

348

I was silent for a moment while his question processed in my mind. I looked up at him and realized a woman was now standing beside him; she was in green.

"Ma'am, how far along are you?" Her voice was harsh; her words, cold.

I focused, "seven months... twenty, twenty six weeks." My jumbled answer trailed off into silence as another sharp pain jabbed my side. I let out a feeble whine as shut my eyes tightly.

"Annabelle?" I heard a female call. Thinking I was beginning to hear things, I ignored the call and took another deep breath in. I opened my eyes to see a familiar woman, knelt in front of me.

"I'm Macie, I was here, with you, the day your family found you. Do you remember me?"

I simply looked at her; the day Allie and Lucas brought me here was a vague memory. I could only remember her face.

She patted my leg with a smile, "it's okay; what's going on? Why are you here?" She redirected the conversation.

"The man that dropped her off said she is pregnant and is experiencing some bleeding." I hear the man in blue answer her question.

"She said she is 26 weeks along." The cold-toned woman in green added. "That's all she has said."

"Annabelle, we are going to get up stairs, right away. I'm going to call up there right now." Macie assured me with a gentle pat on the knee.

Everything around me continued in slow motion. The man in blue moved my chair closer to the counter as the woman in green appeared with a computer on a cart. She began to ask questions that made little sense to me. I could no longer feel my hands; they had gone numb from the grip on the arms of the wheelchair. The cold-toned woman continued to ask questions as her tone grew increasingly irritated.

"You don't need to get her information, she is going up stairs." Macie interrupted the cold-toned woman. I looked up to see her face drop in annoyance as she turned away from me. Another figure stepped in front of me. As my eyes focused, tears streamed down my face in another wave of panic as Lucas came into view.

"It's okay Annie. They are going to take you up stairs." He assured me, rubbing his hands up and down my arms. With that, the wheelchair began to move at a rapid pace. We darted around people in the waiting area of the emergency room, around corners and through doorways. I heard the person pushing me speaking to Lucas but I couldn't focus on the conversation.

As my anxiety increased, my breathing followed. As my breathing increased, I felt myself start to hyperventilate. Hyperventilation turned into a dizziness that began to impede my vision. The walls swirled downward as the chair continued to race down the hallway. My grip on the arms began to relax and I turned my focus to my spinning surroundings. I felt the tense muscles in my shoulders began to relax as I closed my eyes. I knew I was going to pass out.

"Luke," I whispered. I felt his hand grab mine. The walls continued to tumble.

"I'm right here, Annie." Lucas responded.

"I'm going to pass out." I felt my voice trail off. Before I could hear a response, darkness consumed me.

Epilogue

It had been months since Annabelle had made this familiar drive home from work. The fall evening in Fort Kent was crisp and refreshing after the hot summer. The leaves on the trees were beginning to change; bright orange and deep purple began to appear in the fading light of the day. Annabelle squinted at the light of the setting sun, peaking though the leaves, as she turned down Main Street.

Annabelle waved to Chief Michaels as he got out of his car at the police station. As she continued down the road passing the general store and the book store; her mind wondered to that night so long ago. She could never make it pass the bookstore without memories finding their way into the center of her thoughts. Taking deep breath and releasing it slowly, she came to a stop at the light.

The red glow of the light took Annabelle back to the emergency room she had experienced not once, but twice within a short amount of time. She shook her head, looking down at the clock; 5:30. Lucas would have just arrived at home. A smile found her lips as she passed her old apartment complex. She focused on the good memories and sped away down the road towards home.

She made a quick turn down Page Avenue to the sight of both Lucas's and her brother's trucks in the driveway of her small white, two story house. She parked next to the silver truck belonging to her fiancé. Stepping out of her car, the crisp fall air put a smile on her face. She took a minute to look up at the tree in the front yard. It stood tall, also showing signs of the cooler temperatures as is had just begun to drop it's now orange and yellow colored leaves.

As she opened the door to her home, she heard a loud conversation taking place in the family room on the opposite end of the house.

"That's cheating!" Madison screeched.

"Maddy, if you were paying attention, Lucas only played the game by the rules." Allie's voice rang over grumbles of her 6 year old daughter.

"But I was still trying to add the money from Daddy's turn." Maddy added sadly.

"It's ok, Madison. You will have a chance to win again." Evan's voice of reason pointed out.

Annabelle smiled as the conversation continued to encourage Madison that it was only a game and she won't always win. As she listened silently from the front hallway, she slipped out her shoes, shoving them to the side of the close. Her hand found the pocket of her jacket and inside was a folded piece of paper a special someone had put into her bag this morning.

She opened the edges gently and read the bold hand writing,

You are brilliant and beautiful. I love you.

— Luke.

Hearing the floor in front of the kitchen groan, she glanced up knowing exactly who was watching her. As their eyes met, passion erupted; a passion that would never be understood by any other two souls. Two hearts that grew so close, so fast; never to part again. Her smile matched his as she took quiet steps towards him. Her eyes switched to the sleeping child in his arms.

Annabelle's heart fluttered at the small features of this little miracle. Her tiny arms wrapped securely around the neck of her father, eyes squeezed tightly shut, afraid to meet the light of the setting sun. A messy head of dark blond curls that Annabelle couldn't resist to run her hands through. Suddenly, as if switching on a light, the little girl's eye opened with a gasp.

"Mama," Her voice was quiet and sleepy. Annabelle smiled taking her daughter into her arms.

"May Bell," Annabelle whispered, softly kissing her hair, as May Bell rested her head on her mother's shoulder.

Annabelle found her favorite pair of blue eyes and leaned forward to exchange a kiss. Lucas wrapped his fiancé and daughter in the same warm embrace.

It had been nearly two and a half years since Annabelle's last trip to the emergency room; when she was rushed into surgery to deliver May Bell. She remembered little about that day. After the emergency surgery, it took Annabelle hours to wake up completely from the anesthesia and spent the next day under heavy sedation and pain medications.

May Bell was born prematurely at 26 weeks; she weighed less than 2 pounds. The doctor's tried to prepare Annabelle for the worst; explaining her baby's chance of survival was 50%. Annabelle never left her daughter's side. She spent every day and night next to the tiny little girl.

The first time Annabelle held her daughter, May Bell was nearly a month old. She weighed nearly four pounds by this time. May Bell continued to grow, surpassing doctor's expectations. She spent the first two months of her life in the neonatal intensive care unit at the local hospital.

After a tough six months of life, May Bell began to show signs of major improvement. The wires and monitors began to slowly disappear from her nursery in the apartment. Sounds on the baby monitor transitioned from cries for help to normal coos and giggles from the crib. Annabelle returned to sleeping in bed with Lucas after May was nearing a year old.

"Auntie," Madison chimed into Annabelle's thoughts. Looking down at her growing niece, Annabelle waited for her to finish her thoughts. Madison looked up at her aunt, "can I wear my fancy dress?"

Annabelle smiled at the term "fancy dress" that Madison had given her flower girl dress. Kneeling down with May resting on her knee, Annabelle smiled at Madison and said, "Do you remember what I told you yesterday?"

Madison twisted her finger in her hair and looked at her shoes, "Yes…" Her answer trailed into a low whisper as she shyly recited what she had been told only 24 hours ago, "I can wear my fancy dress on October 1st when auntie and Mr. Lucas have their special day."

"Right, and what day is today?" Annabelle watched Madison look at her father who was now leaning on the door frame into the kitchen.

"August 25th." Evan relayed to his daughter with a smirk.

"August 25th." Madison repeated to Annabelle.

"So does that answer your question?" Annabelle asked. She could see Madison's wheels turning.

"But I want to look pretty." Madison replied furrowing her eyebrows, her hands twisting the edge of her t-shirt.

"Maddy, you are pretty." Annabelle reached out for her niece and pulled her closer. "You don't need a dress to make you pretty."

"But I like looking pretty in my fancy dress." Madison pushed her bottom lip out, pouting.

Annabelle smiled and kissed her niece on the forehead, whispering, "When I watch you on Saturday, we can play dress up. How does that sound?"

Madison tucked her bottom lip back in with a grin and hugged her aunt tightly.

"Madison, time to get ready. We have to get home soon." Allie chimed as she walked into the room.

"Mommy! Auntie is going to play dress up with me!" Madison yelled as she ran to her mom. Allie glanced up at Annabelle with a surprised face.

"On Saturday, while you and Evan are out." Annabelle smiled knowing Allie was desperate to get home. Allie stood up, resting her hands on her growing belly.

"Ok Madison, shoes honey." Allie groaned, "Your little brother is ready for a nice foot rub." Allie smirked at Evan who kissed his glowing wife on the cheek.

"How are you feeling today?" Annabelle asked her sister-in-law.

"Big, swollen, ready," Allie laughed as she rubbed her stomach.

353

Allie was due in five days. Today was her last day of work before maternity leave and she was impatiently waiting for her baby boy to make his appearance.

"You look beautiful." Evan added as he helped Madison continue to master tying her shoes.

"Good answer, but I am ready for this little guy to be ready." Allie looked down at her protruding abdomen and smiled.

Annabelle walked with Allie to her car, arms hooked together and whispering quietly to one another. As Evan and Madison followed the whispering women, Lucas held May on the front porch. Madison stopped and turned to the pair. She took a few steps towards them.

"Tomorrow you can play dress up with your Mommy and me, May bee." Madison explained on her tip toes. Lucas smiled at Maddy's nickname for his daughter. He knelt down so Madison and May Bell were now at eye level with each other. Maddy tucked the toddler's hair behind her ear and stuck her tongue out, crossing her eyes playfully.

"Maddy," May giggled happily at her cousin and clapped her hands together. "Play now?"

"Maddy has to go home for now, honey." Lucas explained

"Bye bye May bee. I will see you tomorrow." Madison leaned to give her cousin a kiss on the cheek. She then wrapped her arms around Lucas and May Bell together. Lucas returned the hug and kissed the top of her head.

Madison turned and ran to her mother's car. She flung her arms open to Annabelle who greeted her with a giant hug, especially fit for her niece. She kissed her forehead and promised to see her tomorrow. Madison agreed with a kiss on the cheek and she was in the back seat before Annabelle could blink. Allie and Evan said their goodbyes and headed home to relax for one of their last nights as family of three.

Lucas waited for Annabelle to return to their porch before setting May down. As he steadied her, May quickly walked to her mother's arms.

Annabelle scooped her daughter into her arms and they returned to the living room. She kissed her cheeks multiple times as the little girl squirmed and giggled. As Annabelle held her daughter, she thought of all the things that were right in her life.

Later that night, Annabelle rested her head on pillow, waiting for Lucas to come to bed. She sighed and turned her face toward the ceiling, taking in the cool breeze from the window. The light from the lamp flicked off and she felt Lucas climb into bed beside her. She rolled to her side, the light of the moon reflected off her favorite pair of blue eyes. Annabelle lifted her hand, running her finger tips gently across his bare chest. With a smile, Lucas pulled her close to him, kissing her lips gently. Her hands found either side of his face. She pulled him closer, deepening the kiss. Lucas wrapped his arms around her shoulders, enveloping Annabelle in his embrace. She feverishly kissed his lips, neck and down to his collar bone.

As Annabelle shifted her body on top of his, a small cry interrupted from across the hall.

"Shhh," Lucas whispered, "she might go back to sleep."

They waited quietly, Annabelle straddling his hips. She giggled slightly, looking down at his bare chest. He smiled and whispered, "I think she fell asleep."

Annabelle leaned forward, their lips meeting like fireworks. Lucas ran his hands from her hips, under her shirt to the small of her back. As she sat up from the kiss, he lifted her shirt over her head, removing it completely. She giggled, returning to kissing his neck.

"Momma!" A tiny cry from across the hall beckoned.

Annabelle sighed, falling into his chest, letting all of her weight rest on him.

"I'll get her." Lucas offered.

"No, let me." Annabelle kissed his forehead, stepping off the side of the bed. She grabbed the bathrobe that draped over the door, slipped it on, and disappeared into the hallway.

Lucas took a deep breath, slowing his racing heart. His passion for Annabelle had only grown since the day they met. His heart skipped a beat thinking of the day he looked into her bright, glistening, blue eyes for the first time. He reminded himself this was the path he was meant to take, not the path his parents had laid out for him. Lucas knew his life would never return to the hell on earth it was before Annabelle.

With that thought, Annabelle returned with a tired, crying two year old. May Bell held on as if someone had threatened to take her from her mother.

"What's wrong, honey?" Lucas asked, sitting up in bed.

"Someone had a bad dream and wanted to sleep with Momma and Daddy." Annabelle answered for the sniffing child.

Lucas shifted, making room for Annabelle to lay down with May in between. May refused to let go of her mother, Lucas kissed the little girl on the top of her head.

"You can sleep with us tonight, sweetheart." Lucas snuggled close.

As she began to fall asleep, Annabelle opened her eyes one last time. She looked down at her beautiful baby girl, who was growing so quickly before her eyes. Pure joy filled her heart and soul each time her eyes fell on this little person. Then her eyes fell on the man next to them. His eyes closed, his arms protectively around his family and his heart beating steady against her hand. She smiled with a tired yawned and let her eyes close.

In her arms, she held the sweetest gift from the dark cloud of pain that no longer hung over her life. In her heart, she held the greatest love for a man she never imagined her luck would offer her. In her mind, she knew nothing could ever take away her past. However, her past was the only reason she was able to experience this precious gift and wonderful love. Without pain, suffering or defeat, there would not be healing, happiness, or overwhelming desire to succeed.

The path of person's life is filled with detours, road blocks and dead ends. The path that Annabelle's life took definitely had every detour and road block a path could contain. On the other hand, dead ends did not exist on her journey. Every detour lead to a new road, every road block held a new experience; good, bad and traumatic. Each change made her the woman she became. Annabelle's fate gave her the life she had always imagined but never dreamed of living.

The End

Made in the USA
Monee, IL
22 October 2020